D1321915

RONALD FRAME

Ronald Frame was born in Glasgow in 1953, and educated there and at Oxford. Writing fiction and drama has been his sole occupation for the last decade. He is the author of ten books which include PENELOPE'S HAT, shortlisted for the James Tait Black Memorial Prize, and BLUETTE, shortlisted for the Sunday Express Book of the Year Award. His new book, WALKING MY MISTRESS IN DEAUVILLE, comprises a novella and nine short stories, and is published in hardback by Hodder & Stoughton.

Ronald Frame

UNDERWOOD AND AFTER

First published in Great Britain in 1991 by Hodder and Stoughton Ltd

Sceptre edition 1992

Sceptre is an imprint of Hodder and Stoughton Paperbacks, a division of Hodder and Stoughton Ltd.

Printed and bound in Great Britain for Hodder and Stoughton Paperbacks, a division of Hodder and Stoughton Ltd, Mill Road, Dunton Green, Sevenoaks, Kent TN13 2YA. (Editorial Office: 47 Bedford Square, London WC1B 3DP) by Clays Ltd, St Ives plc. Typeset by Hewer Text Composition Services, Edinburgh.

British Library C.I.P.
Frame, Ronald
  Underwood and after.
  I. Title
  823[F]

ISBN 0 340 56540 3

For the pleasure-seekers!

Acknowledgements

The details offered on the designs and weaving of carpets are owing to the informative, excellently succinct *Oriental Rugs: A Buyer's Guide* by Lee Allane (Thames and Hudson).

I'm also grateful for the picture of rarefied domestic life which Suzy Menkes supplies in her entertaining study, *The Windsor Style* (Grafton Books).

'In China, as you know, the Emperor is a Chinaman, and all the folk he has about him are Chinamen too. It's many years ago now, but that is exactly the reason why it is worthwhile to listen to the story, before it's forgotten.'

'The Nightingale'
By Hans Andersen,
Transl. M.R. James

Part One

ONE

Thirty years later, in 1986, I was revisited by the past.

It slithered through the letterbox one wet Monday morning.

I peeled open the buff envelope over-printed 'Do Not Bend'. From inside I shook out a photograph. I looked into the envelope. There was nothing else, no message.

I held the photograph up to the grainy grey daylight from the window of frosted glass in the hall. A sprawling white house, of Edwardian vintage, in a cedar garden. I recognised it at once, of course, although it wasn't quite the same. But there could be no real confusion, and the sender must have known that.

It was 'Underwood'.

I walked back to the kitchen and dropped down on to a stool. I turned the photograph over several times. I pushed my fingers inside the envelope to check it was empty. I returned to the hall to see if anything had dropped out.

But all I had was the photograph. A black-and-white enlargement. A recent shot, because the car in one corner of the driveway was a current model.

I placed the large rectangle of paper shiny side up on the table. It was a shock, as well as a bamboozlement. Did I really, after the last three decades of my life, want to have this image so calculatedly and so actually set before me again?

The next Monday morning a second buff envelope arrived. It carried a WC1 postmark. I slid my thumb under the sealed flap and ripped it open. But this time I walked through to the kitchen, circled the table twice, and then sat down on a stool to confront whatever was inside.

Maybe I had guessed what the photograph would show. At least it was no true surprise to me this time. A large city villa in a leafy garden. White walls, which it hadn't had then, taken by the camera lens in sunshine, so that through the shadows of the trees they glowed. Like Camelot, a little. The curtains now were – so far as I could tell – ruched. We would never have approved of that, in those days when we had the luxurious confidence of our opinions in such matters as furnishing taste, the social details of how people presented themselves. Everything was in fine and cared-for condition, but international moneyed style had come to Kensington and carried the day, which now put *our* brief sojourn there into a little pocket of time. A desirable residence in a private cul-de-sac, only a backwater after all, and the life we'd had there just a kind of historical footnote.

There was no message included.

I was waiting for the first post the following Monday. No buff envelope came. I was quite sorely disappointed. I stayed in until the time of the second delivery, but the postman didn't stop at the house.

An envelope arrived only on the Friday. I tore at the flap to get inside. This time the photograph showed a terraced house of stucco on brick. Harley Street, I knew at once. The doctor's rooms.

Who else had known?

I turned the photograph over.

If you want to mull over old times, I'll lend you an ear. Then a phone number, with a Putney dialling code.

Was it one of the group, our charmed circle, who had managed to track me down? How could they have made the Harley Street connection, though?

Looking beyond the kitchen door, my eyes alighted on the prayer rug hanging on the wall. Was it by unconscious association? The rug conveniently covered a crack in the plaster work: a Belouch, which I'd bought just because I liked the colours, not because I knew anything about its symbolism.

I started to lose myself in tracking the maze-lines of the pattern, something abstract to me, like do-it-yourself happiness. Inside the maze of red lines on the gold ground figures and places appeared to me momentarily, memory-flashes. I knew already that I should telephone, and I felt my stomach tightening like a fist with the concentration of not thinking about what I might be letting myself in for.

We met in a trattoria near the headquarters of the public relations firm she worked for.

I was walking towards our rendezvous when I remembered having been here before, long before in that other life. There had been a night-club called 'The Fez' roundabout. In the evening the street would be crawling with taxis and limousines dropping off and the music of the live band would pound upstairs to street level. It was one of our loucher social venues, ambience-wise, but expensive none the less and drawing a rich clientele who liked to think they were living dangerously. In fact we were well protected by heavy-weight bouncers, so the sense of hazard was a myth: one more myth in an age of them.

It might have been the site of the trattoria or not. After thirty years, the span of a generation and a half, for one night-club to have gone down and disappeared completely is nothing.

She kept me waiting. When she showed, she didn't quite resemble her clipped and proper telephone voice. I was looking past her indeed when she lowered herself on to the chair opposite me. Short Peter Pan hair, strawberry blonde dyed. A long, tapering face, palely made up. Mauve lipstick, of film starlet glossiness. Mediumly attractive looks being repudiated. Boyish body-line. A bright-green leather aviator jacket, black 501 Levis, and – I just managed to notice – shell pink suede loafers. A girl with some money playing at being her version of a bad one.

'Well, *you* look as I expected,' she began. 'Only older, of course.'

She opened a matt black hard-shell business case. From one of the compartments she produced a photograph. Another of the

black-and-white enlargements. It showed half a dozen of us in
the Cornish garden. Just visible was the sea.

'Where did you get this?' I asked her.

'Can't you guess?'

'Not really.'

She smiled, but not *at* me: away from me rather, towards the
voices from the long table in the corner.

'Among her things.'

'Who – whose – '

'My mother, of course.'

'Your mother?'

'I'm Liz. Fleur's daughter.'

She took the photograph back. I felt as if I'd been felled. I
couldn't speak. But she was in no hurry to either.

She was off-hand with the waiter when she ordered. A tunny
salad, a little bread, an espresso coffee. Quickly, please.

'I can't stay long,' she told me.

I picked from the menu: the first item I could pronounce.

We proceeded with a conversation, very slowly. We were
continually indirect, and I couldn't believe it of myself. She told
me briefly about growing up with her mother. School, university.
'All very boring, really.' I said I'd found the announcement, in
a newspaper, not long after the group of us broke up: the
death notice.

'Oh, my father's?'

She spoke as if it might be a confusable matter, that domestic
deaths happened all the time and were nothing so much.

'What about you?' she asked.

I gave her a few details about myself in the three decades
since. Going off to college 'as a kind of therapy'; getting involved
in a newspaper; then magazine publication, the selling of them.
'Marketing.' Returning to journalism six or seven years ago.

'How did you know?' I asked. 'How to find me?'

'Just a fluke. I read a motoring review you did – in a colour
supp. An Aston Martin, was it?'

'A Lagonda?'

'Was it? There was a lot about fifties cars in it anyway. About
when you used to drive them around London.'

'I don't know why I wrote the thing,' I said. 'Maybe – maybe I wanted to see if anyone would notice? Subconsciously – ?'

She wasn't interested in that, though.

'Your name. The "Ralph" part. And the photo of you. The pose. Just like this, with your weight on one hip and your head tilted.'

I looked at myself in the photograph.

'Just a fluke,' she said.

I stared at her. I didn't know if I could believe her or not.

'Anyway – ' She shrugged.

She ate less than half the food that was brought to her, and there was little enough of that. She took two or three sips of her coffee.

'I have to go now,' she said, and stood up.

'But . . .' I gawped at her.

'I'm sorry – '

'When – how can – '

'I just wanted to see you.'

'We – we'll meet again?'

'I don't know.'

'Please.'

'I never know. That's me. Maybe nothing happens about some things. Other times I go to the opposite extreme and I blow it up into a big event. Main feature. You know?'

I shook my head.

'I'll think about it,' she said. 'Really.'

She removed a credit card from her wallet to pay with. I protested. She looked affronted.

'I asked *you* to come,' she said.

Enticed me to meet her was the truth of it. To what end, I simply had no idea.

I stood up and walked with her, or just behind her, to the door. I felt that with bright daylight shining full on her she didn't want me looking at her as closely as I was. She kept turning her head away. I smelt perfume, something incongruously feminine. Light and lemony.

She pulled up the collar of the apple-green leather jacket. I was reminded of Jean Seberg, a face and attitude of the later

1950s, now tragic and eternally innocent because of her too
early death.

She turned away from me for the last time, as if she'd read too
much of what I was thinking written on my face. She'd wanted
to have the past presented in front of her, and yet she didn't –
I supposed – care for sentiment or nostalgia.

'You'll hear from me,' she said. 'Maybe.'

Outside she raised her arm. The gesture of her hand might
have been a wave, but I couldn't be sure. Her eyes opened
wider and filled with the picture of me, standing in the doorway
of the trattoria: ghosted in a busy weekday London lunchtime,
conceivably on the site of a former haunt, where I had been
content to live ignorantly but gloriously.

Then she disappeared into the tide of pedestrians heading
westwards – back to offices and jobs of work where everyone
needs to imagine they're singularly important and indispensable
– and then, to my consternation, she was gone.

TWO

1956. South Cornwall.

A long shallow estuary of sandbanks. Wide, sheltered sandy bays separated one from another by cliffs. On our own bay at Treswithian we had a vast prehistoric grassed tumulus on one side, as high and green as a hill, and on the other – where we were living – a breezy headland of rock, fissures that filled with pools when the sea ebbed, and up on their heights a covering of soft turf, flowering pinks, and yellow gorse. A small Victorian church with a crooked spire skulked beneath the mound of hill, in a steep-banked churchyard protected from sandstorms by a hawthorn hedge. Behind the church the golf course rolled over its plush acres; palm grasses waved in front of the cream-and-brown half-timbered clubhouse, elevated above the topmost greens and as far as I could see in a northern and westerly direction from my bedroom window. A quarter of a mile or so from the swards and bunkers a lane led uphill, between the shaded gardens of houses, past the public tennis courts, all the way up to the general stores-and-post office, almost on a level with the far clubhouse on one side and Toop's farm on the other sea side: a meandering lane, ill-lit at night by fizzing blue gas lamps lost in the branches of trees and the tangle of ivy or honeysuckle.

The nights smelt of dampening orchards, of the salty mackerel-rich sea. Days smelt of hot creosote on the garden fences, of ubiquitous pine.

My parents had rented accommodation and brought all three children along, for what we knew was bound to be our last holiday together.

I had an older brother and a younger sister, and maybe my

parents thought they could afford to give up with one of us. I wasn't easy to handle, I can see that now. I didn't know what I wanted from life, but anything – I had convinced myself – must be better than being everyone else's man in business. I was at an age, eighteen nearly nineteen, to believe that I couldn't live in that psychotic fashion, dispersing myself among however many people, none of whom deserved me.

They let me go my own way, though, because I gave them no choice. I'd found myself a job – through a friend's friend – at the swimming pool of a massive 1930s mansion block of flats in Chelsea, and I commuted between there and our suburb.

It must have been to make up some of the lost ground that my parents suggested I join them in Cornwall. Presumably they knew, as Nigel and Polly and I did, that it was going to be the final holiday. Since my father was having to take an extended rest on doctor's orders, there was an element of emotional blackmail involved.

We had a swanky-sounding address – simply the house name 'Penelewey' – but before it we were obliged to supply the designation 'Lesser'. (We tried it without, but the occupants of the main house didn't take too kindly to having to walk round to hand in our mail.)

The 'Lesser' rankled. Why not, my mother suggested, something like 'The Coach House', 'The Mews House'? Or even 'The Stables'? But the dozen or so large houses on the headland had gone up in the 1920s, not long after those behind the beach, and garages were simply garages: we found ourselves sleeping in the converted storage accommodation directly under the eaves, with our living space made out of the area once occupied by the cars in what must have constituted a triple garage. The house proper was let out at above five times the amount we were paying, which was no little consolation.

In our dealings with, first, the Ainsworths and then the Markby-Freers, it was I who was the go-between: because I had my grammar-school ways, and because – as my mother said – I had the politest accent of us all. She would brush the hair on the back of my head whenever I had to go into the garden to retrieve an article that had blown off our washing line in the Atlantic gusts, or to fetch our all-sorts dog 'Patch', who must have spent all his waking hours (and probably sleeping ones also) calculating in his wily mind how he could force yet another escape through the fence or under the holly thicket into 'Penelewey''s immaculate herbaceous beds.

My mother had always known about Treswithian, from certain of the library books she devoured. She loved reading about the Edwardian well-born, and intrigued by the various mentions of the place she had extended her reading to guide-books, and to the lives of several Victorian minor poets-cum-curates who had also been attracted here. The name recurred in the holiday 'To Let' columns in *The Times* as soon as the spring notices for summer appeared, and while in those days prices were quoted less often than now the very tone of the notices suggested the locale's exclusiveness: stiffly written in lawyer-ish fashion, with such technical descriptions of the properties as would have stirred the frustrated Edwardian spirit in my mother – seven or eight or nine bedrooms, extensive reception rooms, large and secluded grounds, daily gardener, domestic help (including cook's services) available. A law firm's name might follow, or the owners' central London telephone number.

Even in our former garage, my mother was in her element – even confronted with contemporary snobbery, courtesy of 'Penelewey''s tenants – but she was the only one of the five of us who was anything like comfortable, 'at home'. My father kept bumping his head on the cambceiled portions of the ceilings, and my brother and sister were engaged in a protracted feud about who deserved which bedroom. I'd lost patience with them both, and was perfectly happy to leave my top bunk free (the bunks had disappointed me, but my mother had thought it in keeping, since the nobby sort tend to do down their offspring, in the let-them-suffer-awhile boarding-school tradition). I preferred to sleep instead on the very adequate sofa (not 'couch', my mother would remind us) in the sitting-room (not, she would correct my father, *not* living-room).

We had a wee plot of garden of our own, unhelpfully shaded by the big house's trees for most of the afternoon. My mother was a fiend for washing, which didn't seem quite the done thing on the headland – two vans from rival laundry firms groaned uphill and down six days of the week picking up and delivering to the other houses. (Once they accidentally met, and there was a fracas when neither agreed to budge for the other.) The shadows of washing of a morning afflicted my sister's deep-tanning programme, and made us (I was convinced) embarrassingly visible on our windy height, as prominent in our flapping, sudsy way as the Tregenna Lighthouse in its own.

I'd had my bicycle sent down on the train, however, and I could get away. I would head inland and ride the country lanes for miles in a day, soon exhausting the wisdom of my mother's guide-book. I got to know every little parish church and chapel, every Elizabethan, Caroline and Georgian house of note between ourselves and Boscarne and Outer Tregidden and New Zoar. I learned to recognise wild flowers, and for a suburbanite became astonishingly fluent at distinguishing types of birds from their silhouettes in flight and could even pick apart certain species by the manner of their songs.

I acquainted myself with the rest of Treswithian also. Perhaps I had inherited some of my mother's awe and respect for the lost splendour, imagined or not, of less busied eras than our own. I was attracted to those mysteriously silent and aloof houses that lay behind the beach, built in the first quarter of the century. High hedges and gates, solid or five-bar, kept passive intruders of my sort at bay, and the network of private roads – cracked, mossy, tarmacadam overlaid with soft, seasons-old pine needles and blown sand – were eerily hushed when I cycled along them. Very occasionally, a car drove into or departed from a driveway, crunching gravel beneath its tyres. No one there seemed to peg out washing either: or, if they did, it was hung in kitchen gardens, well out of sight of the houses' owners and their neighbours. A few times I heard the sound of tennis balls twanged into flight; bouncing high on asphalt or crashing into undergrowth, cries of victory or defeat and whoops of laughter. As I cycled on, the voices would become fainter and fainter, turning to birdsong or the slow rush of wind into the topmost branches of a tree. Sometimes a lawnmower might hawk and whine, but rarely, and I couldn't imagine how it was that the lawns were kept in such fine fettle in this ghostly paradise of privilege.

*

'Underwood', the house situated immediately behind the beach, was the one that drew me most. I mean, literally: drew me to the stockade of hedges and the white, solid wooden gates, and the view through a gap between two hinges, of the silvery grey gravel driveway extending to the house beyond. The name to my way of thinking perfectly complemented it, conjuring up a shaded, secretive place, even though the house in direct sunlight shone so brilliantly white.

The building, constructed in the 1900s, was to one of Voysey's earlier plans, without all the stylistic freedom of the buttresses and soaring chimney stacks that came with time. It was more angular, more tied to the conventionally upright, but had characteristically high gables, descending dropped roofs of rosemary tiles, narrow mullioned casement windows and many other traditional English folksy details.

Inside, apparently, the rooms had low ceilings, inglenooks, broad doors (although with handles and locks, not Voysey's usual cottage-latches) and waxed oak floors; the white panelling on the walls was said to dazzle when the sea light shone on it.

I was intrigued. I was my mother's son, but I persuaded myself my curiosity was of a more recondite, architecturally based sort than hers. I was fooling myself and, if I knew, it seemed an innocuous delusion. There, behind the hedges, there was space, and leisure, and deep quiet, and I only had to think ahead to 'Lesser Penelewey' and its cramped quarters to appreciate 'Underwood' – a house of strangers – all the more. Salubrious and gracious, highly detached and proudly arcane, profoundly silent and so mellifluously named, it held me fascinated.

*

I can hardly have been inspiring company that summer. I was

polite, but not very talkative. We had grown too old for games, Nigel and Polly and I.

I watched the women on the beach, of course, the younger ones who crossed my line of vision; I didn't go looking them out, however. I'd never had a girlfriend, let alone any 'experience': that didn't stop my imagination working overtime on impossible hypotheses. A couple of years before, I could have day-dreamed from such a vantage-point on top of the dunes that the future *shone*, just as the bay did when the tide ran out and an expanse of golden sand shimmered. But examined now through a slit torn in a blade of spear grass the shore resembled (in my currently uncooperative frame of mind) something else entirely, it extended like nothing so much as a wasteland of blighted desert.

One afternoon I was congratulating myself on my luxurious negativeness, with a birthday present copy of – surprise, surprise – Colin Wilson's *The Outsider* lying open and face down and unread on the sand and trying to imagine mirages in the heat gases waving over the beach, when I spotted the far-away movement of people, a small party of them, like travellers journeying between caravanserais.

It took a couple of minutes for them to become clear to me. Four or five in a group were picking their way over the ribbed damp sand with worm casts; a little further on they started to run for the softer, paler sand. I heard the sound of their voices, talking and laughing. One woman kept throwing up her arms, and one of the three men preferred to hop forward on either leg. It was those two who fell first, in an untidy tangle of limbs, on to the soft sand, laughing louder together than the other three. Their companions pulled them to their feet and brushed the sand from them while the general mirth continued. Everything was being done in the very best of spirits.

They didn't pass within fifty yards of me but I saw them well enough from my hide among the dune grass. The two espadrilled women wore London styles and colours; one of the men was in stylish shorts, another all in white, and the third – carrying a pair of deck shoes in one hand – in the sort of navy ensemble sold by the chandler's in Cabylla, across the estuary. They still laughed, at intervals, and conversed in accents of the kind my mother would refer to as 'cultivated'.

I was sufficiently intrigued – or sufficiently bored – to get up and, keeping invisible all the while, to follow them. They climbed to the top of the dunes up slithering sand, with more laughter and grabbing of hands and elbows. There was another tumble when they reached the summit, another tangle of limbs, another assisted extrication. Then, all of them back up on their feet again, they started off in their original direction.

One of the men – the one in the yachtsman's ensemble – led the way and seemed a little detached in a more than literal sense. His laughter was more reserved, less robust; he didn't talk as much, and when he did the others tended to fall silent and lean forward to hear. He must have been amusing, because they sometimes laughed at what he'd said, but a little less spontaneously than when some joke or physical gesture of their own set them off.

He led them not, as I was expecting, towards the lane's end where the cars were parked but by a sandy track that wound behind those larger houses closest to the beach and protected from view by walls and holly and thorn hedges. They stopped at the first arched wooden gate they came to, which was the back way into 'Underwood', my favourite of them all. The man in blue opened the lock with a key and stood back while the others walked through. He followed, and the gate was pushed shut behind; I heard the lock bite. Behind the wall and the vegetation the voices were suddenly lost to me; I heard no more laughter. My ears filled with the droning of insect life in the long grass of the lane and some bird cries overhead and nothing human at all. There was no evidence of their presence left, no hint that they had passed this spot not more than half a minute before me. Except . . . just possibly I smelt perfume, picking it out of the various summer-dry sweetnesses of the plant life, a faint thread of the stuff. But the longer I tried to concentrate on it, the more uncertain I became, unable to recapture my first trace of it. Maybe, or maybe not. Whatever it might have been, it wafted away and I was left sniffing at the warm currents of air, clotted in these moments with a too dense profusion of odours and fragrances – vegetal, marine, and the human the least faithful of all.

*

I made copious and – I suppose – not very discreet enquiries.

Little was known about Mr Chetwynd, the owner. He lived in London and only came down, at most, three times a year. The house was regularly aired and attended to, but never let nor even occupied by friends in his absence.

He did have friends, if that's what they properly were: rather, a circle of acquaintances he brought with him, six or seven assorted women and men – the same ones – who enjoyed the house's full hospitality. In addition to them, guests were invited, not usually to stay but to visit for lunch or dinner: London folk mostly, who had taken houses along the coast or further inland. The local Cornish gentry didn't seem to be their cup of tea – or tumbler of gin and tonic – at all.

Mr Chetwynd was employed in some kind of buying and selling business. The 'trade' tag ought to have damned him in the eyes of those working and retired professionals, Services and colonial types, who were his neighbours and who had brought their notoriously snobbish Home Counties ways with them. But 'Underwood''s owner had the supreme advantage of wealth in his favour. He could afford to have little to do with any of them, yet evidently he was polite enough: and both house and grounds were more fastidiously kept up than was averagely so, even here. He had bought the property by private treaty from the widow of the titled builder, and so inherited a tradition of country house largesse by famous repute – from Lady Flett's 'At Homes' to her bathing and picnic expeditions, her weekend parties and yachting forays. The high life for her had tailed off in the days just before the last War; during the next six years the socialising was even more necessary, to restore the spirits of the serving officers who beetled down for a few days of forgetfulness, but ultimately that too became more serious and high-minded – frivolity also had a conscience, and anyway Lady Flett, committedly on the side of youth but with a grandson killed over Arnhem, really hadn't the stomach for it any more.

Chetwynd entertained, but it was done decorously. I was given to believe that he used 'Underwood' more as a retreat – an opulent safe-house – where he and the London coterie he brought with him could relax and revitalise themselves. They bathed in the sea, and took shrimping nets to the rock pools, and sometimes picnicked in the dunes, but for the most part they kept to the garden, behind its palisade of high, clipped beech, honeysuckle and cypress hedges. There was a grass tennis court, and three acres of cropped lawn (including a rolled croquet green) fringed by longer grass where snowdrops and crocuses and daffodils and primroses and bluebells appeared by turns. The company could easily entertain (and lose) themselves within their own grounds and have no need to venture out. Food-stuffs were ordered by the housekeeper or cook and, like the newspapers and magazines, delivered; Chetwynd and his party were seldom seen in any of the local shops – sometimes the garage had dealings with the man himself, but the house had its own pump for petrol and it was only ever the workshop whose services he might require. Once in a while some of them, Chetwynd included, had a round or two on the golf course. They never went to church or partook in any other locally organised social activity. If you weren't to catch sight of them on the beach, at quieter times of the day, then it *was* possible you might glimpse them travelling up or down the village's spinal lane, having turned off or about to turn into the private road – pine needle-strewn and sandy so that it resembled loam – which led to the white, solid wooden gates of 'Underwood'. They couldn't be confused with anyone else: elegant women, somewhere between twenty-five and forty-odd years of age, dapper men of the same (one of them renownedly handsome), and Chetwynd himself, at the upper end of that age range, dressed for Cannes rather than Cornwall, sun-tanned and fit, with a ready smile for any of his neighbours he might encounter. There was a stable of cars, and they might be seen in one – or two, in tandem – of any of four or five.

Naturally the staff spoke a little of the house and its doings, but even they couldn't advance much beyond trivia. Londoners were Londoners anyway, and the new 'Underwood' set (the house had

always had that name) especially so. They could talk about the
food, and the music they played on their smart record-player,
and how they danced around the house with the carpets rolled
up, and how one of the ladies slept and received her breakfast
nude, and how the uniquely handsome young man had a habit of
looking into every reflecting surface he could find. They could
talk about the labels on the clothes that were sent out to the
laundry, and the expense of the perfume bottles that sat out on
the dressing tables, the heaviness of silver on Mr Chetwynd's
hairbrushes and combs and shaving brushes, the extraordinary
soft fluffiness of the French towels, the signed portraits of the
Duke and Duchess of Windsor and other grandees which were
placed on the piano in the drawing-room, paintings by Singer
Sargent, Sisley, Raeburn, and Samuel Palmer hanging – not
in some important gallery as they deserved – but above the
mantelpieces and table-tops the maids dusted twice a day, every
day of the week.

No one complained about working for Mr Chetwynd. When
he wasn't there, the housekeeper and one maid were engaged at
their usual services, and the gardener and his boy spent half their
week there and received corresponding pay, which was London
pay and more generous than any of his neighbours'. When he
came down he brought his cook, major-domo, chauffeur, and
a second maid with him. The bills on his accounts were paid
on the nail, and he was held to be an exemplary customer in
that respect, although unusually demanding in respect of the
freshness of eatables and punctuality of deliveries. Quite often
tradesmen were brought in to tinker with the roof or drains or
whatever, so it was widely known that the house was kept in
tip-top condition.

All in all, he was surely – for all his secrecy – the best news
that the late Lady Flett and 'Underwood' could ever have hoped
to come their way.

THREE

Another afternoon, of that same summer of 1956.

It's as clear to me now as it has ever been.

From where I was standing I had the bay spread beneath me.

If I'd looked to either side, I could have seen from our headland – and across the estuary – to Carbiss Head and the tip of the lighthouse.

It was the best point of surveillance, and I must have known that. The cliffs rose up to a sort of bluff, and on windy days the spot had its dangers. I thought I could see everything from there. And I also thought, with the full folly of unfinished adolescence, that the only dangers lay with the up-gusts of Atlantic wind that came on the tails of Caribbean hurricanes.

Since the thing happened in the middle of the afternoon the sun must have been directly over Kea Hill. Already it would have slipped from its full summer zenith, but still with fury and brilliance in plenty.

That – sun-blindness – might have been a pretext for not running to help. But I had been watching them, even against the glare from the sea, and I had them very clearly in my sights all the while.

There were two men and two women, and I knew they must all come from 'Underwood' since I recognised Chetwynd. He was swimming, plying a steady breast-stroke, while the others splashed one another or tried floating on their backs or tipping themselves over to attempt a doggy-paddle.

When I look back on it all, I read it as having been inevitable, only waiting to happen. I don't see any other bathers in the waves, only those four. And *I* too seem indispensable to the picture, so much so that I can draw back and view myself standing there, on the springy turf of pink thrift and purple burnt orchis above the cliffs, myself watching them.

It took me ten minutes or so to make my way down the track of footholds worked into the cliff. I reached the level of the rock pools and started picking my way between them. The difficult part was over: from there it was an easy descent to the shore. I had nowhere to go, though, no place rather than any other, so I preoccupied myself only with what was in front of me, the clinging shell life I could turn over with the toe of my sandshoe and the darting shapes left behind by the sea in the submerged niches of rock.

But I heard the cries almost immediately: I'm sure of that. I detected them through all the other sounds of the afternoon. I could distinguish the urgency in them from the general frenzy of play.

I was down on the beach in seconds, racing for the sea. Arms flailed, towards a point further out where someone was in difficulty. All the other bathers were at a distance and unaware of anything out of the ordinary. The two who were shouting were of Chetwynd's company; I'd glimpsed him a minute or so earlier walking towards the dunes, tying his beach wrap about him, so that presumably – I give him the benefit of the doubt – he was out of earshot by this time.

The man and the woman called to me, and their shouts told me they weren't able enough swimmers to cope. Their companion disappeared from view, and then the yellow bathing-cap reappeared. It happened again. 'She's drowning! Help her!' The woman's arms thrashed the surface of the water, but I could hear no shouts from her. She went under a third time: but now she didn't reappear.

I kicked off my shoes, pulled off my shirt, ran into the sea, and flung myself into the corkscrew turns of the fastest crawl of my life.

It reads like gung-ho *Boy's Own* action stuff. I didn't mean to be a hero. I had no reason to believe that I was, even after I had laid the woman out on the beach and pumped the salt water from her lungs. She wouldn't look at me, although her eyes appeared to take in everyone else as their heads crowded over her. The man and the woman who had alerted me were now silent. Chetwynd, tight-featured, was arranging for a doctor to be summoned and an old bath chair to be brought down from the house: his principal concern seemed to be to get the matter over and done with, to clear everyone else away, to assure them that the young woman's life was safe.

It took some time, but the people – most of them in their trunks and swimsuits – did finally drift away, with many lingering backward looks. I assisted when a breathless figure in dishevelled livery – striped trousers and a starched, collar-less shirt – appeared pushing a three-wheeled invalid carriage with a wicker hood. The woman still continued to fail to see me and said nothing as she was lifted on to the seat. A travelling rug was draped over her, from the chest down.

She was attractive, I realised, and in a provocative way. I'd noticed the even tan on all the parts her costume had left exposed, and the painted toe-nails, and the knotted ankle-chain of thin gold which I thought she must have forgotten to remove.

Chetwynd had the chair turned round and gave the domestic his orders to return to the house as quickly as he could. He set off, finding the incline of softer sand harder going than the damp. The man and the woman who had called to me from the sea followed behind him, as if their instructions too were understood by them. Chetwynd waved away an onlooker's enquiry. He half-turned round, was aware of me out of the corner of his eye, hesitated, and then turned fully round to face me.

It's his hesitation that I find myself dwelling on now: those two or three seconds of rapid-fire calculation. How many possibilities flitted through his brain in that scissure of time? On what slim fulcrum of chance – or seeming chance – was my future dependent?

The next moment he was looking directly at me. Yet it wasn't really so. His eyes were upon me, but – I can only think to say – they weren't seeing. They were focused not on the specific

22 RONALD FRAME

circumstance but on its significance: what I and my presence might mean to the state of things as they were, to himself, and to the manner of life conducted behind the high wall and rampart hedges of 'Underwood'.

FOUR

Three weeks after our meeting in the trattoria I receive a further enclosure in the post, accompanied this time by a letter.

The letter is brief and to-the-point. She has taken the liberty, she writes, of booking us both into a hotel in Treswithian. She has made enquiries ('discreetly') and finds I am entitled to another eleven days' holiday this year. This will only be for three nights. It's important, she tells me – 'important' underlined – that we two should meet, somewhere not so neutral, and that we should talk. She has something to show me, a written document, which she can't doubt will interest me.

The enclosure, meanwhile, is a shiny brochure. I recognise the building in the front page photograph at once, with a start of astonishment. It's 'Underwood': but with the institutional air of the private hotel it now announces itself to be, called 'Lynton Court'. Bottle-green paintwork, television aerials, a tarmacadam driveway, bathing costumes hanging to dry from an attic window, two top-heavy wire baskets of flowers suspended above the entrance porch, a putting-green on the top lawn, an ageing black labrador pet.

An hour later I sat down to pen a reply. Yes, I wrote, very well, it was possible for me to come. I meant to sound generous, not mystified, and just a little piqued at her presumption. I felt it was a portion of my life not so neatly accounted for as the rest, and I was irked with myself for having allowed the initiative, the higher ground, to be claimed by somebody who must be a stranger to me, and to the situation. Three or four days away, I explained a little stiffly, could (as it happened) be fitted into – or taken out of – my schedule 'without too much fuss'. We'd be travelling down together, would we? (The possibility of reading a suggestive intent into the 'invitation' hadn't passed me by, and I didn't know whether to wonder more at myself or at the unadorned ambiguity of the few words put down on the page in that confident, no-nonsense, larger-than-life script taught in girls' boarding schools.) I signed myself – in my own spikier, less forthcoming, compacted script – hers, with kind regards –

'My real name is Lillias. If that's a real name.'

'It's unusual,' I said. 'I – I like it.'

'I call myself Liz. It's the best I can do with it.'

'Liz-zy?' I suggested.

But she exchanged a frown with her reflection in the driving mirror.

'Liz it is,' she said. She changed gears roughly. 'Lil I thought about. Very *hoi polloi* – and the opposite of what my father wanted the name to suggest.'

'*He* chose it?'

'Indeed he did.'

'He told you why?'

'He died too long ago to tell me anything much.'

'Oh,' I said, 'I'm sorry.'

'Why are you sorry?'

'Because – because you didn't have him there. A father.'

She shrugged.

'There are fathers and fathers,' she said.

The sense was unclear to me.

'Your mother told you it was his choice?'

'Sort of told me. We weren't very communicative, though. She wrote it down, for later.'

'How – "wrote it down"?'

'Not now,' she said, moving the car into the fast outer lane of the motorway. 'When we get to Treswithian.'

*

The windows are salty, as they never were allowed to be in 'Underwood''s day. A drainpipe hangs loose from a wall at the back of the building. There are weeds in the rose beds, and greenfly on the old stippled Piccadilly tea bushes. The garage doors, with the gin-bottle green paint flaking off them, are unsteady on their loosened, rusty hinges. You can pull away dead and diseased red Virginia creeper in handfuls.

The clouds skim the bay at a canter. I watch them, seated at the bay window in one half of the original room that used to be Celia Jepson's bedroom and in which were entertained who knows which individuals or combinations of individuals.

All the same, only different.

The season is running down.

A couple of the waitresses have suddenly realised they couldn't care less, and take as long as they like about things. On the other hand the shopkeepers in the next village along the estuary seem hurried and impatient, not *more* tolerant with the prospect of quiet: they more or less snatch the money out of your hands, and the till drawers are forever being banged shut on these final transactions. Fewer newspapers are ordered at the newsagent's; there's less food on the shelves of the little self-service stores. The locals know exactly what they want, and their needs are the only ones to be catered for now – and even a little grudgingly in their case too. The awnings aren't pulled down on sunny days. The tin Agfacolor and Walls signs topple over on the pavements; half-day closing starts before mid-day in certain shops. Even the wares in the Tyrolean baker's window haven't risen to their usual height, they look stodgier as well as flatter. It isn't the time to have come, that couldn't be made clearer to us. In the hotel, room doors are left ajar whenever the last guests of the summer make their departure; windows hang wide open, and mattresses are placed against walls for an airing and the blankets, quilts and bedspreads folded and piled on the sills. Weeds that must have flourished in the rain they had just before our arrival have got a hold of the herbaceous beds, and the lawns could profit from another mowing session. A night wind has knocked an old nest out of a hedge but nobody appears to have noticed. The gravel would look better for raking, and maybe my expression when the owner's wife walked past told her so: she appeared neither offended nor apologetic, she seemed to be in agreement with me on the point but *she* knew – as I could not – that it isn't worth the effort, not before Easter and the first intake of the year when the whole house will smell of essential retouching with the paintbrush on last year's scuff marks, of carpet shampoo, of Jeyes fluid and Airwicks in bathrooms. Maybe they'll have had the drainpipes cleared and sluiced out; I swear I can catch the sewery stench of leaves, only very briefly each time, whenever the wind does a sort of mongrel's tail and curls back on itself. Maybe too they will see the advisability of hard-and-fast rules on keeping the lids closed tightly on the dustbins on the windward garage side.

*

She was sitting at the breakfast table, with the state-of-the-art black hard-shell plastic brief-case on her lap. When she heard me coming, town shoes knocking on the wooden floor, she made a bid to slide the case to her feet without my seeing. But I did see, and she saw that I did.

I said 'Good morning' and she replied with the same. She could have given the words more warmth, but chose not to.

We ordered what we wanted from the menus. We interspersed our eating with politesse.

Then the brief-case reappeared on her lap.

She opened it. From inside she removed some crumpled sheets of paper covered with script.

There was an assortment of stationery: creamy notepaper, pages from a student's loose-leaf pad, foolscap sheets of typing paper, pages of thinner backing paper, matt photocopying paper.

She placed them on the area of table the waitress had cleared.

'What are these?' I felt I was being prompted to ask.

'A little melodramatic.'

'They're yours?'

'Only – ' She cleared her throat. I thought her voice sounded nervous, notwithstanding the semblance of a cool, sure attack she was taking with me. ' – only in a manner of speaking.'

I looked at the careful ledger script.

'They get messier with time, I warn you.'

'If they're not yours – '

'They're my mother's, of course.' She snapped the brief-case shut. 'She put them – ' Her voice wobbled again. ' – into safe keeping. Someone she knew, a banker. She sent them to him – at the very end, when she'd collected together what she'd written – so she must have been clear in her mind about some things. She told him – instructed him: because she could trust him to keep them from me until after she died. Then he was to give them to me. This is the beginning – '

'There's more?'

'Oh yes. But you have to read it like a story.' She nodded. 'Like a story. She wrote it when it was all quite fresh in her mind – '

'You know it? The story?'

'I know *her* side anyway. Now you have to tell me the other. *Your* side.'

Loaded with more breakfast than I'd meant to eat, I could only stare at her. I wasn't sure of my ability to cope with this.

'I feel,' she said, 'it might have been better if my father *could* have seen them. It might have explained certain things to him. We – people, I mean – must make things clear to one another, mustn't we?'

I couldn't tell if she was being ironic. But I nodded. Then I qualified myself.

'Most of the time,' I said. '*Some* things . . .'

'Oh no,' she told me. 'If he'd known, it might have changed our lives. For the better.'

'And you want me to read these?'

'They're quite legible.'

'But – I mean – you're *letting* me read them?'

'I think you must,' she said. 'If, that is, you can tell me what I need to know.'

'Of course,' I replied. 'I'll do my best.'

'Why "Of course"? Aren't there some things you'd rather not tell me?'

'I – '

'Or not tell yourself?'

I stared at her. I shifted in my chair.

Over the years, since my time at 'Underwood', I had adjusted
to what I decided suited me as a version of events I could own to.
By this means I empowered myself to dwell on certain aspects
of the past and not on others. My own Vulgate was truthful
inasmuch as I wanted it to be the truth. Memory is seasoned
by the thought of the might-have-been: at which point guilt will
obtrude if it's given a chance, so the most important priority is
not to give it a chance. Life is best lived, for stability's sake, in
the mental equivalent of a vacuum.

FIVE

I've tidied up the things Fleur wrote. Sometimes she produced sentences; sometimes she was reduced to just phrases and key words.

She muddled her chronology, confessed to forgetting, unwittingly contradicted herself, sidestepped the main issues with non-sequiturs.

I can see that I've ended up giving her too much of my own voice. She thinks with my mental inflexions. I've lent her my vocabulary. It began unconsciously: but later, when I tried to tone down my contribution, I found I was implicated more than I'd ever meant to be the case.

Or am I being less than fair and honest to myself as I was? Maybe thirty years later I wanted this, to be more implicated in her account, more than I chose to judge in retrospect I really had been at the time?

Maybe.

The business starts with adverbs, with 'really' and 'honestly' and their deceptive simplicity. This is going to be a very Gordian knot to unravel.

*

A young man presented himself at the house this morning. It was *the* young man who saved Melinda's life. I came to have a look. He seemed awed by us all, and by 'Underwood'. I felt sympathetic, even though he ought to have been the hero in our midst. His arms hung so rigidly by his sides.

C. made the introductions, in rather a shambling way. He obviously wasn't expecting a visitor. It must

have taken courage — a *proper* hero's — to open the
gate and walk the full length of driveway. Everything
in this heat is so still, so solemn, so weighted with
expectation.

He asked after Melinda's health. C. told him she's
confined to bed and very lightly sedated, as the doctor
instructed, and that a nurse keeps dropping by. (A
circumstance which Melinda — only C. didn't say —
has willed herself to put up with. As needs must.)

When he'd finished explaining, C. asked the young
man if he would like to speak to her. The visitor
replied yes, yes please, thank you, sounding dis-
tinctly nervous about us all.

                              *

It was a strange performance of invalidhood, and after a while
the patient forgot and started to smile. Chetwynd had left us; she
pulled open the drawer of the table and removed a box of choco-
lates. She nibbled at a few, remembering every so often to offer
me one, until I couldn't refuse any longer. She talked of nothing
very much – the shapes of faces in the draped pelmet at the window, the effects of different light on the glass water jug and its
contents, the cost of half-way decent Swiss chocolate – and not
at all of the sea and what had happened. It occurred to her to lie
back on the pillows, in a Victorian swoon. In the sunlight that fell
across the pillows, I saw that she was heavily made up, like an
actress. Her fair hair winnowed Ophelia-like about her head.

Downstairs again I glimpsed Chetwynd's friends in the drawing-
room, as The Invalid had referred to it. I paused on the last
tread of the staircase to look. I stood watching them for perhaps
fifteen or twenty seconds. Although I was aware of a floorboard
creaking behind me I didn't turn round. Then I heard the squeak
of shoe leather and it was that which alerted me.

I spun round. Chetwynd stepped forward from a passageway
somewhere behind the staircase. He made no pretence that he
hadn't been watching me. He only smiled when he saw how confused I was. He placed his hand on my arm, and turned me, not
towards the front door but in the direction of the drawing-room.

'I imagine,' he said, 'Treswithian is pretty prolific with its speculations. About how we live here.'

He didn't need to hear a reply from me.

'All this, of course – ' His eyes made a circuit of the hall, including the staircase. ' – is on condition that you don't satisfy their curiosity. *Compris?*'

I nodded. When he looked at me for a spoken answer I told him, yes, yes, certainly.

My words were wound around by silence, which only confirmed – for me as for him – the significance he wanted them to have. Then it was his turn to nod, more purposefully than I had done, in the sober acceding manner professionals use to seal the parties' contract.

*

I was in the sick room on the second day – with Johnnie Ray singing on the radio – when the half-sleeve of her nightgown was caught back.

I noticed marks on her arm. Little perforations in the skin like needle pricks.

She saw me noticing and immediately pulled at the fabric.

I stepped back. Her face was bright red.

I hadn't seen them at the time of the accident, but there had been too much else to think about then. They studded the upper arm, seven or eight scarlet aureoles, some slightly crusted.

I turned to look out of the window. The others were outside. I heard their lazy laughter. I smelt honeysuckle; blue wistaria fringed one side of the window. It was perfect, or it ought to have been.

*

Could I drive? Chetwynd asked me at the conclusion of the next visit, which I had been invited to make.

He was accompanying me to the front door. He opened it himself.

I told him yes.

He led me outside and, when I was preparing to say my parting words, turned me towards the garage.

He rolled back the doors. Inside were five cars.

'Serious and not so serious,' he said, nodding to the selection of sports and staider models.

I gazed in admiration, especially at the Aston Martin: a DB2-4 Mark II.

'I'm on a sticky wicket here,' he said.

He explained, briefly, that he'd been let down by his driver, who had decamped back to London without giving him any prior notice.

'It's cramping our style a bit.'

I replied yes – like the man of the world I was not – I could quite appreciate that it would.

Then he made his offer. Would I be interested in taking the job on myself?

'Part-time,' he said. 'It shouldn't take it out of a strong lad like you. You might even find it's the making of you!'

First of all, I had to get in touch with Randolph Square, from whom I had already taken extended leave.

Chetwynd let me phone from the house, and offered to speak himself if need be. But that wasn't necessary.

I was in luck. My swimming-pool supervisor told me he was even relieved by my call, because the management committee had decided during my absence to overhaul the pool and mezzanine lounge areas: it would have to be closed for ten or twelve weeks while new changing-rooms were built.

Whenever I wanted to come back there'd be no major problem, he'd be happy to have me: I did my job well, he only had to tell me something once and I remembered.

Chetwynd assured me this was the best possible outcome. He discussed wages – it was superior pay to a pool attendant's at Randolph Square. *And* I should be fed. So – all told, and given the nature of 'Lesser Penelewey' life – it seemed to me that this was providential treatment indeed.

*

Driving wasn't likely to take up very much of my day, unless there was an expedition along the coast a little way or inland,

to whichever house they had been invited for lunch. Since I was
quite interested in mechanical matters, I was told I should keep
an eye on the cars and an ear cocked for any faults, and wash
them and brush up the interiors and not just wait for Chetwynd
to give me the word.

In addition we agreed that I should be an extra pair of
hands when and where they were required, wood-hewer and
water-drawer in emergencies. The gardeners had their own
province, and Tuitt (the major-domo) and Mrs Millard (the
live-out housekeeper) had a list of tradesmen and available
handymen, so any duties I had indoors would be of the domestic sort.

Everyone could swim who wanted to – even Melinda, when
she remembered not to over-reach herself – but, just possibly,
my services might be required as lifeguard also.

All in all, I thought I was going to have my work cut out.
But then and there I couldn't have wanted anything better to
happen to me. The opportunity was ideal. Even chamois-drying
and waxing the Bristol or cleaning the tines of forks in silver dip,
even waiting for the call to act as a watcher on the beach, I was
never to be less than wholly grateful.

                                    *

Thereafter he called me by my Christian name.

'Ralph.'

He pronounced it 'Rafe'. At first I thought he was merely
making fun of a previous generation's pretensions. But I came
to realise that he actually meant it. Dressed in the blazer and
flannels he'd provided me with, my neck over-heating inside a
collar and tie and my feet sweating in town shoes, I was not to
be the 'Ralph' I'd always been but this other one, 'Rafe', almost
a travesty or parody.

SIX

'Downstairs' wasn't quite that. Half a dozen shallow steps led down from the back of the hall to a short corridor, a baize door, and – beyond – the kitchen quarters. They were light and airy, a welcome hybrid mixture of the conventionally formal (towering dresser, serried rows of copper pots and skillets and jelly moulds on shelves) and the easy and informal: stockings hanging from a ceiling pulley, a fragrant marmalade hash with pith and pips tied up in a muslin bag simmering in a pan, a wireless turned very low and playing 'Memories Are Made Of This' and 'Whatever Will Be Will Be', the same tunes to which they would dance upstairs in the drawing-room. 'Downstairs' and 'Up-' were conveniences of expression used – I have to say – quite freely by Tuitt and Mrs Millard and by our cook Mrs Wragg, but not by Chetwynd and his guests. Our own generals seemed comfortable with the terms as with the distinction, however, and we left them to it.

I was accepted straightaway, and unconditionally. There was no profuse show of inclusion, but neither was there any wariness on anyone's part or any sly testing of this unknown quantity, myself. Few enquiries were made about my background, or my life before 'Underwood'. It was assumed that, even if I had no formal qualifications for what I was doing now, Chetwynd was too canny to allow himself to be wasting money on a bad bet. If there was slacking it wasn't admitted to, and nobody took me under their wing to detail the Do's-and-Don't's, what could be got away with by skimping on and which corners could definitely not be cut. I learned that my predecessor as chauffeur and factotum had talked too much, of fast cars and of the fancy human types he saw and studied on his travels around London, but – I was left to infer – it hadn't cut any ice with the present assemblage, and the only person who'd given an ear to him (a maid called Mavis) and who'd swallowed it hook-line-and-sinker had walked out and was working now, for her sins, as a skivvy in a sea-front hotel in Weymouth.

'Foolish girl couldn't recognise luck with bells ringing on it,' Mrs Wragg warned me in her summing up. 'Didn't realise when she was well off. This is as good as what any of *us* are ever going to get our eyeful of.'

*

Simply, it was the brightness of the rooms upstairs: the white panelling and the white friezes and ceilings, the exotic glowing islands of rugs on the wooden floors like rich harbours, the quietening blues and pinks of the upholstery and curtains. It proved an eye-opener to me after a British upbringing, that anybody in a land of grey stone cities in a drizzly climate should be capable of such lightness of touch. Chetwynd shrugged his shoulders and admitted to me, as a special confidence, that the colour scheme was a designer's doing and that you were required to 'consult' about these things. But even if that were so, he had wanted it and recognised what he wanted when he saw it, and I guessed that nothing major could have been done without his express approval: so while he disclaimed responsibility, I penetrated that ruse of modesty – he must have been instrumental after all in producing this resplendent but understated, scintillating décor.

There seemed to be no corners, no hiding places. Everything was candid, apparently. The house looked astonished by its own transformation. We were all a part of the mood, the ambience, and I soon realised that we were meant not to disappoint. Chetwynd had chanced on some potential in each one of his friends, and – I watched them – it was up to every individual, in gratitude to him for remarking their capacities, to be luminescent for him.

*

'Upstairs' they dressed for dinner, because – Chetwynd had told Mrs Wragg – that was how things had been done in the old days, when the house had belonged to its original owners.

They dined with candles on the table, and with the table laid in the confusing English fashion, each place setting chock-a-block with silver implements and several glasses laid out in a file. The ritual had been got exactly right, and in that sense was earnest enough. But why then should I have had the notion from my vantage-point hovering behind doors that the business was also a facsimile, Chetwynd's pastiche of dinner in a country house? I had heard how Chetwynd would examine the table in advance of the meal, sometimes repositioning certain items of cutlery or glassware but more generally just walking a circuit of the table, then another circuit and another, taking in the grand spectacle. Apparently he was most insistent that everyone was dressed correctly to the smallest detail, but he didn't object in so many words when debonair Patrick Durran forgetfully propped his elbow on the table or handsome Clive Melchett pushed his chair back on its hind legs or elegant Drusilla Cowper emptied the contents of her petit point evening bag into her lap to find her cigarette lighter.

The aesthetic effect was all. I couldn't know if anyone seated at their host's table suspected it was as mock as it was. They dutifully dressed to the nines, and as far as they could (posture excepted) watched their P's and Q's and politely allowed Chetwynd to pilot the conversation for themselves and their guests.

Wasn't it, I asked myself, just too much of a re-creation? Outside Oxbridge colleges and the Inns of Court, whoever heard of such formal antics being respected in *this* day and age?

*

My father became too easily tired to really care about my summer employment. My sister and brother were too busy trying to make new friends – quite separate friends – down on the public tennis courts. It was my mother's reactions I attended to, therefore, and I couldn't decide what she thought. She was interested, of course, but also a little alarmed, since all her library reading matter had been located in a world quite different

to our own. Maybe she was in some ways envious of me, and
even somewhat peeved that the luck should be mine. But if she
couldn't understand the reasons why *I* had been selected (she
had me repeat to her, several times, how it had happened, that
I'd made their acquaintance down on the beach), she must also
have been flattered not a little that her son was capable of making
an impression on such types. Chauffeuring, of course, was only
a holiday stop-gap: she had no doubts in her mind that I should
be going on to university after I'd taken the year 'off' which I
had insisted this next one would be, with my schooldays now
behind me. She must have told herself that the Chetwynds of
this life are very fussy about who drives them, who is sitting
there to be spoken to. She attributed my success to my voice,
my nice accent (which meant, really, having less recognisable
accent to 'place' me than did those of my contemporaries she
knew), my looks, my neat appearance, the constant parting in
my hair, my politeness.

I just smiled. I smiled, and said what she expected me to and
what she wanted to hear from me, and for most of the time I
was away from it I let myself think back to, and forward to,
'Underwood' like a sanctuary.

*

I ate in the scullery, off the kitchen. At supper-time we sat at
a deal table: Tuitt, Mrs Wragg, sometimes Mrs Millard, Iris,
Jen, and myself. We usually had the pickings of the previous
evening's upstairs dinner; it involved some deft stretching on
Mrs Wragg's part, but we dined very well – absurdly well – on
partridge, venison, lamb, lobster. Our lunch was taken early,
an hour or so in advance of the upstairs serving: it was a much
simpler affair, bread with cheese and chutneys and strong tea
from an urn. Tuitt and Mrs Wragg could drink gallons of the
stuff between them, our gardener Kestle not much less.

This was our little band. There was something pleasantly
mindless about physical toil and then savouring your rest,
especially when the sun shone and good food was so abundant.
Before we cleared away, Mrs Wragg would doze lightly, Iris
would read a library romance with her head supported by her

hands; Jen would buff her nails or trace the whorls of wood on the table with her fingertip and be content enough, Tuitt would read the racing newspaper, and Kestle would deliver a commentary on the state of the garden, as it was and had been and might be, and would only interrupt himself to remark on what was visible through the window: sometimes the lower portion of a body walking past, or a change in the weather, or a pattern of clouds, or a butterfly's colouring. I thought I might fall asleep like Mrs Wragg with the very pleasant and dependable, very welcome tedium of it all.

SEVEN

First of all, there was Chetwynd.

He was just below average height.

Neat, trim torso; small-waisted.

Elegant hands and (perhaps) under-sized feet, but medium to stocky legs.

A tight face; clear-complexioned. Moderately good-looking, in a rather anonymous way.

High cheekbones, a thin priest's nose; a confusing mouth – wide, but with spare ascetic lips, and with a small crooked lift on the right-hand side; cleft chin.

The eyes, as blue as the eyes of the boys who went off to war. The left one seeming to balance the right-hand side curl of the mouth with its slight cast. When he was talking to you, one eye – the perfectly good one – fixed on you totally, but the other was, if not its own master, then somewhat wayward, seeming sometimes (when he was tired, for instance) less to look *at* you than *around* you. Dark eyebrows that met in a scatter of darker hairs over the bridge of the nose.

Black hair on his head, not fine or flyaway, regularly cut short, receding on top; clean-shaven.

Does this all add up?

In the flesh, the effect of the man was his completeness: his full command of himself. He had never a hair or a crease out of place; I didn't once see his shoes unpolished.

His clothes didn't draw attention to themselves, which meant either that they'd been very carefully thought out beforehand or had been purchased on an infallible instinct. Three-button suits in charcoal cloth or herringbone tweed, double-breasted blazers with dark-enamelled buttons, white or hair-line stripe cotton shirts with starched collars and cuffs, flannel or cavalry twill trousers, black or navy socks, Oxfords or demi-brogues. He dressed in accordance with a social fashion, but perhaps more faultlessly – more neatly and bespokenly – than is usually the case. Only bachelors with valets to lay out, put away, and press and launder clothes can achieve that studied artlessness.

His composure was an object lesson to the rest of us. He wasn't exactly a point of stillness, though: I had the sense instead of a very tight-packed energy committing itself to seemliness, sublimated to the unexceptional appearance of ordinariness as it was accepted within a certain restricted, august social grouping. His voice was proof of a special sort: as if it was a mechanism held back on a taut string, pitched very slightly higher during a longer interlude of talking than it was with just a handful of words, neck sinews strained, diction as precise as a foreigner's, accent as such non-existent. He spoke quietly, but quite often with what I can only call an understated degree of urgency, which – coupled with the steeliness he could convey by his eyes – was able to silence a conversation of much louder voices.

Does this all really add up?

A description of the external can't include the fact of his charisma, which was conveyed from the inside out. His money may have been more charismatic than anything, and the real apologia for the authority he exercised over us. And yet while I can't disentangle that vital aspect of the man from our other perceptions, I can't accept either that there wasn't another valid reason – to be found in natural science, in the workings of body and inter-body chemistry, in the operation of electrical waves expelled by his person – why he exerted that sheer *physical* hold on us that he did. When I dream about those times still, we are – as my imagination has it – literally revolving around him, always and forever in the clear and unequivocal orbit of his influence.

I didn't see him looking in mirrors – or he didn't let me catch him looking – and yet he must have been very self-aware. We, and our guests, were his mirror.

He affected casualness, and yet the type of image given of himself to others was of the utmost significance to him, socially and professionally. He understood that, in this democratic age more than ever, appearance counted, that – before everything else, even home(s) and car(s) – clothes and poise and dulcet, euphonious vowels make the facsimile man, the subtly distinguished variants of the 'Anthony Chetwynd' he meant his small, enclosed world to perceive him to be.

*

Clive Melchett was in his thirties, and stunningly handsome. Prior to his current life he had been an actor, although the name was unknown to me. He occasionally took on modelling assignments, and the work was apparently enough to provide him with something resembling a healthy income.

Mitchell Ogilvie was in his late forties, with a very distinguished RAF service record, which included a DFC. The battle over Béthune had left him with a limp and two steel pins in his back. Thin-faced with a clipped moustache and brushed hair, blue-eyed like Chetwynd and lean and sinewy in build, he exactly looked the part, dressed either in flannels and blazer with squadron crest or in cavalry twills, corduroy waistcoat and sports jacket.

Patrick Durran, beanstalk high and broad of shoulder, had almost, but not altogether, eliminated his South African provenance from his accent. He resembled a rather weathered, fatigued version of the popular film actor David Farrar, with the same powerful brooding manner but not a full complement of those dark, smouldering looks. His patrician nose was the result of various rugby breakages, and women seemed to go for that, irrespective of the sardonic mouth. He was also reputed to have a virility the rest of us might envy, and indeed after an afternoon or an evening in his company, certain favoured women would reappear wearing a deliriously sated expression which told us of the secret state of play.

Celia Jepson was the most senior of the women, in status and at the age of forty-five or so. She had lived too full a life to have retained her looks, so that now she patched and infilled and painted over to keep up a front. She was Chetwynd's head-of-house, and nothing escaped her eye. Her past was a mystery to us, but presumably not to Chetwynd. She had possibly worked in department stores, perhaps as a buyer; she dressed impeccably. At some point she had made the acquaintance of Patrick Durran, but no one knew how: in the man's biography, Mitchell Ogilvie told me, there were always the same two or three missing years, which had caused him to seriously wonder if he could have been serving time at the pleasure of His Majesty.

Melinda Myer's background was pukka – an Army General father and Rear-Admiral's daughter for a mother, boarding schools (plural, which suggested expulsions she never admitted to) – but it hadn't reached to the débutante ritual and coming out. Somehow she had got through the years and now – a little *too* freckly, at least a stone overweight, but with a good-natured laugh to (figuratively) pull the ceiling down on us – here she was.

April Purris was quieter, but she had clever, determined eyes: they mightn't have been as practisedly shrewd as Celia's, but they were kinder. Her accent was as manufactured as Celia's, and yet – sensibly aspiring to be, not Knightsbridge, but merely neutral – it seemed to me more excusable. Those vigilant green eyes under clipped arc brows were her best physical feature, and hinted to me at a rare quality like integrity at the heart of her. There was nothing about fashion, hair and make-up that she didn't seem to know.

Beyond them, in their lesser orbits, were the others.

Of those, the friendliest to me was Howard Kimble. He was the chief rival Patrick Durran had in the tennis stakes. He worked for an estate agent in Chelsea, and Chetwynd enjoyed quizzing him. Fair-haired and happiest in a hacking jacket, he didn't speak like a toff; he had a good memory for jokes, and didn't need to tank himself up like Durran before he began on his audience.

Christopher Lester-Jones, although younger and an Oxon. MA, had something against Durran, and it seemed to prohibit his being included as often and as fully as I guessed Chetwynd would have liked. A rumour did go about that he and Durran had crossed proverbial swords once in love. Maybe he also had too much of the demon vice pride in his make-up. His expertise at mixing cocktails would have been invaluable. More than that, though, Chetwynd missed being regularly plied with stories of legal life, seen from the young man's fairly lowly position (as yet) in a hugely reputable outfit where he was serving his articles.

Of the secondary women, the one we saw most of was Drusilla Cowper. Her life had seemed complete and unperturbed. A wife and mother – palmy days in Cuckfield, attractive, educated, moneyed, holidayed – she was someone on whom the sun of cliché ought always to have shone. But suddenly, with no forewarning at all, her husband – a company accountant – had informed her that their marriage was at an end. Even worse, she was to discover that he had set up home – a new home, after they'd sold the one in Cuckfield – in a flat in racy Brighton, with a girl he had established in the fancy goods trade. Drusilla – for all the suburban pains she took with her presentation of herself, for all her mature attractiveness only flawed by the insomniac's rings under her highlighted grey eyes – lived very close to the edge. Chetwynd might have been tempted to include her among the closest disciples if she hadn't been possessed of that strain of unpredictability which marked her apart from the rest of us: she prised people from their shells, but she was too openly cynical to fit quite comfortably with the group our host had gathered about himself.

If he hadn't been able to exercise control over every imaginable contingency of life at 'Underwood' and his grander London home, then what would have been the earthly merit of the enterprise?

*

She was vaguely familiar to me, the afternoon she walked in through the french windows, framed against the baked blue sky. I thought I was possibly remembering her from the first afternoon I'd called at the house. She was fair and pretty, in a quiet and undemonstrative way the personalities of the others were bound to eclipse.

Chetwynd had told me there was an Ordnance Survey map on the shelves somewhere. The others gossiped happily enough among themselves even with me, a menial, there: admittedly Celia watched me carefully, while I guessed the actor Clive's attention was of another sort.

Someone spoke her name, 'Fleur'. She smiled, a little uneasily, looking past us into the hall.

'His Lordship's somewhere or other,' Melinda said.

An arm-chair was found for the visitor.

She sat down.

'Too hot for walking,' she told nobody in particular. 'Today.'

'How far is it?' April asked her. 'That you have to walk to get here?'

'Oh, just a mile or so.'

Melinda laughed. '"*Just* a mile"!'

The arrival smiled again, although I realised that the laughter puzzled her.

'You should bring your little girl along,' Patrick Durran said.

'Someone comes. And looks after her. They go down to the beach together.'

'Sandcastles and things?' Clive Melchett said. 'I think you're very wise to leave her there, Fleur.'

The young woman's smile faded a little more, as if she was unsure how she should be responding.

'You'll make Fleur feel guilty,' Mitchell Ogilvie admonished, maybe jokily or maybe not.

'Christ, Fleur. Have I?'

The question received a head-shake for an answer. In the next couple of seconds I followed the direction of April's eyes. Chetwynd was standing in the doorway.

'Mrs Simmons, you've managed to get away. Excellent!'

The arrival leaned forward in her chair. Her face was suddenly animated.

'Are we going out somewhere?' Melinda asked.

Chetwynd moved into the room.

'Bunty B. has taken Praze Place for a month. She rang this morning.'

The others were in no confusion as to the identity of the person being referred to.

'Some of her friends have come down,' Chetwynd continued. 'I thought we might present ourselves. She wants to show the house off.'

'I'll bet it's expensive enough,' Celia said.

Celia was the closest to Chetwynd. But the slight chill with which her remark was received informed me – and was meant as a reminder to her – that there were limits as to what she might feel herself at liberty to say.

The woman called Fleur – and 'Mrs Simmons' – was looking at the others. The name 'Bunty B.' seemed to be as new to her as to me.

'Now we can all go,' Chetwynd said. '*En famille*. We'll take two cars. Ralph, you can drive Mrs Simmons back from Praze.'

She glanced up at Clive Melchett, then at Patrick Durran. Chetwynd placed his hand on my shoulder.

'May I introduce a new member of our staff. Ralph Witton.' He pronounced it, as ever, 'Rafe', and the fact seemed to register with her. 'He is our new driver.'

Her eyes alighted on me. I merited a pale, guarded smile. Clearly she failed to recognise *me*. Did I just not look like a 'Rafe'?

I was still intrigued. Where had I seen her before? Somewhere in London?

Chetwynd reached up to a shelf behind me and retrieved the Ordnance Survey map of our reach of Cornwall.

'This is what you're looking for, I think.'

Now that I had the map I had no alternative but to take my leave. She was the person in that room I looked at last as I closed the door on them from the hall. The gap narrowed between jamb and the edge of the door, until only she was left. At the very final second, even though her face was turned towards Chetwynd, her eyes traversed the room and found me, through the crack.

I recognised in that instant what I tended too easily to forget later on, that the two essential aspects of the life she was living then were fear and daring.

Sometime shortly after six o'clock we left Praze Place and I drove her the seven miles back to Treswithian in the Bristol. Chetwynd had told me that she wanted me to take her to 'Underwood'. From there she preferred to walk.

To walk home without arousing undue suspicion, I deduced.

On the drive over mid-afternoon, it had come to me where I must have seen her: back in Chelsea, at Randolph Square, one memorable face among the hundreds I'd watched come downstairs into the pool area.

She did live in London; 'in the north' was the best answer I could elicit. I asked her if she had ever visited the flats at Randolph Square. She hesitated before she said 'no'.

'It's been a wonderful summer for weather, hasn't it?' she said, quickly changing the subject. 'Cornwall can be unpredictable, I've heard.'

She told me, when I enquired, that this was her first visit. A – she hesitated again – a 'patient' of her husband's had given them the use of a house for a while. Her husband was staying on in London; he had his work to attend to. She didn't say if she was expecting him to visit.

The information she did impart was cautiously given. I suppose she realised I could have found out, even if she had refused: I had my eyes, and a question or two voiced in the kitchen would have produced an answer.

Driving with one arm propped on the sill, I mutely tried to impress on her that I wasn't 'merely' staff. But I doubt if she noticed, because she hardly once took her eyes away from the windscreen.

'Now you'll have to drive all the way back. On my account.'

'That's my job,' I said.

'But you're Mr Chetwynd's driver.'

'It – it's a lovely evening.'

'Maybe it is – but . . .'

Since our setting out to return I had wanted to ask her about

Chetwynd, how she had come to make his acquaintance. She might have heard my thoughts in the silence; maybe she took pity on me.

'Mr Chetwynd's been very kind to me. Asking me to join his friends.'

Maybe she was also wanting me to impart some information in return. I obliged: hinting at the extent of their social life in London, where their existences evidently revolved around Chetwynd's own and his grand house in Kensington.

'I know very little about *objets d'art*,' she confessed. 'I believe his work is something in that line.'

'Nobody else knows much either,' I ventured.

'An *antiquaire*.'

'I wonder when he gets the time for his business. What with everything else.'

She didn't reply. Maybe she thought I'd gone a little too far, over-presumed, as Celia had done earlier.

When we reached 'Underwood', she got out, thanked me and smiled, and then set out for home by way of the side-gate.

I stood watching her as she followed the sandy track through the grass. The sun had sunk low in a pink sky, but she didn't raise her head to look. When she reached the foothills of the dunes she opened her handbag and took out a headscarf. She placed it over her hair and knotted it under her chin. She might have done so to protect herself from blown sand or from the chill that would start to rise from the beach at sundown. Or – another possibility occurred to me as she looked back over one shoulder, then the other – she might have done so for a more acute reason, for the strategical sake of disguise.

EIGHT

It was during one of my washing-up stints in the kitchen that I heard them discussing Chetwynd's wealth. There was this place – and the house in London, in Kensington – and the other house nobody, not even the regulars upstairs, had ever seen, in the Balearics or North Africa. He was rumoured to own a racehorse, and an Englishman in a Bugatti was said to drive the stretch of coast road between Juan-les-Pins and Cros-de-Cagnes. Not long ago a photograph had appeared in a magazine showing him at a party on a yacht, off the rocks of Capri, and apparently he'd been very annoyed about it.

'The party?' Jen quipped. 'Why, wasn't it any good?'

'The photograph, lass.' Tuitt drew himself to his full six feet to put her quite straight. 'The disregard of a man's privacy.'

Mrs Wragg cut in. 'You don't take your position here seriously enough, my girl.'

'He can't hear us.'

'Oh, can't he?' Mrs Wragg glared at her.

'Walls have ears, do they?'

'Put a thought into words,' said Tuitt, 'and who knows where it can fly to?'

We all fell silent at the elusive wisdom of this observation.

*

The newspapers were all hidden from me, so I was never to know where in Cornwall Mother had her accident in the car.

Perhaps we passed the place on the taxi journey from the station, the point where it happened. We drove past and may have been looking in the other,

wrong direction. Wherever the car went off the road,
vegetation must cover the spot now, the hedges must
have grown back in a long time ago. I wanted to ask
the driver, do you remember an accident? Do you
recall hearing of it, of a woman's death, you know
where such a terrible thing took place? But I didn't
want to ask him in Lillias's hearing, not in front of
her, as if the matter was really an obscenity.

So we have to live with this ignorance, all of us
– of what it was Mother lived and died for. The
responsibility, I feel, is mine: to discover. Yet she
was as secretive about it as she might be with me, her
own daughter. Shouldn't *I* respect her reticence? At
the time I could see the evasions in her eyes and hear
the silences in her voice. She refused to be explicit:
she knew I would understand, by my blood intuition,
just what I would, what I needed to understand.

Gilbert hasn't made the association – that Lillias
and I have come to the county where Mother died. I
have chosen not to tell him about C. and 'Underwood'.
All he knows or cares about is that Treswithian is one
of 'those' favoured places where the knowing folk
and their sort come – Home Counties professionals
who turn into summer yachtsmen – so it passes the
respectability test. He can have no complaints.

*

The banks of rhododendrons and the long, dense honeysuckle
hedges and the drystone slate walls stood between us and the
life on the other side. Occasionally I heard children's cries
from the beach, a stray curlicue of adult laughter. But hardly
anything reached us where we were, sunk low on immaculate
lawns beneath the mass of vegetation. Occasionally a gull or a
kittiwake floated above the garden on its way to or from the
dunes; once a bi-plane mewled overhead and inland, from the
other side of the estuary. For families holiday afternoons raced
by, recorded for future reference in photographs, to prove
that they had happened at all. For the 'Underwood' set the

afternoons were leisurely, tranquil, exclusive – and, even for us 'downstairs' folk by association, mysterious.

'I advise people,' I overheard Chetwynd telling one of his smart dinner guests as I waited at the table, 'on acquisitions and, of course, sales.'

'Do you,' the woman with the dished face asked, 'have a shop?'

He didn't allow himself to look offended by the question.

'I *do*,' he said, 'have business premises. A showroom. But I'm a sort of mobile business. I move about to do my consultations and purchases. To – to give my advice.'

'I see,' the woman replied. 'I see.'

I wondered at her emphasis.

He straightened his cuffs and pulled at the links.

'It is, as they say, a living.'

A good one too, I was aware.

He smiled again, in the cryptic way he had. It might have been a defence mechanism, I was starting to realise. There were things that couldn't be taken quite on trust, I felt: simple gestures which were somehow complicating themselves into riddles.

On the hottest days, it was as if Chetwynd and his party were all on reduced wattage. They might have appeared to be as before, but in fact there wasn't enough energy to go round and to keep a conversation in operation. Sentences became sequences of disjointed phrases that petered out . . . Even smiles were hardly that, but like little last gasps of frayed etiquette. Cigarettes were lit and forgotten, burning themselves out in the ash-trays; cups of coffee were sipped at and then placed out of thought range where they turned cool and streaky.

I realised then just how much dynamic momentum it required to keep life at 'Underwood' in its – for want of a better adjective – 'normal' condition.

The rushing sound of tyres on gravel: the pedal gently braking to a halt. An interim silence. Then the car doors opening –

shoe soles and heels touching the granite chips – the doors being closed. The crunching of gravel under the footfalls. The contact of steel tips and/or stilettos with the slate steps. The brief, ritual delay before the front door is opened. The fading of the footsteps over carpet on parquet. The heavy closing of the door.

Silence, that is, apart from the chortles of the wood pigeons. And the soughing of the tallest trees – the cedars and the pines – as a breeze reaches us from the beach and turns tail to travel out again, towards the estuary. Birdsong from the shrubbery. Insects' droning. A voice, a fragment of speech, carried from the dunes. The low, muffled echo of the breakers running on to sand.

Silence which is not. Sounds inside sounds.

And that enveloping whiteness: white-painted panelling and frieze and ceiling, a white fireplace, white loose covers, white net curtains at the windows. The other colours were pale pastels: scatter cushions, sheeny Persian and Chinese rugs, delicate water-colours, the garden flowers arranged in silver bowls.

The drawing-room was the most beautiful room I had ever seen. I was bedazzled by it every time I found an excuse to walk in. Perhaps what impressed me most of all was its impracticality: it wasn't suitable for either ordinary life or ordinary people. Even time seemed to have a different measure in that place: languid, elastic, unaccountable.

*

When I wasn't there, when I was back in our house, I seemed to carry part of its atmosphere with me, and it seemed to have taken and to be holding a part of me. My mother noticed my dissatisfaction with things as we had them, even in another person's home. She was probably asking herself what it was going to be like when we were back in London. I told myself I wasn't thinking that far ahead, but necessarily I was, because in three more weeks we should be gone. This prolonged summer

was a luxury for us: the mean duration in our modest suburb
was ten days or two weeks. But owing to my father's having
had a 'shock' to his heart shortly after Christmas and a number
of giddy turns since, he was taking very seriously the doctor's
firm advice to rest. Yet this too would end and we should return
to our mock-Jacobean semi-detached, Dad would try working
again, I'd hang around with my old pals from the Grammar
school, and Mum would probably nag me about not having put
my back into chasing a university place when I already had the
qualifications on paper.

No, I was in no hurry to leave Treswithian and 'Underwood',
none at all, and certainly not to return to that.

*

I had a whole afternoon off every Wednesday as well as on
Saturday and Sunday, and on one I made for Doiles' auction
rooms in Wadingford. I wasn't really well enough off to buy
anything, but I was fascinated by the artefacts of other people's
lives, especially when they were seen so out of context, in
Doiles' linoleum-floored halls with their paraffin smell.

That Wednesday afternoon I was looking through a pile of
dusty *Country Life* magazines from the thirties. I was turning the
pages of one when I saw a photograph of the Gainsborough 'conversation piece' that hung above the fireplace in 'Underwood''s
drawing-room. I blinked: stared at it. I had no doubts it *was* the
same painting. I'd taken advantage of moments when the house
was deserted to acquaint myself better with the appointments
in the public rooms.

The article was on the subject of Thomas Gainsborough's
patrons. It stated that the portrait of the Lamond family of
Lincolnshire – the newly wealthy Mr George and nameless
wife, and their three anonymous, lounging young lads – hung
in the old saloon at Hexby Abbey. I also had a memory for
the conversations which I would hear as I served dinner or
poured coffee, and the name of the house had cropped up
before. I only remembered the name, not the circumstances.
Now the painting belonged to Chetwynd, to 'Underwood', and
its pedigree was – truly enough – a thing of the past. But

the coincidence intrigued me, I wasn't sure why: sufficiently
so for me to fork out twenty-five shillings in order to outbid
the Bookshop man and buy myself the stack of forty dog-eared,
musty-smelling magazines which would be my express reading
fare over the next ten days.

I pored over the magazines with the myopic application of a
scholar.

  I was rewarded: with sightings of several objects whose
whereabouts 'upstairs' my mental eye could exactly place as
I read. In each case they appeared not in a salesroom's advertisement but in features that either concerned an artist or
craftsman or described the architectural details and interior
decoration and furnishings of a stately home or grand country
house. I recognised the commode of West Indian satinwood,
the Chippendale break-front bookcase, the oak court-cupboard
of the 1640s. Each was ascribed with a location and a history of
ownership. A few of the owners referred with some pride to this
or that heirloom, but others were quite matter-of-fact, as if afraid
in the British way of giving too much credence to 'culture'. Too
many of them seemed to be clichés – clipped moustaches and
whisky complexions, or else racehorse features and the extreme
leanness of over-bred Celtic hounds – and I wondered if it could
be a Haw-Haw perpetration. But the objects themselves, the
œuvres d'art, those must have been genuine surely, to prompt
such reverent attention from the writers, and the prominence
of their display photographed on the page, sometimes straddling
four or five columns of print.

NINE

I lag myself in woollens and sit out on the hotel's sunken terrace for tea. The sun is warm reflected off the wall, but it isn't swimming weather. Liz hasn't appeared; I am alone – except when the waitress, another of the temping students, brings the tray – but all the time I seem to be hearing ghostly footsteps behind me.

I sit remembering my first visit, discovering tiny initials furtively scratched in a corner of a window pane, and a certain dark stain on the morning-room's parquet. Then also I had imagined I could hear footfalls on the sunshine terrace, which had only been – like now – the blowing hither and thither of the papery husks of dead summer blooms.

The house's transformation to hotel has been only averagely done, with the inevitable lapses of taste and – tapping the walls – reverberating hints of chipboard conversion where sizeable rooms have been divided for profit's sake.

I shouldn't have come. It wasn't desirable and I haven't been wise.

A spindly-legged Siamese cat stalks the garden, and it seems to me a sinister, ever watchful presence which I should have seen – that first afternoon, on my arrival, crossing my path on the front steps and hissing at me – was really warning me away from the place.

*

Fleur continued to be different from the others. It was the difference that appealed to me. I was intrigued also by Chetwynd's keeping an eye open for her every time footsteps sounded on the gravel of the driveway. If she did appear, he took great care that she shouldn't feel her domestic responsibilities with her daughter were excluding her.

She said less than any of the others. Her smiles were quieter, more reflective, sadder even, but perhaps more necessary to her. I had the sense that she unwrapped a little in their company. I had the impression also that Chetwynd recognised this psychological dependence she had on the time spent at 'Underwood'.

Because only Chetwynd appeared to notice apart from myself, I felt jealous – possessive – of my curiosity. I savoured my involvement with her enigma.

*

Liz walked me back to the house where they'd stayed and found it without any wrong turnings. I didn't tell her that I had three or four times followed her mother home in the evenings, shadowing her from thirty or forty yards away.

The lane was darker than ever. The track was still flint and sand with a ridge of coarse grass along the middle between the wheel ruts. From either side vegetation encroached, and the air was close and polleny.

Closer to habitation the tops of the trees grew together. The lane narrowed like a tunnel, and the track acquired the greenish tint of underwater, or of a dream.

We reached the half-dozen houses. The first ones had the charm of the Bates' residence in Hitchcock's *Psycho*.

'Do you know why your mother came here?'

'An estate agent sent her the details. Ambiguously worded, I suppose.'

'Why Cornwall, though? Why that summer?'

'My father was busy with his patients. Building up the practice in Harley Street. He told her she should take me away. I'd been a bit poorly. The area had its associations, of course. Although she hadn't ever seen it for herself, it had meant something to *her* mother – '

We stood outside the house once called 'Lanteglos'. The name had been removed from the stone gatepost and a blandly

harmless one, 'Holmhurst' – the sort you buy ready-made in
wrought iron at a garden centre – fixed on top. Its life now
appeared as a picture of the conventional: bathing-wear drying
from a line hung between two trees, a child's BMX bicycle lying
on the grass, an unattended Peugeot estate car with its rear
door left open, the faint sounds of a radio tuned to the *Top
Forty Show*.

She pointed to a yellow plastic bucket moulded like a small,
square, self-contained sandcastle.

'What a bloody cheat! We had to make our own castles. Pat
out the towers and join them together with walls: ramparts.
These days children have to get it all *now*. No bloody imagination at all.'

She sounded like an *Any Answers* correspondent, as radical
as the best – or worst – of them. She smiled to hear herself.

I kicked at some pebbles at my feet. They skittered into
the neglected verge, where the grass had been left to grow
and had seeded with red campion and white camomiles and
stonecrops. Beyond that was the hedge and the garden with its
roughly scythed outer field and the machine-mown lawn closer
to the house.

As I looked again at the arrangement of windows and stood
trying to recall which of them I was used to finding lit, she spoke
over my thoughts.

'I knew you by sight,' I heard her say.

I blinked several times. Then I turned my head and looked
at her.

'I'm sorry – what did you say?'

'I recognised you. When you came along here. At night. Of
course I didn't know *who* you were. But I knew someone used
to stand out here under the trees, behind the hedge, and watch
us. Watch *for* us. It *was* you, wasn't it?'

I stared at her. But I couldn't deny that it had been me.

'Yes,' I said, a little indistinctly. 'Yes, I came – '

She nodded. Her face was quite serious now. Her eyes
travelled a slow double-circuit of the garden that was visible
to us, one way and then the other.

'I would hear my mother coming back. Sometimes I pretended

to be asleep. Then I'd get up. You only appeared at night. It was better than being told a story. Better than having the scary bits left out, how my mother did. I couldn't lie in bed thinking you might be out there. I had to get up. I was drawn to look.'

She paused. She gave me a tight, inattentive smile.

'So – you see,' she said, 'I already knew you quite well. This isn't the first time we've encountered one another. Sort of, anyway.'

I nodded, but I didn't speak.

'But in London too,' she said.

'What?'

'You came out to Hampstead. At the end. Didn't you?'

'I . . .' My heart skipped several beats.

'On your bicycle.'

'I thought – I thought in a city – it would be different – '

'How did you discover where we lived?'

'I took a taxi. I had it follow your mother's.'

'How they do in films?' Her little smile was tighter than the last.

'It was the only way I could think of.'

'And what did you learn from that?'

'I just had to see the house,' I said, 'that's all. I was curious. It happens to people. You know – ?'

'To those in a certain frame of mind?'

'"Frame of . . ."?'

'The love-lorn, you mean? Stricken swains?'

'I . . .' I lifted and dropped my shoulders. 'I don't know.'

'You don't know? Or you don't *care* to know?'

'I was young.' I swallowed hard. 'If I seemed confident, it was a lie.'

'You were a cowardly swain?'

'You want me to believe that?'

'That you were a coward? Or a swain?'

'I thought, somehow my – my curiosity – it would protect her. It would keep her from harm.'

'Someone – ' She half-spoke, half-sang the title of the song. '" – to watch over me . . ."'

The tempo was wrong. She made the sentiment sound hollow.

'What – ' I spoke without permitting myself even a glance. ' – what would she have thought?'

'About being a cowardly swain?'

'About – about keeping an eye on her?'

'I expect it was a sort of vague comfort. When she did discover. But that was too late.'

She was looking at me. I saw so out of the corner of my eye. Maybe she was concerned about the epithet: either the vagueness of it, or of my having been anything in particular to her mother.

We seemed to be on the point of broaching an understanding. At very long last.

I was turning to look at her, quite frankly, when quite suddenly the mood changed. Her eyes were concentrating on the flinty surface of the track at her feet. Her face had hardened.

'I'm walking back,' she said, and moved off. 'Come on.'

She didn't speak until we'd put a couple of hundred yards between ourselves and the houses.

'She was a fool.'

I thought I'd misheard. I hurried to catch up with her and match my stride to hers.

'What was that?'

'Here was the last place to come. She was a fool not to know that.'

'But your grandmother's accident – '

'That was ages before, it was history. What good did visiting *this* place do?'

'You couldn't help it, what happened. The "Underwood" set-up – that was an accident.'

'She'd never have met them. If she hadn't come. Never met any of you.'

'When – ' I tried to slow her pace, but she wouldn't be held back. ' – when you saw me – from the window – did I frighten you? – '

'I hated you too much for that.'

'"Hated"?'

'The only frightening part of it was imagining the best death for you. The *worst* death, that is. There was an old well roundabouts that was talked about, overgrown and so deep you couldn't hear a stone strike the bottom, and I used to picture you falling into that.'

She set her face in the direction of the hotel, its green retiled roof just visible where some trees in the garden had been lopped low.

'For your mother's sake,' I said, 'you wished that on me?'

'My mother left me alone. With those women she paid to look after me. I had no forgiveness in me for them either. When she came back I'd hear her singing little bits of songs. When she came into my room, I could see through my eyelashes how she was smiling; her cheeks had a high colour in them. If she thought I was asleep she started undoing the buttons or the zip on her dress, she took her party shoes off. My father must have been aware of what she'd asked Mrs Thorold to pack and send on to her from home – fancier clothes – and if he didn't know the full extent of it . . .'

She wouldn't continue. I asked her to, I asked her several times. Then I stopped asking.

I had to scamper after her to keep level. She took the track like an infantryman on a forced march. Pebbles skidded from under her shoes: navy leather Timberland deck shoes, as the fashion required; the narrow trousers were white cotton cut-offs, the sea island shirt was pastel matelot-striped, the peach cardigan in a revived twenties shape. She was dressed to, in a leisurely summery manner, kill. But her face would have done it first – her looks alone – with the angular features she hadn't inherited from her mother: with a mouth ruthlessly pinched and primed to strafe, with those raging, deadly laser eyes.

*

Today I've lied for the first time.

Gilbert rang in the evening and asked the usual general questions. But secreted in among them was a more particular one. I told him I'd gone over to Cabylla again on the ferry: to look about the shops, I said,

and that sort of thing. Then he jumped. Somebody who knew we were here had asked him if Wilkins' was still in business, on the quayside. The grocer's. I hesitated, I couldn't think where I'd seen the windows of hanging hams and stacked biscuit tins. And because I didn't think it could matter, I told him 'yes'.

Later, I asked Amy — not very casually — as she was putting on her cardigan to leave. I held the door open, and she told me Wilkins' was the ironmonger's, on Breja Street, and it had been gutted by a fire the year before last. 'But there *is*,' I asked her, 'a grocer's? On the quayside?' 'On Tolver Street,' she said. 'There's nothing like that on the quay. There's the Electric Board. And the chandler's, and the wool shop. And the WI window. With baking and flowers. Oh, and the old fish shop, of course.'

Of course, of course.

'But that's it. That's all — '

I gave her a wide smile, while she had to wriggle an exit between the wall and the door I was holding only half-open. I noticed and apologised but it was too late, she must have seen I wasn't concentrating.

Just a detail, I tried telling myself, Gilbert confused the question and I confused my answers. I've heard his question over and over, however, and his manner of asking it, and each time there is the same sly, intense aura of silence around the words, framing them.

Guilt's expertise is a terrible clutch-hold on the heart. You breathe too hard, thinking of nothing else, and you start to colour. I feel that even Lillias is aware, in the virtual darkness of her bedroom I can't adjust to quickly enough; she watches me with her eyes glinting in the scatter of lamplight from the landing. I looked in twice and couldn't think what to say, and waited until I could decipher her mouth, that sullen gash on her face, a breathing-hole.

**Just a detail, I'm telling myself, we were confused.
Why should it bespeak anything, unless my belea-
guered conscience is willing it to?**

*

'One – two – three – four – Right up to sixteen.'
  'Always,' I asked her, 'sixteen?'
  'Sixteen footsteps. From the bottom tread to the top of the
staircase. And on to my room.'
  'Did your mother know you counted?'
  She stared at me.
  'Would that have made any difference?'
  'I don't know,' I said. It was a lame reply.
  'I loathed the house eventually.'
  'It wasn't an unattractive house. Its neighbour was the ugly
one – '
  She shook her head at me.
  'I loathed it,' she said. 'Don't you see that's all that mat-
ters?'
  She sighed.
  'I could have burned it to the ground.'

*

One morning I had the Bristol out on the driveway for a cleaning
session. I thought the house-party were all down on the beach,
and I'd turned on the radio in the dashboard and wound down the
windows. At some point Iris appeared, taking a breather from
the kitchen. The garage doors were wide open. I asked her,
in a fruity fol-de-rol voice, didn't she want to go in and have a
look at my stable of little beauties? I was in a mood for a laugh,
for letting my hair down. Whyever not? She smiled at me in a
tolerating kind of way – how puerile I was, the smile said, but
too harmless to get bothered about – and she ambled, hands in
apron pockets, into the garage.
  The tune on *Workers' Playtime* changed to 'Stranger In
Paradise', one of my favourites. I left the car, crept into
the garage on tiptoe behind Iris, and grabbed her round the
waist. She cried out – a theatrical little squeal – but offered no

resistance when I took her hands and led her into a dance, a kitsch dance.

They were roughly the steps of a tango. She must have known them too, and with the second chorus we launched into what was actually quite a passable rendition. I performed a mock bow when we'd finished; she curtsied, but didn't turn away. The next tune that came on was a waltz. I bowed again, she curtsied to me; we took our position, then started to dance a second time. There was sufficient space between the Bristol and the Frazer Nash to travel an easy, complete circle.

When I was turning her round on our third lap I happened to look towards the connecting door to the house at the back of the garage. Chetwynd was standing there watching us both. I immediately stopped. Iris asked me what was the matter. She followed my eyes.

'Oh, Mother of God – !'

Chetwynd, however – never quite predictable after all – was in generous spirit. He indicated that we should continue. I was embarrassed to death, but I thought a far greater offence would have been to refuse. So we started again, awkwardly, but soon enough we caught the motion of the music and found ourselves dancing as before on the garage floor, maybe a little better now.

The kitschiness forgotten, we concentrated on keeping our gaze on the walls and rafters and nowhere else, picturing the precise geometry of our feet on the floor. When the music stopped we did also. We both turned round. Chetwynd still stood watching us. He nodded his head. 'I'm impressed,' we heard him say. Then it was his turn to show some awkwardness. He seemed to become aware how stiffly his arms were hanging by his side, and he brought up the hands and stuck them into his blazer pockets. In another three or four seconds he was gone and the connecting door had closed behind him.

The upshot was that, a few days later, Chetwynd came to me in the garage where I was waxing the Aston Martin and asked if I would agree to be a 'frog prince for an evening'. 'Some people' were coming over for dinner, friends from London who

were staying in these parts, and for entertainment afterwards
he proposed some dancing. Would I be available to assist Tuitt
beforehand with drinks and dispensing wine at table – and then,
when dinner was over, to present myself in the drawing-room?
Some of the group were very fond of dancing but they didn't
have their usual partners with them –

I realised he wasn't going to take 'no' for an answer, that
he was only formally presenting me with a résumé of what my
duties were to be. One important question did occur to me,
however, about what I should wear. 'We're much the same
height,' he said. 'I've a dress suit I can let you have. The
trouser waist is adjustable, just re-fasten the buttons at the
sides. It'll do you quite well, I'm sure – '

He stood nodding, then and later when I presented myself
to him in his study. The trousers were still a little loose on the
hips, even with the waistband adjusted to the skinniest setting
the buttons allowed, but the jacket was undeniably a good fit.

He had arranged that Clive Melchett would give me one of
his starched white dress shirts to wear. There was a black silk
bow tie in one of the jacket pockets.

'Be so good as to dance,' I was told, 'whenever anyone
asks you.'

'Would the ladies be expert dancers, Sir?'

'*Enthusiastic*, let's say.'

'I may not be good enough, Sir.'

'If you follow what they do – or better, *you* lead, whatever
you choose to dance, and let *them* follow *you* – '

On the evening I danced: better than I thought I was managing
to, to judge from the comments and smiles in the room.
The reflection I caught in the mirrors didn't really resemble
myself, but was a temporary improvement. I hardly sat out
one whole dance, and my colouring in the hot room flattered
my complexion. Two of the non-dancing women asked me to
light their cigarettes, twice each, and one of them chattered
away to me as if I were a bona fide guest.

When it was over, I felt as Cinderella must have done,
the monumental let-down of having to undress and get back

to normality. The tunes from the record-player were still unravelling in my head, I smelt the perfume of my partners on my lapels, cuffs, the skin of my hands and neck.

I was standing in front of the wardrobe mirror in Mitchell Ogilvie's room when the door opened and Chetwynd walked in. He congratulated me, with a wary smile. His eyes passed over me slowly and critically, from my shoulders all the way down to my shoes. His eyes, it seemed to me, lingered a moment or two longer about the slightly problematic thighs of my trousers.

'Keep the suit for just now,' he said. 'Wear it home if you like. Put it on, get used to seeing yourself in it. Then you'll feel you're quite the part.'

I had already noticed him a couple of times watching me consulting the mirrors for a verdict on myself. He anticipated my question.

'If I want it back, I'll tell you. And if I'd like you to dance again, when we have company, I hope you'll feel you can oblige me.'

This time he stood awaiting an answer.

I nodded.

'Oh yes,' I said, relieved to think that I might have carried off the fetch. 'Oh yes.'

I still have the dress suit, nearly thirty-five years later. The trousers are an easier fit to me now than the jacket. It's of a style – satin shawl collar, ventless – that has survived the whims of fashion.

I still have the business card I found in the outer breast pocket where it must have been overlooked. It's the card of a dress-hire firm in Hamburg. In the centre is a line illustration, printed green, of a top hat, crossed opera gloves, and cane. Above is the name of the company 'Ottenbacher' – the same as that sewn on the jacket's label – and beneath the illustration is the address, 52 Lorettostrasse, Hamburg. On the back of the card are two words, scribbled one below the other. 'Jägerstrasse', 'Ulmerstrasse'. The capitals 'J' and 'U' are each circled. Underneath the second word is a single circled 'I' with two question marks placed beside it.

It was an intriguing discovery, but there was a great deal

else to intrigue me in those days, and I suppose I too, in
my turn, overlooked the card. It was the design of it which
principally appealed to me when I came across it again: the

now archaic motif, and the green and silver border, ,

and the Germanic script. I had forgotten also about the words
on the back, and the arrangement of initial letters:

J

U

I ??

*

Suddenly, between one day and the next, the weather turned
turtle. There was a feeling in the air: I can only think to call
it 'negative' where previously it had been 'positive'. I felt the
change in the clarity of the atmosphere, in the noticeably colder
touch of objects to the skin. Everything had a *there*ness, insisting
on its three dimensions, where – before – definition had seemed
to matter less, things somehow not being so exclusively themselves, and distances blurring. The world was compacting itself
around us, and over breakfast 'upstairs' Chetwynd announced to
the group that he considered it time they all shook the sand out
of their clothes and thought of making tracks back to London.

*

It always happened just like that, Mrs Wragg assured me, without any more warning. It meant that their departure – and I was
to mark her words – was no more than thirty-six hours away.

*

The next morning Chetwynd took me aside and asked, would I
be averse to continuing the chauffeuring up in town?
    I had told him I already had a job, or half a job, at Randolph
Square. The hours, though, were variable –

He explained to me that it would be work for the evenings only, four or five evenings in the week. Could I manage that? If I was willing, the routine was this: I should present myself at the house about five-thirty; I would be fed and watered, just as I was at present, then I would change into the livery uniform and await my instructions. Mostly I would be carrying a party from the house, up into the West End: there he might have arranged for them to eat at a restaurant or go dancing at a club. I wouldn't be required for Chetwynd's own evenings out alone, when he was quite capable of driving himself: he drank little, he said, and the concentration needed for the journey home always prepared him for sleep afterwards.

I found myself answering yes, when he formally asked me if I was willing to accept the job. He nodded approval, he even smiled with quiet satisfaction. I felt I must have acquitted myself decently thus far, that I should be considered worthy of trust.

I repeated my answer. 'Yes Sir, certainly Sir.'

Chetwynd shook his head. 'Sir' was unnecessary, he told me.

'Mr Chetwynd,' I said.

He nodded, quickly, as if embarrassed. I conveyed gratitude in the features of my face. I told him, 'Thank you. Thank you, Mr Chetwynd – ' He waved his hand, as if to imply he was such a modest man that these unwonted civilities were quite mortifying to him.

I knew he could only be bluffing, but did he honestly believe I was bluffable?

TEN

Finding my bed-sit in Pimlico was a stroke of luck. Now I was supporting myself. My parents were no nearer and no further than a call on the telephone downstairs in the hallway. It was my own territory, notwithstanding that I rented and that the house's future was forever being 'talked about', as it had been for years, so that none of its tenants could effectively plan further than a month ahead.

It would continue to be my home in fact for a further twenty-odd months. It didn't matter that it was at the other extreme from the circumstances in which I came to spend my evenings. Indeed part of its charm was owing to my keeping it such a close secret from the others. My reasons for finally leaving had to do with growing up, not shame – with my wanting to shed a skin, to let time do its work and to enter another phase of my life.

I acted as chauffeur until early December.

It tied in with my swimming-pool roster; or, as the case became, vice versa. Latterly, though, it wasn't always an easy matter to find someone at Randolph Square yet again willing to switch duty turns with me.

My parents, my mother especially, became anxious that I wasn't settling to anything. I suppose she was impressed to a point that I was experiencing the modern equivalent of a world of which she continued to read in her library books. Her own speciality was aristocracy, and I talked to her about some of the guests. The more she heard about Chetwynd, however, the less regard she seemed to have for him – he was my means of access, my conduit to observation, that was chiefly all. It amused me and irked me, both together, to see how her mind worked. Her reaction only inclined me further towards my abstruse employer.

When I drove the group anywhere together, we used brand new transport: a Lagonda 3-Litre and/or a Daimler DK400 limo. Sometimes the cook's husband also drove when we were an especially large party. The two cars would have paid for a new Rolls-Royce Silver Wraith we could all have squeezed into, but there was a certain type of ostentation Chetwynd shrank from. He also indulged himself with sports cars, but only the experts appreciated what each marque represented: Rolls-Royces were somehow a very common form of exclusivity, because everyone was familiar with the name and the legend had become tarnished by its obviousness. So our transportation was attended to with a little more anonymity, if that's what it was: or rather, with more discernment.

*

The other chauffeurs I encountered showed only loyal pride, never resentment, in the goings-on of their employers. There was some gossip, of course: yet not a great deal, and what there was was respectful. They stood in the tracks of their cars' headlights, smoking in that unobtrusive way they had, holding a cigarette concealed behind a cupped hand; they talked with their voices pitched low of the rituals they observed from the outside, of who had been dropped in favour of whom or – say – the comparative obesity of Lord X's daughters, but they spoke at greater length and with more evident relish of well-endowed maids-of-work and pin-ups in film magazines and likely nags in races and of the pubs they frequented. I chipped in whenever I thought I could, to keep my end up, and they gave me the time of day. I was years behind in the gossip stakes, however – even when I remembered the names of paddock fillies Patrick Durran had mentioned – and my presence during those long waits was chiefly tolerated, which was sufficient for me.

Gradually I came to feel in my bones that, if I didn't wholly fit in, it hadn't all to do with myself and my temperamental make-up. My employer also didn't quite accord with the norm in those high-falutin' circles. He had acquired the social connections despite the absence of a pedigree, and he was very regularly 'seen' in the places deemed worth being seen in; and yet while invariably present, he somehow wasn't as apparent as the others. He certainly wasn't spoken of in the same breath, and it sometimes happened that I had to bring up the name because otherwise it would have gone unsaid. Were the conversational omissions on account of his being between trade and profession, and a commoner instead of titled, and more intellectual than not? Oddly the drivers weren't snobs, socially or otherwise, and I think their neglect was owing to no more than their inattention and to Chetwynd's paradoxically reticent manner of passing himself off as a socialite.

*

I had a good many hours of waiting.

I would park in a side-street and go off to a pub. An instinct would tell me when to hie back, and I'd drive myself to where I'd left them, at a restaurant or a night-club, and I would park either at the kerb or alongside the other limousines and cabriolets. While their drivers fraternised, I preferred in the end to keep my place behind the wheel, listening to the radio in the dashboard. I could whistle along to all the musical hits of the day: 'Cara Mia', 'Three Coins In The Fountain', 'Secret Love', 'It's Almost Tomorrow'.

But then my chauffeuring days suddenly stopped. Chetwynd told me he'd hired other help. He waited until my face fell before he smiled and told me my services weren't being dispensed with. My duties, he announced, were being changed.

I stared at him.

'If,' he said, 'we require you to dance, then dance you must. You will, of course, eat with *us*.'

I continued staring at him.

'In the house you might lend a hand just now and then, in emergencies. But I'll get you measured for evening wear, and we'll order some tweeds while we're at it. A blazer and flannels. And ties. I could get you any school tie you like.'

'Oh, I have one,' I said. 'But – '
'Well, no one will recognise it, I dare say. Which colours?'
'Crimson and yellow.'
'Is that anything?'
'"Anything"?' I repeated.
'Crimson and *gold*?'
'No. Sort of lemony yellow.'
'Hmmm.'

*

I didn't see much of my family that Christmas season. My brother taunted me with references to my *other* family, whose company I seemed to prefer to theirs. He was largely right, but I was annoyed that he'd said it. I denied I understood anything of what he was talking about – it was just a load of rubbish, I told him.

My father was indifferent; my sister too taken up with her boyfriend. My mother surely was the one most affected: she appeared pained, hurt, and not for effect as my brother was. She stopped asking me if what I was doing was 'wise'. And yet her Christmas present to me was a pricey green silk cummerbund from Jermyn Street. I was astonished by the daring and also the implications of her choice.

I'm not sure what Chetwynd thought about my accessory. Celia told me it was (she swallowed a little breath) 'very festive': which was probably an indication that it was legitimate for this brief season only, and only because I was a novitiate. So I deduced at any rate, and I didn't wear it after the last party of the old year – a luncheon in the final week of December. Chetwynd was due to leave London for a while, to join some proper high fliers in St Moritz: Celia informed us he wasn't a great ski-ing enthusiast, but he did venture a little on the pistes – he walked rather more, though, and attended to a good deal of 'business' in the restaurants, bars and lounges of the Palace and Carlton Hotels.

When he came back at the end of it, back home to base in Kensington, I was ready and waiting to begin.

ELEVEN

Chetwynd's house was one of five similar domiciles in an exclusive cul-de-sac of the Royal Borough called 'The Circus'.

In size each house approached the interior volume of properties in Eaton Square or the Regent's Park terraces, but their stone exteriors had been left in their original worked condition without stucco or plaster: the external effect was quieter, less showy and more discreet. The finish of the rooms inside was inferior to none of those in the more familiar addresses where wealth resides.

The drawing-room was referred to as the saloon. It ran the full breadth of the house between two deep semi-circular bay windows, with mid-way an arrangement of panelled doors – four in all – which could be pulled across to convert one vast room into two very generous spaces.

The dining-room was truly formal, with – like the saloon – two fireplaces but – unlike the premier room – only one glass chandelier instead of two. Both rooms had access to the paved garden terrace and pergola.

Behind the dining-room was the morning-room, where breakfast and private suppers were served, and a large cloakroom of the sort found in restaurants – with rails and lines of wall-pegs and shelves for parcels.

The lower staircase whorled upwards with *Gone with the Wind* grace. On the first floor was an elegant sitting-room (called the 'drawing-room') with an aerial conservatory behind; also, a room called the 'accounts' house', and Chetwynd's capacious library and study. In addition there were two full bathrooms for guests, and a dressing-room for the women.

On the floor above were five bedrooms, and on the top floor, accommodation for the resident staff.

There might have been more furniture, but Chetwynd had an eye for quantity as well as quality. Its choiceness wasn't in question, and he must have known that his informed selection would be seen to best effect because the rooms were uncluttered.

The furniture was of English or Irish derivation, in glowing woods – golden West Indian satinwood, honey walnut, coffee-coloured Brazilian rosewood, bronze Jamaican mahogany, ginger-brown elm – and sometimes they were inlaid one into another. There were pieces of proven authenticity (he assured us) to original designs by Marot, Shearer, Sheraton, Chippendale, Hope and Smith, the clockmaker George Graham, and nobody had any reason for doubting him. Everything was in near-perfect condition and, without exception, exemplified Chetwynd's exquisite taste. The various citrus- (lemon or lime) or ivory-coloured walls and silk papers – he consulted with experts to be certain that the shades and patterns belonged to the period of the furniture – made the surroundings seem much *less* like a museum interior than they might have done. The furniture was grand but functional: robust bookcases lined with books and cabinets of porcelain service-ware, stout console tables of black or green marble supported on lion's legs of gilded oak, escritoires replete with stationery, commodes that earned their keep by storing linen, cutlery canteens, and art magazines kept for reference. The carpets varied from kelims and Russian runners on the second floor to assorted silks and Kashans, Isfahans and Tabriz' in the first-floor semi-public rooms to Aubussons, Flanders and Gobelins in the ground-floor reception areas. The great if not the good had walked there before us, which was the true reason for their seeming so intimidating at first; but events were to redefine our situation, with a corresponding and prismatic shift of emphasis – because we dined on those carpets like islands and couldn't walk off them in the saloon or sitting-/drawing-room without conversation becoming inaudible, inevitably it was on the same carpets that we 'performed' and so it was there too in consequence that we always seemed most alive, in the shine of candles and the soft glow from the silk shades of the table-lamps. The carpets had us trapped with the aura we required to believe, that of our own usefulness.

Two of the houses in 'The Circus' were embassies. The other two were residences, one constantly occupied as was Chetwynd's, but the second seldom visited by its owner, a Cuban tobacco baron.

The house hardly merited the epithet 'home'. It had been intended for a specific manner of living which, by fortunate chance, Chetwynd's mode of existence was able to do some sort of justice to. Perhaps these rooms had never been designed for proper ease, and only Chetwynd could give a masterly impression – his successful impersonation – of being comfortable in them. We all of course 'adjusted', but merely by dint of our coming together; none of us could have claimed this was anything remotely like our natural habitat. Truly it was as unreal to us as Tibet, or the moon.

I preferred, as an aesthetic choice, the airy whiteness of 'Underwood'. Already I could remember those days as a delicious, balmy hiatus. In London, by contrast, the frequency of the entertainments, like the imposing location, would not allow us to relax to that degree – and in addition there were the constant enigmas to keep me keenly tuned and on my toes.

*

Some of the chauffeurs did a double-take as if they recognised me when I walked past in Chetwynd's party, but I doubted if I had been memorable enough for them to be sure.

Chetwynd preferred that we serve a very formal luncheon in Kensington when it was an entertaining day, and on our social evenings that we should dine out in restaurants and supper-clubs. I wouldn't have thought it possible when I began, that I should soon feel so – comparatively – blasé about it all. After six or eight weeks I grew used to the décor and the à la carte choices and the quirks of the service wherever we went, and was already familiar with the faces of the habitual customers we re-encountered on that circuit of glamorous night-spots.

I danced whatever was required of me: waltz, foxtrot, old-fashioned palais-glide or valeta, rumba, paso doble, a sort of cha-cha-cha, a mild impromptu samba. I had invested in a 'teach-yourself' book during my last year at school and studied again but more intently all the steps, detailed on the pages by broken lines indicating the progress of either a pair of matt black, infilled dancing pumps or else their outline only, like footsteps in white sand. In the event the floors were too compact for anyone to notice if I was step-perfect or not: certainly I was proficient, which seemed to give satisfaction all round.

On average there would be two formal lunches or dinners at 'The Circus' in a week, for between ten and fifteen or sixteen: that is, 'ourselves' plus up to half a dozen guests. Invariably the group swelled in night-clubs when other parties lost members to ours. We ate in restaurants and supper-clubs once or twice a week. On a second or third evening we might eat privately in Kensington, 'en famille' as Chetwynd had it, and then go on to a night-club – those forays were a lesser expense, comparatively speaking, involving the cost of entrance and drinks, and always billed to Chetwynd. At the same time that I was enjoying his hospitality, it should shame me to confess, I lost sight of the cost to him. He never once appeared to concern himself, and we all too happily succumbed to forgetfulness, which was really a kind of collective madness. It sounds improbable, but perhaps Chetwynd was quite aware of the group mentality: if he'd meant us to view the practicalities, he would have offered us clues and portents. But he hardly cast eyes on the bills that appeared on plate-silver salvers; he deposited a wad of notes, or hastily dashed off his signature, and – with the matter so easily disposed of – the maître d' would be dismissed with the briefest smile. Some bills would be sent on to the house, in the fullness of time. But I didn't once hear the accounts' room door open or close or see a light appear from beneath.

It was understood that otherwise, away from 'The Circus', we each of us were self-supporting, in our very modest way, but that it was only a case of tiding ourselves over, paying for the accommodation we rented and saving up for this or that article of clothing. Celia did some mornings in a dress shop in King's Road; April removed her nails and typed letters for a firm of lawyers; Mitchell Ogilvie stood in the showroom of a Bentley distributor part-time and tried to collar prospective buyers into a test-drive; Clive modelled at a famous school of art and did photographic work, in the clothing and male jewellery lines, for manufacturers' catalogues; Melinda was relief telephonist in the Army & Navy Stores and then Lillywhites, but was always having run-ins about her hours; Patrick Durran was his own man, compulsively secretive, but needing to secure the contents of his bulging wallet with an elastic band. Meanwhile I continued with my job at the Randolph Square swimming pool; I was able to work over a week in shifts of four hours with three others, any block in the day from 6 a.m. until 10 p.m.

Chetwynd himself came in one afternoon, quite soon after I'd started attending lunches at 'The Circus'. Perhaps he was checking up on me, but he did so under cover of accompanying a parliamentarian acquaintance, one William Plynn-Gore, who was there as the guest of a colleague and resident.

The two guests swam with their host. Chetwynd was lean for his age but athletically built. He wore a pair of loose-fitting colourful madras cotton trunks, American-style. At that time he was still tanned from one of his jaunts abroad; the hair on his head was lighter than that of his chest and on the small precise 'V' above his buttocks, on the small of his back.

As I watched him swim, quite effortlessly, with suppressed power, my mind went back to that other afternoon at the bay, on the day of Melinda's dream-drowning. Probably he really had been out of hearing range of the cries. Anyway *I* had been on hand, to go tearing into the surf like a story-book ace, towards the spot where Melinda might have been about to give up the ghost. Yet I couldn't quite convince myself on the point, not wholly, watching from the pool-side.

As he emerged Chetwynd nodded over to me but that was that – he gave no other hint of familiarity. The trio dressed, collected their valuables from the boy at the desk, and left.

They all reappeared behind the windows of the mezzanine lounge upstairs. They seated themselves at a table where I could be more clearly observed by them than they by me. Through the glass they were constantly crossing with their shadows.

The next time I was asked to dinner, Chetwynd said nothing to me about his visit, nor did I mention it. What went on when I was away from 'The Circus' was a closed book to me, so to speak, and intended to be: and yet I wonder if *he* didn't keep tabs on *me* more closely than I could ever have known.

The business of which of us came when was clear-cut. It was effected with the minimum of kerfuffle and euphemism. Chetwynd simply found an opportunity to ask us – singly – would you care to join us for luncheon/dinner/an evening up in town. One waited to be asked; one did not presume.

Three or four times a week was usually the way of it for the regulars. Only occasionally did someone appear unenthusiastic, but the reason would be no more than fatigue. I'd venture that the combination of familiars and guests was never twice the exact same in the eighteen months during which I was there – with increasing frequency – as a witness of the ceremonials.

The house at 'The Circus' ran like clockwork. It was by no accident, because that was Chetwynd's skill.

He was a vigilant host and staff-musterer, who was equally careful to be seen underplaying all his consummate attention to detail.

His purpose was to put us at our ease, and – as far as he was able to – he did so. In the early days at least, a recognisable Name or a formidable pedigree would intimidate me a little, but Chetwynd made the occasion of our sharing a table at his home or in a night-club a not unnatural happening. He didn't want any frights, and nor did he expect any of us to be over-confident and forward with his guests. We hadn't to be servile either, or obviously grateful, but somehow sufficiently *au fait* to allow the guests to think that they were giving the best of themselves. Of course we were there to flatter the guests, but also to slightly deceive them with our social savvy. We were to be the quintessential country house party transposed to the city, in a decade when nostalgia was possible only because we were supposed to have worked automatic respect for the old ways out of our collective national system.

The service was Limoges or, on days deemed special because of the company, Sèvres. The best glass was a combination of blue Venetian with two-hundred-year-old, funnel-bowled English crystal. A clutch of the cutlery might have snapped weak wrists. The napkins were Irish linen, embossed on one corner with Chetwynd's entwined initials sewn in gold thread. Silver pheasants trailed their plumage across the sheeny Virginia red walnut. Orchids or arum lilies were delivered from a florist's in Sloane Street. The candles came from Goode's, and stood in either two or three George II candelabra, fashioned in the famous London workshops of William Kidney. Our eyes rested, when they needed distance, on pastoral views by the likes of Cotman, Crome, Millais, Wilson Steer and De Wint: chaste and not immoderate representations, in oil or water-colour, of the classic English landscape – valley floor, sylvan drop, forest sward, watery cascade falling into mist, the landscaped naturalness of a rich man's estate with sheep cropping beneath mammiform hillocks and a lactic gushing at a well-head in a corner of Albion forever green and innocent. A three-tiered chandelier hung from the ceiling, hovering overhead like some enchanted organism in nature – salt-less ice crystallised to glass, as if in a dream. The chips of transparency glinted aureate and imperial and pale fire, and the sight and the sound – a very faint, elusive tinkling whenever a draught blew – transported us from SW10, as we were, into a wonderland remoter still.

*

The 'outside' guests – whose specific benefit our entertainments served, nominally at least: they were supposed to be the purpose of the whole damned, splendiferous routine – were of two main sorts.

There were the representatives of the *noblesse*. They bore old and hallowed family names, and practised all the courtesies. I was puzzled, I have to confess, as to why they should have elected to be regular guests of a man clearly of a lesser caste, rather than suppose on the mutual grace and favour of similar scions of vintage blue blood stock. But they came, and in their decorous way made free with their host's fare, and took care not to give the impression that they wished to be anywhere else.

The more sizeable group belonged to the genus they presumed Chetwynd to belong to, the upper middle-class. The men as boys had attended respectable public schools, the women as girls had boarded away or, less often, been educated in the style of the true *noblesse* by governesses. Their parents, as they themselves, were professional or Services or farming. A common condition, one passed down through the generations, was to live in a manner not quite justified by funds or social position, which suggested a tradition of landed status and resources. Their manners were a little more particular than those of their betters, and their accents frequently extended to drawls. What the *noblesse* did instinctively, they did as policy and intent.

*

Some unlikely types condescended, but only by invitation. A few prevaricated about accepting, but fewer still did not come.

It was up to *us* to make them welcome. I watched how expertly our group attempted to put them at their ease. No spinster was too mothballed, no bachelor too set in his ways, no backwoods m'lord too crusty, no inbred county dowager too conversationally limited. Eventually most of them warmed and opened up. They remembered the taste of good food, they mellowed after a few glasses of fine wine, they rediscovered that they could dance. No one could resist flattery when it was practised so consummately, so effortlessly, even when – in the colder light of another day – the social presumption might have been considered so great.

TWELVE

Gilbert took me out to dinner, to Prunier's. He said he had chosen the courses for me, that everything had been arranged beforehand, over the telephone.

The main dish when it came was Cornish lobster. He told me, and I think I must have hesitated before I smiled.

'That's — appropriate,' I said, or something as anodyne.

'Did you eat any when you were down?'

'I can't think. No.'

'Lex said they sell them on Cabylla quayside.'

I couldn't remember, of course.

He handed me a skewer and a pair of claw-crackers. I'd eaten crab, but never a lobster in my life. The thing lay on the plate, crimson and blue. I was remembering C. showing me a photograph in a magazine, of Dali's lobster telephone.

'*Bon appétit!*' Gilbert said.

(The words should carry an exclamation mark after them, but I didn't hear it in his voice.)

Chrome skewer in hand, I delayed. Then I started. A proper dog's dinner I found I was making of it.

Gilbert pretended not to notice. Probably he considers himself an expert at not letting you see what he doesn't want you to, but I know him a little better than that after our eleven years of marriage. I scrabbled away and kept chattering while he looked all round the room. The clientele were well-heeled predictably, and I caught his eyes scavenging among

them – on the look-out for faces he might be familiar
with, I supposed.

It was an evening of not-so-sweet irony. In the end,
as we were folding our napkins and pushing away
our coffee cups and saucers, it was I who spotted a
familiar face, familiar to *me* – Anthony Chetwynd's.
He was at a table on the far wall, but I recognised him
from the very absence of gilt buttons on the blazer
cuffs and (more so) from his habit of crimping the
cloth along the table edge with his fingers, as if he
were sealing the rim of pastry on a pie. His companion
was a woman of mature years, grey hair turning to
white and skin hanging loose on her arms above the
elbow; a sapphire necklace glinted on the weathered hide of her upper chest, matched by splendid
three-drop earrings. They were in animated conversation; or rather *she* was, while C. attended most
diligently to what she was saying, as if he was afraid
to lose a single word. A champagne bottle rested in a
bucket on a stand, and C. smoked a thick cigar. Old
rubies gleamed among gold on the third finger of the
woman's left hand, but she was of an age to have lost
a husband – and to be seeking sympathetic, elegant
consolation in her widowhood.

I couldn't watch them all the time, of course. I had
to (ever so casually) happen to slant my gaze in their
direction. But I must have made slits of my eyes with
concentration to observe, because I'm quite certain
that I gave myself away and let Gilbert cotton on.
He referred to this person or that he could recognise
from the newspapers and would half-turn round to
glance at them. C. and his companion were behind
him, so he could only allow himself to look at last
when he stood up and came over to pull back my
chair. I lifted my eyes and saw him looking. I let
him be a screen between that side of the room and
myself; he walked just in front, and I followed behind.
I even put my hand up to my hair, so that the palm

concealed my cheek, lest I should be spotted. I knew
C. was too discreet – his favourite quality in others –
to do anything even if he were to catch sight of me;
but I also guessed that the talk which so preoccupied
him was a one-sided conversation he wouldn't have
allowed anyone to interrupt.

Our coats were fetched. Gilbert dropped a ten-
shilling note into the concierge's saucer. He saw me
stare at it; my (unintended) expression must have told
him I thought the extravagance bizarre, and vulgar.
His mouth pursed, shrank. I smiled, much too cheer-
fully, but was unable to confront those needle eyes of
his with my own.

*

Here in London we all lived out. When we left the house we
dispersed, to go our separate ways. I didn't have anyone's
address, but that was no accident. I didn't ask because I had
an instinct that I shouldn't, and nobody offered. We only met at
'The Circus', and we were as intimately uncommunicative and
self-preoccupied as actors assembled in the wings to walk on
stage and play our parts.

When I wasn't at 'The Circus', I felt I was living a very diminished
life by comparison. I thought less and less about the practicalities
of existence in Pimlico, and in my imagination I relived the one in
Kensington.

On my 'nights' I was never in bed until two or three or four
o'clock in the morning, and I couldn't sleep until the ordinary
world started to waken: when I heard the first milk-float rattling
into the street, my eyelids were suddenly heavy and my head
sank like a stone into the pillow. Sometimes I had pool-duty
starting at ten. If not I slept for seven or eight hours and woke
slowly in the late morning, feeling solid and thick as if I'd been
drugged. I got up, turned on the hot water, and breakfasted on
whatever was to hand – which might be cheese on tea biscuits,
flat lemonade, the remains of a bar of chocolate. After it had
settled, I tackled fifty press-ups and thirty sit-ups. After that,

if I was 'on call' I would lay out my clothes for the evening,
unfolding a fresh white shirt; I would take care brushing the
suit, I would press my trousers if it was required, and always
polish my shoes until I could see the colour of the objects in the
room reflected on the toe-caps. Then I'd set off for Randolph
Square and my afternoon shift.

When I knew I was going out in the evening, anticipation
was everything. I turned on the radio, to dance music (if there
was any) or to classical, and paced the room in my underwear.
Sometimes I might pull on trousers and my pool tee-shirt and
go outside for some fresh air, but even in the streets there
weren't enough distractions to take my mind off the prospect
of the evening ahead. I felt I was privy to a secret world, and
that I had to demonstrate pity in my face – knowing how other
people would envy me if they could only find out.

*

Christ Almighty alone knows what the entertainment must
have cost.

But at 'Underwood' I'd heard the kitchen gossip about his
wealth, and before me I had the evidence of the house, another
house, and a garage of cars to indicate he was a man of ample
means. Presumably he knew what he was involved with: and
even if he couldn't afford his behaviour, that was his responsibility also. *We* must be absolved, I assured myself. The matter
was thus simply, and painlessly, settled in my own mind.

*

**April took me upstairs to a bedroom and seated me
on the stool in front of the dressing table. She stood
behind me, with her hands on my shoulders, and
began without asking, dabbing at my face with wads
of cotton wool wetted with a sweet cleanser. She
must have known that I wouldn't offer her any resistance. I sat and watched while, in the mirror, my face
was transformed by make-up.**

**She told me, the years hadn't been wasted com-
pletely: there were a few things she'd learned.**

I started at the results. I looked older, more worldly and experienced, more in command of myself.

'I've brought out your eyes,' she told me. 'Taken the shine off your cheeks. Quietened your mouth a little.'

I nodded.

'Nothing major, though,' she said, to reassure me.

I nodded again. I smiled with my pale albertine lips. It had taken a lot of applied effort – with foundation and cream, cheek colouring, mascara and liner – to understate me. I looked more collected and assured but in a soft, uninsistent, even chaste way. I resembled an artist's crayon illustration of myself, a likeness made to flatter. And yet – I lightly touched my chin, my cheek, my nose – it was real enough, using those merest components from their phials and tubes.

April smiled at my naïvety and in approval of her own handiwork.

'Now what?' she said, speaking for me.

I stared up at her, at her reflection above mine in the tall mahogany-hooped oval of bevelled mirror glass.

I told Gilbert it had happened in a shop: a very persuasive woman in the cosmetics department had dragooned me into it.

'Couldn't you have stopped her?'

'Don't you like it?'

What he was thinking was as clear to me as if I were seeing the thoughts through glass.

'Do you want an honest answer?' He spoke without a smile.

'No,' I said. 'No, not really.'

*

We were in the 'Seventy-Seven' one evening when there was a sudden mêlée of activity on the stairs. A party entered; capes

and furs and overcoats were taken by a posse of attendants, and
a group of a dozen or so began their descent of the staircase.
In their midst, surrounded by smiling flattery, was Princess
Margaret. She was wearing – 'resplendent', as the newspapers
would have it the next day – a lilac silk gown and white silk stole.
She pointed one white-gloved arm to indicate where in the room
she wished to sit, and waiters went scurrying.

Later in the evening a figure appeared at Chetwynd's shoulder: it was his summons. He left us and was escorted across
the room to the royal party's table. The Princess had been
dancing and was standing to receive him. Chetwynd bowed
and had his hand briefly taken. Her Royal Highness, who
could only be answered and not spoken to, started to speak.
Chetwynd nodded; the Princess continued to speak, smiling as
she did so, and fingering her magnificent sapphire necklace.
The (conscious or unconscious) turns of her head showed off
the matching three-drop earrings to very best effect. Chetwynd
was granted his opportunity, and he replied. Another comment
or two, another response. Then the Princess inclined her head
away, to indicate that the audience was at an end. Chetwynd
bowed, and took several steps backwards.

Back at our table, he informed Patrick Durran – who asked
for us – merely that the talk had been on a professional matter:
the Princess was a keen connoisseur of the fine arts, antiquities
included, and had a shrewd eye: had she not been Who she was,
she might have been able to make quite a successful career for
herself.

That was all we were told. We were obliged, as is the form
on those occasions, not to pay the royal party specific notice –
but always of course to be aware. The Princess passed among
us, so to speak, at a five or six yards' remove; when she danced,
we clung to the edges of the floor. It was an irresistible fancy, to
imagine that we had 'arrived' at last, but for Chetwynd it was a
somewhat truer state of affairs. (And truer still, I was to realise
much later, when I made some discoveries about the distance
he'd travelled in life.)

I suppose this was the point at which we could believe
ourselves claimed by a real-life fairy tale. Even the Princess

herself must have had faith in a future which might offer
more than flurries on a night-club staircase and a band to
play whichever tune she requested. I saw her many years
later, making her early exit from a charity event through a
parted curtain, dressed in lilac silk and with a white silk stole
draped about her shoulders, glove-less and with the gleam of
fine old rubies in gold about her fingers, still in the midst of
smiling flattery – but the fairy-tale days for the rest of us, if
not also for herself, were long, long since gone.

*

Chetwynd in his good moods tells me about the carpets. It
must take a wealth of knowledge, I think, to make sense of
that world of sign and symbol: the Buddhist fishes of plenty,
the figure of the wheel that 'is' the efficacy of jurisprudence,
the unending knot of fate, the Taoist bamboo betokening the
reading of fortunes, the fan which resuscitates the spirits of
the deceased, the flute whose music weaves an enchanting
seduction, the five bats of happiness – good health, high calling,
quietude, rectitude, and a reposeful exit from life.

He has seen the finest carpets that money can buy, but he
hasn't forgotten the pleasure of discovering what 'his' speciality
was to be – or forgotten the excitement of his first modest
acquisitions. I feel a keenness of pity for him when I glimpse
something simpler through the sophistication – the joy and
pride of his learning, a profound satisfaction with objects well
and honestly crafted and whose form and function harmonise
impeccably.

'Isn't it complicated to understand?' I asked him.

'Not if you appreciate what it is you're looking for. It's no
different from learning a language. A sign language.'

I thought he was being merely self-deprecating. I wasn't
able to see that his meaning was quite seriously sincere. To
him the process really *was* an academic one, of learning and
remembering and applying, and only instinctive in the sense
of practice rendering perfect. He *read* his subject by a grid of
reference: that one flat dimension yielded its meaning in terms

the Chinese understood, but which are doubly foreign to such a bland, unspiritual race as our own, consorting always with the manifest and surface. Peonies, forced only in the gardens of rich men, denote breeding, fortune and tenderness; a pear probity and excellence, an artemisia leaf high decorum, peach blossom (as does a tortoise) long life, a pomegranate fecundity, a duck faithfulness, a butterfly betterment and conjugal delight, a vase solace and rest, a table stillness.

First of all, though, one has to quite literally 'see', to be able to pick out a symbol from the copiousness of the pattern, and to distinguish between the outer form of a medallion in a Chinese rug and the meaning of the inner composition. I could at least identify the repeating swastikas, which he told me was a device of seemliest intent: betokening the Buddha's heart, the numeral ten thousand, and (the most constant aspiration in the weavers' art) joyfulness. On a brief tour of the first-floor rooms he pointed out to me what I would have failed to observe for myself: the Persians' cosmos upheld by four swimming fish, the several interpretations of the almond-shaped *boteh* emblem of our Paisley pattern (leaf, cypress tree, pine cone, male sperm, foetus, Zarathustrian fire), the similarity to the *gul* (at its simplest reminiscent of a playing-card diamond) which may have developed so in Turkmenistani (southern Russian, north-eastern Iranian) mysticism as a device constructed to deflect (as might a mirror) the evil eye. The Afghans' elephant's foot or pug echoes the octagonal totem in which the sexual yin-yang wheel is held: the eight sides, the Pa Kua, symbolise heaven, earth, fire, water, wind, cloud, mountain and thunder.

He nodded to my feet. He had me pick out the border of . . . linked swastikas.

'This,' he instructed me, 'is the carpet of the ten thousand joys.'

He turned the carpet over with the toe of his Lobb shoe.

'A good weaver used to manage a thousand knots in an hour. Two threads from the pile are tied together to work every knot.'

He explained about the Persian knot, about pile yarn and ward strands and single loops as distinct from doubles, all of which was far beyond me.

He stooped down to replace the fold of rug on the floor. I pointed to a tadpole-like squiggle in the pattern.

'That's a sceptre,' he told me.

I didn't see the resemblance.

'It's God's sceptre. Or at least, the Chinese thought of Him as head of all the deities in heaven. So elevated is he that the top of the sceptre becomes a cloud. That becomes a cloud with a little trailing tail.'

'And means?'

'And means a wish. Wanting a wish to be achieved. To come true. "J". "U". "I".'

Then, so to speak, he lost the thread somewhat. He tipped his cuff back and consulted his watch. Such a thing as a business card for a Hamburg dress-hire firm didn't then, or for many years, occur to me.

'So endeth the lesson,' I said.

He had mistaken my remark for flippancy, I realised not quite immediately. He looked at me in a way that told me I had betrayed the trust of these few minutes, that it was granted only to those he assumed would treat it with full respect. He had presumed better of me, to bring himself as close as he had to something like a confidence.

Or maybe he simply lacked a sense of humour. He might have been an ironist in the important things and yet also incapable of recognising an immature attempt at a joke when it was made. Perhaps he had too much egotism and was at the same time too defensive by nature to respond to what was merely, in the most mundane fashion, obvious.

Our luncheon guests had all gone. The other regulars who were still left were out in the garden taking some air. I had realised I was being honoured with his attention. At the back of my mind was a certain suspicion – but very muted – which I sometimes had at the swimming pool, when single men made their way to the attendants' room to enquire about opening times or the chlorine content of the water.

Christ, how much less self-respect I had than he, and how

uncertain were my own defences. He surely hadn't judged me
well at all, but grossly over-rated my personal qualities.

And all the time I was conscious – as he surely wanted me
to be – that it's a matter of sign and symbol, what French
intellectuals would shortly relaunch as semiology. I was inclining
to the notion that – despite his own playing down of the intuitive
element – the business required not just a trained eye and
encyclopedic memory but, every bit as importantly, a *disposition*
to decipher and understand.

*

He never mentioned the War, that I can recall.

Everyone else talked about it. Mitchell Ogilvie, of course,
because he had decorations as a conversation-opener; Clive
Melchett, because he'd played sailors in films and served on
fire-tenders in London; Celia had sewn parachutes, and Drusilla
Cowper done a stint in a munitions factory; before he became
an estate agent, Howard Kimble had been in Fuel and Power
administration supervising coal supplies; even Patrick Durran
claimed to have worked in various bunkers in the vicinity of
London, on official decoding exercises; Melinda too remembered her school's evacuation and helping out on farms.

The War was blamed for so much. To the traditional sort we
came into contact with, nothing would ever again be how it had
been: their houses were now burdens to them, but they saw
themselves obliged – in the face of too much indifference – to
assert the *modus vivendi* of yore. The War to others had been
a salvation, rescuing them from social anonymity and allowing
them, through ingenuity and a ready eye to the main chance, to
get a proverbial leg-up: when they looked back, it was only to
remind themselves of where they wanted never to go back to.

Chetwynd remained quite reticent. I have no memory of him
saying specifically where he had been or what he had been
doing. He didn't discuss his origins with us, or anything prior
to an apprenticeship he'd served in Paris, which I worked out
must have occurred in the mid to late 1930s. The years which
followed that were only referred to in obliquest fashion. He
remembered, say, the reputation of a restaurant when it had

had another name, or he could tell us that 'not so long ago', 'in its recent past', this street or that block of apartments had had a more distinguished ambience. My impression of Chetwynd's War was of a ghostly city and a manner of life which – ironically – didn't seem to my imagination so very different from our own one, except that style and breeding had been more in evidence. I had no other impression to gain from the verbal evidence. He might have been a hero himself, or a pimpernel, but the secret stayed secure.

*

In restaurants Chetwynd was able to give his instructions in French every bit as well as if he had been born a native. Ersatz-y French waiters knew better than to try anything on with *him*.

That's how I first discovered he had learned the rudiments of his trade in Paris; he told us that he'd had no option but to pick up the language. He knew formal front of shop, the aristocratic measure, the market slang they spoke in the streets, even the Franco-Yiddish compounds. He didn't clarify why it had been in Paris, there and not in London or another city, that he had served his time.

Subsequently I noticed how, occasionally in the general conversation at table, he would mention the name of a town he had visited in France – usually a resort, La Baule or Vittel or Évian-les-Bains – and I would presume that his sojourns had been in the line of business: he had gone there to inspect the treasure troves of lowering *belle époque* villas, to have privileged access to the darkly shuttered apartment of some 'embarrassed' *comtesse* or returned exiles from the colonies.

*

'Knowledge,' Chetwynd told me one evening as he nursed his customary whisky, 'is everything.'

We were left sitting at the large round table that was ours when we visited the 'Hungária' in Davies Street. I'd only missed half a dozen or so dances, so great had the demand on my services been.

'Do you think I should gain some?' I asked, taking the

opportunity to seek his advice on a pressing matter. 'Go to university?'

'Is that what your parents say?'

'They've said it, yes.'

'They think you're wasting your time?'

'I . . .'

'Have you told them about your evenings?'

I shook my head.

'I never,' he said, 'associate you with your parents.'

I didn't answer him.

'You look thirty,' he told me. 'Do you realise that?'

I didn't know how to take the remark.

'It's excellent camouflage,' he said, 'so far as your fitting in is concerned. You don't seem out of place at all. But I always forget how young you actually are.'

I had the impression that he was really addressing himself, speaking his private thoughts aloud.

'So you think,' I said, 'I should acquire knowledge?'

'If you haven't already.'

'Hardly – '

'Modesty is very becoming.'

He didn't mean I should believe him. I smiled without much conviction. We sat back in our chairs and made a pretence of watching the couples out on the floor. I waited for him to say what he would.

'If not knowledge,' he told me, 'then knowing in a different way. From other people.'

'Knowing more?'

'Knowing alternatively – in a different way from the norm.'

'To appear cleverer?' I responded.

He corrected me.

'I'd say, to afford yourself protection.'

He looked past me, and I realised that he'd imparted as much advice as he was prepared to. The last admission had been in the way of a clue, about himself but also about the limitations I should place on my self-confidence.

Meanwhile couples were circling the floor, in a slow waltz. The band, bedecked in Hollywood-inspired Magyar costume, were providing an emotional rendition of 'Goodnight, Vienna'. I felt nostalgic myself, and vaguely tearful for a city I had never even visited. By contrast, Chetwynd – who had told me once that he judged the Hungarians 'better at dreaming than the messy business of living' – was quite unaffected, clear-eyed indeed, with his thin, fastidious lips set straight on a perfect horizontal.

THIRTEEN

I preferred when Fleur was there. Like me, she was an amateur. Sometimes I felt I didn't quite fit in with the others; they were perfectly pleasant, I didn't imagine that they were talking about me behind my back, and yet I knew I didn't have access to that full lore I was certain they would have been able to share among themselves. Fleur was in the same boat as myself, I believed. It was true that I had adapted more easily than she, and the puzzlement that regularly articulated itself on her face confirmed this for me. Let me put it this way – she made me feel an outsider when it suited me, and suggested I was half-way to acceptance when, rather, it was that which I chose to think.

*

Two or three evenings in the week, on average, and one or two lunch-parties. I have no difficulty finding the energy to go through with it when I'm there. But much of my time at home is spent in nervous anticipation – of Gilbert cancelling a journey, or Gail or Hazel being unable to come, or Lillias taking ill . . . or of some unthinking, accidental betrayal of my own intentions. Tiredness might overcome me afterwards, once I'm back home, but I've had my vitality and verve when I've needed it.

The only time that is my own has to be savoured behind the locked door of the bathroom, when I'm lying soaking in the bath. My ablutions are taking longer and longer: up to an hour sometimes. I don't know how the time passes: exploring the geography of heat and coolness in the water, surveying the

**contours of my body like an aviator watching the land
spread beneath, tracing letters and patterns with my
right index finger on the condensation on the yellow
tiles. My mind is anything but empty, and yet these
are the only occasions in the week when I approach
a condition like calm, a languorous hitching loose
from my moorings and floating in delicious, otiose,
aqueous limbo.**

*

I would watch Fleur's eyes, to catch the moment when she might
turn them to look towards me. Unlike the others', I couldn't decide
what they were thinking. Sometimes her attention was like an
electric prod, and I would force myself to be more animated with
whomever I had been paired off. At other times she seemed to
be quizzing me, wondering what it might be that I was about, and
then I'd consider just what it was in fact I was doing and to what
possible end – prattling away, trying to dredge up old jokes from
memory or to select the aptest *bon mot*, hoping to pass myself
off as a paragon of erotic charm.

She could be flirtatiously charming herself, and respond well
to jokes, as ably as any of us. But those occasions were the
exceptions – holidays from herself. Mostly she was quiet and
demurely lady-like, but that appeared to be a strong element in
her appeal to certain of our guests and to Chetwynd also. She
was different, and that was appreciated – she wasn't the type you
expected to come across in a night-club on a weekday evening, her
eyes didn't look as if they were rimmed with kohl and her mouth
wasn't a scarlet slash, so that made her all the less forgettable.

They remembered all that she wasn't. I describe it as if it
were a negative achievement, and it must be the case that
she didn't work on making the effect that she was able to.
Chetwynd didn't concern himself with the psychology of it all, he
just extended an open invitation to her and she came whenever
she possibly could.

So far as I was aware, no one enquired too closely about her
home life. She was married, lived – she said – in Highgate,

had a daughter. Her husband was a doctor; presumed by us to be a GP in their own neck of the woods. Her mother was dead, her father lived somewhere near the river, not too far from the Embankment, where one of the guests said he had chanced to see her, making at a smart pace in the direction of Cheyne Walk. She'd blushed when he told her, and Patrick Durran nudged Celia's elbow so that we should all see, which precipitated a second rush of blood to Fleur's face – at which point Chetwynd stepped in, literally, and informed us he'd considered buying a house there, in the days before Kensington, but the ceilings had been painted blue with white clouds adrift on them and he'd found wall-crucifixes at every turn and, really, he'd felt he didn't have either the spiritual essentials to take it on or the freedom from superstition to paint out Heaven and repaper the Saviour's shadow on every wall. Ha-ha-ha.

*

I order my life by Gilbert's diary.

Most weeks he spends two or three nights away from London. I receive the news of his movements quite impassively, and commit them to memory, the dates and his destination. Sometimes he will put himself up at a hotel, but more often – by his own preference – he will be invited to spend the night on the premises by his host, who may or may not also be his patient. Being there on hand might seem to be part of the professional service, but I know my husband a little better than that. His patients are hand-picked, and he wouldn't find himself at anywhere less than a manor or dower house.

He returns with some sly comments to make about the accommodation and the company, but that is his way. I can see quite well that he relishes the change of scene. On the first day back he is more irritable with little things than he was just before he left, and I know that in his imagination he is still *there*, in that other place he has newly come from. I do my best, but it's not quite enough, and I'm probably too late, in this our twelfth year.

Of course he must speak of those whom he met — names he may have mentioned on other occasions, but I forget. Not so long ago my forgetfulness used to disappoint and irk him. But now he only wants someone to talk to, to receive what he tells her, who makes no social demands on him so that he can pace the bedroom or sitting-room with his shirt collar hanging loose and slippers on his feet.

I am quite glad to be of some use — it assuages my guilt a little. My real usefulness occurred at an earlier point of his life, however, and this is the next best thing.

When he isn't here, I go out. It's usually Mrs Thorold's niece who stays to look after Lillias and, not as circumspectly as she thinks, to pick her way through the larder foraging for tit-bits.

I can walk down the steps and along the street without needing to take a backward look.

I wait for a taxi at the corner. The expenses of the journey add up, but there's nothing else to be done. C. has offered to send a car for me, but eyes would be watching from the shadows of rooms along the street. As it is, I'm over-dressed for a dinner party or a bridge four or — it's my most frequent excuse to Gilbert — a visit to father in Chelsea. The evenings aren't dark enough yet and I feel nothing is hidden: of my finery, or even of my intentions, my neglect of my child. Preferably the taxi rides pass in silence, and on spacious avenues and crescents I look through the windows for the evidence in all the fine houses of other high-living peregrinations about to be embarked upon.

*

Chetwynd protected her. The rest of the company had to look

after themselves – and take the consequences for any social gaffes. I was effectively on probation, but the guests seemed to understand that I hadn't the liberty of the others. *They* pencilled in 'appointments' in their diaries, but Chetwynd made sure that he knew about the few later engagements that came my way, to approve or to veto them.

Calling her 'Mrs Simmons' was one way he had of establishing a separate status for her. I couldn't believe she was on trial in the same manner as I was. He was waiting for something, an opportunity, in respect of her: but it might have been that he wasn't even sure himself of what just yet. He had to be very careful, though, lest he lose her, lest he rush things and she take fright and his ulterior plans, whatever they were, fall through.

*

Nobody would expect to see me in those places C. takes us to, so they don't see me. That's how I can explain and justify it to myself. The car drives there with the others prepare me – such unlikely progresses through the night streets in the back of the Daimler, smelling of leather and thick carpet and the super-efficient heating system. Arriving is vaguely a shock to the system, stepping out into pungent or chill fresh air, but it's only for half a minute or so, until we're swept up and escorted inside the premises of whichever restaurant or night-club I've allowed myself to be talked into coming to.

Anyway, I look different in the artificial light. I don't look myself: or not the person that passes as myself, should I say. The light dramatises everything. My face is pronouncedly oval, from somewhere I acquire Slav cheekbones, my eyes are greener. I have the lower lip of a sensual woman. I never see these things when I am not in these places, at home. I've considered myself always an unexceptionally English composite, with little to distinguish me, dutifully adhering to type: thankfully a good clear skin, a tendency to flush in a hot room, not a round face but geometrically undefined, blue eyes with a little green in them, a quiet and precise mouth. But it seems I have been labouring under a misapprehension all this time. This, I must suppose, is living and learning.

*

Chetwynd could home in on her from several places away at dinner if she was getting into difficulties, and steer the talk around the rocks. Usually she was no more than four chairs away, and I noticed that it never happened they were at opposite ends of a table, or diametrically placed at a circular one. She and I, I also noticed, were kept apart, both at 'house' entertainments and when we were taken to the supper-rooms and dance-clubs. When things were more relaxed – foregathering, for instance, or seeing the guests off – and when I attempted to draw Fleur into conversation, Chetwynd had an unfailing, and to me wholly irritating, knack of interrupting us, always with some perfectly sound pretext for doing so.

Twice I plucked up courage and suggested to her, well out of Chetwynd's hearing, that we might meet somewhere outside. But on both occasions the request clearly alarmed her, her pupils loosened in the whites of her eyes and scanned the room behind me, and I hadn't the grit to ask her again. If she'd given me any sign, any at all, I should have swooped on it.

She would make her departures unaccompanied. Chetwynd was always there to see that she did. I'd watch her go, and hope every time that she might show a change of heart.

*

C. appreciates my difficulties – even though to him I'm the wife of a GP called Simmons – and he is perfectly understanding. I've explained that I have my other duties, and he couldn't agree more. He asks me what 'Donald''s movements are, and I try to remember the details of conversations with family doctors I've been introduced to over the years. A

GP for a husband occurred to me on the spur of the moment, and maybe I could have chosen more wisely, but it's only later we become the subjects of our impulses. I think he's trying to see how I fit into the perspective of this marriage, and 'Donald' and Gilbert fill the bill equally. He has commented that my husband is very particular about his social acquaintances, and my silence must have told him that he'd hit the nail exactly on the head. He has used a number of names which sounded half-familiar to me: some I *can* recognise, and when I tell him I can he nods thoughtfully – not in approval surely, but because it's helping to slot together a jigsaw picture in his head. I take it as an expression of his interest, and I appreciate that gesture of involvement very much.

*

I would have protected her myself if I could have done, if she had only given me the opportunity to. I envied Chetwynd that he was able to, that – presumably – she would allow him. Was that all – my jealousy gnawed at me – was that all she allowed a rich, unmarried, not unprepossessing man to offer her: his protection?

I kept them both under continual observation. I could believe that it was as much my duty to keep alert for her sake. I learned to watch in mirrors. It seemed to be a houseful of eyes sometimes. But, in this advancing summer of 1957, it was no more than how we charmed ones found ourselves living now.

FOURTEEN

When I became as regular an attender as the others, I noticed how at every second or third meal someone of the intimate inner group would be missing and a place would have been removed from the table-setting. No reference would be made to the absence. It was as if – very curiously – the person remained unknown to us. I felt I could only take my cue from the others, which might have been my weakness: but their cue surely came from Chetwynd, and it did me no good not to heed him. I didn't want to be on the receiving end of one of those piercing stares of such reasonable incomprehension I had learned to recognise.

The absences didn't usually last longer than two or three days at the most; some only necessitated the surrender of one dinner. At first I'd thought the business – especially the ignoring of it – odd, but as weeks went by it seemed less so. It just became a custom. The absences weren't discussed by the absentees afterwards, which was odd too: they were sidestepped, as a bout of illness or drinking or depression might have been. Our reticence was unanimous.

Meanwhile the summer was passing. Pollen came and went. Rooms grew warmer again, briefly, in September, and I perspired rather more. But then the trees started to lose their full green glory as I cycled to and fro. We saw a little less from the back of the Daimler or the auxiliary Lagonda in the evenings. Stars appeared earlier in the sky.

Chetwynd was absent for some weeks. Exiled from Kensington we bided our time, all in our own little burrows.

Then we returned. The rituals recommenced. It felt as if many months had passed.

I noticed a dropped leaf one lunchtime, as I got off my bicycle
and wheeled it to the garage: it was still green, but some force
in nature had caused it to fall on to the polished toe-cap of my
patent black pump.

*

On the floor of the drawing-room of the Kensington house was
laid a Tabriz carpet, showing in rich detail one of the royal
gardens of ancient Persia. Held within walls was a formal but
idyllic pastoral scene created out of the unpromising landscape
that surrounded it – ponds, pathways, trees and shrubs, birds.
The borders were a riot of floral growth.

To Islamites, as to Christians, the reward offered for faith-
fastness in this earthly life is an eternal existence in Paradise.
I read in a book about carpets that the Persian word for
'Paradise' is the same as that for 'garden'. The trees depicted on
the Kensington carpet were the trees-of-life, bridges between
Paradise and this world beneath. The weavers, devising their
sanctuaries 'of foliate plenitude', were engaged in a spiritual act
of faith.

*

We were at the Brazilian 'Caipirinha', famous for its sugar-cane
brandies with lime juice.

I was returning to the main room from the men's cloakroom.
My route took me along a corridor of burgundy velvet walls.
Before I reached the corner I saw Chetwynd emerge from a
room and close the door, marked 'General Manager', behind
him. He didn't see me coming. I wasn't the only one to spot
him, however. A woman customer approached and spoke.
Chetwynd stopped to reply. I came upon them slowly, creeping
forward on the runner of carpet so I shouldn't be heard.
Chetwynd was replying 'no, I think not'. He smiled as he
shook his head – a courteous smile but a firm head-shake.
He repeated what he'd just said. The woman was reddening,
with too evident embarrassment. 'I didn't say *that*,' Chetwynd
answered, attempting to sound jocular. 'We sometimes went,
you see,' the woman explained, 'to the restaurant. When we

were in Hamburg. And I said to my husband when I saw you this evening – ' 'I'm very sorry to disappoint you,' Chetwynd apologised, and started to move off. 'Would you excuse me,' he asked, 'if I return to my shepherding duties with my party?' 'Oh, of course, of course,' she replied, but I heard how intense her disappointment was, to be told she could have mistaken him for someone else entirely.

*

When Chetwynd smiled, his face would somehow become *more* serious, not less. It was a curious accomplishment, and I was fascinated – and disturbed – to watch. He smiled even more at the concentration on my face, as if to deny the fact of his own. But I told myself I couldn't be fooled: or only up to a point.

Sometimes I asked, and on a very few occasions Fleur said yes, and so we danced. She would let me decide the step, and I led. But I lost my fluency. I didn't acquit myself nearly as convincingly as I could usually manage. My hand rested on her back, and yet we didn't draw close. I'd be thinking how like the six-inch rule at school dances it was. Even at our coy distance she must have felt, surely, the excitement her ceremony was causing me, a spate of it, conducted along my shoulders and arms.

Whenever it happened that we danced – no more than four or five times, and snatched at, such were the demands on me – I had the presence of mind left to sense Chetwynd was watching me. And when I turned to search him out, I discovered that he was. Always watching, missing nothing. *This* wasn't the point of the exercise, I realised from the dead-pan expression: and you know it very well, lad. This doesn't pay anyone's keep.

*

'They're so polite,' Patrick Durran told me.
'Who are?'
'The waiters. Nothing could be too much trouble. But I know for a fact . . .'
He paused to tantalise me.

'Yes?'

'They hate the customers. It's a ghastly, grotesque game.'

'How do you mean?'

'They put bromide into the sauces. And the chef opens his flies and pisses into the soup tureen.'

'I don't believe you.'

'They do worse things than that.'

'Well, please don't enlighten me – '

'You *certainly* wouldn't believe me if I did.'

'Why did you have to tell me?'

He laughed, then said 'You shouldn't believe what isn't worth believing in.'

'But *you* come. To these restaurants. Don't you?'

'I'm a hypocrite?'

'I just – don't follow your reasoning.'

He laughed again.

'I never take the soup. Haven't you noticed? That's my reasoning.'

'And nothing with sauce either, I suppose?'

'Oysters. The brine kills the taste of anything. And the sole's grilled, which lessens the chances.'

'Expense no object?'

'Don't be a killjoy, Ralph.'

He pronounced it as I'd been christened – 'Ralph' not 'Rafe'.

'Isn't it expensive?'

'Chetwynd doesn't say anything. Wouldn't raise an eyebrow.'

'Why not?'

'What? And risk losing me?'

'Would he?'

'I get my oats. And he gets what *he* wants out of it, I suppose.'

'How do you mean?' I asked him.

I found he was staring at me: listening to the implication of his own words. His eyes were terrified.

'Mean what?'

'What you've just said.'

'Forget it.'

'About Chetwynd getting – '

'*Forget* it, Witton.'

He snatched my hand and made to crush it inside his. I doubled-up with pain. When he let me go, my eyes were squeezing out tears.

*

Inevitably I wondered about Chetwynd's sexuality.

I would see him kissing some of his guests on their cheeks, and receiving a kiss sometimes, but the gesture appeared wholly social. He *watched*, of course, but somehow they didn't strike me as appraising looks in the sexual sense. When he kept us under observation, he never forgot himself, and what is the erotic if not (temporarily, at any rate) self-forgetful. It seemed to me that he always knew exactly what he was about. The longer I studied him, the more scientific I could conceive his surveillance of us all was.

Was he queer? Ambivalent, then? It was possible, but neither could I find evidence to that end. He wore no signet ring, no jewellery at all, not even a tie-clip. He donned a cravat occasionally but most certainly showed no fondness (that I could see) for the green chiffon sort, which was the famous – because deliberate – give-away in those closeted days. Might he have pederastic inclinations? That *was* a possibility, but I couldn't recall ever having seen him in the presence of even one little boy to be able to judge from. Would little girls have been his province, rather? Or slightly older girls, just as the physical changes out of childhood were upon them?

I was spoilt for choice, in a manner of speaking. But he was far too careful, for me or for any of us. I tried to lead my companions into speculation, but they were curiously loyal and non-committal: or maybe, more simply, they were as much in the dark as I was. Or indifferent. They would discuss with me his likely wealth, but not his sexual orientation. It was as fruitless, as wholly dead an area to them as his previous personal history prior to his Kensington self.

Anyway, they had their own affairs to occupy themselves with.

I knew that there were comings and goings with our guests, but I still thought then that it was all quite casual and accidental, that – maybe – it didn't much signify. How could I have supposed the extent that it did matter, that in fact it was the point of everything? At that time I didn't imagine it to be more than a pastime, my companions playing at being the famous actors and actresses they would go to watch in the films. We were all living charmed, not quite real existences, courtesy of Chetwynd, so why should they believe in the peripheral business? We survived on secrets, what we didn't admit of ourselves – that was true of all of us. Now my acceptance – my failure to enquire further – doesn't seem credible to me, but that is hindsight's judgement on the most bizarre interlude of my life. Over the twenty-three months I picked up my leads from observations let slip in conversation: the geography of certain quarters of London seen from the speeding comfort of the taxis they travelled in, the quality of food in certain restaurants I knew they couldn't have afforded to eat at out of their own pockets, the failure to explain a stylish new hair-do or manicure or the purchase of a silk tie or pair of cuff-links.

*

Celia stands so close to me. I pretend that I don't notice, but she knows that I do. I might attempt to move away, but I stay exactly where I am. The side of me which is closer to her takes a sensation like an electrical charge. It's heat and cold simultaneously and it numbs me. I can't think where to look, and so my eyes fix without my realising while I seem to be seeing the situation from outside myself, which can only disable me more. I feel I'm locked into this moment, and every time the situation comes about I seem to be further and further from the possibility of understanding and of doing anything whatsoever about it. I can impute anybody else with lack of honesty, but not myself. That doesn't seem to me a fit and proper way to be living. Now I am being consistently disappointed in

**the person I can least afford to be let down by —
myself.**

*

I realised that Chetwynd was making contact with people he
thought it important, for his own reasons, that he should make
contact with. I realised, also, as I've said, that I didn't especially
want to know. This was conscious policy. After all I worked at
a swimming pool, and it was no job for a greenhorn: the veils
wrapped about human nature were, one by one, stripped away,
to reveal the complexity of our character beneath. You trained
yourself to spot the glad eye, so you were ready to handle it and
to have the eyer-up – be it woman or man – let down easily, with
as little offence taken and rendered as was possible.

And yet, while that was the state of affairs in Randolph
Square, no more than two and a half miles away I persisted in
resolute, stubborn thoughtlessness about the implications of it
all. Curiosity had brought me to 'Underwood', and my curiosity
would return to me in the later days, but for that long middle
period of my service in Kensington I went into mental neutral.

A programme of non-stop activity kept me fully preoccupied.
I saw my parents sometimes, and my brother and sister, and
friends, and I had to buy food for myself, and there was simply
all the business of living, which gave me very little free time for
reflection.

It did occur to me that Chetwynd must be a social climber –
that probably he was looking to do business with those types
we encountered – that the programme for his advancement and
the assiduous trading pitch were one and the same thing, and
bound up with the man's personality. If we were using him –
taking the hospitality offered by him – he could be said to be
using us, couldn't he: we being a means to an end for him?
Should we have felt at all guilty about merely going along with
the mutually undeclared arrangement? Everyone, so to speak,
was getting what he wanted out of it: we a prodigal taste of high
living, and Chetwynd by our complicity a coterie of bona fide
titled acquaintances and variedly influential luncheon-favourites
and dinner-intimates. All parties appeared to be satisfied: and

if not, why else should we continue? Perhaps I was taking a market assessment of affairs, but I was of a generation with an obligation to assume a modern attitude.

There came a point when I understood that my parents acutely disapproved of my life. The swimming pool was bad enough, but I think they saw my existence at 'The Circus' – the little I told them about it now – as positively effeminate. It was achieving nothing in their eyes because it was distracting me from the only business which could possibly matter, that of winning an academic degree for myself. In her letters to me my mother was always reminding me of my results and report cards at school. She pursued me, even in my dreams, like a spook. I didn't know – for all my so-called cleverness – I just didn't have a single clue how it all could possibly end.

*

I used to sing Lillias the nursery rhymes I remembered from my own childhood, and something in me turned not sentimental but melancholic when I heard myself, in that nursery with the rosebud wallpaper and the stencilled furniture. I would stop half-way through a verse and look about me and wonder how Gilbert could have talked me into such mawkish taste. Lillias would outgrow the surroundings, but never forget, and I didn't see how it was really any preparation for life. Then I would become conscious of Lillias tugging at my arm and asking me to finish the rest of the rhyme. 'Have you forgotten?' As early as two or three years old there was already a frostiness in her delivery I found unsettling.

It was then I felt too young and too ill-equipped to be dealing with a child. I seemed to have run a lap of myself, when I hadn't yet had time to fathom my own early childhood. But there wasn't any time for being so abstract, because practicalities were forever rushing in. My real dread was that Lillias was already able, with those eyes open so wide, to observe so much – her father's irritability with me, and my being always seconds, whole beats, behind where I should have been with them both, so preoccupied with my own suspicions of my neglect of love.

FIFTEEN

On one of the drawing-room walls, out of the reach of direct sunlight, hung a fetching water-colour by Winston Churchill.

Someone asked Chetwynd how he had come by it. He was vague. I couldn't make out if it had been a gift from the painter himself, or from a mutual friend. The guests seemed just as unsure as myself, but had the tact – or the wish not to appear slow on the uptake – to let the matter of its provenance go.

'Isn't it Morocco?' another guest – Laurence Breen the couturier – asked.

'Yes.'

'Churchill stays at the "Mamounia", doesn't he? Or he did. In Marrakesh.'

'That's right.'

'So, those are the Atlas Mountains – '

'Quite correct.' Chetwynd, smiling, held up his hands in a mock gesture of surrender. 'You're in quite the wrong line of work, Laurence.'

'Not *work* surely!' The man seemed a little piqued, notwithstanding his levity.

'An art connoisseur, I meant.'

'Oh, I can't say if it's well-painted or not.' Breen had his little revenge. 'It's very pleasant, which is all that I care about really.'

'Have you been, Anthony?' asked Celeste Hillier, mistress of an earlier prime minister. 'To Morocco?'

Chetwynd returned his most unyielding smile.

'Certainly.'

'You've been to – '

'The painting sums the place up for me.'

He walked across to it. His words became fainter. Something about 'terrain', an 'African sky', (perhaps) 'a shimmering
uncertainty'.

*

Once the woman on my arm (so to speak), the jaded spinster
daughter of a peer who only came alive when the music played,
told me 'Sometimes you remind me so much of Raoul.'

I presumed Raoul had been encountered on a foreign hop, to
one of those highly-professional resort towns where her type
go to be briefly winkled out of their shells.

'Whereabouts was that?' I enquired.

'Not here, I'm sure.'

'Which country – '

'In *London*!' She laughed in the overstated, uncontrolled way
she had. 'I just can't remember which club.'

I didn't reply.

'Anthony introduced us.'

'Chetwynd?'

'This is four or five years ago. I don't think they knew one
another very well. Anthony had his flat then, and didn't seem
to have the company he does now.'

'And *he* introduced you?'

'Me to Raoul. And Raoul to me.'

She smiled at the recollection.

'I remind you of him?' I asked.

'The way you dance,' she said. 'You're both excellent
dancers.'

I simulated being flattered. But I knew quite well that dancing
was my strong card. I had also suspected that without it my
patent pumps would have been filled by somebody else: not
necessarily a certificated life-saver, but another in the vein of
Raoul perhaps.

'The name,' I said. 'Raoul – '

'He was French. A very good English-speaker, though – '

(A dancer *and* a linguist?)

'You could tell his nationality by his appearance. But he was
handsome – in both languages – '

She had shed weight as we danced to the music. When they danced, women lost their ungainliness as they did some of their inhibitions. Her eyes glittered like mica. She was floating across the Hollywood dance-floors of her imagination, at a quick-step, in a close-fitting gown of white taffeta and in silver shoes that had wings to them. I didn't have it in me to disappoint her, not for a single second, even though the floor was cramped and the lighting inadequate. In Hollywood the floors were polished like fury, until they resembled ice. Yet we too were encountering no obstacles to our progress, no friction. After three consecutive dances she seemed to me years younger than the forty or forty-five I had guessed her to be; we mirrored each other's every movement, and two might have been one. That was the masterly illusion of dance, effected to the Tin Pan Alley rhythms of paso, bongo, turkey-trot and rumba. But I was a virgin, still, and she was old enough to be my mother.

'What happened?' I asked her.

'"Happened"?' she repeated.

'About – Raoul.'

'Oh . . .' The shine in her eyes started to dim. 'I never discovered. He went out of circulation. Sometimes people will seem to be always there, then all of a sudden they just – disappear. And . . .'

'Didn't Chetwynd tell you – ?'

'Anthony?'

' – where Raoul had gone?'

'Why should he have known?'

'Didn't they know one another? Didn't you say that?'

'He introduced us. But introductions were always going on. Ice-breaking. I didn't suppose they really *knew* each other. Just socially – '

'*Could* they have done?'

'Anthony wasn't always there when Raoul was.'

'And vice versa?'

'I . . .'

But she couldn't be sure. Her eyes dimmed a little more. She was losing the rhythm and starting to drag against me.

'Was Raoul there when Chetwynd was?'

'Does it matter?' she asked, sounding pained.

'Perhaps,' I said.

'I think he was. Now when I think about it. I can't be categorical . . .'

She considered. She nodded her head, but looking away.

The dance had finished. We were standing in the middle of the floor. Slowly our arms dropped to our sides. I was my own inexperienced, not very confident self again. She was definitively forty-five again, a plainer woman with thicker ankles and a tendency to stoop and a terribly staid sense of dress. Ivory clanked heavily on her wrists.

I led her back to our large table. Through the blue cigarette smoke I caught sight of Chetwynd watching us both. He was talking to somebody else, lifting his cigarette from the ash-tray, fingering the stem of his wine-glass – but unmistakably he was watching us.

She and I met again soonish, sometime within the next two or three weeks, at 'The Circus'.

'Please don't think,' she whispered as we stood up to assemble ourselves for the progress towards the dining-room that evening, 'I was talking about – ' she nodded towards Chetwynd, who was instructing – 'behind his back, because really I wasn't.'

'No,' I told her. 'I didn't think that.'

'Thank you.' She smiled, replacing her cigarette case in her monogrammed evening bag. 'They were good times with Raoul, but they're over.'

I nodded.

'Anthony has been so good to us.'

'"Us"?'

'My father and myself. I couldn't begin to thank him.'

'How exactly – ' I embarked.

She shook her head.

'I can't talk about that, Mr Witton.'

'Ralph, please – '

We walked across the drawing-room, towards the opened doors and the gallery beyond.

She lowered her voice.

'He's proved a good Samaritan, if ever there was. We'd quite given up hope.'

'"Hope"?' I repeated, feeling that she was surely inviting the question. 'About what exactly?'

'Oh . . .' She shook her head, more vigorously this time, against temptation. Her jade earrings spun. 'It could all have ended so differently for us. That's all I meant. *Now* – ' She turned us towards the head of the staircase. ' – will you or won't you accompany me?'

Sometimes she forgot about her gaucheness, the ungainliness, the evidence of middle-age she powdered over, and merely became a flirt. Any metamorphosis, she made me think, might be possible at the house of Anthony Chetwynd.

The house seemed even larger inside than the outside lay claim to being. It was a veritable palazzo, especially at night when it was illuminated by lamplight and candles and the rooms grew to the unspecifiable dimensions of caverns. In such a place, I could believe, sorcery of the ancient sort might be done. Circe and Calypso would have been quite at home here.

Then my dancing partner was gone.

She didn't appear one lunchtime when Celia had informed me she would be coming. A place was removed from the table, and I realised there was no expectation of her coming. I would have asked why not, but it was one of those occasions when Chetwynd hadn't addressed a single word, nor spared even a glance, in my direction.

She had told me she would be up for an exhibition of Mary Potter's paintings at a gallery in Cork Street. I had expressed an interest in them, and she'd said, We must have a rendezvous. The showing came and went, however.

I continued to hear nothing from her. Eventually I asked Chetwynd, when I thought I could: and where better than at her favourite of the supper-clubs, where she had first told me about Raoul. Over his brandy (a whisky man's concession to his guests) he turned the most charming and harmless of smiles upon me, which was how I knew to be on my guard.

'I gather,' he said, 'she has gone out of circulation for a while.'

The words induced a shiver of recognition.

'Has she,' I asked, 'told you where to?'

'I only heard from another source. She likes to have certain secrets to herself. That is her right, of course – ' He looked at his fingers, turning the stem of the brandy balloon. ' – but it makes things a little difficult on the social front.'

He glanced up at me again with the same artful expression of reasonableness.

'I see,' I said.

He knew quite well that I didn't.

'You will find, I hope,' he said, 'consolation. Among the company.' He was gently ridiculing me, of course. But I was familiar enough with his multiple ambiguities to recognise when the tone of his voice carried a warning in it. 'Others attend your skills. You have quite a following of devotees – fans – you know. They're only waiting for an opportunity. When it comes to the light fantastic, you're in a class of your own.'

They were flattering words, but I prided myself that I was not to be won over that way.

Chetwynd sat watching me for a reaction. I wondered why it should matter to him. What had he overheard of my last conversation with Lord Liddington's daughter?

'So you mustn't,' he said, 'disappoint our good friends.'

'No.'

'Their disappointment would be mine.'

He spoke in a lower register and more quietly. He remembered to keep smiling, over the rim of the balloon glass.

*

I was in the Gents of 'The Fez' one night. Someone came and stood at the stall next to mine. I turned round and saw our Adonis, Clive, in dinner jacket like myself. He was looking down as he unbuttoned his fly. A smile widened on his face. I followed his eyes. His penis was unfolding in his hand. In four or five seconds it had swollen half-way to a full erection.

He said nothing. Blood thumped in my chest. I felt a motion

inside my own hand. I panicked, and crammed myself back inside my trousers.

Still Clive didn't speak, didn't look at me. I had no idea what to say. I turned, turned and fled.

*

Then there were times – more times – when Chetwynd seemed bored and exhausted by us all, and the fact wasn't concealed. He shrank further into himself and observed us from a greater distance even than his usual. Our behaviour, I felt, became quite tangential to his life then. He might have been waking from a sleep to find his rooms occupied by strangers, when he could only stare mystified, in unblinking incomprehension. It would occur to me on those occasions that our secondary lives were unplotted and accidental, and that I had quite erroneously ascribed to him the capacity for meticulous, arcane organisation. Perhaps there was far less reason for it all, either because he was lonely or because he took pleasure in what he saw as our ritual humiliation.

He didn't stop watching us. Sometimes that was all he did. He'd be drinking but not eating any of the expensive food, smoking a Camel cigarette or cigar instead. He might explode with anger over some trivial matter. He never left us, though; and none of us ever left the group. There must be these deeper silences, I attempted to convince myself, these troughs with their atmosphere of conceivable treachery to unsettle us: reasons must exist in nature, and there was nothing on that account to be uneasy *about*.

And yet I was. The opening up of that greater distance did unnerve me. I felt from it the sort of coldness which is carried across a lackcolour winter sea. He appeared to study us all without regard for personality, but – it's the best I can describe the effect, and doing so in retrospect – as a confederacy of integers, a sum of abstract parts. We continued to perform, and he was a silent, unimpressionable audience. It was preferable, I realised, not to look at him, not to be caught looking. And yet there was an irresistible temptation, to intrepidly dare the intensity of that blankness

in his eyes and somehow set into all the other features of
his face.

*

I was turning the pages of a magazine – *Country Life* again
– in the mezzanine lounge at Randolph Square, after a shift.
As the pages turned I saw the image of my erstwhile dancing
partner, Petronella Liddington – an artist's painted portrait –
looking out at me.

I stopped and thumbed back through the pages. I found the
illustration, in a gallery's exhibition advertisement. It wasn't her,
in the end, because the clothes – and the style of the portrait
– were another generation's taste. But the face was surely a
relation's: her mother's even.

The painting, by a celebrated portraitist and Royal Academi-
cian, was one of the effects of an Anonymous Titled Gentleman
being offered to the market. They included paintings, silver,
porcelain, also fine netsuke and rare lapis lazuli and soapstone
carvings.

There was no mention of carpets or tapestries.

SIXTEEN

It was always to be a great disappointment that we never returned to Treswithian and 'Underwood'. Chetwynd had planned it for September, but it transpired – when September was upon us – that he had more urgent 'business' to attend to, in Paris, so he flew off there. A photograph in a number of newspapers showed Marlene Dietrich and Orson Welles, arm-in-arm, descending the steps from an Air France plane, at Nice Airport, and who should be just visible, next in line to emerge into sunlight from the cabin, but Chetwynd.

When he returned he knew all about the photograph. Before we could contrive to ask a question, he asked if we'd seen his press agent's work. It was a joke, and he happily enough (it seemed) told us he'd spent a few days at the Eden Roc Hotel on Cap d'Antibes. We made the only deduction we really could, namely that 'business' had gone very well indeed. He was wearing with his dark business suit a bold new floral-patterned tie, and April showed me a current photograph syndicated to magazines of the Duke of Windsor tilling his garden at the Chevreuse mill-house, wearing a tie very like it or even its exact double.

But I should have preferred, for my own selfish sake, if we had gone back to 'Underwood'. I knew I'd have enjoyed it. With the passing of the months the house was acquiring more of a lure for me, certainly not less. The bay scintillated in my memory. I almost – almost but not quite – forgot the indignities of 'Lesser Penelewey' suffered with my family, and my earlier cycling trips about our corner of the county, and the vaguely constructed plans in my head to try to secure a place at university for next year. However, the recollection of 'Underwood' shone through all the rest; every time I read it clearly – and with increasing pleasure – as if it were a private watermark indented deep into my truest past.

*

It's a pity that Father can't come up to Hampstead and the house, or to walk on the Heath as he used to. It's a long way, and he isn't so fit. Chelsea living has softened him, I tell Gilbert. But really it's age, and there's nothing to be done.

I visit him instead, when I can, but not as often as I should. Whenever Gilbert asks me about my nights in Town, I mostly tell him I've been over to Chelsea. If I think he has his ears and eyes especially open, I say I took a walk along the Embankment – to think, or to clear my head – before I went looking for a taxi. The taxis are an expense, all the way to Kensington and back, but I can just about cope with it. I only have to think what the alternative is, really visiting Father or staying at home with Lillias in Gilbert's house with its address which he considers so desirable.

Lillias deserves better of me. She deserved another name, since it was Gilbert's choice, and since I couldn't think of anything else – except Mother's 'Rosamond' – and since the birth had left me bloated with fatigue: I couldn't think how to object.

But maybe this way, because we're not confined together – since she doesn't have to see *me* as the prisoner of the house – we can have an easier, lighter relationship. It's hardly honest, but it allows us both some space – even in such a large house – to be able to be ourselves. *By* ourselves. If we were always here, we should start taking the other for granted, which can become the final assassin of respect.

This is what I tell myself. But I don't know if I believe it. I survive on a structure of moral conveniences I pretend are logical premises, and I stolidly trace them back – sitting in a rattling taxi cab – to verbal aphorisms I can't decide if I'm remembering or making up. I start to lose some of my guilt when we reach, past Kensington's borders, the signs that announce 'Royal Borough Of . . .': and it recedes further the closer we come to 'The Circus'. I am as effortless and – finally – as unrepentant a traitor of myself as that.

*

The carpets had a transcendent beauty and order which may have seemed to excuse the untidiness of our times, and the scrabbling shenanigans that accompanied them. They existed on a purer plane, which was also – confusingly – a much more literal one than time's contemporary history.

The carpets were his high ground: or alternatively they were islands of detachment from which he could view the follies of others, and from which he could plan forms of retribution that had nothing to do with morality but everything to do with the affirmation of his own purchase and intelligence.

*

Some London afternoons we had spent in the garden. It was a haven of quiet, and felt like a secret garden. The traffic sounded, not several dozen yards, but miles away.

The dimensions are probably beside the point: half an acre or so of lawn fringed by colourful azaleas and magnolias, with evergreen conifers behind. Above us dense Lebanon cedars shivered in every draught of cooling breeze and I would suddenly be hearing the sea. A few lichened stone urns and small statues merged into the greenery. The shrubbery seemed utterly indigenous to the spot. The trees had gnarled and knobbled boles and made me think – for some reason – of blind Milton being read to, in the jasperous shade of acanthus leaves. A single judas tree blossomed resolutely lilac.

One afternoon, though, at the very end of the formalities and

just as we were all leaving, I saw what I had quite failed to notice
earlier, on any of the other afternoons: that the encircling outer
wall (of dressed stone to match the house's) was – where the
eye wasn't invited to look, under the profuse, disguising cover
of creeper and tree branches – topped with four rows of taut
and tensed barbed wire.

SEVENTEEN

Liz and me.

All this fuss, her handling of the crockery tells me. Tea pot, china cups and saucers, ditto side-plates and milk-jug and sugar-bowl. Scones, butter, jam, cream, cutlery.

She's doing it for my sake, but I don't want it either. She hates the domesticity. She is irritated with herself for interrupting me before I have the chance to offer to pour. She is so determined that she won't be a victim of sexism that she only compounds the offence, done by herself to herself.

We carry it off, but the afternoon tea is a travesty of what it purports to be. We are frightened of its implications, and yet tempted – in spite of ourselves – to try, to test this vital aspect of ordinariness that is absent in both our lives.

*

She had a crooked finger.

It was the fourth finger of her left hand, where a wedding ring would have gone. From the knuckle to the tip was askew. It partially rested against the middle finger. The joint hardly bent at all; when she curled her other fingers it remained stiff but twisted.

I tried not to let her see me looking at it. I couldn't tell if I succeeded or not. I wasn't even sure that I *shouldn't* mention it. I wanted to come closer to this woman, the daughter of that other: to offer the proof of my discretion, my protectiveness, if only she would take it.

But I dissuaded myself. I merely looked, attempting to divert my eyes quickly enough not to be noticed.

As ever, though, where my dealings with Liz were concerned, I got it all too wrong.

*

'"Concerts," I'd hear her telling my father. "I go to concerts."'

She rolled up her paper napkin and dropped it with relief on to her plate of crumbs. The stupid tea party was over.

'He didn't care for classical music, although he made himself listen to it when he felt he had to. But his face went rigid with boredom, and you could tell it was just a faint faraway background to his thoughts. She knew that if she said "concerts", that she went to hear orchestras and chamber groups in his absence, it would be a further confusion to him. He couldn't ask her all the questions of where and when and why without betraying his ignorance. I don't doubt he was conscious of it as a grave failing in himself.'

'How often did he ask her?'

'I've no idea. One day it just happened, I was there to overhear them.'

'It interested him, I dare say, to know – '

'But you didn't see him.' In an instant her tone was angry. The purpose of the tea was completely undone. '*You* didn't live with him. You can't *possibly* say a thing like that – ' She glared at me. 'You've no right, no right at all – '

'I realise,' I said, 'I have no right. It's not my place. But I'm only trying – '

*

When she came down to dinner I thought she looked red-eyed.

She spilled water from the jug as she poured into our glasses. 'Shit!' At that one of the other guests glanced round. Liz scowled at her, and thumped the water-jug back down on to the table. The waitress serving us leaned forward to return it to the mat. 'Leave it where it is!' Liz barked at her. The girl jumped back.

I thought the reprimand was quite unreasonable. But something prevented me from speaking, a certain – I euphemise – disinclination, only too familiar to me. Liz didn't look at me all the while. I sensed that she understood I would say nothing in the girl's defence. My sort of gallantry only went so far. To be chivalrous you need to be possessed of honesty, fealty to a code which you single-mindedly cling to like faith.

Yet even if she suspected I was a squeaking weathercock, morally speaking, it was *she* who had sought *me* out.

Somewhere, she must have known, there were some salvageable nuggets in my recollection, which had to be dredged up from the sediment.

I'm wreathing myself in metaphor. I have always preferred to dress up the raw and naked probities. If Liz was uncomfortable, she knew I was just as much. No one was unsinkable, and if she was to be scuttled she'd see me hulled too.

Neither of us could win at this.

*

'I know I wasn't *wanted* much.'

'What?'

'By my parents.'

'How can you – '

'Except strategically, I mean. As a ploy. A very calculated move. I was very necessary for that. But not as a person – if you understand me – '

'Can any child say that about their parents?'

'They've the right, haven't they? For what they have to suffer, for what's done in their name.'

'What was the strategy, then?' I asked.

'To make bricks out of straw. I'd be something their marriage was *about*. Something to keep them – committed to one another, I suppose. Something to hold them.'

'Or – couldn't it have been because they cared enough – to lose themselves in one another – '

But she shook her head. It wasn't a feasible hypothesis, however incoherently I was expressing myself. It didn't even remotely come within the bounds of possibility.

*

She removed her plate from the raffia place-mat and laid her left hand on top of it. For a moment or two I thought – with complete stupidity – that she needed the contact of warmth for the good of her crooked finger.

I just kept on getting it wrong, time after time.

'Well . . .' she said.

'What?'

'I've seen you looking at it.'

'Looking?'

'Well, you were. Weren't you? Or just trying to work out why I wasn't wearing a wedding ring?'

'I . . .'

'I did it myself.'

'Yourself – ?'

'You *do* want to know how?'

'I don't mean – I'm not pry–'

'I slammed a car door shut on it.'

'Jesus – '

'As hard as I could.'

'But it was an accident – ?'

'No.'

'What?'

'No, it wasn't an accident.'

'But . . .'

She sighed: not at the fact, but at my reaction to it. Then she started again.

'It was quite deliberate.'

'But why?'

'Why what?'

'How could it be? "Deliberate"?'

'Well, if it wasn't an accident it must've been.'

'You're not sure, though?'

'Oh yes.' She sighed again. 'I'm quite sure.'

'Why would you shut your hand in a car door?'

'To hurt myself. To hurt others. To make *them* cry too.'

'Make who cry?'

'My parents.'

'When – when did you do it?'

'When I was seven or so.'

'Didn't you realise how dangerous – '

'Oh yes. I think I realised quite well. But I still did it. The pain was incidental. The gesture – the act – that was everything. It was like those fire-walkers in – in New Guinea, you know? – an act of will.'

'But it must have been excruciating – '

'I don't think I felt it so badly. I'd closed my mind to that aspect of it. To get them to open their minds to me, I had to shut mine down. That's just how these things work.'

'It is?'

'Have you a better theory?'

'No. No, but – '

'Well, then. There we are.'

'A car door?'

'The Jag. It had beautifully fitting doors. So neat and flush. So smooth too, I wasn't even cut. But my finger – the nerves – it must've been the angle I caught it at. Something or other was severed. I twisted the bone trying not to think about pain. I must've pulled so hard on it.'

'Christ Almighty.'

'Oh – ' She even managed to smile. 'I don't think *He* had anything much to do with it. God had other things on His mind. Wars. Famine. Drought. Floods. He was overseeing all that mayhem.'

She spread the fingers. The fourth inclined inwards from the knuckle, in search of the third. I felt then that she deserved me to be wholly, utterly, unutterably sorry for her. It was the sort of too evident disability that might have distorted a young girl's life. But – hadn't she just told me – it was distorted thinking that had come to cause it in the first place?

'What happened? With your parents?'

'My father was very practical, asking me what I could feel. He went off afterwards and called someone very important he knew, to have a look at it. My mother went into hysterics.'

'What did it achieve, though?'

'A crooked finger.'

'No, I mean – '

'A crooked finger. That's what it achieved. Not that my father

was alive much longer to have the sight of it to contemplate. My
mother did, of course. She had years to worry about it. We didn't
talk about it. But I'd catch her looking. How *you* were looking at
it, just now.'

'I'm sorry.'

'Why should you be sorry?'

'Can't you even allow me to be?'

'For *my* sake?'

'Why the hell not?'

She didn't reply, but she dropped her eyes from my face, to
consider her finger where it lay, on the cooling place-mat. The
pain was still just as real, if not in her material substance then in
the vast and reverberating mental construction which effectively
is the life of all of us.

*

'My mother and I never really got on.' She shrugged. 'It's just
some people's lot in life.'

'Are you sorry?'

'Of course. Life shouldn't be about avoidance.'

'How "avoidance"?'

'We developed ways of skirting round a lot of subjects. I was
sent away to boarding schools. Friends' families invited me to
stay with them in the holidays. Every school trip that was got
up, I was on. When I went home, we often had company in the
house, at meal-times. Second-billing people, who really didn't
mean much. But they were there, as social conveniences, and
that was enough: that excused them.'

'You didn't like that? Or did it matter?'

'It just *was*. The state of affairs between us. We'd got so
used to it. It was habit. Habit – it pardons so much. I went
along with the arrangements – as she did – because it was
easiest.'

'Your mother didn't want to marry again?'

'She had proposals, I'm sure. Two at least. But perhaps
marriage frightened her off. Even with decent types. Could
she be sure that they would always stay as they were now?

Marriage does complicating things to people. She must have felt that quite strongly – to have inculcated me, I mean. Not that we ever discussed it – had the time or opportunity to, or the disposition – but I just knew how she felt. I *knew*.'

*

Fleur died, messily, of a slow, seeping secondary brain haemorrhage, in 1983.

At first Liz was oddly phlegmatic describing the business.

'I gave her as much care as I could. It's nothing you can plan for. I don't know if she understood what was happening, that I was there even. But I stayed on until the end. After the first attack. It was only a few months.'

She came back to the subject later when we'd driven over to Bojewyan to pick up lunch – pasties and custard tarts – from the Tyrolean baker's and came back to eat them down in the dunes.

'I had to do it. Look after my mother.'

'I can – '

'It was just a compulsion. To make up. For not having been closer.'

'Do you wish you'd been closer? Before?'

'We couldn't have been. Our natures were what they were, that was how we were made. I don't know if it matters about wishing. I learned to accept that's just how things were between us.'

'You felt you wanted to make up, though?'

'Oh, that was a luxury. An indulgence. Imagining I might be able to put things right.'

'Didn't you?'

'But she wasn't in any condition to realise. Not properly. I needed her to recognise it was *me* there with her.'

'Wasn't it enough that you were helping her?'

She shook her head, dropping some pasty crumbs from her fingers.

'It *should*'ve been enough. But it wasn't really, not for me anyway. We'd lived too long by our routines, you see.'

She picked out some specks of sand that had got into the pasty's filling.

'I tried to make it as easy a death as I could.'

'She must have understood.'

'How? How could she?'

'Somehow,' I said weakly, 'she must have done.'

She returned the remnants of the pasty unfinished to the paper bag.

'We didn't have that kind of – empathy.'

'Not even mother and daughter?'

She shrugged. A fistful of sand was slowly expelled from her fist through a tiny point formed by the angled joints of her little finger.

'I was thinking,' she said, 'all the time, what it would be like for me. When it's my turn. To have no one to do that for me, even that.' The soft sand trickled over her bare foot. 'To come crawling back at the very end of the day. Like a messenger of death.'

She was sitting with her knees drawn up to her chin. One hand, laid flat with the palm down and fingers stretched, was skimming the sand beside her, smoothing the surface flat: like the gentle, rhythmical raking of a Japanese garden.

I meanwhile, cross-legged, was holding a half-eaten pasty in my hand. I was hungry – I had been ever since we'd arrived on the beach – but I didn't have the heart to finish it.

'That's two of us,' I told her.

'What?' she asked without looking up.

'Who'll have to make our departure unaided. Without a dependant there.'

She didn't reply, but placed her arms around her calves, hugging her legs closer to herself. The action only confirmed her solitude, and also the pride she felt in it.

I returned my wedge of pasty to the paper bag. Overhead a laggardly cloud had drifted in front of the sun. Without direct sunshine, the temperature would dip immediately, which told me what I checked later from the calendar notes in my pocket diary, that we had passed into a different season. Even the sand swiftly lost its heat, when it wouldn't have done in the proper full flush of summer, when you could have closed your eyes and imagined Africa was boiling under the pads of your feet.

*

'What do you think,' Liz asked, 'it would be like to be happy and only happy?'

'Oh,' I said, with the smugness of the cliché-dealer, 'there would be no edge. It would be sedation. Or – or like drowning in – in swathes of – velvet.'

But she wasn't listening, quite wisely. She was trying to imagine the prospect of uninterrupted, incontrovertible happiness and joy. It was, perhaps, the ultimate fiction. Yet it presented itself as a hypothetical imagining, so it must have had an existence of some sort, even if it was only an abstraction of an abstract.

EIGHTEEN

For good or bad, I have given Fleur my voice. It's how that welter of history which Liz unloaded from her brief-case has resurrected itself. I can't remember how conscious some bits of that process were. But now I can own to this. I *want* her story to read like my own. That way, if I achieve nothing else, I can lay claim to my fair share of the blame. I reckon there is more of that than glory, on an overview.

These words are her words and my words. Our stories start to coincide, or at any rate to blur together. It didn't quite happen so then, but life throws up these little ironies as we live it. I could have depicted Chetwynd as a monster he was not, but I mean to be faithful to him also.

We are all of us condemned to be characters in the one same story.

*

Would it have been better if we hadn't mentioned Mother?

We tried too hard to keep the memory of her alive and all that did was to take us further and further from the truth of her. We acted — Father set the example and I dutifully conformed to it — as if the dead are to be revered and shown every respect. And yet the person we would speak of was less and less the one either of us remembered. We had the tiny details (almost) right certainly — of a place, weather, the clothes we were wearing — but the large and important things (Mother's attitudes, her behaviour) we stalled on, we didn't know how to tackle, so in the end we

were left talking about ourselves with this third presence, a marionette's. Vaguely we did ascribe to her the virtues of a wife and mother, but only trivially: preparing sandwiches for a picnic, filling hot water bottles hot but not too much so, knowing how to catch a daddylonglegs and to eject it alive from a window without crushing it, spotting that a button was loose and sewing it tight in a couple of minutes, being able to wash my hair without letting any soap into my eyes, having green and growing gardener's fingers. We took it all for granted, and that was the reason why I would cry in those first years after she died. I cried for selfish reasons, for ourselves, for our not having her anymore. A little later I could weep tears for *her*, for the time she hadn't been given to live, but by then I could better control my emotions and I never wept in front of Father. Anyway, by that point I was in my teens and finding myself involved in other people's lives, away at school, and starting to realise that Mother's death hadn't received – *then* or at a subsequent juncture – anything like an explanation. It had hardly been even a fact – simply a reported state of non-being (a car accident, driving Father's car on a private holiday she didn't explain to us, in a distant county I'd never been to, Cornwall). I hadn't ever been offered any valid proof as to what took place. She *had died*, and – merely – everything that concerned my own or Father's life was accepted by us as having happened before or after that fateful date – the third of May, 1938.

Father would look at me sometimes, when I was shedding one of my female skins, and I'd see him catching resemblances in me. There was nothing I could do. It made me feel so empty, talking so breezily to divert him.

I coped well enough when we had company to the house. It was (more or less) my function to be the hostess, and I had the talkative manner. But I talked about nothing. When I look back and see and hear myself, I wish I might be capable of it now, that imperturbable social ease. But it's too long ago to recover the knack, and I'd experienced too little then to know better, that such shallowness in adulthood is a native accomplishment of the irredeemably cheerful and unconcerned. I shall never have that ingenuousness again.

In that red-brick pile on the heights of healthful Highgate there are just the two of us, plus domestic help. Father and I share those twelve rooms, rattling about like two sorry peas inside a tin can. Yet even that privilege of space isn't able to compensate me for the confinement, not when Father grows silent and moody.

I watch very carefully the single women who come to dine, the friends of friends. They have lost their first (and probably also their second) youth, but they cultivate the illusion, and I think Father sees through it and — inside himself and behind his ready smiles — is offended and dispirited by it. Occasionally I see him give them — when *they* quite fail to see — a look of, certainly not condescending pity, but irritability, of disgust even. And then to me those unattached, unclaimed women become what they really are: overdressed, too heavily doused with perfume, groundlessly and untenably optimistic.

Now and then I'd even hear myself talking like him: in that deliberative, circumambulatory manner he has, which poses as intelligence and precision. It was only one step away from *thinking* like him, and that really would have been the world's-end of everything.

An assistant in the store's day-wear department is

watching Father out of the corner of her eye, so I know to whom she is referring.

She calls him at one stage 'the gentleman, your grandfather'.

I stare at the dress in the mirror. It's only a schoolgirl's outfit after all, supposed to hint at maturity. I'm — what? — sixteen? I lift my eyes to my face. It looks even younger than the one I'm so familiar with. There are how many points in the day — almost every time I pass a mirror at home — when I long to have reflected back at me what I hear other women complaining about when I take them upstairs to the bedroom where they can lay their coats and have the use of the dressing table: just a line or two, hair that isn't so unmanageably thick and so uniformly brown.

'No,' I tell the assistant. 'No, I don't think so. Not at all.'

'*I* was thinking, how nicely — '

But I turn my back on her and try to remember in which changing-room I've left my own clothes.

I have been this person, preserved in my childhood, for too indefensibly long now.

By the time I was sixteen, I could wear Mother's clothes with some degree of conviction.

They had stayed in the house, and I couldn't think why unless it was in anticipation of my showing an interest some day. But when I did, and asked Father if I could look in the wardrobe he kept locked, I sensed that he was unhappy letting me.

After that first time I didn't ask him again. I didn't need to. I found that the wardrobe wasn't locked — either because he'd forgotten, or because he thought I had a right to look but on the unspoken understanding that he and I should not discuss the wardrobe's contents. I wondered if I had reminded him too much of her, too painfully, walking downstairs in the marine-blue spring suit and black basque beret. I caught sight

of him scrutinising me in the mirror before he could
make a performance of turning round and seeing and
giving me his verdict on how I suited my ensemble.

I only tried the clothes on when I knew I couldn't
be interrupted and he couldn't be surprised, when
I had the house all to myself. For one thing the
house felt less oppressive when I exchanged clothes.
I persuaded myself that nothing had been cleaned
subsequently, that I was wearing what had last been
worn next to Mother's skin. It was an intimate, sensual contact. From the sweet talcum and floral eau-
de-Cologne worked into the fabric I could believe I
was smelling the life of her.

I continued to observe those women we entertained,
when I was there to see them. But nothing ever
happened to suggest to me that the presence of one
meant more to Father than that of any other. I came
to see only the silliness they had in common: their
predisposition to be flirtatious, to be liked by one
and all. They seemed quite desperate to be popular,
to be wanted, to make themselves indispensable. For
a while I wondered if Father was skilfully disguising
his intentions by focusing his attention on women
who constantly spread themselves so thin and lacked
the self-awareness which would have betrayed their
knowledge of his purpose.

Even by inviting them to Highgate, he wasn't – I
came to the conclusion – really 'about' anything at
all.

I doubt if I was disappointed; I doubt if I cared enough
for that.

It took me a long time to learn how to be so honest
with myself. At least by then I wasn't having to live
my double life beneath the same roof as him. A while
before that, though, I did suspect what my feelings
actually were, and occasionally I would exquisitely

skewer myself on guilt. For a spell I was a veritable martyr to unhappiness. At the eleventh hour I would cancel an invitation to go out, and stay in the house to keep him company. I let my frustration show, so that he couldn't fail to recognise it and suffer too, but *my* suffering was much more delicious than his because it was volunteered, sacrificed, because it was the purest strain of masochism.

It didn't last so long, yet it occurred at an interlude of my life when friends from my school days and their parents were trying, not quite selflessly, to pair me off with various young men deemed eligible.

I've imagined the consequences too often, brilliant hypotheses, what would have happened *if* . . . if I'd acted on my introduction to Derek Trescott or Nigel Flemyng (with a 'y') or the providentially named Norrie Younghusband . . . if I'd actually dared to tip my cap at any of them. Any one would have been more suitable than the husband I have. It would hardly have mattered *which* one. In a sense they were inter-changeable anyway. Even the least of them, should any have shown a retrogression from the norm, could not have caused me to be less contented than I am.

Gilbert knew none of the friends I'd kept from school, nor any of *their* friends, and in the mood which possessed me at that time that was a supreme rec-ommendation to me. Worcestershire, Evesham fruit-growing country, a public school in Shropshire called St Ronan's, the Oxford Medical Faculty — I was unfa-miliar with all of these, so he came with the inesti-mable advantage (so I judged it to be) of his novelty. He was quite good-looking enough and somehow I thought that his undemonstrativeness mattered less when it was considered against that. He had a cer-tain charm, of a chilly kind — hiemal and frore — which I merely thought formal. He was equipped

with manners, and he knew all the ways to flatter
Father – about his professional wisdom as a lawyer,
his clientele, his taste in furnishings, his memory for
cricket matches and scores.

He has never spoken to me – when I've persevered
– more than a sentence or two at a time about his
parents in the rural Midlands, in their fertile Vale.
It was at a soirée at the family home of a fellow
medical graduate that he first heard about me and
was introduced to Father. Father was won over by
him, I can only suppose. He showed up at our home
not so long afterwards, at one of those evenings when
I still, but a little mechanically, was going through my
party paces.

He was young. I didn't see the snobbery in him,
much more advanced than Father's sort, which was
essentially professional, a by-product of his legal
skills and the prestige his practice had acquired. I
didn't perceive Gilbert's motives, not at all. I had no
conception of how ambitious he was, nor – at that
juncture – how poor. Highgate must have gone to his
head: the house, its size and run-down good taste, the
cosmopolitan talk. He can't have been impervious to
my presence, and it's the case that I did very little to
dissuade him.

There was a kind of stasis then which I was conscious of, 'à trois', which I simultaneously wanted
to end and not to end. Long summer evenings with
the french windows open to our tangled garden. The
low gas-lamp with the fringed Finnish shade of brass
and fabric over the dining-table lit, and ourselves
seated beneath it, just the three of us. An unconscious aural tapestry – the hissing of gas in the
wall brackets, the dragging pendulums of assorted
clocks, the drowsy droning of bees, the sounds of a
tennis game carried to us from somewhere. I simply
drifted, I let myself be carried. Ophelia wasn't more
helpless than Fleur Mayhew, and like her I gathered

flowers, lazily made chains before the daisies closed
their heads, and like that poor lost girl I finally laid
myself down.

He was a doctor, just newly become so, and maybe I
shouldn't have been surprised he was as clinical as
he was in his – as the expression is – 'love-making'.
A virgin expected a little more – *ardour*, I suppose.
It wasn't how I had imagined in my most feverish
fantasies beforehand, not at any rate to have his
head below my waist. I only ever had a picture of
myself looking up into my beloved lover's enrap-
tured eyes.

   He would talk about women – those he'd known – in
an impersonal way. No names, no identities. I knew
he was specialising in gynaecological matters, and I
did feel – oddly, literally – the *object* of his physical
desire. None the less the moment seemed right for
what we were doing, even if the emotions did not
quite. He was acquainted with aspects of my interior
which I was not – and showed me with his fingers
and a tiny angled mirror. On the third afternoon in
my bedroom, with Father again out on business, he
brought me to what he explained was an orgasm, and
then to another. He knew some short-cut or other,
but it felt deliriously real enough, and I wondered
if bodily gratification would always be just like this,
so utterly involving, so devouring. I felt I wanted
to claw at the walls, to wrench off the ceiling. I
thought that, like this, I should be capable of loving
him for ever.

   How little, how sadly and abysmally little, I really
did know.

Father wasn't unaware of how things stood. He
encouraged the situation, I believe, by doing nothing
and – I dare say – by convincing himself he was
allowing me to make up my own mind. But all it

really was was evidence of his mental ineffectual-
ness.

While I continued to drift, supine, I had no other
plans for myself. Those of my kind, my tribe, simply
supposed that marriage was to be their lot, and their
right, and all we had to do was wait. Even as my
mother's daughter I understood that. You can make
your move too soon: the trick is not being tardy.
Maybe I had left everything over-long, out of some
absurd, fastidious intent. What on earth could the
point of that have been?

Father was very quiet at the wedding. I thought it
must be because he was recalling what he inevitably must.

Some of his clients were persuaded to attend. Back
at the breakfast in Highgate, Gilbert had me introduce him to every single one of them. His own parents
came from their fruit farm: two slow, polite, softly-
spoken, quite amazed persons. I was introduced to a
colleague, Lex Elson, and to his fiancée. They both
told me when Gilbert's back was turned that my
husband was bound for medical fame – or else a very
lucrative living. I remembered to smile, thinking the
remark just another of the day's ritual compliments.

Father continued to look vulnerable. I spent what
time I could with him. I linked my arm through his,
and felt I was doing so because I must have seen the
gesture performed in a film. I made sure that he
was left alone as seldom as possible, even in rooms
where almost everyone knew him, where he was the
connection we all had in common.

On the fringes of these same rooms which had
always been 'home' to me, I felt I could detect Mother's presence, her wary vigilance. I went upstairs,
lifting the tumble of white satin and lace. In the
oriel-windowed bedroom I discovered that the door
of the wardrobe was locked. I stood in front of it,

staring at the lock. More than I ever had before,
I wanted now to have the fragrance of her in my
nostrils, even after fifteen years. But it wasn't to
be. I was to be denied, on the day when the disappointment scraped right through me to the raw
bone.

It made some sense that we should all share the one
house, at least for a while. So in Highgate I remained.
That was a crucial error, but I was still at the stage
of thinking I must oblige.

The three of us stayed there for three or four
years, until Gilbert's career took off, when no less an
eminence than Sir Marcus Urban, flouting convention
and precedent, ruffled any number of feathers by
inviting Gilbert to be his second. Gilbert soon heard
about a house with a good address for sale, on a
road off Haverstock Hill, so – now that he said he
could afford it – down we moved to Hampstead. He
persuaded Father, and myself, that he would prefer
the convenience of life in a flat further in, and again
– through his contacts – heard of a spacious apartment quite a good bit further in, in Chelsea, at the
Randolph Square complex. I wonder if it wasn't done
rather to remove Father from our circuit than as a
humane kindness? Gilbert did tell me it would make
things easier when Father dies: the Highgate house
would have had another few years' deterioration to
its discredit. All we shall have to deal with – Gilbert
assured me – is a well-preserved flat in a popular but
exclusive, expensive development for which there are
always buyers.

How merely logical Gilbert can make everything
sound that serves his own advantage best.

Lillias was, strictly speaking, an accident.
Gilbert blamed me. And how *could* a respected
gynaecologist not have known to be thoroughly exact

in his methods of contraception? By necessary implication I had let him down badly in a professional sense also.

But since we had already settled that we would have a family, at a future point, did it honestly matter that it happened a couple of years before we meant it to? No moment would have been 'perfect' surely, not for both of us.

Now, after five years of marriage, we were mother and father.

What was a child supposed to do for us?

With the crying and wailing in the house at night, loud enough to disturb the sleep of our smart Hampstead neighbours, it was hard to imagine. To compensate, Gilbert invited our unnervingly accomplished neighbours to dinner, where they made earnest conversation with his medical colleagues. Father wasn't included at these evenings, which I thought a pity and rather ungrateful, but Gilbert had the excuse of the distance from Chelsea to offer me. Father would have recognised some of the names my husband now dropped of his own accord, and maybe that was part of the trouble vis-à-vis Father: Gilbert wanted to be master – uncontested lord and master – of his own walnut (with cherrywood inlay) dining-table.

But what was a child supposed to do? For *us*?

Poor Lillias. She is the bridge between Gilbert and me. Yet when I think of 'bridge' it isn't some clever, dependable cantilever construction that comes to mind but the St Bénezet, that haunted broken structure of crumbling stone at Avignon which Gilbert and I saw on the honeymoon Father paid for, its four arches uselessly straddling only half the breadth of the River Rhône.

Lillias has had to function as a link between us, a support, but it has been an insupportable burden.

Poor Lillias, forgive me, forgive us both. One day you may be able to understand the paltry but significant truth, that certain events will come into being despite our best intentions. A situation composes itself around us, and by cold reason of our character and temperament, we find ourselves fully implicated, framed.

A 'family'?
I try to work myself into the word, to get the feel of it – to expand myself until I can fit the whole space of it, from the bracket of the 'f' to the little final cusp of the 'y'. But I have never belonged to the word, it is as unaccommodating to me as any in Portuguese or Serbo-Croat or Hebrew would be.
Family, famille, familie, familia, famielia, familj, obitelj, οἰκογένεια.

*

A whole year passed. I still hadn't gone to university.
Another Christmas came and went.
How can I explain? We were under a spell, that's all there is to say. The spell of Chetwynd's life. Of London by night. Of our voluntary desensitisation to everything except our own pleasure.

Then, after Christmas at home – with Chetwynd away for the season, but now returned, untanned and cashmere-overcoated and fur-hatted – 1958.

*

I arrived early one Sunday lunchtime. My watch was running fast.
Tuitt pointed out my mistake when he came to the door. I offered to go away and return, but – forgetting his usual formal reserve – he shook his head complicitously, as if we were just old mates together. I had the sense I had interrupted him about something and – for the first time in our acquaintanceship –

he winked at me as he departed on his way to the back
quarters.

Ten minutes later I was sitting in the morning-room when I
heard an exchange of voices. I distinguished them – Chetwynd's
and Melinda's. She sounded excitable, and he displeased. The
door was ajar and I stood up and tiptoed forward to hear.

They'd gone into the library, leaving the door open. I wasn't
able to hear clearly enough the words they were speaking, only
the tone: now indignant on his part, protesting on hers. The
voices became more and more clamorous. His own resolve was
unmistakable, as was – finally – her defencelessness. I did hear
him call her a 'careless, idiot bitch' and at that words failed her
and she started to cry. I was taking another few steps forward
when the library door was closed tight shut and the sounds of
Melinda's sobbing were masked as much as they could be.

At lunch Chetwynd was in slightly sprightlier form than his
usual.

Melinda gave no evidence of tears, but she did appear to be
paying only intermittent attention to the conversation. She drank
no wine and spilled some water from her glass as she sipped.
She ate, but no more than half the food on her plates, and she
tried to disguise the fact with her main course by covering the
partridge breast left with the uneaten vegetables.

Every now and then Chetwynd's eyes sought out hers, but
she was assiduous in not looking towards his end of the table.
The closest she came was to the floor at Chetwynd's feet, to
the carpet. But she wasn't seeing it, or any of that glory of the
Paradise garden.

*

She came – Fleur – to Randolph Square one day, downstairs to the pool, carrying a superior soft leather *trousse
toilette* under her arm. She knew one of the residents, she
said.

I was quite taken aback. I spoke, but too much. Handing
her two pink towels, I dropped them. I found her another
two.

She smiled, in the vague way she had. She seemed to have caught Chetwynd's habit of making a smile seem significantly serious.

She had an eccentric, unmethodical method of swimming: changing stroke mid-length, crawl to breast and turning over from her front to her back, and vice versa. On her front her breast-stroke was clean and elegant. Her backstroke was thoroughly individual, arms spinning behind her like a windmill's sails and her feet pedalling forwards as if she were cycling. She would sink from view for up to ten seconds, trawling beneath the surface, and reappear at the other end of the pool. She would suddenly lose interest, and doggy-paddle or float on her back or make for the side and rest her forearms and elbows on the tiled edge. Then she would return, her method changing every few moments from one stroke to another. She swam very ably, but the erratic disjointedness didn't make for easy watching.

I tried to appear busy when she emerged. She used the chrome rails to pull herself up the steps. She loosened the seat of her yellow costume, running two fingers under the seams to let out a little water, then she prised off her matching bathing-cap and shook out her hair.

She was slim: more so even than the run of younger women who regularly swam in the pool. I could see the muscles pulling in her thighs and upper arms. Perhaps she was *too* slim for one to be wholly comfortable with the sight. It might have been the finicky thinness of a woman who kept an anxious eye on her weight; but possibly it was really the other sort, where the nervous life is its own physical arbiter. She swam in the disconnected manner I could understand a woman who lived far inside herself would do.

She wrapped the larger towel about herself, loosely, in wrap and tuck-over sarong fashion. As she was making for the changing-rooms she looked over her shoulder. I was taken by surprise again and she saw me watching. Her reaction was the same modest, serious, preoccupied smile.

Before she left she sat upstairs in the lounge and read a

newspaper – or pretended to, holding it open and turning the pages with unlikely regularity.

Every so often as I went about my work I glanced upstairs. I was mystified. At the same time she could be detached and also suggest familiarity, rise above me and come as close as social propriety made possible. I knew I didn't comprehend her. I appreciated from this practical demonstration, my object lesson, that women were hugely, but quietly and almost casually, complex.

She remained seated, suspended above me, splendidly unfathomable. Her legs were crossed, and she had lowered the newspaper a little. One shoe hung loose from the back of her restless foot.

*

Chetwynd discussed cars with me. It was a subject he knew I knew something about.

I accompanied him a few times when he made short journeys in his London sports cars. First the Allard, then the AC Ace, then the Salmson, then the Interceptor. He would let me take the wheel for a while, round a couple of blocks. Once Howard Kimble spotted us, en route to dealing with his fancy freeholds; he waved over, but I don't think news of the business – Chetwynd's act of favouritism – got back to 'The Circus' afterwards. Or if it did, no one thought for a moment to be envious.

Chetwynd told me that down on the Corniche he had a Bugatti-France: a Type 101 Coach, with 8 cylinders and 3.3 litres. I only knew it from a sketch I'd seen in a magazine: a sleeker version of a Bentley Continental Mulliner with inverted horseshoe radiator and a two-piece windscreen. Evidently he had his eyes on a BMW 507. He said it had a top speed of 140, that the hard top was detachable. Or an Aston Martin Superleggera Spyder, except that there was a waiting list for them. Or if not either of those, a Pegaso Berlina: he had never owned a Spanish car, even though the body was worked in Milan.

Then came the ultimate assertion of his confidence in me,

when he allowed me behind the wheel of the Ferrari Super
America. Down in Putney I took her out, on a quiet road beside
the heath. 12 cylinders, 5 litres, 340 brake horsepower. He told
me, if there was another one in London he hadn't seen it.

I felt that afternoon with the prancing black horse was like a
gift from the gods. How much had the car cost? It terrified me to
think. But I was aware that I must have been considered worth
the risk. I also realised that just as a spin in a Super America
isn't offered lightly, I must find myself beholden in some way.
Nothing is given without, at some date and somewhere along
the line, an equivalent cost being exacted.

NINETEEN

We had gone to 'Le Paris Noir' one evening. Some familiar faces were already there, by accident or design, and we formed a nucleus of a dozen or so persons at a couple of round tables beside the square hardwood dance floor. As usual my skills as a dancer were in demand, and I obliged. Most of our own group seemed to be in a party-ish mood, and I didn't have an opportunity to eat much, caught up in the tastefully Africanised rhythms from the band stand. I stayed on my feet for a good three-quarters of the evening and changed my step accordingly with each number: 'I See The Moon', 'Oh! Look At Me Now', 'I Believe', 'No One Ever Tells You', 'Unchained Melody', 'Nice Work If You Can Get It'.

At several points I found myself leading a guest I thought was called 'Mrs Garewode'. Or should I say, she took me up those several times and I – as ever – dutifully obliged. That evening she presented herself as a not unattractive, not unvivacious woman. I use the negatives because I had the sense she was less being herself than carefully according to a toned-down image she wished, or was required, to present. Her clothes were expensive but rather too elderly for a woman in her thirties; her face was made up, but with old-fashioned blusher and tangerine-tinted lipstick; her conversation was as pernickety as a diplomat's.

I saw Celia watching us dance. She lacked Chetwynd's subtler means of observation, but I knew that whatever she saw was bound to be relayed back to him.

'You two seem to have hit it off,' she remarked later in the evening. 'You and Mrs Yearwood.'

'She's a very good dancer,' I said. 'She enjoys it.'

'She's got a lot of spirit.'

I frowned.

'Good or bad spirit?' I asked.

'Her school expelled her, so they knew what *they* thought.' She tried to be jokey about it. 'I think differently – I think.'

I made the connection concerning her name.

'She's married to the politician?'

'Before he *became* a politician.'

'But he became one,' I pursued the point, 'when he was already married to her?'

When he knew – in other words – the sort of woman she was, which he could depend on her being.

'She – she's different,' I said.

'I think you *should* dance with her.'

Celia smiled her encouragement, perhaps imagining that she'd said too much and might be reported back to Chetwynd, by me or another, as having tried to dissuade me.

'How did you know?' I asked. 'About her being expelled.'

'I met someone who went to the same school. Her parents were well-off – *are* well-off – so they indulged her – '

'Does that follow?' I asked.

'Usually,' she replied, quite tartly. 'In her case, certainly.'

'What else? What came next?'

'Another school. Then a finishing school. They went about picking up the pieces. Probably still do. Someone's sister introduced her to her brother-in-law. Yearwood. It seems she was just what he was looking for. That's the official version I heard, anyway.'

She smiled, rather cryptically. She wasn't telling me 'no'. If she had done, it would only have been an incentive to me, and she probably appreciated as much.

'If she thinks I'm a good enough dancer – for a junior Minister's wife – '

She raised one eyebrow. 'I expect she could teach even *you* one or two things you don't know, Ralph.'

I'd picked up dancing from a manual. I wouldn't have known how to get a woman into bed even if I'd waltzed or cha-cha'd her there. Maybe I was too romantic to be lustful. Celia was making fun of what she perceived quite well was my unworldliness.

I smiled, so that the mood wouldn't darken between us, so that we might blandly continue as we were, as colleagues in this eccentric arrangement if not anything friendlier.

*

Lavinia Yearwood and I met again, at the 'Blue Hand'. We danced again, another four or five times. By the fifth (if it was) I had naïvely started to forget she was married to the man that she was.

Glancing past a mirrored column on that same fifth dance, I noticed Chetwynd watching us both – us in particular out of two dozen couples. He continued to watch even when I didn't look away. Slowly, against the accommodating tempo of a leisurely romantic shuffle, he permitted himself this time to very seriously smile.

On that second occasion we were standing outside on Charles Street waiting for our drivers to recognise us. A school of gleaming black cars had collected beneath the trees in the square. We were claimed by the tracks of headlights; clutches and accelerators were engaged. As the engines turned over, as approaching tyres sizzled on the wet tarmacadam, my arm was grabbed. I looked round, into the face of my fellow shuffler, Mrs George Yearwood. I held my spread umbrella over her.

'What a dismal climate,' she said.

I moved my umbrella arm further towards her.

Then she spoke again, in a voice pitched so quietly I could scarcely catch her words.

'Meet me at "The Carioca" next Tuesday,' I thought she said. 'For lunch.'

I stared at her. The expression of anxiety in her eyes told me that I *had* heard her quite correctly.

'But don't tell anyone.'

I continued staring at her. She turned her head away and spoke out of the corner of her mouth.

'Nobody has to know.'

She moved away before I could reply. In no time at all she was la-di-dah-ing with the others, chewing out little Belgravian questions and over-reacting to some remark with a whoop of mechanical laughter. Settled into the back of her car she raised her hand to wave, to all of us and to no one, and it was done a little too much in imitation of the Queen Mother, a tiny opening of the palm like a vapid sea frond.

I was waiting for her at 'The Carioca'. I failed to recognise her when she arrived, out-of-breath and more excitable than I had seen her before, and as complicatedly proud of her achievement as a schoolgirl playing hookey. Accidentally (I suppose) she brushed the back of my hand with hers as she moved past me, to her chair against the wall. Away from the dance floor, however, we comported ourselves with exemplary propriety. We talked good-humouredly, and without any stagnant pauses, about everything that was not personal. She didn't once mention her husband, nor I Chetwynd. There were no holes in our conversation to have to talk over, and viewed from the other side of the room we doubtless appeared as old friends or as very amiable kin.

Outside on the pavement, she didn't need the cover of an umbrella. But with the two of us caught in brazen sunlight and our reflections bold in the taxi's windows, the cycle was repeated. She asked – *sotto voce* – might it be possible for us to meet again? She added, how grateful she felt towards me – so that I believed myself vindicated by the virtue of charitableness in replying, almost immediately, 'yes' to her.

'Yes, of course. I should be delighted.'

'My father gives me an allowance. To do what I like with it. *This* is what I like to do – giving myself a treat.'

We met for a drink one evening at the Basil Street Hotel. She was on her way to meet her husband, at a colleague's 'At Home'. In Hungary's wake, with Algeria fermenting, and while events in the fiery Middle East still simmered away, while pot lids rattled on that steamy situation and Hussein got the jitters, routine domestic life in our own temperate clime was conducted as per usual.

We chatted as easily as before. Although dressed much as she had been at 'Le Paris Noir' she had loosened up a good deal from that initial image. Now she was vivacious and jokey, and not quite so discreet.

Again we talked of everything except the most significant presences in our two lives, her husband and my social provider. She allowed herself to laugh at my puns, and the sound seemed harmless in that mezzanine lounge two storeys above the hooting of car horns in the narrow canal of street.

When we left the doorman was busy, and I called her a taxi myself. I opened the door for her. She leaned sideways as she was climbing in and, taking me quite by surprise, planted a kiss on my cheek.

Even when she'd gone and I was left standing on the pavement, I could feel the contact of her lips on my skin, I could still catch the bewitching amalgam of powder and perfume. I had received kisses before from partners, but they'd been given as elaborate stagey gestures of thanks after a dance, in the half-light of night-clubs beyond midnight.

I stood smiling down at the pavement, in full public view. How could I even think to care?

I needed the change perhaps. Or I needed to think I was as capable of a clandestine life – of a fairly public sort – as the others in the group were.

She asked that I accompany her to see a couple of films. At first I hesitated. But that only encouraged her. She persisted until I agreed. She was always to work on me like that until I relented, until I'd learned not even to try to deny her.

I bunked off pool duty at Randolph Square to be with her.

She was loosening up all the time.

She liked to go into shops and try on the most extrovert outfits she could find on the rails, swanning about in front of the mirrors but always – quite suddenly – losing interest in the game, like a volatile child. She preferred shoes, and did buy two or three pairs. My presence must have emboldened her to buy for herself, from her allowance, and not for her husband – why else a pair of (what she called) 'hyacinth' blue lizard court shoes, with their matching coloured heels? Twice we went to Derry and Toms' roof gardens and ambled beneath the wistaria-less, laburnum-less pergolas and she told me about sumptuous gardens – perfect dream-gardens – she claimed to remember from her childhood.

In Bendicks', in the middle of one afternoon, George Yearwood's wife ate scrambled eggs and a banana sundae in tandem, a forkful of one followed by a spoonful of the other. In the National Gallery she took up the attitude of the sitter in front of each painting she stopped to stare at. She gave a mint five-pound note to a tramp in St Martin's Lane; he said nothing but he looked after her with a disturbed – and disturbing – air of recognition. She found us an empty pew at the back of St Martin-in-the-Fields as Evensong started and she sat quite motionless listening, scarcely breathing. Another day, on Kensington High Street, she helped herself to a Mackintosh apple from a tray on a fruiterer's delivery bicycle and walked off eating it. She caught a stocking on a branch of straggling holly hedge, and it ran to a long untidy ladder, so she turned off into a mews and, leaning against a wall, quite calmly proceeded to unhitch both stockings from her suspender belt and to roll them down and remove them altogether. She bought us each a bag of salted hot chestnuts and, hugely to my embarrassment, aimed every second one of hers at the open windows of houses and cars travelling too fast in traffic to stop. She walked round the cosmetics department in Barkers' very matter-of-factly making herself up from the sample wares – to look like a tart, I was astonished to see – and before returning to the Ladies' Room turning the courtesy hand-mirrors this way and that to inspect the result. She asked me somewhere on Queen's Gate, was I a nancy-boy? I told her hotly 'no', but she didn't ask me what I was going to do to prove that I wasn't.

By then, though, I think she'd frightened me off: from any move of an amorous nature, at any rate. There was never a dull moment with her, but what confused me – in addition to the alarms of her behaviour in public – was not knowing how much to believe of the personal history she confided to me. Somehow sections would ring bells in my head: as if I'd made their acquaintance before – heard something similar on the radio or read a nearly parallel story in a newspaper. Yet I couldn't be sure. She deserved a very much better listener than someone like me, who treacherously suspected she might be a wholesale plagiarist.

Chetwynd took me with him to look at a new model in a Jensen dealer's showroom, the 541. I guessed that it must be an excuse, because he was attached to the Interceptor. If I hadn't known already, his careful, loving handling of it on the way there would have told me.

Stopped at traffic lights, we both noticed a weeks-old discarded newspaper hoarding. It referred to an urgent late-night Cabinet meeting in Downing Street on the Lebanese menace.

'Yearwood's on that committee,' Chetwynd said.

I turned my head and looked ahead of me.

'He's considered quite a high flier. Has the ears of our rulers, by all accounts. He got quite involved with Suez.'

I didn't respond.

The lights changed to green. Chetwynd pressed on the accelerator and we pulled away.

'Our lives are being decided upon,' he said, 'in midnight rooms. The final particulars are worked out there while the spade-work takes place at dinner-parties. Between the cheese and the pudding, between pudding and coffee. While the whisky's being poured.'

I must have made a sound in my throat.

'It's quite true,' he said.

'I see.'

He didn't mention Yearwood again. Nor, more significantly, did he refer to his wife. I couldn't know what *he* knew, but it would have been strange indeed if he hadn't appraised himself

of more than a little information about our movements round
London. Nothing he ever said or did was purely accidental.
Even the newspaper hoarding might have been providential,
just as the traffic lights had been fated to change against us –
that was the tenor of Chetwynd's existence.

Everything connected.

She made no mention of her husband to me, and since I
presumed that was deliberate I didn't enquire. I thought she
might be trying to find a way of eliciting a question from me,
so I became doubly determined not to capitulate.

*

Is it possible?

We are walking out of Bendicks', Mrs Yearwood at my side
sated with scrambled eggs and a banana and butterscotch
sundae, and definitely a little green about the gills.

Outside, on the other side of the street, a woman is about
to step off the kerb, into the back of a taxi. Can it possibly be
Fleur? She is looking over towards the coffee room – or it's
quite feasible, at ourselves. She hesitates, holding her head
steady. Her hat with its little trailing net is intended to conceal
the wearer's identity. Her gloved hand rests on the taxi cab's
roof, the fingers sculpt air for two or three seconds. We've
moved off, and her head turns to follow us.

Then, in an instant, it's gone. The door of her taxi bangs shut.
A figure moves behind the reflection in the back compartment.
The driver finds an entry into the stream of traffic. It's only
an incidental matter: four or five seconds at most. But why
am I suddenly left acknowledging what I've resisted admitting
to myself all along, that I'm being a deal less true to myself,
equivocating and compromising and in the end only selling my
honour cheap. There is the whiff of corruption in the air, and
no fallen leaves in spring-time to blame.

*

When we were travelling downstairs in the lift on our second
visit to Derry and Toms', she said she had to meet someone.

Her husband, I presumed she meant, the rising star Yearwood. But as we were walking out of the store she mentioned 'Daddy'.

'You know what it's like,' she said. 'Family council sort of thing.'

She sighed. She must have heard herself because she immediately and falsely brightened, lightening her voice.

'I'm still very close to my parents,' she said. 'I think it's sad when someone isn't, don't you? When a family grows apart. But we're not like that at all.'

So, inevitably, I was left wondering.

I didn't leave the area. I caught sight of her again, walking thirty or forty yards in front of me, on Kensington Church Street. I was following her when a Rolls-Royce, being driven in the same direction, slowed down and stopped a little ahead of where she was walking, strolling along the pavement. The front passenger door opened and, with no unnecessary ceremony, she got into the car. It immediately pulled away.

Twice it passed me as I started my return journey home. Once it was negotiating the corner into Wright's Lane, and the other time emerging towards Town from Palace Gate. The driver was of an age to be her father certainly. On both occasions they were talking animatedly as their heads moved both ways to observe traffic. It was a distinctive model of Rolls-Royce: a two-tone silver-and-grey Mulliner Silver Wraith with sweeping wings but a stately dowager aspect, and a luggage boot which seemed appendaged to the bulbous body. The car was defined as being a 'touring limousine' and designed to be driven by a chauffeur. The man wore no uniform, however, so I presumed this was one outing on which a chauffeur would have been considered an encumbrance, a hazard to privacy. My last sight of the car, all eighteen feet plus of it, was of its rising regally above the lesser vehicles as it proceeded along Kensington Gore.

TWENTY

For a while I wasn't averse to giving Fleur the impression that I wasn't watching, wasn't listening, wasn't caring. I wanted to gauge her reaction, of course, but that would have involved my watching, listening, being seen to care. So I missed the indicators. I tried to catch a feeling in the atmosphere, but it wasn't forthcoming. I wanted her to be conscious that she was being denied: deprived of something she had come to depend on without realising so.

Did she notice? She doesn't say so anywhere, among her other observations and concerns. Was she attempting to play me at my own game? That was her subtlety? Did she mean her scripted version of our life to reach my eyes one day? Or is that a gross distortion of the evidence to placate my own vulnerable, floundering ego?

*

Once I mentioned to Gilbert something about Father never having married again. His response was a kind of inattentive snicker. I thought the matter deserved a more sympathetic hearing than he was giving it.

'What does *that* mean?'

'What does what mean?'

'Was I making a joke?'

'Weren't you?'

'I was talking about Father. Not marrying again.'

'You're being serious?'

'Of course I am.'

'So you think he's a ladykiller?'

'No, I don't. What a vulgar expression.'

He smiled, as he invariably does when I rebound on him with a matchless demonstration of middle-class morality. Privately, and perversely, he has a zest for it: I know *something* about him at least, even if he imagines I don't. It's one of the reasons why he married me, to be taunted by the superior airs I adopt when I'm riled.

'He's extremely gentlemanly,' I said. 'I presume you can see that much.'

If that was a response to him, in a sense I was giving *myself* away. I had realised very well before we married what our appeal to an *arriviste* such as Gilbert was: that we lived in the old way, by certain traditions of courtesy and decorum.

'Your father isn't a ladies' man?'

'All I said was, I used to wonder if he might not marry again.'

'You must have had the evidence, though. Things he did to make you suspect so.'

'Not – not really,' I said. 'He was married once. Why not again?'

'Once might have been enough.'

I didn't speak. I had never discussed Mother with Gilbert. But by some means or other he had known: always known, in fact, from the time he first came calling to the house in Highgate. He'd expressed his sorrow, his sympathy, his pity for me, et cetera. But I was left thinking, had he been waiting all along, for me or Father to tell him, to impart what it was that would bring him fully into our confidence. But, independently, Father and I had both lacked the courage. The issue of Mother and her death that was probably suicide was, essentially, a complication.

'Your father may,' I heard him say, 'have preferred to live with his memories.'

There was an unconcealed serrated double-edge to the remark. I didn't know what to say in reply.

'I haven't noticed,' he said, 'a disposition for the ladies.'

Something in his tone – something deeply and allusively mocking – unsettled me. My eyes lost their focus for some moments.

'He doesn't . . .' I cleared my throat. '. . . he doesn't have to be eyeing them all the time.'

'Just *some* of the time,' he said. 'A little of it. *Any* time.'

I couldn't fathom his words. I couldn't get to the bottom of this at all.

'Maybe,' I ventured, 'maybe . . . with age . . . you know . . .'

'May-be,' he said, in as sceptical a tone of voice as he could manage.

It was the end of the conversation. I was careful after that – with a scrupulous attention I couldn't explain to myself – not to embark on it again.

I watched Father. I watched him like a spy in his own house, and I felt my treachery as heartburn: a long, hot, deep pain over that part of my chest.

At whom he looked when we had company. (And, on average, half as much at women as at the men.) At whom he looked when we walked round Highgate: younger people mostly, and as much at men and boys as at women and girls. How discerningly he continued to dress: well out of anything resembling fashion, but with a little of the dandy-ish air he'd admired in his elders. How artistically he held his knife and fork, how carefully he handled a stemmed tumbler, how precisely he placed his lips against the rim to drink, how exactly he was able to calculate each measure that went into his mouth. How assiduously he now failed to mention Mother at all.

Father has brown eyes. They are round and moist and staring – although the irises are hard to distinguish in the pupils – with long soft lashes, and I have been reminded (not very originally) of a cow's eyes. They move slowly, and somehow generously, unlike Gilbert's, which become needle-sharp in an instant. Gilbert's avoid the stage of appearing hurt, and will directly become scathing, or cruel. Father's belong to a milder, more troubled, perhaps haunted man, and it may be that the look I sometimes saw as I was growing up and which I hadn't a hope of identifying then was, in fact, the harrowing personal demon of his guilt.

Guilt about what?

I try to decide, watching him where he sits in the Randolph Square flat, out of the direct light. He doesn't see me looking. One hand – pale, not large or long-fingered but neatly, even daintily proportioned – hangs from the end of the chair arm. On the little finger he wears a signet ring. His nails are kept trimmed; once I spotted an emery board on the bathroom window sill. His cuff-links half-show beneath the sleeve of his jacket. His fingers fan a little, then close, spread like fan spokes, then close again.

                              *

At the 'Tic-Tac' Club I defied Chetwynd – I was irritated that he hadn't offered me an explanation for Lavinia Yearwood's absence – and stayed on after he'd gone. I danced the last five dances with Fleur, until they were putting the chairs up on top of the tables. The band dwindled to a trio, who presumably had no homes to get back to. But we danced well and maybe they had satisfaction in blending their music with our movements. I forget who led, we or they: we were like hand and glove, let me say. The music filled our heads, and we understood the lyrics – in their essence – inside out, as only two o'clock dancers can. We were dappled in pink and blue light, and I was in heaven. Yet there was no intimacy, even now. Fleur was somewhere else entirely. Not until I let go my concentration and our feet collided would her eyes at last show recognition, of who I was and where we were. Temporarily she would will some rigidity in her arms, but it drained away again as she lost herself in the music, in the requirements of the dance.

I was her servant, her vassal, but I don't know if she once realised, not properly. Sometimes she smiled, at the very earnestness I couldn't disguise. But above the smile her eyes were so strangely distanced, seeing me and not seeing me. The carnation and violet played across her irises and pupils like caressing flames, like inveigling deep-water.

*

C. had used the name before I was aware he had.

'If someone were to say to you, "If you buy half a dozen of *these*, Mrs Tobin, and . . ."'

Not 'Mrs Simmons'.

It was dropped into the sentence so effortlessly, his voice was so seductively even-sounding –

We were alone. The others had left the room, drifted off into the garden.

I sat bolt upright in the chair, poker straight. I didn't know how to respond. I couldn't think what he had been talking about, how I could fake an answer.

I saw Ralph looking up from the terrace, watching us both.

Should I carry on as if I simply hadn't heard?

But I was taking far too long to decide. I was losing the little grip I had, second by second by second.

'Have I said something . . . ?'

I shrugged. He knew the answer to that. My manner of surrender told him.

'Don't hesitate to put me right, Mrs Tobin. About . . .'

Maybe it amused him. His own manner was almost jocular, and quite unrepentant.

For the first time I saw the full extent of my folly
– allowing myself to be befriended as I had – but even
so I couldn't regret it, I shall never regret it.

*

We reached Marlow, C. nodded, and I caught my first
sight of the hotel over the stone parapet of the bridge.
I knew of its reputation, but it was prettier than I was
expecting. Pedestrians stood on the high pavement
looking down on the river garden. Swans swam, and
ducks and coots strutted on their orange feet on the
grass. A motor cruiser puttered past.

Inside the restaurant, at our window table for
two, I had a view of all the river life. Birds were
continually landing and taking off; I don't know how
many pleasure-craft of all sizes and designs went
up and down; even rowing sculls flashed by, as if
somewhere very close to us a film was being shot
in celebration of picture postcard England. This was
the view on a calendar, or a tin box of biscuits. On
the other side of the river was a church, a thatched
cottage, a red-brick house with half-cross timbering,
a spreading oak.

C. saw me watching it all. He smiled, bemused.

Then – we just talked: talked together in a rambling
kind of way. He seemed interested in my doings. Or
rather, my doings appeared to interest him chiefly
when they referred to Gilbert. Or maybe he was just
trying to get a rounded picture of me and my life.
I answered his questions; I didn't deliberately hold
back, because I trusted him to keep the information
to himself. I'd had nobody to talk to for so long.
We seemed far away from that existence anyway;
and far enough away from the other tables in the
room, in our window bay, for nobody else to be
eavesdropping.

I told him about Gilbert's hours, his absences,

the sort of patients he seems to prefer, something about his attitudes, his tastes. I told him about the company we keep – Gilbert keeps – in London. I told him about Lillias, and my troubles with her. I talked a little about my life with Mother, my memories of growing up.

C. was smoking a havana. He let me speak, and I talked through little cloudlets of blue smoke. When Gilbert smokes, I make sure he sees that I object to breathing in the detritus of his lungs. But in sunny Marlow, by the river where all life flowed past, it was part of the atmosphere, the ambience.

I kept talking, on the journey back also, settled deep into my seat. We were driving so fast, I realised no one would have an opportunity to see through the windows, into the low car. The speedometer needle reached 80 several times. I decided I liked this fast motion. Gilbert is always so diligent about the limits specified on road-signs; he's told me he can't afford to lose his licence. Nor, I suppose, can C., yet he did it, breezily flashing past the markers on their posts. I could feel I was taking to this, to this perilous adventure. It's like a little storm whipped up inside my head: this devilment, deliciously anaesthetising all my organs of judgement.

'I can smell cigar smoke,' Gilbert said when he walked into the drawing-room.

I was still wearing the dress I'd had on for lunch in Marlow.

'Can you?'

'Yes.'

He smiled, as if the remark had no significance really. But several times he came into the corner of the room where I was sitting, where I'd retreated when he'd made the comment. I could tell he was returning for a breath of the evidence in his nostrils.

'I went up into town,' I said. 'I had tea in Harrods. I expect that's where I got it.'

'Ah.'

'I didn't notice.'

'Buy anything?' he asked, with sly keenness to know.

'No. No, I was just looking.'

Pause.

'By the way,' he said, 'the Elsons are going to invite us for dinner again – '

'Oh, Gilbert – '

'Don't say you don't want to go – '

He knows what I think of Christina, but he asked me last time, please would I not make an issue of it again. Her husband is his good friend as well as a colleague, and it's true – I have to bear this in mind – that Gilbert can't have a say in what sort of wives the males in his circle choose for themselves.

I sat in my far chair, looking – I have no doubt – very gloomy. Gilbert sighed. The Elsons are not only social, they're a professional consideration, which is the rub. Medicine also, even in Harley and Wigmore Streets, is a trade.

*

Talk of the she-devil. Whom should I meet on the stairs in Simpson's but Christina.

She immediately apologised for our cancelled dinner engagement. I asked after Lex and the children. She seemed rather quiet: quieter even than she normally is with me. Then she suggested we go off and have tea somewhere.

It was an odd and stilted conversation that ensued. The questions mostly came from her. Some were about Gilbert, and I doubt if my answers proved very satisfactory to her. Lex could have given her more information about Harley Street than I was able to, since he is only three doors away. I just tried to

appear a little scatty about it all. But I could see
that she was thinking, what an ignorant woman for
a wife. I've never felt she had a very high opinion of
me at all.

And then all in a moment the whole point of it
became blindingly clear to me, during a discussion
of our social movements.

'This may sound awfully strange – but Marcia
Palmer told me she was quite sure she'd seen you
at the "Hungária". One evening when she was taken
there – '

I concentrated on keeping my face quite straight.

'The "Hungária"? The restaurant?'

'You were with some people.'

'Was I?'

'She didn't recognise any of them.'

'Really?'

'Well, Lex said, what would Fleur be doing there
with strangers?'

I smiled, not at all warmly.

'He said, it must have been a case of mistaken
identity.'

I didn't reply.

'Lex prefers hotels, the grills there. To restaurants. He thinks they're classier.'

Of course she believes Marcia Palmer's story,
because it's what she wants to believe. She needs
a little melodrama in her life, just a little, and I'm
the one – the familiar non-entity – to provide it.

'Yes,' I said, 'they probably are.'

'We must have dinner more often, the four of us.
We don't see enough of you both, not together – '

'Gilbert is very busy just now.'

'That must be rather a bore for you. Isn't it?'

'One – one adjusts to it.'

'Does Gilbert still go away?'

'Yes. Sometimes.'

'House-calls?' She laughed.

'What?'

'Lex sees his lights on when he leaves. When Gilbert's in town, that is — '

'Does he? Well, yes, he works late.'

'Often?'

'Quite often, yes.'

I can see what she's thinking. How inconsiderate of him. And how uncomplaining *you* are. But how venal of you both. Is that why he does it, for the money, and why *you* allow it?

Her eyes swept over me, from the top of my head to where I stopped, at table-top level. She sat considering the expense of the stones in my rings.

She has never failed to underestimate me. But I am partly responsible for that. It has suited me perhaps, that she shouldn't suspect too much. There may have been other sightings, but she can ply me with those some other time. This was to be a preliminary testing.

'Or *we* could meet and eat,' she suggested. 'How are you placed with your lunchtimes?'

Maybe my suspicions were written on my face for her to see. She looked at me like a schoolmistress who has realised she has been indulgent with her charge for too long, that I'm clearly not responding to treatment.

'You know how people are,' she said. 'How fast the news will travel — '

'"News"?' I asked. 'Or "rumours", do you mean?'

'Oh, *I'm* no good on — what's the word? — on *semantics* — '

'It's just the difference between "news" and "rumours" I mean, that's all — '

'Perhaps it's obvious to *you*, Fleur dear — '

I accept Lex, for being the decent man he surely is, even though he is also a friend of Gilbert's. There is no earthly reason, however, why one should have any respect for other men's wives. It ought to reflect adversely on Lex, and yet . . . He may have failed to understand women, or (to be fair to them both) even someone like Christina might have undergone a change of nature with the years – too many domestic responsibilities, the crowding in of the years, the realisation that the future plays cruel tricks of perspective on us, tempting us to invest our trust in possibilities as fickle finally as mirages . . .

TWENTY-ONE

I waited for her to come back to the swimming pool. At 'The Circus' she always seemed preoccupied, and I had a sense that Chetwynd was keeping her apart from not just myself but everyone. Whenever he rescued her in a conversation, she looked intensely grateful.

She didn't come in, though, or not when I was on attendant's duty. I felt that fate – or whatever – meant Randolph Square to be one existence, and 'The Circus' the other, and that its previous mistake of confusing them wouldn't be repeated. When I wasn't in Kensington, I wanted to be. I never experienced the converse, concerning the swimming pool. I longed to be with those people I knew so little about but whom I'd got to the stage of recognising in all sorts of strangers' faces, either in the street or at the pool. I could almost believe it hadn't been Fleur after all who had appeared that day. I wasn't sure if my wanting her to walk through the doors was on her account or because she represented to me possible access to Chetwynd's enigma, which we might have tried to discuss over a coffee in the mezzanine lounge upstairs.

It remained academic conjecture. She didn't come. The two realities, the greater and the lesser, didn't collide again for a while, and I was no more than a spectator when they did.

*

We had been invited to the Urbans' youngest daughter's wedding in Oxford. I had no wish to go, but Gilbert merely presumed, since he owes – and knows that I know he owes – a great deal to Sir Marcus, for his confidence in him in the early days.

The reception was held in New College. Gilbert seemed to enjoy being back in Oxford, especially among Wykehamists, and I thought the day came to us in the way of a remission. He drank liberally, and found more than enough people among the guests he thought deserved a social acknowledgement. We were among the last to leave, at the tail-end of the afternoon.

On the drive back I took a headache, not helped by Gilbert's erratic driving. He suggested (more for his sake than mine, I was sure) that we stop and look for some reviving tea for me and sobering coffee for him.

I realised what his choice of stop was going to be when we were crossing the bridge over the Thames at Marlow. He swung into the hotel's driveway, taking the corner faster than C. had in his Aston Martin.

I tried to stay composed, but I could only sip at the tea. The lights came on, the first diners appeared. Gilbert asked, what were we going to do about eating? When we are by ourselves, he doesn't like supper or dinner late. Even when he stays on in Harley Street, he goes out for what he terms 'a bite' around seven o'clock and returns to his rooms.

His digestion isn't of the best, and I have adapted to eating rather earlier than we used to do at Highgate.

'I suggest we have something here. A bite.'

'Isn't it . . . ?'

'Isn't it what?'

'Rather fancy? For the purpose?'

'It's been a fancy day.'

'We had lunch – '

'It wasn't rich, though, and very light. If you like, we'll just have a couple of courses – '

He decided we would, even though I didn't confirm that my headache felt any better. The head waiter was the same one, and I panicked. I saw him look

more closely at me as he approached. When I pushed
my arm through Gilbert's, the man slightly inclined
his head, as if, yes, yes, in this job of work he learned
to – understand certain things . . .

My head felt huge like a pumpkin – a great gawping harvest lantern – as we were shown across the
room and seated. But that was the least of it. I
thought when the menus were brought to us there
was something unusually calculating about Gilbert's
eyes, even for him.

'I shall order for you,' he said.

I knew what the order would be before he'd given it.
Game pâté, poached salmon with hollandaise sauce,
honey syllabub. It was as close as he could have come
to the choice I'd made at C.'s suggestion from the
luncheon menu.

'I presume you have no objection?'

'I . . . No, no, that's . . .'

We weren't seated in the window this time, but in
the centre of the room. I looked past him to the view
of the river. My heart was up in my throat, a metal
clasp was fastened round my head. I couldn't see, I
couldn't breathe.

Gilbert was saying something. He must have said
it several times. When I switched my eyes to him,
he was laughing: the driest, falsest of laughs. Swans
he'd been talking about. Swan-upping.

The square of pâté on my plate was only picked
at. The wine went untasted, and Gilbert took my
glass from me, to supplement his own. I thought I
was going to be sick in the interlude between the
courses. Gilbert talked on, about the wedding, about
guests he hadn't thought to introduce me to. The
salmon arrived, two cuts of a pink, very dead fish
laid out on two monogrammed bone-china plates. I
heard Gilbert say something bitchy and unbecoming
about a colleague he'd graduated with: and hint that
Urban wasn't quite the doctor of doctors he'd always

imagined he was. I fed the fish into my mouth, little baby portions on the tines of my fork, which crumbled into flakes and were mulled around and around before I was able to swallow any of it.

Afterwards Gilbert kept looking at his watch. His face was grim. The thing had been done: presumably without the full confidence of a prior reservation, because then he would surely have gone the whole hog and put me in the window table, to let me know that he was in no doubt whatsoever of what he was engaged in, that coincidence doesn't merely follow on coincidence.

In the ladies' room I started to cry, but really I was too frightened to let myself go. I returned to the car. The river shone in the darkness. The birdlife hooted, screeched; a few solidly silver swans lurched drunkenly on the lawn. Gilbert turned on music, Bach (which at any other time would have had him reaching to retune to another channel), only so that now we wouldn't have to speak to one another. The headlights came up; they ranged across gravel like a continent of arid stone desert. The engine whined under the bonnet, his foot stabbed on the accelerator. I reached up for the grab handle above my door, and then we were off.

*

Surely you'll regret all this? my mother would say.

Oh no, I would tell her.

Will you be better for it? she meant. Or wiser?

But it's living, *I* meant, it's all part of the learning process. How could I be a *lesser* person for any of it?

*

After a 'Circus' lunch on another day C. asked me, quite plainly but in the same quiet tone of voice, what Gilbert's 'area' was.

'Gynaecological.'

I thought I had explained to him, when we'd had our lunch. But I explained again.

He nodded, slowly. But some gestures deny themselves.

'That's all I know,' I said.

'You discuss it?'

'No.'

'So, you've told me what *he* has told you.'

'Yes. Yes.'

The repetition rang in my ears. I stood up, to clear my head.

'And he stays on in Harley Street of an evening?'

'Sometimes,' I said. 'He's kept very busy.'

'Do all consultants work as hard as your husband?'

'He has so many patients.'

'They're content to come in the evening? If that's the only time they can acquire his services?'

'I suppose so. He goes into the country quite a bit. To patients. His time gets used up, you see.'

'He has a fine advocate in his wife, Mrs Tobin.'

I closed my eyes, to dispel the thought.

'The evening offers confidentiality, perhaps,' he said, 'in private matters? All medical business *is*, of course, but for certain women . . .'

'Perhaps,' I replied in the silence.

'Our worries can cause us to side-step convention. Make us even a little –' he paused. ' – a little irrational sometimes – '

I considered; then I nodded.

'I'm glad we agree, Fleur.'

It was the first time he had ever used my Christian name. I couldn't prevent myself from smiling – a smile that spread wide across my face – even though the topic we had been discussing was so painful to me.

TWENTY-TWO

That afternoon turned out to be the last time she visited Kensington.

I walked with her to the end of the road, to find a taxi. She was as tense as she'd been all through lunch. Had she been crying? She looked unslept.

I felt she wasn't really aware that I was there. That it was me beside her. But I told myself, that meant my presence was only the more necessary, as a protection.

A taxi came. By some uncommon fluke, a second appeared in view as hers set off. I hailed it and asked the driver to follow the taxi in front.

'Friends?' he asked. 'Or is it a chance?'

'Somewhere between the two,' I told him.

He snatched at the hand-brake.

'I've waited all my life for this, squire.'

The expense started to bother me as we reached, not Highgate, but Hampstead. Nevertheless I told him to wait a few moments before we moved into the road her own taxi had turned into.

The houses were substantial, detached, turn-of-the-century properties. Three storeys, grey brick, with high sash windows. There was something lowering about them, ranged along both sides of the road, even though they had leafy front gardens behind railings. Drawing-room territory, with half a dozen or more bedrooms apiece, and poky staff quarters up in their attics. The very substance of respectability, it has to be said.

At Number 8 lights went on at the side. A staircase window was already illuminated. A small shadow passed across it, flaring for a split-second before shrinking back into the stonework.

For a moment I thought I caught a movement at one of the unlit square windows on the second floor, above the garden. But I might have been wrong, it may have been a bird or a bat just flying out of my range of vision; or the briefest reflection by moonlight of a vanishing cloud, like the parting whisk of a horse's tail.

*

His consulting rooms are in a building as seemly as any of the well-preserved palazzi along both sides of Harley Street. He has the best position in the building, architecturally speaking, on the first floor: a suite of airy, high-ceilinged rooms with tall, leaded-glass windows and two balustraded balconies to the front.

Gilbert has never once invited me inside the building.

The entrance from the street is that shared by the other consultants. A stout oak door with a round of stained glass somewhere above average head height is somewhat intimidating, as its purpose surely is to be; it is also, by design, a very effective guarantee of privacy. When a car or taxi draws up to the pavement and the passenger makes his way – in Gilbert's case, the passenger if 'sola' will always make *her* way – to the four shallow steps and the small causeway of terrazzo on stone above the deep railinged area, someone must be watching through one of the stained-glass side-panels or through a spy-hole elsewhere because the door will already be drawing open to admit the caller. Momentarily a passer-by might catch sight of the interior: light caramel-painted walls, white stucco friezes, a standard lamp with a gold-coloured bowed silk shade, and always a spray of seasonal flowers placed in an alcove. Then the door is closed again, with no audible sound of locks, but closed – very decidedly and very firmly. The car or taxi has driven off, and inside the building the net curtains at the windows further protect the privacy and anonymity of the visitor. The front offered to the world is one of perfect professional discretion.

Yesterday morning Gilbert told me he would be working late. He has been late home at least twice a week for the past three or four months. It has happened too often for me to be required to show any reaction. I can give as little of myself away now as the façades of the buildings in Harley Street. What I'm thinking is quite another matter.

Normally, though, I can forget. When he tells me he will be late, that much registers, but then I put the fact out of my mind. Yesterday, for some reason, the fact was not for that easy automatic expelling. It stuck, stuck fast, like a burr, like a twist of fleece on a thorn-pricket. Nothing I did could divert me. The idea of it – what was delaying him, why he had to spend another evening in Harley Street until ten o'clock – obsessed me all morning and afternoon, when properly I should have done what I usually did, forgotten about it except to appreciate the quiet it brought to the house for a few extra hours.

C.'s talking about things hadn't helped any. It seemed to have concentrated all my thoughts on the subject.

Why couldn't yesterday have been like just any other day? Why couldn't I simply have let my pernicious, calamitous fancy go?

The building – the relevant portion of it – was still lit.

Through the fanlight the glass chandelier in the hall was visible. The stained-glass window in the front door dribbled ruby and indigo streaks across the high paving between the areas on either side. A light was on in one of the front rooms on the first floor, but dimly. Just once, while I stood looking up from the opposite pavement, I thought I caught sight of a figure, but it was only a faint, fleeting shadow on the white net curtains.

I must have spent twenty minutes waiting, watching, pacing the pavement, selecting vantage points from which to observe the same five windows on the building's conforming brick and stucco front to the street. I waited and watched until a second lamp went on in an inner room. I now felt I could be certain, Gilbert *was* there.

After that came the first real signs of activity. Firstly a girl in a raincoat, wearing a nurse's starched cap and flat shoes and black stockings, rounded the corner from Queen Anne Street and hurried, half-running, to cover the distance to the front door. This must have been the new girl Gilbert — for once — mentioned to me he'd taken on. She consulted her wrist-watch as she reached the railings, then sprinted up the steps and let herself in with a key, slinking between door and jamb. Nearly fifteen minutes later a silver-and-grey Rolls-Royce approached; it purred towards the kerb and stopped directly before the steps. A uniformed chauffeur and another man in a fitted overcoat emerged from the front of the car, and then — when the chauffeur had opened the back door on the pavement side — two women also, one middle-aged and the other younger. A valise and vanity box were removed from the boot by the chauffeur while the other three — with darkness a three-quarters cover — walked up the steps, the young woman being supported. The door of the house drew open, and the nurse — in starched white — stepped out to lend a hand. The suitcase and boîte-bouteilles were deposited in the hall, and when the chauffeur withdrew the door was closed behind him.

For another fifteen minutes the chauffeur sat outside in the car. I had to move further off, towards a bus-stop, so as to eliminate myself as much as I might from the panorama he might have had beneath that peaked cap.

I wasn't in the best position to see, therefore, when the front door of the building opened again. Against the golden light in the hall only two figures emerged, the older couple, and they returned forthwith to the car. The chauffeur was on hand to open the back door for them, and they hardly needed to lower their heads even as one followed the other into the luxurious seclusion of the rear cabin behind the glass screen.

The car departed. The turning of the engine was almost inaudible. At the very top of Harley Street the driver turned right, in the direction of Portland Place, and then the car vanished from view.

I kept up my watch for another ten or fifteen minutes, until I started to feel chilled. There was no other evidence of life at all from the building, not even a shadow falling on a curtain. Only the windows on the first floor showed a light, and the fanlight in the hall. I don't know why I then started to doubt myself, my conviction that Gilbert must be there in the building after all. Perhaps my suspicions were aroused by feeling I might myself be the unwitting object of other people's suspicions. I started to think that the same cars were making their way up and down the street.

Gilbert kept the Jaguar in a mews lock-up at the rear, I knew. I relieved myself of my post at the front of the building and made my way, via New Cavendish Street, round to the back. I hoped I might see the car parked on the cobbles, but it wasn't there. I found the garage by counting along. Its doors were locked, and there were no means of seeing inside from the lane. I looked up at the back of the building. Heavy drapes had been drawn across the windows, but I could distinguish smudges of light along their edges.

Nor do I know why I should have turned the handle of the back gate. It was idly done, in a wispy mood between confusion and despair. But the handle did turn, and the wooden gate creaked open, like one in a story of childhood. I hesitated, then I stepped between the posts, into the yard. Several stone urns had been positioned on stone slabs, and in them — high walls notwithstanding — bloomed moss pinks and early geraniums. I looked over my shoulder and noticed that at the back of the garage there was a window. I went over to it on tiptoe, and recognised the familiar sculpted lines and chrome trim of the Mark VIII. So he *must* still be here . . .

I spotted a wrought-iron bench placed against a side-wall hung with cane trellis-work, out of viewing range of the upstairs windows. I was tired, so wearied, the small of my back was aching, how I longed for a rest. I sat down. Everything was starting to feel quite unreal. The buildings roundabout loomed with cartoon menace, slanting into a black sky of stars. What was happening to us? The day of our wedding had proclaimed itself a sesame to all manner of contentment. Our fulfilment through mutual obligation. But it seemed — it seems — such a very long time ago, almost a different woman's experience.

I dug my hands into my coat pockets. I pulled out a sheet of notepaper. Written on both sides was a list of things I wanted to remember to buy for Lillias's birthday party. But it seemed a pointless mission. It took me several moments to realise what I was doing, that I'd been tearing the page into pieces. I was shocked to see the scraps in my hand. I suddenly felt a terrible surge of guilt.

On the other side of the yard were several dustbins. I closed my fist tight on my debris and stood up. I must have disturbed a cat, because an elasticated shape shot past me before my eyes could adjust.

I felt myself shaking with the speed of its movement. I had to get away. I should discover nothing more tonight. I might never discover anything more, however many nights I took up my watch in future.

I could have put the litter back into my pocket, but I just wanted rid of the evidence. I'd have to begin a new list. The party was only a fortnight off, but the days slid away dangerously.

The dustbin lid I took hold of wouldn't budge. I should have given up, there and then: I should have done. But I felt everything was resisting me, I had to declare myself somehow. I tugged and tugged at the handle. Eventually I won, the lid came away in my hand and I was left with the shudders reverberating up my arm.

Some of the scraps of paper had fallen out of my palm, on to the paving. I threw the rest into the hold of the bin. I watched them snow reluctantly, confetti-drift, clinging where they could to the sides.

Looking down, though, my eye was caught by what I thought was the silvered wetness of a fish. It glimmered in a parcel of newspaper that had burst open. When I looked a little closer I couldn't see scales. The substance of the thing seemed to be jelly-fish rather, and faintly diaphanous: pinky-bluish, by the lamplight from the lane. I leaned further forward. Not a fish, I thought: someone had been planning to eat a small rabbit — a skinned and gutted young rabbit or leveret — but an interruption or a postponement had happened to prevent them. I reached into the dustbin. I pulled back a fold of the newspaper, like a petal. I turned my head to examine the object from another angle. I couldn't find the shape of a rabbit, decapitated and belly slit. Instead I thought I caught the resemblance to a head, a rather squashed but domed, bald human head, showing cracks on the temples — and in miniature the oval of a swollen body, like a starveling's bloated belly, with a tiny shrivelled squiggle lying on top, like a signature. I pulled back another corner of paper and saw, obtruding from the body portion, another curlicue of the same flesh, like a little tail, like a question mark. A piglet, I was reminded of. Then quite another picture came into my mind — the archetype of all the photographs I'd ever seen of such a thing — and I realised, I identified what I hadn't been able to.

I froze, paralysed, in that scrutinising pose. I stared and stared. I had never seen one and yet I knew for a certainty that this was what it was. A foetus. I stared at life in a raw dollop, ripped untimely from its growing place. Pinpoints of black, the size of peppercorns in the spawn, were eyes. Little fringes on the squiggles were potential hands and feet. If I could have seen, I should have discovered the body and head marbled with veins. The cracks must have been where the forceps or wrench had reached to, to do their crushing work. Seeing what I was able to by the yellow lamplight, I spotted the smears of dried blood on the newspaper.

A life but not a person.

Somewhere along the line, on the mother's part, there had been a fatal lack of confidence.

I wanted to cry. I couldn't. I was too shocked. Too frightened.

Next to that dustbin was another one. And another next to it. And then another two still.

I stood staring at them.

What could those have shown me if I'd dared to look inside? Had the new nurse not understood the way things were done here?

But I would have needed courage to look, and I simply didn't have it. I see now there was really nothing anyway that I could have done. It was too late, far too late. We had come too far. The stakes now were metaphysical.

*

I followed her from Harley Street to a café. She knew it was me behind her, trailing her. Her pace slowed, she undid her headscarf and shook it out. She wasn't caring about protecting her identity from strangers.

She pushed on the door and walked – or stumbled – inside. She slumped down on to a bench. I opened the door quietly and stepped across to the table. She didn't look up – her eyes were on the silk scarf being played between her fingers – and I took the absence of a gesture for approval.

She was in tears. Her shoulders shook silently for several moments. Then she let out a sob. She clasped one hand to her mouth. I leaned across and took the other hand. I wanted to wrap her up and whisk her away to some place of the spirit. Oh, I wanted more than anything to be the essence of kindness itself. I pressed her hand tight, so tightly it must have hurt her. But she had too much else to think about, and she may hardly have noticed my presence at all.

When she did talk at last it was in scraps and tatters of sense. I realised she was referring to her husband, but the gist wasn't very clear to me. Of living too well and of having known too little . . . A car passed outside and momentarily distracted her, but she was really an age away, in her youth, in a past of (still) seductive potential. And all it had come to was this, to now, to a late-opening café and her reflection cast cold in the glass on to Marylebone High Street in all its smug antimacassar-and-beading unconcern.

She started to cry again with tiredness and was too weary to know how to stop herself. It didn't matter who saw, because there was no remaining ideal of herself to live up to. She spread her hands flat on the table-top and opened the palms wide.

Her head swivelled round on her neck, her eyes returned to the window. Out on the street two cars passed, illuminated in the tracks of one another's headlights. The pavements were deserted. I glanced down at my watch. It was twenty minutes to eleven.

She didn't move, though. Then a thought occurred to me. Was it possible I had interrupted her? Had she been planning to meet someone, and I'd only put myself in their way?

'I'll have to go now,' I said.

I needed to repeat myself before she heard. She turned her head round but her body stayed angled away from me, in a position to better watch the window.

'Where to?' she asked.

'Home.'

'Oh,' she nodded. 'Yes. Yes, of course.'

I pushed back my chair and got to my feet. She viewed my movements, I thought, with alarm.

I stood – stood still – in front of her for several moments.

'You *will* be coming back sometime?' I asked her.

'What?'

'To "The Circus"?'

'I . . .' She shook her head. Not, I felt, to signify 'no', but because she wasn't able to fix on the matter at this moment.

'Sooner or later?' I said.

'Oh . . .'

And so the conversation just petered away, ran down to suspension dots, silence, nothing.

From outside on the pavement, I looked in at her through the window. Now she was facing where I had been sitting. She looked forlorn in the bleak fluorescent light, just like an image of solitude in an Edward Hopper painting of a bar or automat counter in an American downtown long past midnight. But I couldn't make the connection unaided: between the image from the land of 'Nighthawks' and the few facts of her history which I knew.

*

Kensington life went on without her.

A luncheon or two. A couple of evenings on the town. All I had to do was be charming, and dance, and make my partners feel adept. Round and around. Their perfume clung to my clothes and smothered the coating of swimming-pool chlorine on my skin. Round and around, like a dervish dance.

Chetwynd didn't refer to her absence. I was irritated that he didn't. Every time I was irritated with myself that I'd come.

Only Howard Kimble seemed to realise. He was the estate agent by day, busy and prosperous, but it was he who had the savvy in reserve to recognise there was something wrong. Badly wrong. His eyes passed between Chetwynd and myself.

He came and took a leak beside me in the Gents of 'Le Safari'. His penis, I noticed with relief, was quite flaccid.

'You're a bright lad. I don't get it.'

I didn't need to ask 'get what?'

'I suppose,' he said, aiming an arc of hot piss past his feet, 'everyone needs time to get their priorities sorted out.'

I started buttoning myself up.

'A year or so, Ralph. To get things in focus.'

'*You* come along with us,' I said.

He shrugged. 'Lush life. Easy pickings.'

'But what's in it – '

He interrupted my question.

'It's only so Chetwynd can pump me about work, of course. About who buys what. Which property. And for how much. Leases, loans.'

'Don't you mind?'

'Being used? That's life. I'm using Chetwynd. We all are.'

I instinctively pulled a face at the white porcelain.

'We're all useful to *someone*,' he said.

'*I* am?' I asked, and must have sounded incredulous.

'Why else would he go on inviting you if you weren't?'

I didn't reply.

Kimble looked over his shoulder.

'Why get guilty about being a freeloader?'

He laughed. Laughed so hard he spilled piss on to his patent shoe.

'Fucking hell – '

I had never encountered treachery of this sort before. I was intrigued to know more. Kimble shook his head, still smiling. I hovered between him and the door. He could see my physical displacement and read the uncertainty of thought and conscience behind it.

*

Everything in the house seems to defy me. *I am here in spite of you, bought on the profits of shame and quick-fixes. The subterfuge skill of the scalpel has provided your comfort — aren't you grateful?*

I don't touch anything. I can't eat the food, I can't put the tines of the fork into my mouth, the blades of the knives are all too keen. This is the House of the Dead, and no mistake about it. I turn my eyes to the wall, to a chair, to the fire, and I see instead the dustbin and its contents. There's too little food in my stomach to bring up, but I have the taste of it in my mouth, in my nose. It takes an age to get to my feet and make for wherever is not here, this room with the recurring picture in the gas flames, it's waiting for me somewhere else too, and I don't know where to go to avoid it, but any other room is worth trying. I sleep only in fits and starts, and the scratching begins before I'm fully awake, the recollection that something is terribly wrong, so irredeemably wrong, and the scratching turns to gnawing, and I suddenly lose the little release of sleep and start to shrivel up again. I lie on top of the mattress like an embryo, tilting round on my axis. I have no consolation I can think of, but closing in on myself is the strongest instinct that remains to me.

How might it be possible to ever trust anybody again?

There's no place to go back to, to wish myself there. I only have the space I occupy, the cowering embedding itself into the mattress, which will be the only impression I can leave on events. There is this and there is nothing else.

C. knew. Somehow he knew.

How long has he known? Since when? Since I came to Kensington, or since I first encountered them

all on the beach at Treswithian? Or since before then, even?

Somehow he knew too that I should discover for myself. He could have saved me from it, but he wanted me to discover. He needed me to understand the sort of man I'm married to, that for however many years of our marriage Gilbert has conducted his lucrative trade and no one has dared to stop him. Acquaintances in very high places have ensured that no harm has come to him. C. wanted me to understand that too. He could have saved me the knowledge, but he thought better of me than that. I had it in me, he knew, to retrieve the situation: to save Lillias and myself.

*

Possibly. Just possibly.

She says no more. I asked Liz, but she told me that's all there was about it. She herself wasn't willing to delve deeper than that into Chetwynd's involvement.

Perhaps, though, other darker shadows of suspicion had occurred to Fleur. She may have perceived that Chetwynd was counting on a stronger reaction than anger: a venomous desire in her for revenge. Now that she knew the little – the most significantly little – that she did know, she should have found the means to learn more. As her husband's wife, she had access to certain confidential information without previously realising it. Information, Chetwynd had always assured us, was security and control: command and power.

I imagine her waiting by the telephone: hoping that it will ring and she will find Chetwynd speaking to her. If he doesn't ring, then the obligation is surely hers to call him. But her confidence (if that is what it truly is) waxes and wanes. There are moments – more and more of them – when she sees opportunities reducing themselves, when she can't view the situation clearly, not through a mass of obtruding and shrinking angles. Her predicament is closing in on her all the time she is left to think about it. Minute by minute Chetwynd seems

to be distanced further and further from her, even Chetwynd
with his concern and sympathy. She has been given access to
an existence she thought had come to her by mistake, from that
very first afternoon on the beach at Treswithian: come to her in
default of its being granted to someone else. But she had always
sensed that Chetwynd's life was greatly complicated, where
none of them could properly see: that it didn't compose itself by a
sequence of accidents. She had accepted his hospitality and been
too grateful – like me – to allow herself to enquire how and why.
There was so much money involved, but Chetwynd was the
most disarmingly generous person she had ever encountered,
without a single thought for the persistent economies of other
people. Yet nothing in life is so straightforward, or so casual.
Beyond the age of four or five or six, no fairy tales are possible
in the world that stretches ahead of you on waking up, which
becomes less and less certain or clear-cut as the day advances
inexorably towards the twilight and shadow-time and then, all
over again, into the bogey kingdom of darkness and night.

She sits beside the telephone in the hall of that grey-brick
house with its good address, surrounded by similar residences
where their smart and accomplished neighbours conduct their
own lives. Her husband isn't in Harley Street tonight, he is off
to the country, on one of his obscure assignments that probably
cost the patient or her parents or spouse an arm and a leg, at
any rate a damn sight more than the crumpled, bloodied foetus
alone.

The memory of the dustbin has sent her to the bathroom so
often, there's nothing left in her stomach to be retched up. She
tries to focus on the fact – the Fact – as pragmatically as she can.
But she is a mother, with a child of her own who is also Gilbert's,
whom Gilbert delivered himself, and it must be different for her.
She can only think hard, very hard thoughts. She sits waiting by
the telephone, while what remains inside her – the bludgeoned
mental and exhausted physical life – is a turmoil of rage: fury
at all the deception and steel-cold necessity in the world, and
impotent sorrow for the victims, for those who stupidly and too
trustingly give themselves to the superior wills that dominate
and oppress them.

She has never, even as a bereaved child, hated as she does now, in the enviably commodious, centrally heated, over-furnished and sound-deadened desolation of something a little less than life on Rosslyn Hill.

TWENTY-THREE

I returned to Harley Street on another couple of evenings. On the first, the Rolls-Royce again drew up at the door. This time only the older woman and man emerged, and they hurried into the building. They stayed for about half an hour. They made their exit a little less hastily, but went straight from the front door into the back compartment of the car.

Lights remained lit on the first floor and in the hall until eleven o'clock, when I left. A Jaguar Mark VIII crossed the street at New Cavendish Street, several houses further down, and I thought it might be Simmons'. The girl in the nurse's white uniform, who'd made the same dash – consulting her watch – to reach the premises as she'd done the previous evening, hadn't come out again, and I went away with a sense that the building – its first-floor rooms at least – weren't unoccupied.

I couldn't be sure about the registration plates. But how many silver-and-grey Rolls-Royce Mulliner Silver Wraiths were there on the streets of central London? I had tried to catch a resemblance in the woman being led inside, but it was too dark to see. That was not accidental. Her parents, Lavinia Yearwood had told me, indulged her; they also, Celia had informed me, went about picking up the pieces of a disjointed life. She never came dancing now; I hadn't set eyes on her for some weeks indeed. Guests were always dropping out of our evenings: the point of everything was that an arrangement could only ever be temporary. I knew, to judge from all the other precedents, that Mrs George Yearwood would not be back.

*

'What would you like most in the world?' Howard Kimble asked me, when the two of us were alone in Chetwynd's blossoming garden and out of anyone's earshot.

I didn't have to think.

'A car,' I said.

Kimble nodded, and seemed approving.

In the silence I said, 'To give me my freedom.'

He repeated me.

'Your "freedom"?'

He stood considering the word.

'To get me from A to B,' I said. 'And C.'

His reply was instantaneous.

'And back again?'

Coming back must always count for less than the journey to wherever it happened to be.

'Just a car,' I said.

He repeated me again, surely lending the remark some irony.

'"Just a car"?' The smile wouldn't stay off his face.

I was mildly irritated. But I concentrated on not giving myself away. Or so I thought I was doing. He had the measure of me, however. His smile remained. That only irritated me more, and had me straining to show nothing at all in my expression.

'Any particular car?' he asked me.

I shrugged.

'Some make or model?'

'An AC,' I said immediately, because that was the first name that came to mind.

'An Aceca?'

It was the fastest and priciest, and I thought he could only be laughing at me, through the demure smile.

'Not necessarily,' I told him.

'But maybe?'

'Or an Ace,' I said.

It was the middle model of the three. I had read an article in *Autocar* about it some months back.

More than anything, I didn't want his selecting for me a car's aptness, and his presuming to know my fancies better than I did myself. It irked me that he should so perfunctorily prejudge the matter.

'It's good to have hopes,' he said. 'Aims.'

'Is it?' I replied.

He nodded.

'When you're young,' he said. 'When you're – flexible. It's important, Ralph, to know what you want. What you want to get out of life. What it can give you – '

'Are we talking,' I countered, 'about the long term or the short?'

I preferred him to know that I wasn't a wholesale fool. But the question must only have confirmed his verdict on me.

'I can see you in one,' he said. 'Driving it.'

The remark, I assured myself, was a miscalculation, and a bad one. The person he was talking to was a year off twenty-one, not half that age. Did he really think I could be taken in so easily?

In the days afterwards, though, the less I tried to consider the matter, the more difficult the business became, until I swear my mind's eye was seeing a low, round-tailed AC two-seater turning every street corner, gears changing and six cylinders revving, trailing in its slipstream – along with the pufflets of exhaust – notice of glamour and, I deduced, unremitting fulfilment.

*

Fleur didn't reappear. I wondered if it was possible that she had somehow failed Chetwynd's expectations of her, and after her period of probation he had decided against including her in our number?

I considered getting in touch, taking the trip out to Rosslyn Hill. But she hadn't given me her address, and even after the minutes I'd spent with her in the café – minutes of such high emotion – I didn't feel entitled. I hadn't understood her reason for being out so late, walking these streets long after dark and directing herself from the mews lane to that empty diner, in Hopperland-cum-Marylebone.

I didn't have the courage finally, confronted with all the mystery of another person's life. I shied away from actual

contact with the complexities. Perhaps I simply didn't want
to run the risk of being excluded again, as had happened in the
café, however unconsciously done on her part. I had a young
man's pride, but also – what I didn't appreciate at the time –
a naïve young man's stupidity in plenty.

*

C. telephoned me here, at the house, on Sunday when
Gilbert was in. It was only by good luck that I reached
the telephone first.

I think I was shocked to hear him more than
anything. I couldn't make myself sound in any way
relaxed. I told him it wasn't at all convenient to
speak just then. He told me we had to speak some
time very soon.

'What about?'

'About what's making you unhappy.'

I couldn't have denied I was unhappy.

'You must remember who your friends are, Fleur.'

I don't know why I then replied so irritably.

'Everyone thinks *they* know best for me – '

This wasn't how I had envisaged our conversation,
not in the least.

I asked him, 'Why have you rung?'

'I knew you were upset.'

'How could you know that?'

'You should hang on a while longer, Fleur.'

'I don't think it's *your* place – '

'Your unhappiness distresses me. Very much.'

'Thank you,' I said, 'but – '

'What's unforgivable is that people should be capable
of causing distress. Wantonly, callously. Especially
when their public persona is quite a different one.'

'I can't,' I said, 'talk to you. Not just now.'

'You are a woman of conscience, Fleur. Of integrity.
I know you well enough to understand what your
virtues are. Never let them be compromised.'

I realised I was going to cry. I said 'goodbye'. I replaced the receiver on the cradle as undramatically as I could.

'Who was that?' were Gilbert's first words afterwards.

'Father,' I said.

He didn't look as if he believed me. I didn't care, not really. At that same moment I was looking down into the dustbin. I thought I was going to choke up my lunch, right there in front of him.

I'm falling apart. This is the beginning of the end.

*

One afternoon Howard Kimble, on his way back to the estate agents where he dealt in such very desirable residences, drove me directly from Kensington to Randolph Square.

I found he was quizzing me long and hard about life at 'The Circus', and earlier at 'Underwood'. I told him most of what I knew, but it clearly wasn't all that he was wanting to hear.

'Why don't you ask the others?' I put it to him, in part to shake him off me.

'They'd let slip something to Chetwynd. I know that you'll be – discreet.'

'How can you be so sure?'

'Oh . . . I just know. Experience tells me.'

At last he came to the point.

'Have you any evidence?' he asked. 'Of goings-on?'

'What sort?'

'Immorality.'

'Immoral goings-on?'

'You know what I mean, Ralph.'

'I do?'

'Is he running a brothel?'

I stared at him.

'Of course,' he said, 'it's being done much more subtly. Nothing so crass.'

'Are you asking me a question?' I said. 'You sound as if you're stating a fact – '

'Do you think it's possible, then?'

'*You* seemed to be sure about it – '

'I *am*. But I need corroboration.'

'Evidence?'

'Yes.'

'Why?'

'To be able to make a charge.'

'Why, though? If you've to hunt around for the evidence – '

He smiled, at my incomprehension.

'Chetwynd is a very slippery chap.'

'But immoral?'

'Running a brothel is the least of it. But it'd be a start. A spring-board. You see? We charge him with that, hold him for a while – '

'What have I got to do with it? I haven't been there as long as them – '

'Seventeen months isn't a long time?'

'Not compared with the others, though – '

'Wriggling out of it, Ralph?'

'No.'

'*You*'ve less to hide, I should say. And you've less reason to think you're dependent on him.'

'What?'

'Get up and go – '

'I don't understand.'

'D'you really not?'

His smile was wholly sceptical.

'It's not never-never land, Ralph. Nothing comes free in this life. Everything costs, it has a price label attached. But I don't need to tell *you* that, do I? You're a smart enough lad, I'm sure.'

I could tell from his tone of voice he certainly didn't believe his last words.

'You can start again. Your life – your real life: your adult life, I mean – it's just beginning. This'll just be a little memory soon.'

'What will? Being at "The Circus"? Or having to go through all this questioning?'

'Everything. The whole of it. It'll be immaterial.'

'But – ' I persevered. ' – but it's not immaterial to you at this moment, is it? It means a lot to you, a hell of a lot – '

'It's my job.'

'So, what *is* your job?'

'I – I'm an investigator.'

'A private dick?'

I meant my delivery to sound sneering.

'No. For the police.'

As I was about to speak, the final climactic word brought me up short.

'*What?*'

'Police. But we don't need to go into all that, do we?'

'Why – why the hell are you telling me? If that's what you really are?'

'Oh, it's a risk. A very calculated risk. I just hope – for both our sakes – you don't let me down. Land us both in the drink.'

'How? How could I do that?'

'By not assisting me, Ralph.'

'To do what?'

'Help me and bring our friend to book.'

'Why? So you get promoted, I suppose?'

'So Chetwynd receives the onus of justice he so richly deserves. His fate – his meet end – after dispensing it to so many others – '

'And what's in it for me?'

'Ah, now we're getting there! Now we're coming to it, my lad – '

'You think I haven't got a conscience?' I asked.

'Oh, indeed I do. Establishing so – that's the point of the exercise, is it not?'

'"Exercise"?' I repeated.

Moving into the inside lane on King's Road, Kimble changed his tack.

'I hear that Fleur hasn't been seen at the house for – two weeks, is it? Three?'

'Three.'

'I gather she's upset.'

'What?'

'Disturbed.'

'Who told you that?'

'I don't have to be told, Ralph.'

'Disturbed about what?'

'Chetwynd would know.'

'Why Chetwynd?'

'Could there've been a falling out?'

'Why? What on earth about?'

'Or, might I suggest, something he chose to disclose to her has unsettled her. She has no desire at any rate to find herself back at "The Circus". That is *one* source of her unhappiness – '

'So . . .' My head was a welter of thoughts. '. . . how can *I* possibly "assist" you?'

'Are you offering to assist me?'

'Christ – '

'It *would* be worth your while.'

'You really think you've got me sized up, don't you?'

'I have a job of work to do, Ralph. And soon. Loyalties to – '

' – to yourself?'

' – to the truth, Ralph.'

I shook my head at him. But he continued.

'You're too cynical, too modern a chap for concepts like "truth", is that it?'

I was still shaking my head, staring down at my feet beneath the dashboard.

'*Is* Fleur coming back?' I asked him.

'I doubt it. Doubt it very much.'

'What did he say to her?'

'I don't know.'

I glanced over at him.

'Honestly,' he said. 'But it must have been as insinuatingly done as ever. Knowing the bastard – '

'Chetwynd?'

'Who else?'

'How "insinuatingly"?'

'A matter of suggestion, but lethal with it. Something she doesn't have the proof – yet – to deny. But also something she knows she *can't* really deny. Her heart's got there before the head, but the proof of the two will be overwhelming.'

I let out a deep, plaintive sigh. Perhaps it was more eloquent than words would have been, however. Because how could I have conveyed to him by the mere vehicle of language all that I was feeling – my anger on Fleur's account and my pity for her, my past gratitude to Chetwynd and all my continuing unsureness about him, the history of my unwillingness to consider the subject of myself, to confront the nebulous zones – at their worst, black holes – where personal ethics are in perpetual abeyance.

*

Father is the only person I have left.

I've let him be alone too long. But we have less and less to say to one another. I don't recognise our old furnishings in the flat. His address book contains names and telephone numbers I don't know anything about.

We've been walking about the gardens. I feel as old as he, and nearly as frail. I can't decide if my lassitude is the 'fluey sort, or purely exhaustion.

Father and I have sat a few times in the mezzanine lounge, at a distance from the glass window but able to watch activities in the swimming pool beneath us. It's shot with bright underwater lights and looks other-worldly, emerald-green and seductive. Ralph is there still, quite calmly going about his work. The first time I saw him, the coffee spilt out of my cup. I haven't the heart to confront him. It's over, all that, over. Quite over.

Then . . .

But it's impossible. Isn't it?

I'm looking down from the window of Father's sitting-room. A car stops at the kerb. A fancy Salmson thing, Father's voice is saying at my shoulder. It's C.'s manner of walking, with the knees a little raised. He makes quickly for the canopy and the doors into the vestibule. I spill my coffee again; it drips on to the window sill.

'It's all right,' Father says, 'it's all right, nothing that can't be cleaned up.'

'I'm getting so clumsy,' I tell him. 'I'm sorry, I don't know — I don't know why — '

I saw them through the mezzanine glass, just the two of them. Fleur and Chetwynd in the empty lounge. She was in tears. He tried to touch her arm, but she stepped back. He tried again; momentarily there was contact, but she shook him off. A pot plant toppled off the top of a table. She turned and ran. Chetwynd watched, considered, then got down on to his knees and started to pick up the dirt.

*

[At this point a page of loose-leaf paper has been torn in half; only the bottom portion survives.]

I waited until nightfall. Until the car had gone. Then Father rang downstairs for a taxi. I hugged him as I was leaving, which seemed to surprise him. The lights in the corridor made the flat seem dingy by comparison. I hadn't noticed while I'd been inside. I blinked in the coral glow. A door opened, and from another flat a couple emerged, dressed for the opera. They looked back at me and smiled. I smiled at them, stupidly, like someone who only dreams about life.

*

I stood under one of the pergolas to watch her leave.

Outside the block she looked up, at the windows on its east

side. A good number were lit; she gazed up but there were too many for her to be able to work out which ones she was looking for. She pulled her jacket about herself and seemed to shiver. I stepped forward. At that moment, though, the taxi driver leaned across and opened the back door of his cab. She hurried towards it, with relief to be gone; she ducked her head getting in and pulled the door very hard shut behind her.

'Ever heard of someone called Chetwynd?' Gilbert asks.

My breath is sucked out of me.

'Lex said he came to see a friend of his for an appointment.'

'Why – why should – '

'This bloke's as rich as Croesus, he guesses, but he'd never heard of him. He asked Lex, and I was to ask you, if *you* knew.'

'Why – why me?'

'If you'd seen his photo anywhere. In a magazine.' He nods to a pile. 'Christina wouldn't know about anything like that – '

'"Chetwynd"?'

'Well? Have you?'

'I . . .'

He looks at me so intensely, his eyes trail me. They want to fell me, to see me down. They want to slash me, to shred me like a ripper.

*

One night – or, rather, in the early hours of one morning – I returned to the lodging-house to find my door standing open and the room in chaos. My neighbour was sifting through the debris on the floor – ripped bedding, slashed clothes, torn books, shards of mirror glass, a grated lampshade. The bed had been overturned and the mattress gutted with a knife. The uppers of a pair of shoes had been separated from their soles. A fist or a knee had gone through the cheap reproduction paintings I'd bought. Even the contents of the ash-tray had been flung on to the floor.

I couldn't believe what my eyes were seeing.

A neighbour mentioned a car parked outside on the road. A 'fancy' sports car. It hadn't been there long.

What did the chaos mean? That I wasn't to meddle? That there were ways and methods, and I'd already forgotten the debts I was owing?

But loyalty to whom?

And why should the lesson have been insisted upon with such venom?

*

I heard Gilbert's car draw up in the road outside. That was unusual, since at night he drives in by the back lane. He doesn't put the car in the garage, of course, when we have a dinner engagement; or when he's going out again later by himself. He's very particular about such things, and has never parked in the road for the simple sake of laziness. Did that mean he had another engagement tonight? It was already ten past nine.

I have to prepare myself mentally for his arrival, to find an attitude for him. I *am* particular about that. It's easiest standing in front of a mirror pulling my hair back into shape. I can strike a pose and see how it looks. The glass is as cold and impassive a scrutineer as my husband ever is.

I returned to my chair and sat down. I picked up the magazine I'd been reading. I turned some pages. My ears were open for the sound of him. The sounds I know by heart.

The striking of his steel tips on the pavement. The click of the gate. His footfalls on the path and then on the steps. Five steps. The jutting of his key into the lock of the front door.

But it didn't happen, any of it.

Instead I heard heels, the sort I wear. The high

heels. Running. And possibly, just before the running
– but I can't be sure now – a cry. A single cry.
It sounded to me like the low, suffering bark of a
dog, and maybe it only registered subconsciously, or
maybe I have come to imagine it.

I continued to sit, turning the pages of the magazine. I turned them more quickly, then started to
riffle my way to the end. Beautiful women in pristine
fashions in immaculate settings.

At last I got up to look. I switched off the lamp by
the wall and pulled back the curtain. The Jag was
still in its usual place outside the house. The driver's
door was open, on the road side. Gilbert seemed to be
supine on the seat. I saw the shoulder of his coat, and
his arm up on the steering wheel. I thought he must
be leaning out to investigate under the chassis. But
I couldn't see any movement.

I went downstairs and opened the front door. I
paused for several moments. Then – I don't know
what caused me to do it – I ran down the flight of
steps and along the path. I threw open the gate. I
hesitated. Then I ran out on to the pavement, on to
the road and round to the open door.

His right arm and hand hung straight out.

His throat had been sliced through. I saw the
severed windpipe.

Blood dripped on to the road. There was already a
pool of it gleaming on the tarmacadam.

I screamed. Screamed and screamed. People appeared from somewhere. They lifted his body. I freed
myself from someone's arms, and stumbled forward
to help them. Blood still flowed from his throat, from
the ragged hole. It had soaked his coat, his shirt; the
leather of the seat was sodden with it. 'Stop it,' I told
them, 'stop the blood!' It never seemed to end, the
constant oozing of blood from its source. His eyes
were wide open and fixed with terror. 'Close his
eyes,' I shouted, 'close his eyes! Please, please – '

They were wanting to take me away, but I couldn't leave, not even when my knees buckled and I had to be held up. Supported, I stayed there, until the ambulance screeched to a halt with its bell ringing. The drivers couldn't close his eyes either, though, and he saw it all, in its horrific brazen detail. His left arm had worked its way under the horn dish at the centre of the steering wheel and had to be gently extricated while the body was pulled forward on the seat and rotated. They laid him on a stretcher although it was too late to do anything to save him. The police who'd arrived were taking charge. They wanted me to go inside, back into the house, Gilbert's house. The little lake of blood on the road reflected the blue of the flashing emergency lights, and looked – it occurred to me – like something molten on a furnace floor. I was promised some tablets to 'help' me, if I would just allow myself to be taken inside. But I must have had a harpy's strength in me.

Two of the policemen were examining a shiny object. When all the blood was wiped from it, it was revealed as a steel scalpel. I heard a neighbour's voice say it had been recovered from the road. The policemen let me see, but not touch. It resembled a surgeon's implement, and I duly said nothing. What was the point?

Gilbert was dead. They kept the fact from me for as long as they could, until the ambulance doors were closed and the engine had been started.

Our life together, it was finished, it was over.

*

'There's still a file on it,' Liz said. 'It was considered such a shocking crime. For a man with his professional connections. Apparently they found the heel of a woman's shoe, not far away, in the camber of the road. An elegant heel, thinnish, covered with the skin of the shoe: a certain shade of lizard, a fashionable French lavender.'

. . . A younger woman's shoe. Or a woman of an age where she's capable of bearing a child, let's say: and it's thought of lesser significance if she's required to 'lose' it, that life she's carrying. Talked into not giving the child birth, that is, although it may be against her principles, or anyway against her better judgement.

Liz pulled herself up in the deck chair.

'The police, I expect they were seeking a male culprit for their crime. My father was strong and healthy after all.'

. . . But a woman – one he couldn't immediately recognise from Harley Street, whom he was seeing in these quite different circumstances – she would certainly have had the advantage over him of surprise: with a stolen scalpel secreted in her sleeve.

. . . And thus Death had come storming out of the world of too-knowing adults – of wads of hush-hush banknotes – of a razor-sharp scalpel and snicking surgical scissors and a rubber mask of anaesthetic gas in the whitest, whitest room in the whole of Harley Street, West One –

TWENTY-FOUR

When I got back, I knew something was wrong in the house. I smelt more than ourselves – damp wool, perhaps, soap on the skin. There was such a numbing silence, I knew the unexplained presence had been and gone, and that I was alone.

I walked upstairs with no more trepidation than at any time in the last few years, since things had become complicated between Gilbert and myself. I noticed that the door of his study stood a little ajar. Since he'd died I hadn't been able to bring myself to go in: its darkness was forbidding, excluding. I stood by the banister rail. Reflected rain-runs from the staircase window pitted the walls with excrescences and carbuncles on the rich man's slubbed silk paper. The house felt like a depository of coldness and that eerie liquid silence, of rain striking glass. I could hear the blood pulsing inside my head and singing in my ears. My breath was caught in my chest, bundled tight into a ball that made my bones ache holding it in. The rainy coruscations on the walls started to drop like sun spots in front of my eyes, flare traces on a pale moonlit ground of vague, floral arabesques. The curdy blue light lay on the surfaces like provocative satin.

I crossed the gallery and pushed open the door of the study. The unrecognisable odour was clearest to me there, standing in the entrance. When I turned on the light I was already – in part – prepared.

The operation had been attended to very tidily. I wasn't even aware until I reached the desk and noticed a white index card lying on the carpet, under the shadow of the desk's top. The drawers had all been closed, but when I pulled the handle of the top one it slid open. The drawers were always but always kept locked. Gilbert would never have left an index card lying on the carpet; I simply knew — in my gut — that he would have spotted it, something so vital to himself. In his study he was a most conscientiously orderly man, forever re-shuffling papers and aligning them exactly: on the desk the papers, notepads, pens and blotter at more or less precise right-angles to one another. He wouldn't have left the desk like this, I was certain. An ash-tray sat on top of the blotter and several blank index cards were casually fanned, and a propelling pencil's leads were scattered in a little pile on the leather.

I sensed that the other corners of the room had been disturbed also, but in the same subtle way. Some of the books were pulled forward of others. A Meissen figurine presented by a grateful patient stood just a little clear of a dustless square. The campaign chest which held back-copies of medical newspapers must have been moved to leave those faint secondary imprints of its castor feet on the carpet. The chintz pattern on the armchair's cushions didn't run the same way, and Gilbert wouldn't have allowed himself to sit in the chair unless they had been.

The room, I realised, had been given a thorough going-over. I couldn't believe that I wasn't more surprised, that I could be almost calm about it. And yet . . .

I dropped on to the chair on the landing outside. If there had been chaos I would have been less sure that the search had been for one specific and (to someone) most necessary purpose.

*

The evening activities seemed to have been suspended, and

there were fewer luncheons at 'The Circus' than before. I greedily snatched at any messages that were left for me at work. I couldn't connect Chetwynd with the burglary, not at all, but I felt everything had been set skew-whiff. The world generally had that sharp, bleak, too definite look it does after rain. I wouldn't admit it to myself – which was wholly typical of me – but I already missed the enveloping vagueness, the smothering hedonism of our prodigal evenings on the town: the food and the wine, the music, the warmth of the rooms, the aroma of perfume and cigars, the ready and effortless transportation through quiet night streets.

It so happened that I spotted him, Clive Melchett, walking out of a pub in one of the little Chelsea squares I went home by. I had a forewarning as the heads of the drinkers at the tables on the terrace, under the trees, turned to look at him. Crushingly, heartlessly, despair-makingly handsome as ever.

I hadn't seen him for several weeks; we hadn't coincided at 'The Circus'. This evening he was accompanied by an elderly man with a spa-clinic complexion, coiffed hair tinted evenly grey, and a camelhair coat thrown over his shoulders, who fixed a proprietorial claw-like clutch on his arm with a liver-marked hand. Clive did a double-take, then stopped – even though his companion was attempting to urge him forward – and smiled, a little awkwardly. Maybe his embarrassment compelled him into the disclosure. It was the first thing he said, even before we exchanged names or could ask one another how we were doing.

Had I heard about Fleur Simmons' husband, the doctor?

Immediately I was wary, but also intensely eager to know.

'"Her husband"?' I repeated, as if I might only be establishing for us the fact of her marital status.

'It's a real horror story.'

His companion stood glowering at me and breathing heavily. The man's hand still held Clive's arm, the fingers wrinkled the light plaid cloth; his plans had taken no account of familiar strangers such as myself cluttering their path. He tried to move them both forward, but Clive resisted.

My eyes must have been so full of curiosity, and alarm possibly, that he would have been unmovable. He could get his own back on me for this ambush, equally unexpected to both of them.

'Murdered.'

'What?'

'Throat cut.'

'*What?*'

'In front of the house. Carved up. Some razor-man.'

'Jesus Christ – '

His companion slightly inclined his head at the invocation.

'When?'

'Nine or ten days ago.'

'Where did it – '

'In front of the house.'

'In Hampstead?'

My instinctive reaction was of the plain incongruity of it all.

'Yes. Yes, I think it was there.'

'Jesus Christ – '

'We really must – ' The man spoke in an airy voice, hitching his coat up on his narrow shoulders with his other hand.

'Where,' I started again, 'where is she?'

Clive shook his head. 'No one knows. She's gone off evidently. Who can blame her?'

I stood watching them as they made their departure, walking together in step. Clive automatically moved his head from side to side, for passers-by to have the pleasure of his profile, while his companion – steering them both towards a white Austin Princess – kept his quite steady and fixed ahead. A few coloured lights, left over from some long-gone Christmas celebration, hung in a tree, but the effect was oddly cheerless. Beery smells and laughter wafted about me.

The car doors slammed shut and the side-lights were switched on. The car's high grille resembled an open jaw, with cruel steel teeth bared.

It was a predator's world.

The house in Hampstead was not only unlit but empty. There

were no curtains at any of the windows to hide prying forms.

An estate agent's notice fixed to the storm door with drawing pins announced that the property was for sale.

Her neighbours couldn't put me right. They eyed me up and down suspiciously. Why should I be interested in an empty house – or in such a ghoulish story? I didn't look like a medical man's type of acquaintance at all. What was the fate of a young widow and her daughter to me?

They called her 'Mrs Tobin', not 'Simmons'. She had left the district, that was all they knew. Naturally, they replied, she had been distressed, how could that not have been so?

*

I had to supply Howard Kimble with lists of guests' names, and to discover what I could – in the course of idle conversation with Chetwynd's protégé(e)s – of the frequency of contact between both parties. I was required to supply information in advance of Chetwynd's business programme: the times of day or evening when he expected to be absent from the house.

Less straightforward was locating Chetwynd's keys.

The solution in the end was spontaneous, although I had unwittingly helped set it up for myself.

At a group lunch at least a fortnight before, and prior to my room being burgled, Chetwynd had been discussing exercise with our parliamentarian Plynn-Gore. He suggested that Chetwynd come to use the swimming pool at the RAC Clubhouse as his guest: he would ring to arrange a time. When the MP and the others had gone, I ventured to bring up the subject with Chetwynd. I told him he could use Randolph Square's facilities if it could be timed to coincide with my being on duty when my supervisor was absent. (Our pool was actually reserved solely for use by the residents in the blocks and their guests. I didn't think I could do myself any harm – and it was a paltry way of having Chetwynd owe me a favour for once – by turning a blind eye.) Chetwynd nodded at my proposal, and appeared genuinely interested. He was in the habit of visiting an osteopath regularly to have him straighten out a mis-alignment in his hip bones, but he felt the need of something else between these sessions of manipulation: massage wasn't somehow *active* enough.

In the same week of my 'arrangement' with Kimble, Chetwynd telephoned me out of the blue at Randolph Square. With that menacing charm of his, he held me to what I'd said. I complied. We fixed on a time the next day, and he duly arrived, walking rather stiffly.

He had come once before as a guest, after I stopped chauffeuring, so he knew the drill. Managing to look cheerful – although the impulse had quite left me of late, after Kimble's confidences – I handed him two towels and a pair of rubber sandals. I took his valuables from him – wallet, steel oyster watch, keys – and placed them in a locker drawer and handed him the single key with its number attached on the disc. It was as he was undressing in the changing-room that something so simple, so novelettish, occurred to me. My conversation with Kimble had been occupying my thoughts for the couple of days since we'd last spoken. Now an opportunity – melodramatic admittedly, 'B' film-ish – presented itself. But this existence had all along been unlikely, as I'd been appreciating too well of late: a film noir escapade of supper-clubs, dance music, cigarette smoke, sheeny taffeta and high heels, car headlights shining on wet roads, so-so scripted lines. Everything fitted into the picture that was meant to: nothing was occurring that hadn't, by fate or by some other mechanism, been intended to. There were no pure accidents in this story of ours.

We had doubles for the drawer keys. I'd always felt they rather defeated the purpose in one sense, but evidently in the early days the wrath of regulars who mislaid or lost keys had made this additional security very necessary. All I had to do was unlock the drawer in question and remove from the contents Chetwynd's keys in their leather pouch.

Some I recognised – those for three of the cars, the front door of the house, storm doors, back door, terrace doors. Brief-case and luggage keys were kept separately. Three others were left on their clips.

All it required were three mint bars of the medicated soap

we supplied in the showers. I lightly dampened them, then I set each of the keys into the white soap, making sure the impression was sharp and clear, every indentation exact. Before Chetwynd emerged from the changing-room, I had wiped the keys clean, replaced them on the links in the same order in which I had taken them, and returned the pouch to the drawer. I wrapped the soap in tissue and deposited the three cakes in a cool place, at the back of a cupboard. I proceeded to busy myself by untying a net bag of the larger towels, freshly laundered on the premises, and arranging them on the shelves.

I felt as smooth, as dextrously furtive, as any Culver City or Hacienda Heights private investigator in Hollywood's hey-day.

Kimble agreed to call round and take the bars of soap from me when I came off duty. He said a colleague could make up keys, overnight, and he'd get them over to me, here at Randolph Square, for first thing in the morning. Then, he said – I knew what I had to attend to next, didn't I, he was trusting me to do my damnedest.

With access to the study, I removed correspondence and accounts books. I took them to a bathroom to read through. I couldn't always be certain what was important and what not, but the tone of many letters left little room for misinterpretation:
Appreciative notes of thanks (and assurances of all prompt future attention, et cetera) to 'clients' on whose behalf Chetwynd had recently sold articles as requested, and courteous, not bashful enquiries as to their state of mind (presumed, rather, *peace* of mind) now that they were re-established on a surer financial footing than of yore –
Polite but noticeably non-committal replies to those from whom he had bought in the past and who wrote to suggest that he might be interested in making further acquisitions –
Purportedly after-thought letters to the same (above), in which Chetwynd offered to inspect and value, not the objects suggested by their owners but those which his own eye had previously picked out as likely to appeal to certain prospective vendees –

Curt correspondence with dealers to whom he sold, reminding them that he had contacts on the Continent with whom he frequently did business and who had a more trusting opinion of his valuation methods –

Extremely dry, technical letters outlining terms for short- and longer-term loans offered in the most discreet fashion and tailored to the client's personal requirements –

Several hand-written, self-excusing replies to correspondents in embarrassed circumstances (or, most probably, to their wives or other kin), who complained of a lack of 'understanding'/'patience'/'sympathy' or 'compassion'/'reasonableness' or 'practicality'/'straightforwardness' or 'fidelity to his word'/ 'decency' or 'gentlemanliness' in his dealings with them –

Instructions to financial agents to demand, either with the issue of a penultimate verbal reminder by telephone or immediately and 'vigorously' and 'by quite explicit personal communication', overdue payment from X or Y or Z –

I had three trawling sessions in all. They were fraught with hazard, but on each occasion I had a clear run of ninety minutes to two hours to sift through what the desk drawers (those which I could unlock) yielded. The picture that emerged from the paper-work was an increasingly unattractive one. I became more and more curious to uncover all I might, and my initial guilt was replaced by a no less intemperate sense of exculpation.

With each haul of incriminating evidence, Chetwynd forfeited more of even the most basic articles of respect.

TWENTY-FIVE

Now it's really over. I can't believe I've had the courage to leave. But all the options have really been taken from me.

On one of the last days my neighbour Mrs Sugarman drew me aside. A young man had been spotted hanging about in the road. She'd seen him herself, she'd stood watching from the shadows at the back of her dining-room.

Young. Fair-ish. With a bicycle.

I said that I really had no idea, no idea at all . . . I don't know if she believed me or not. I smiled, tepidly, but didn't wait to talk with her any longer.

She meant Ralph. How did he discover where I live? And why should he have come, if not to satisfy his curiosity? Where does his curiosity begin and end, what are the lengths he'll take it to?

But why stand outside — why allow himself to be seen? She was quite definite, Mrs Sugarman. With a bicycle, and fair-haired. She tried to pink me with those unsweetest of eyes, but I wouldn't let her.

'A *young* man. Quite strongly built.'

No, no, *no*.

The two are fixed in my mind, in spite of myself. The disturbances in the room/the observing stranger on

the pavement. He must have followed me, that's all he can have done.

What am I *supposed* to think, for Holy God's sake?

*

For Liz now the memory was as constant as it had ever been.

'My mother threw some clothes into a suitcase, slammed the door of the house behind us, and off we went in the Jaguar. The police had gone over it for fingerprints and I suppose it was still meant to be under wraps, or whatever the expression is, but my mother can't have cared. We left one evening. She was a crazy driver, and on the quiet unlit roads down in Sussex she went way over the white lines in the middle, on to the other side. I sat in the front, beside her. She'd scrubbed the seats herself, although probably she shouldn't have. But they were a deep claret red anyway, so the blood wasn't so evident on the leather as it might have been. She sat on a cushion, and grabbed the wheel tightly. Sometimes she seemed to be flat up against it, at other times it was as if she was trying to push the wheel away from her – and herself right into the back of the seat.

'It was the journey to end them all. Rabbits got caught in the headlights' tracks, owls swooped low and towards us and only missed us by inches sweeping over the roof of the car, moths and insects were splattered all over the windscreen. It was too late to hear anything on the radio, and she snatched at the button so hard the top part came away in her hand. The corners were worst – the tyres slithered about and the brakes squealed. I kept thinking she was going to lose control, that she wouldn't be able to hang on to the steering wheel.

'It was terrible, all of it, but I can't remember being frightened, only fascinated. By her behaviour. Because she wasn't speaking. By the violent motion. By wondering how much faster we could go without having an accident. It was an adventure; and we were together; and we were away from the place where the dreadful thing had happened which I couldn't quite get my brain to engage with. I asked her where we were going, and she could only say, "Wait and see". Not unkindly: she just meant it literally. She wasn't hiding anything from me. I'd have to wait and see because *she* didn't know yet either.

'By two or three o'clock she was so tired, she had to stop. We roared into the yard of a small hotel beside the road from Ashford to Hythe. I went back to it years afterwards, and the owner still remembered us. He'd come to the door in his dressing-gown and suspected the worst. I couldn't blame him, what would anyone have thought? Two pastiche runaways?'

She sat shaking her head at the madness, the lunacy, of the recollection, as if it couldn't really have happened.

'For several days we drove about. We must have kept changing direction. We drove west, to Dorset or so, and then north, maybe up to Gloucestershire. We could have gone on to Wales, or the Midlands, to Evesham in its Vale, but my mother started to tire – *really* tire. She was exhausted – and the crazy resolve seemed to leave her. Maybe she heard something on the radio, because I saw her from the window of our hotel bedroom one evening: sitting out in the car with the aerial extended, turning the channel button. She sat in the driver's seat for half an hour or so – I actually thought she was going to start the engine, rev up and take off and leave me. But she didn't. She got out, closed the door very firmly without slamming it, and walked back. Everyone in that hotel – we were somewhere near Cheltenham, on a steep hill – they seemed to be eyeing us with suspicion, so maybe we were now newsworthy and our names and descriptions had been circulated.

'I never talked about it afterwards, and my mother wouldn't discuss any of that terrible time with me. Any of that craziness.'

*

I did receive my reward, and Kimble dropped the keys into my hand.

It was a car, as I had been told it would be.

An AC.

A second- or third-hand 2-litre two-door saloon.

Not an Aceca, not an Ace. Rather a cumbersome affair indeed, with a two-piece windscreen and rear-window and front-opening driver's and passenger's doors. But even so with an Aceca-sized

engine, and a machine far beyond my dreams, not withstanding
rust spots.

I realised at once that I was going to have to explain it away
to everyone I knew.

He led me out into the street. I lowered my eyes to the
key-ring. A pad of green leather carrying the emblem of the
marque. On embossed and coloured metal. Art deco-like initials
inside a closed circle.

I couldn't think what to say. At the same time – I appreciate
now when I try to recall – I was managing very well to forget
the stages of the story which had brought me to this point.
All that concerned me was the car, my having the keys, the
embarrassment of gratitude. I doubt if I even had any prospect
in my head of what I might do with it and where I might go.

There had been no more summonses from 'The Circus' – no
entertainments were taking place there or up in town – so I
had time, far too much time, to kill.

Not infrequently I drove up Hampstead way. Whenever I
went, there was no sign of the Jaguar parked outside, or
anything equivalent. The 'For Sale' bill had been removed,
the house appeared to be in darkness, and the positioning of
the curtains at the windows didn't alter. The metal gate that led
to the footpath was never closed; in the wind its latch handle
rattled against the fixed catch on the gatepost.

Kimble didn't contact me in the interlude and I hadn't the
nerve to visit Kensington or even to get in touch with any
of the old set. I cut myself off from that life. I drove around
London instead, up to Highgate and Elstree and Bushey Heath
in the north and west, just drove and drove.

                              *

By special delivery I received an envelope at Randolph Square.
I recognised Chetwynd's handwriting from the address. Inside
was a short letter of commiseration. He'd been very sorry to
hear from Mitchell Ogilvie, who'd picked up on the grapevine
. . . I was even more astonished to find, attached to the back
of the letter, a cheque for the sum of one hundred pounds and

payable to myself, 'to help put things straight' with my landlord for the burglar's work.

I could have replied, but I didn't know what to say. Either the letter and money were an act of extreme hypocrisy: or all along I had been wrong in my suppositions about who had caused the damage. Was it likely that Chetwynd would have done such a deed himself? Was he stricken now by conscience? Or did he truly know nothing about it?

If not Chetwynd, or a hired hand, then who? One of the others? Kimble, meaning to apply some pressure? Or a perfect stranger to me?

What had Kimble's talk of brothels meant? Had he detected some disposition in myself for, of all things, moral rectitude?

If only I could have raced ahead, to read of what was happening from the future, how I would have read a book –

*

Less than four months after I received the gift of it, with my Kensington life over, I sold the car. I doubt if I got a fair price. The garage owner kept a close eye on me from the showroom while the car was gone over, and when he absented himself I guessed that he was on the telephone, making enquiries to his source about recently stolen AC saloons. But the following day the sale was finalised, and the money was paid, on a cheque. I left the garage with relief, but after two or three hundred yards I could feel the money burning against my chest. A cock crowed twice. I sensed every pair of eyes I passed turned upon me, that the situation was perfectly understood by them because my crimes were branded on my face. The heat rose from my chest to my face and my scalp; my back ran cold with sweat. The hardness of concrete through the soles of my shoes on Pelham Street was indescribable.

*

Selling the car only compounded my guilt. I couldn't get my mind emptied of what had happened, what I'd let myself become involved with. I missed the distraction of speed I'd had when I went out driving. I felt weighted to the ground now, on lead legs; all my actions and thoughts seemed to be slow motion.

I'd heard no more from Kimble. I'd done my bit, and received my reward. I'd had no 'explanation' of what it all amounted to. It occurred to me that the only person who could expiate my guilt would be the one who had helped to cause it.

I went to Scotland Yard in person – one afternoon I simply rolled up at the doors. I asked for 'Mr Kimble' – he hadn't told me his rank – at the front desk.

A forehead crumpled.

A register was consulted.

I was asked to repeat the name.

A second register was consulted.

'Kimble?' Was I sure about the name?

'Quite sure,' I said.

Might I be confusing it with something else?

'Oh no. Definitely not.'

An officer?

Yes, an officer.

A telephone call was made, someone was spoken to. The receiver was handed to me. I waited a while listening to silence. Then the voice at the other end told me, there was nobody of that name either working in the building or employed by the Metropolitan police force.

Why did I want to speak to this person?

I was vague in my reply.

'My car was stolen,' I said. 'Mr Kimble – he was dealing with it.'

Papers were rustled at the other end of the line. I heard several grunts.

'He says he's an estate agent. That's his ploy.'

'"Ploy"?'

'His alibi.'

'Alibi for what?'

'Discovering things about people.'

'Which people might these be?'

'I – I can't – '

More pages were rustled.

'It may not have been "Kimble". The name. Maybe he wouldn't – '

It hadn't occurred to me. The silence berated me for my stupidity.

'Describe him. Can you?'

I tried. But when I gave the description, it evaporated into vagueness. I could have been talking about anybody.

Without waiting for another question I very quietly replaced the receiver on the telephone, smiled apologetically at the policeman behind the desk, and turned myself for the front doors.

But if not a police officer – then who *had* he been? Might I not have expected to hear something from him since?

Chetwynd must have had enemies. Any of those would have been capable of infiltrating 'The Circus'.

Without the flimsy prop of legal sanction that I'd had, I grew more fearful in the days after my visit to Scotland Yard. The business suddenly became shapeless, with the possibility presented to me that it wasn't over, that I might be revisited, that further requests would be made of me, that my involvement might prove never-ending. I started to panic. Looking back, how absurdly easy my misdemeanour seemed, and so blithely done: if I could only have got the fuller picture into my viewing range, scanned beyond the puerile novelty of the AC with its sweeping curved radiator grille . . .

Then one of my neighbours remembered something that had slipped her mind. High heels scraping on the staircase on the day my flat was knocked about. She'd gone to her own door, opened it, heard hard breathing from the staircase as the shadowy figure descended, smelt a trace of perfume. But that was all.

That – I was starting to realise, to my intense frustration – is only ever 'all' in this life.

TWENTY-SIX

'It was the end of everything,' Liz said, 'I can see that now.'

We were sitting high in the dunes. She pulled her knees up to her chin and wrapped her arms around her calves.

'No one could pretend after that. After the screaming, the blood, the police, God knows all what.'

'"Pretend"?'

'That we had been normal. A family. Like any other family of our acquaintance. We weren't. We never had been. It was only a ruse. A farrago.'

She shook her head, staring past me, out across the bay. She hugged her legs tighter.

*

Fleur sits a little apart from the others: only noticeably so to me, I dare say. She has positioned herself so that she can hear the general conversation but at the same time look across the bay, over half a mile of wet sand towards the thin strand of silver that is the sea at its lowest ebb of the afternoon. She's wearing a white cotton dress sprigged along the hem and shoulder straps and around the waist with little yellow sunflowers. Because she wears it, the naïve, charming decoration is also sophisticated, because her manner of dressing shows how over-accoutred the other women are: Celia in her navy-and-cream cartwheel hat, Melinda in her rope espadrilles, April in domino cotton shirt and too tightly cut shorts. Fleur is simply herself, and with only the minimum of make-up her attractiveness is the freshest and purest of anyone's. But this afternoon she is quiet and introspective, as she quite often is of course, and sits bare-footed at the top of a long slide of soft dune sand with her knees up to her chin and her arms wrapped around her calves. Her hands are long and – sometimes I think – disturbingly thin. She smiles every so often at some remark spoken behind her, and she contributes her own whenever an opinion is asked of her, but she is contained as none of the others is. She even lets the sand-flies land on her knees, her ankles, her arms, she doesn't squeal as Melinda does or vex herself with them like Celia. She is thinking of other things, and I doubt if they give her much satisfaction because now and again her face acquires a gravitas: not a solemn sort, if I can distinguish, but one which composes her features to the quiescence of sleep, when she briefly forgets to smile and to play this unfailingly harmonious game they all of them play.

*

'My father was going to leave my mother,' Liz said.
'Do what?'
'Leave her.'
'But why?'
'Because of what I'd – '
She clammed up. She looked away.
'You know that?' I said. 'Or you're imagining – '
'He told me he and I were going away for a time – on a journey – that we'd come back in a while, but when we were home again things would be a little different.'
'How – "different"?'
'He didn't say. Didn't specify. But I had a feeling.'
For the first time she was smoking – a cigarillo, which seemed a quirky choice.
'I wasn't to tell my mother, so what else did I need to know really? He knew me well enough to be sure I wouldn't blurt it out. That it was a secret I was bound to keep, since I'd shown him – he thought – where my loyalties lay. But . . .'
'"But – "?'
'But once a traitor, why not again? They're not fussy. Wherever they can win the most for themselves, or make most trouble – '
'He told you what?'

'He said he would tell me what I needed to pack. When the moment came. But he had to "check up on things" first. And he kept reminding me I wasn't to discuss it with my mother.'

'Wasn't – couldn't he have meant just a holiday? A surprise holiday?'

'Oh no.' She shook her head, very positively. 'No, not that.'

'And did the moment come? To pack and go?'

'I waited. I waited and waited. But it didn't happen.'

She considered the cigarillo she was holding between her fingers.

'My father took on that preoccupied look I knew quite well – which had to do with his work – he got very far away. But I knew he hadn't forgotten. Just from certain little smiles he gave me. As if we were colluding in something very specially secret – '

'But – but it didn't happen?'

'It's the thought that counts. Isn't it?'

'I . . .'

'The principle. That we should leave. That we were to abandon my mother.'

'How – how did you feel about that?'

She blew out some smoke.

'I don't know,' she said. 'Indifferent at first. Maybe I even thought she deserved it. Then I started to wonder how it was going to affect me – practically – afterwards. I didn't really think of my mother's – discomfiture. I spent a lot of time lying on my bed looking at the ceiling, I remember. Maybe I was trying not to think too hard. About what I'd done, and what was going to happen. About my mother. About how the bits had got tangled up – fairy tales all out of order, and your bike down under the trees. Two different types of tree, in Cornwall and Hampstead. I knew the ceilings very, very well – I must've given myself neck cricks, but I don't – I don't recall – '

Her voice trailed away. She leaned back in the deck chair, cigarillo in hand, and craned her neck to look up. The sky was an imitation of summer's – the softest hue of blue, with very high strata of white feathery cloud – and yet there seemed to be a rime, like crackle-glaze, all about its edge. A cameo sky.

She drew in her breath.

'But that's not the worst of it,' she said.

'No?'

She watched the little meandering plumelet of smoke.

'You see, if she'd only finished the story . . .'

'"Story"?' I repeated. 'Which one?'

'About the soldier and the tinder box – '

'The children's story?'

'Hans Christian Andersen.'

'Why didn't she? Finish it?'

'She'd been reading it to me two nights running. Then she forgot. If it had been the first time she'd forgotten, then it wouldn't have mattered. But it had happened regularly. Too often, I decided: once too often.'

'And . . . ?'

She hesitated. She tipped the cigarillo downwards between her fingers and watched the cusp of ash drop and scatter on the grass.

'That,' she said, 'is the awkwardness.'

'How?'

She snatched at a fly.

'I told him.'

'Told who?' I asked.

'My father.'

'You "told" him?'

'That I'd seen you. That I was quite used to seeing you. On holiday, the year before last, and now in London – '

'Me?'

'Oh yes. Definitely you.'

'Why – ' I swallowed. ' – why did you say that?'

'But it was true.'

'To tell him that, though? Putting it like that? Just when he – '

She shrugged.

'Then was the time I wanted to say it.'

'You mean – it was mischief?'

'Only a part of it was.'

'You didn't know,' I said, excuse-searching, 'what the implication – what he might read into it.'

'Oh yes,' she said. 'I think I really knew quite well.'

'So it *was* – just – mischief?'

'Not really.'

'But how could – You were a child. A little girl.'

'Was I?'

'You were – what? – seven years old.'

'But I wanted to hear about the soldier who found the tinder box – and fell for the princess in the copper castle. *You* wouldn't let me, though.'

'*I* wouldn't?'

'Somehow you were to do with it.'

She inhaled on the cigarillo – then slowly blew out smoke. 'Why my mother couldn't concentrate. You became the reason why she couldn't.'

'But – '

'When I thought of the soldier – who was going to be hung on the gallows for loving the princess and stealing her away at night on the back of a giant dog – I don't know why but *you* became superimposed on top. By association, from Cornwall. Your nights in the lane, and now in the street. I didn't think of one of you as separable from the other. You and the soldier *were* each other.'

I could only stare at her. I stared so long that in the end she imitated me, gawping back at me with – as one of the decade's hit songs put it – those big Bette Davis eyes. But she did it without smiling.

'Well . . . ?' she said.

'I don't know.'

'Say it.'

'But you *were* just a child.'

My reaction was only an irritant to her.

'Why can't you be more angry with me?'

'Is that what you want?' I asked her.

'It would let me know what I should be feeling.'

I was quite lost. Her eyes shrank as she watched me, as if

incredulous that I could be so stupid, so wholly insensitive to
her situation.

'Did . . .' I began again. 'The story – You heard it all in
the end?'

Then she did smile, quietly, just to herself. She nodded her
head, as if in agreement with some private opinion. More ash
dropped on to the grass.

'About the soldier,' I said.

'Yes. I know what you mean.'

'Your mother – '

'No, I never heard the end of that story,' she said. 'Whether
he was saved from the noose or not and what it had to do with
the magic tinder box.'

'There were other stories, though?'

'No,' she replied, 'there weren't many other stories. Not after
that. Not children's stories, at any rate. There were lots of little
fictions – between us, my mother and myself – but that's not
what you mean, is it?'

She duly received the stare of incomprehension it seemed
she was expecting.

'And that,' she said, 'that really – to confuse the issue – is
quite another story, isn't it?'

*

'Where to now?' I asked Liz.

'Well, I don't think I'll stay on here.'

'In Cornwall?'

As ever I failed to understand.

'England,' she said, denying herself the solace of a sigh on
my account.

'Any place in particular?'

'Somewhere warm maybe.' She nodded after she'd said it.
'Yes. Somewhere warm.'

'Has this . . .' I began. 'Has it – '

' – been useful?' she said. 'Oh yes, I think so.'

'But does it explain anything?'

'I never thought it would.'

'You didn't?'

'I'm my mother's daughter. That's what I needed to have confirmed. Before, I couldn't be quite sure.' She nodded again. 'Yes, I know now.'

*

I couldn't sleep. I got up out of bed, and went and sat by the window.

If this were a story calculated to serve its characters best, I could write – what? – that I heard faint sobs through the wall, from Liz's room next to mine. But I didn't hear sobbing, from that room or any of the others still occupied. I sat listening instead to nothing: or, if not to nothing, it was to a roaring silence that held the centre, of the house and its garden, like a turbo. In it reality and invention, truth and hypothesis, admission and concealment were endlessly promiscuous, in a night gyre.

I fell asleep, in the chill comfort of confusion, with my head resting on my arm. At dawn I woke in the other blue-hour, to the clean scraped cries of gulls, to the pristine swell of surf, supposing I'd been beached – firstly in a future, then in the past, anywhere rather than in the imbroglio of my present time, this ravelment of guilts and declarations and evasions.

*

For Liz, conscience had been tackled at last. Her eyes had lost their redness, but they looked no gentler.

During most of the journey back to London she listened to her Walkman or, for variety, she slept. With the critical revelation over, I presumed she must have no further need of the cigarillos.

For a while she drove, through Wiltshire. She sat close to the wheel and held it very tightly. She saw me looking several times and seemed displeased. But I think that very little I could have done would have given her any satisfaction at all. She preferred to be like this, I decided, hard and implacable. I'd been an echoing wall rather than a confidant, but either way my usefulness was at an end.

We stopped for tea at a Little Chef near Newbury. Now when I had convinced myself she was unchangeable, I had the unforeseen spectacle of her bursting into tears over a blackcurrant waffle which she was served by mistake but didn't return. She said nothing and retreated to the Ladies'; when she came back she had patched up the damage to her face, but still she said the minimum. Back in the car, in the passenger seat, she placed her headphones over her ears and slotted a cassette into the player. The sizzle of percussion seeped out of the foam pads. Her face set again, like plaster. She turned her profile away and looked out the side window. All there was to see was the tedium of English provincial life. The motorway verge, patch fields, smoking house-chimneys, signs to a hypermarket, pylons with some sheep cropping beneath, a poplar break. I heard her sigh, between the drum tattoos.

*

Now I remember, from that other drive down only four days before.

'I like this one,' she suddenly said, turning up the volume knob on the radio in the fascia.

It was her admission of an enthusiasm which surprised me. I only noticed what the tune was after that, and of course the choice didn't mean much to me, although I recognised it.

The Marrakesh Express.

Crosby, Stills & Nash.

The dream-train. International hippies and little old American ladies in blue.

She sang along. The call was going out, the train's ready for boarding. This was one trip she wasn't going to miss. Climb on board, destination Marrakesh . . .

*

'*Did* you love her?' she asked.

'What?'

She uncorked the little speakers from her ears.

'Couldn't you have loved her?'

'I . . .'

'I could understand my hatred then. Why I hated you so much. Why I had to suffer.'

Blaming me for that too seemed grossly unfair, after everything else. What about her father, and his plans to abandon her mother?

'You're putting me in a corner,' I began.

'For Christ's sake,' she said, 'just be honest with yourself. For once in your miserable life.'

I didn't deign to reply.

She plugged the speakers back into her ears and turned and looked the other way.

Lovers are committers, I wished I could tell her. Lovers are darers. I've always been a step or two away from where I needed to be. In 1957 I was young, I lacked confidence . . .

I watched my fingers tighten on the steering wheel.

Even if Fleur had rebuffed me . . . Maybe my life would have been a very different one after that. The fact of being rejected, as gently and pitifully as she would have done it, would have been the trial by fire. The worst would already have happened, I'd have got it over with, and if something similar were to happen again in another circumstance it couldn't ever matter in the same way . . .

I stared and stared at the stretch of motorway ahead.

That was the positive, upbeat scenario. Character is character. That's what will 'out'. Fleur's disposition had been to hope for some small measure of happiness or relief while she was suffering. Destiny had prearranged Gilbert for her, as she for him, he to torment and she to be tormented.

For a while, though, as 1958 drifted by I tried to believe I could be reclaimed by her innocence. Maybe, beneath my coy surface, I wanted something more selfish than love, to me more urgent. I wanted her to be my conscience and to forgive me. But I would have needed commitment and daring to bring myself as close: the closest I came was a café table in Marylebone High Street. It wasn't close enough, not when I was looking for her to change my existence for me.

My vocation in this life was determined by the personality I was born to have. For a coward, it's a kind and indulgent philosophy. 'I was made this way' is the paragon, the absolute of excuses. I was made to be a weak link, consistently the weakest in the chain, but also to carry on trusting that another finer purpose would be revealed to me in time, when my excuses too would simultaneously fall away, by the wayside. It might take forty, fifty years, but the point of my own existence must become, if not clear, then less obfuscated.

I could never have expected that my journey to Damascus would begin on the M4, between Junctions Twelve and Eleven in Berkshire, but fate to the end plays its cards flat against its chest.

TWENTY-SEVEN

We did go back to 'Underwood' once more as a group, but – the point being – only for the sake of an absentee, without whom our old manner of living was now over and done.

Chetwynd's beach-wrap wasn't found placed neatly on a rock, close to his bathing place – as I expected that it would have been – but thrown down anyhow on the dry sand some twenty yards from the highest point the tide would have risen to at the time of morning when he was in the habit of taking his swim. In one pocket was a carton of cigarettes and a gold lighter engraved with the linked initials AC. There were no keys. He had walked down from 'Underwood' to the beach leaving the drawing-room french windows open and unlocked.

In the dining-room at one end of the long table, a breakfast setting was laid for one. A half-grapefruit sat on a dinner plate, and beside it was a pot of Epicure marmalade. In the kitchen the bread-crock had been moved to the table in readiness; the slices of loaf for toasting, once he'd cut them, would have been placed on top of the Aga, which he used to say always made the very best toast. There was no newspaper for that day, but a copy of a Simenon novel lay face down, with covers spread, beside the crock on the table. A washed but unstarched and unironed shirt was hanging upstairs in an airing cupboard. About the floor of the master bedroom were strewn yesterday's clothes and the day before's – underpants, socks, shirts – which, Mrs Millard had told us in the days of my serving, was his natural way. A copy of a pink racing newspaper was found in the bedside-cabinet, with ink crosses marked against certain runners in races for the rest of that week. When his watch was noticed on the mantelpiece, it was still running, which meant it must have been wound up on that last morning of waking. The sash of one of the windows in the bedroom had been raised, presumably to give the place an early airing.

'What is it?' I asked the detective inspector's assistant, 'that makes such a thing happen? The tides?'

'Not in the bay. Out in the estuary, yes. It would be possible to get swept along there.'

'Are they so fast?'

'There might be a current of much colder water. You have to be very hardy to attempt it. Or foolhardy.'

'People do swim, though,' I told him. 'Quite far out. I used to watch them from the dunes, before breakfast.'

'In the summer.'

'Yes.'

'Did Mr Chetwynd swim then?'

'I believe so,' I said. 'I'd see him leave the garden sometimes.'

'In his wrap?'

'Yes. Probably when he couldn't sleep – he'd get up early – '

'How often did that happen? The sleeplessness? Do you know – ?'

'Every so often he'd say he'd had a bad night.'

'*How* often was that?'

'A few times in a month maybe.'

'Was he fit?'

'He once came to the swimming pool where I work. No, twice. He was a good swimmer – strong, easy strokes – '

'And you should know?'

'Yes. But I don't know about the cold. If that could have affected him – '

'How did he appear to you latterly?'

'Tired sometimes. Thinner.' I thought some more. I was given the time to consider. 'A bit paler. But it was a long, dreary spring – we all got that way.'

'Did he take holidays?'

'A few short ones. He'd just go off. Partly they were business. He was also talking about the West Indies. To somebody at dinner. But I don't know when that was to be. If they were firm plans even – '

'Or just dinner-party talk?'

'Possibly.'

We both nodded.

'Then what happens?' I asked. 'If they're swept away?'

'If they're swept away – ' The Welshman turned to get his bearings on the bay from the garden. 'It hasn't been the case very often – since I came here to work. We've had bodies being found up to ten miles away. Or around the headland. But not many. Although they've tended to be the able swimmers, who've over-reached themselves, or they've been hit by some freak wave, or run into a channel. One was stung to death not so long ago, by jellyfish – '

'Jesus – '

' – a great white school of the things. Like a cloud under the surface. I saw them myself – '

'Could that have happened again?'

'Well, we'll just have to wait and see about that, won't we now?'

*

It was the first time we had gathered together without Chetwynd. In a certain sense he was still here. 'Underwood' was his house, and he was the reason why we were congregated in our city clothes, with our London pallor, in what the vicar assured us was our 'grief'.

There was little we could do except stand or sit about and appear to be suffering. His body hadn't been recovered yet, although we supposed it was only a matter of time until it was. The white rooms were incongruous, I felt, when we had all taken care to bring newly dry-cleaned dark suits and dresses with us. As it was, though, without steady sunshine the white rooms were colder and starker anyway, and the place had a clinical feel I hadn't been conscious of before. Even so soon as this, it wasn't the same house as in my recollections. The rooms rang hollow as we walked the block floors in our heavier street shoes. The carpets had been rolled up and stored somewhere, but islands of darker staining where they'd lain were mapped out on the Oregon pine. The net curtains needed to belly in a light breeze blown in off the dunes: hanging so stiffly, they looked as if they were there to keep prying eyes from observing what was intended to be kept secret. The airlessness caught the throat; upstairs indeed there was a suggestion of mustiness as well. I felt very strongly that I didn't want to be here, for a variety of reasons. It was a haunted house, and in part the haunting – I see now – was by a knowledge of my own inadequacy, past and present, my free-wheeling and an act of betrayal.

Chetwynd of course had recognised that I was essentially one of the group, that I would let things drift too far before I felt a responsibility for my own actions – my inactions, rather. He understood how committed we all of us in his hand-selected clique were to the convenient art of forgetfulness. We too, in a cruder sense, were instantly forgettable – I had parents certainly, but they were on the point of giving up on my future – and he must have realised that it was our haziness and vacuousness as individuals that was the fact we were trying, at any cost of conscience, to put right out of our minds.

Perhaps some strings were pulled, because the search for the body was exhaustive. But the time and energy put in produced in the end no results.

The body's non-appearance was a continuing mystery, but in his lifetime Chetwynd had been a man apart, so why not in death too? While the beaches and rocks were scoured along the estuary and on each of the headlands, and as far as Truas Bay and Pengylli Point ten miles away in either direction, we were left to imagine – every one of us – the body's fate. I saw it tumbled into weed, arms and legs inextricable; it was turned on its back and the colours of sky were reflected in the cold jelly of the open eyes. The fancy recurred to me in my dreams, and I slept less and less well the short time – three or four days – we stayed in the house. Without rest I became edgy and irritable. The same condition afflicted some of the others. By the third and fourth mornings we weren't the best company.

The house no longer ran like Kensington clockwork, which was another problem. There was no staff – the locals simply didn't appear, and Tuitt, when we told him we were going down on the train, had decided to stay put in London. We cooked for ourselves, and had to make sense of essentials like plumbing and hot water. Nobody thought to attend to general cleaning and dusting. The floors showed ugly shoe-prints, and I wondered if Chetwynd could have foreseen our carelessness, which was why he had arranged to have the good carpets and rugs put away.

I did at last locate them, along with the pieces of felt underlay, stored lengthwise in rolls on the floor of a room off the hall which might once have held riding-tack or fishing-tackle. Their being there was a further puzzle to me: either he'd taken them up off the floors before his disappearance, or he had failed to replace them when he'd come down and spent the time with the floors bare.

He hadn't notified any of the summer staff who lived round-about, not even Mrs Millard. Other than tins on the shelves, we had found only a few eggs, a paper bag of apples, a grapefruit, and half a loaf in a crock; the refrigerator stood unplugged, with its door wedged open. Nobody we spoke to remembered having seen him, not in person. Lights had been glimpsed behind the windows, but it was presumed that Mrs Millard's husband was on one of his regular tours of inspection.

No one – as the police requested – went into his bedroom. From the door one saw the unmade bed, clothes replaced over chairs or on hangers suspended from the top of the wardrobe. A newspaper lying on the tallboy hadn't – in all probability – been bought locally, so predated his occupancy. The entire chronology of the business was still guess-work.

There was an open verdict at the inquest arranged by the most elevated of Chetwynd's West Country connections: Death by Misadventure. We had to be content with that, although it left every single question still unanswered.

We had returned to London and gone our separate ways.

There was talk of regular 'reunions', but nothing was to come of that. Celia and Patrick Durran probably kept up for a while, but they too were each adrift in that buyer's market for labour.

I did hear through Mitchell Ogilvie – the closest we had to a nostalgist, who telephoned me with the news not long after I returned – that the Kensington house had been sold and 'Underwood' was currently up for sale. He was telling me, I suppose, that the end was very final now it was here and that there could be no hope of our ever getting back to that time and how we had been. He didn't even mention the matter of the missing body.

*

At 'Underwood', as we waited, I found myself falling into the old ways quite readily: sitting at the kitchen table watching the old brass bell-stops on the wall, walking the corridors pitched forwards on the balls of my toes so as not to disturb, running a hand over the bodywork of the four cars still kept with tanks topped up and engines tuned.

For no good reason I was investigating the back quarters of the garage when I discovered – relegated to a cupboard mounted on one of the walls, concealed behind canisters of oil and lubricating fluid and anti-freeze – a couple of matching car number-plates, black figures on a white ground. I lifted them out. I recognised them at once as German.

I returned to the Mercedes-Benz coupé. The car couldn't have been more than a couple of years old. It hadn't been here the summer we'd visited, however. The steering wheel was on the left, which contributed to the un-British, narrow-windowed Aryan look of the machine. The liberal use of chrome detracted from its old-fashioned appearance: the raised grille, the shaped front and rear wings, the dipping tail-line, scuff-plates, rocket indicator lights over the back wheels. Chetwynd had always been enthusing about the SL Sports, which was as modern as the day by contrast with gull-wing doors and 140 m.p.h. marked on the speedometer. He would talk about 'those Stuttgart wizards' with the greatest respect, as if they could teach the British a thing or two about building cars.

I opened the door and fitted myself into the driver's seat. The cabin smelt of leather, carpet, under-use. I had no key for the ignition lock so I could only sit with my arms stretched out to the wheel and my hands placed wide. The windscreen and side windows were high and the rounded coupé roof enclosing, designed for privacy: for expensive, discreet, *altmodisch*, decadent seclusion. All in front of me was arranged in continental order, with no concessions to our native way of things. I ran my hands round the wheel, passed my fingers over the polished silken wood, and considered again the German number-plates. The interior carried no evidence of the car's previous whereabouts, whether it had been bought in England or abroad. In the glove compartment I did find a manual printed in German.

I caught sight of the number-plates again as I was preparing to leave the garage, on my way over to the light switches. I picked them up and returned them to the cupboard, to where they'd been lying at the back. I blew off some of the dust. I could tell that at some prior point in the car's history they had been used on the road: on the autobahn at any rate, or on one of those twisting mountain roads corkscrewing up through a Bavarian forest, which the newsreel footage of Hitler's cronies' home-movies had made cinema-goers familiar with.

I took a note of the numbers. Back in London I must have thought to place the piece of paper somewhere safe because years later, by some most curious chance, I found them transcribed into a notebook. I consulted the German Consulate in Edinburgh, where I was living in the late seventies, and they informed me that the car's registration centre had been Hamburg: the date, 1956. I wasn't so surprised to be told. 'Yes,' I said, 'I see . . .' It was from there – directly by ship, I supposed – that the car had made its journey. Of all German cities it had to be that one, situated on its great conduit of trade, the Elbe, by which both officially and unofficially colossal fortunes in goods – some worth several kings' ransoms – travel by day and by night.

*

On what was to be our last evening at 'Underwood' I left the others in the drawing-room. An inexpert fire had been lit in the grate and it burned only half-heartedly. Some of the furniture was still shrouded in dust-sheets, and I found the sight of it dispiriting. So I mumbled an excuse, made my way through the house, and walked outside.

On the garden terrace I suddenly felt very alone. I shivered, down into the 'V' neck of my pullover, and found the usual warmth of the jacket's tweed lacking. The sea beat a slow rhythm on the roughcast walls of the house, and the sound was remorseless and cold. As the clouds overhead parted and moonlight drifted in the dusk like smoke, the walls loomed sallow and – I could imagine – frosted. From somewhere in the house a single peal of laughter reached me, but I heard it ring as hollow as our footsteps. We were *all* alone now, we were each of us – singularly – vulnerable.

*

Only I knew – as Chetwynd had been aware – how good a swimmer he'd been. He had let me see, twice, at the Randolph Square pool.

Something wasn't right about all this, but I couldn't say to anyone. Wasn't such a manner of dying too lacking in subtlety, too *arrant*? It seemed to belong between the covers of a paperback thriller. I couldn't believe that I was meant to believe it.

I felt that the unseen presence forever behind me was, could only be, one man's. It was as if – I can say now, seeing from thirty years away – for all my ignorance and second-rateness he had perceived a rough potential in me, to set the story – *his* story – straight. I was the only one he understood as inclined and, possibly, able. I sensed it in my bones, even then, that something was weighing on me: a hypothetical onus of responsibility. In the silence of the house a voice was trying to find the voice to speak.

It would take another thirty years, and a return to 'Underwood' aka 'Lynton Court', to see what my purpose was finally to be: as the weakest link in the chain, and also the hesitant historian.

Chetwynd must have intuited that, suppressed as it had been until then, I had the makings of a dogged, plodding searcher out of data. Except for Fleur I had gone less far than any of the others in reconstructing myself, in turning myself into the Ralph Witton who would be most things to most men. To have the facts, those that could be, salvaged from history was as much as he could hope for. He took a risk, that I might prove the least prejudiced of our number in laying them out. Maybe he visualised me one day married and a father, but with a nagging impulse to wrap up all that past time and to put it to rest. I came close to marrying once, but I didn't, and I never fathered a child. The impulse remained, however: he guessed correctly there, *that* part was significantly true. He may have underestimated the complexity of motives: I began by wanting to justify and also exonerate myself, but the prevailing and most insidious influence was to prove Gilbert Tobin's flinty daughter, the Jean Seberg lookalike, who if she couldn't forgive me did drop – metaphor of metaphors – a depth charge into the recesses of my conscience.

Facts. Impartial truths. To render us as we were, in England's broken idyll. To state rather than to interpret. But, from my own experience, to hint at that roaring silence that lived inside each one of us.

*

I found a bag of apples in the kitchen, on a shelf in the larder.

One of them was bad and had begun to rot the paper. The apples next to it had taken its disease.

The bag started to disintegrate in my hand. The apples fell out before I could open my arms to catch them.

The bad apple splattered soft brown pulp on to the floor and the others rolled in every direction.

I stood smelling the thick, over-sweet odour of orchards, deceiving me with a mental picture of normality, of the cyclical harmony of the seasons, which was what I had always and too easily presumed to be the benevolent logic and system in nature.

Part Two

TWENTY-EIGHT

The house in 'The Circus' is now in foreign hands.

The curtains at every window are ruched; a gardener attends to the flower boxes on each outside sill. The furniture in the rooms appears to be a *mélange* of gilded and reproduction – studded green pristine leather, the Charles Rennie Mackintosh 'look', lighted circular glass shades growing out of alabaster acanthus plants painted gold. The paintings are presumably the genuine articles – modern filter-lit landscapes and life-sized nude women being 'natural'. The garden has been overhauled by a landscaping firm, bouldered and re-terraced; there's an all-weather tennis court with floodlighting; gravel lies deep on the driveway, which is stocked with a small fleet of transportation, all West German in origin and uniformly black – a Mercedes, a Porsche, an Audi, a VW Golf GTi.

*

I've sat for dozens of hours in the green glow of computer windows.

The past, if it hasn't exactly come alive, has asserted itself in print reminiscent of fretwork: a formal dance of symbols staccato-jigging across the screens.

Consider the carpets.

The concept of the whole is determined in the very first stitches. The entirety is contained in the merest part, and the final effect is a state of mind. Just as important as the aesthetic balance of colours and shapes, fields and borders, is conveying the implications of all the symbols in your head, or else – if that lore is lost to you – appreciating the circumstances of the carpet's production, seeing the ground at your feet as a spiritual as well as a material plane.

Carpets flew in the Arabs' tales because they were metaphysical conceits.

Chetwynd's story, I have to remind myself, consists of more than the factual. It's historical, and of its time, but the man's personality and behaviour disclose only too many confusions for anyone who probes it. His story's 'time' is the middle to late 1950s, one of ambition and material progress, of convictions and equally – as the nature of progress was exposed, with its negative drag, the under-tow of old rivalries, envy, want, hedonism, and empty display – of illusions. The 'clue' is not to be found in any *one* thing, not even in a particular incident of his childhood. The story, I feel, can't be unpicked and disentangled easily. The man of forty is four years old in the mirror, and similarly the little boy sees through the rich man's covertly watchful eyes.

Dancing across the computer screens of England, France and Germany, everything – every single item – conspires to belong to the total, to the story as it has to be told in the round. Out of a hundred thousand words of stylised computer print, the semblance of a face takes shape. As I conjure more information from the memory banks, I mentally trip over certain words and the life reduces itself to glowing and – depending on the state of the source-current – not always consistently stable caps: KT BACH, DFC, DB, ISFAHAN, 1956, PCL, S'UNG, FEZ, AC, JU-I, ROMA-DA VINCI, J & B, HRH, CD, % INT, ALTONA.

*

I found photographs of an actor called Clive K. Melchett. They dated from the late forties. If I hadn't had two, I should have supposed they were wrongly captioned. The face bore little resemblance to that of the Clive Melchett *I* had known. Only the eyes – under lids that must have been surgically altered – were the same, piercing and ambiguous.

If it hadn't been for the evidence of the eyes, I might have imagined the names accidental: or been led to surmise that the Clive Melchett I was familiar with had appropriated that of the other.

As I came to discover, 'my' Clive Melchett was and was not the face in the photographs, inked on to the dots of newspaper.

He was making his way, as they say. He had only landed small roles but he was working in films, which he felt was the place to be. Little would lead to bigger and better.

For a few minutes of screen appearances in toto, he had to put in many long hours waiting about on and off the set. The fourth film was called *Fair Runs The Tide*, which explained itself, and in it he played a naval colleague of the star, Kenneth More. Even more waiting about was required than in the previous three – because the part was more substantial – but he was willing enough to have the time consumed for his career's sake.

His career, however, meant nothing when, without any forewarning, a hot lamp crashed down from one of the studio's lighting gantries immediately overhead. He was felled and concussed. In seconds a fire was ablaze. It took another three-quarters of a minute or so to pull him out, pleached in flames.

In hospital he was found to have eighty per cent burns. Even worse than the scorching to his limbs and torso was the disfigurement to his face. The full impact had been to his skull, and shards of glass had spiked him like cloves a pomander. The furious white heat had melted the cornea in his eyes and peeled the skin from his cheekbones and nose. At that temperature some of his blood had merely evaporated.

It exceeded anyone's expectations that he survived, and lived on. Plastic surgeons got to work at the very first opportunity, and the patient underwent several operations. After seven months, unrecognisable as the man he had been, he left hospital; but ten days later, at the expense of an anonymous benefactor, the firm of theatrical agents he was with organised his transfer to a clinic in Switzerland. There, in Lausanne, a plastic surgeon of world renown began again on the long task of reconstructing his face.

The results this time were nothing to cause the sorrow and shame of before. Over a period of eighteen months the features' remouldings were painstakingly perfected. The cost might have been prohibitive but, for the German surgeon, the process of treatment was in the way of a major, protracted experiment in technique, and he voluntarily renegotiated his customary charges to the purchaser's considerable benefit.

Back in London, via a spell of social adjustment in Nice, the patient – startlingly handsome as he hadn't been before the accident – had to cope with essential problems of attitude concerning his work. He didn't see how he could ever step on to a film set again, beneath a gallery of arc lights, and he found – to his distress – that he hadn't retained the degree of nerve necessary to perform in front of a theatre audience. All in all, despite his magical metamorphosis and the acquisition of Hollywood looks, his immediate future appeared bleak.

But that was only one element of the scenario – that he should appreciate his own limitations – until he had an opportunity to meet in person the man who had been his (faceless) benefactor, directing operations (in every sense) from afar, one Anthony Chetwynd.

*

It wasn't so difficult. One of the big London stores was celebrating its centenary, and I read that (figuratively) no stone had been left unturned in an effort to find former employees. In this case I had little investigative work to do. In fact Celia Jepson had written in to the firm herself, requesting an invitation to the festivities. It was judged by those who saw to her welfare likely to prove too unsettling a journey for her, however – even though she'd had her best, but not so recent, jersey wool dress sent to Bollom's for dry-cleaning in anticipation.

Mentally she was as bright as a button (gilt or chrome, from haberdashery), but now she lived inside a body that was between seventy-five and eighty years old, after a full and fairly turbulent life. She recognised *me* immediately, while I had trouble picking her out from her companions in the Home. She shook her head at me, but smiled notwithstanding.

She could talk about that first afternoon on the beach at Treswithian, and even of afternoons before that, when she'd seen me watching their group. I was embarrassed to hear, but she didn't understand the reaction.

'We were very exotic, I'm sure,' she said. 'That's what it was all about, wasn't it?'

She was still as directly to-the-point as ever, and her eyes simultaneously missed no detail of my middle-aged appearance.

'They'll make me my own tea if I ask them nicely.' She picked up the telephone. 'It'll be extra, of course. They're very obliging, these Indians – or Pakistanis, or whatever they are – but they make sure they're paid for every favour. It's revenge for our colonial past, I expect. They're sharper than the Jews ever were – '

We retired to her own room in the nursing home, and tea was duly served to us. Glossy magazines, I noticed, were stacked under her high-backed chair. A copy of *Hello!* was open at a colour feature on a super-rich Texan couple who had bought the mansion next door, as it were, to Balmoral Castle.

Apparently she had indulged in a sapphic embrace in a public place – or one that was more public than she had supposed – and an onlooker had summoned a policeman. The onlooker turned out to be the wife of a circuit judge, and a fundamentalist Christian to boot, and she threatened all sort of legal and divine retribution. The police proved unsympathetic in the extreme, and in their custody she had thought this must be the miserable end of everything.

But, providentially, from somewhere a lawyer appeared in the nick of time. There was a good deal of brisk toing and froing. She couldn't really dare to hope, but in the end the unthinkable happened and the charge (of causing a public affray) was suddenly, by a stroke of a pen, dispensed with.

The woman with whom she had been so foolish as to compromise herself had been married to a scientist.

'I naturally supposed he must've been able to apply some pressure. Human physics, sort of thing. But when he heard, evidently it just shattered him, and he didn't know *what* to do.'

I asked her how the lawyer had become involved, why she had been let off the charge.

'It took me months to discover. By then I'd met Chetwynd, and because everything was so different it didn't surprise me.'

What, I felt obliged to ask, had failed to surprise her?

'Finding out it was his doing. A stranger's doing, at that time. It was he who'd got hold of the lawyer so quickly. The right lawyer too, who knew the ins-and-outs. He must've been able to address a few timely words into suitably cocked ears, though. Linney, the judge, was in some Masonic Lodge, and Chetwynd probably did some diplomatic work behind the scenes. I got to hear there were also some Scotland Yard bigwigs in the Lodge.'

I asked if Chetwynd had been a Mason too?

'He wouldn't have left himself so vulnerable.'

'He could have learned about people, couldn't he?'

'Maybe. But he didn't want – I don't know – people to protest their loyalties. They mix blood, too. He had a distaste for all that. The physical intimacy.'

I said, I hadn't realised that he'd been especially so.

'Being touched? Didn't you notice? Or being too close to people? Even us?'

Well, I told her, well maybe I had . . .

'However, it happened, anyway – '

'Chetwynd saved the day?' I asked.

'Like Saint George, you mean? Well, those days are *long* gone – but I was very grateful. I owed him . . .'

She paused.

'Your freedom?' I prompted.

For a couple of moments her eyes were as scathing as Liz's: at my own glib innocence which I had revealed by the remark. But just as quickly her eyes cleared – or rather, they were how I had always been used to seeing them, observant and shrewdly assessing but at the same time guarded, as if viewing at long range, from a safe and marginal distance.

We did talk some more, over the teacups, but she was alert enough in her old age not to be drawn further. I had always supposed her to be more in Chetwynd's confidence than had perhaps been the case. What she knew, at any rate, she wasn't willing to impart to me – I had only been a minor and late addition to the group after all. Much more important than my enlightenment was the continuation of the myth, with its hierography of secrets.

*

Mitchell Ogilvie's career lasted for another eight or nine years. He was seen eating quite conspicuously in certain London hotel restaurants: never alone, but 'à deux' and always in the company of women of more mature years. The women varied, but seldom the type: well-to-do, left by themselves because of death or neglect, needing the solace of attention. I'm sure he assured them very well in the short term. But it must have been a somewhat thankless task also, dealing with that unending stream of dissatisfied, frequently tranquillised females whose thoughts could never be prised from their – happy or disconsolate – pasts.

He briefly became involved in the financial organisation of a Knightsbridge night-spot: dis-organisation rather, because the enterprise didn't recover its initial costs and drifted into reefs of debt. One of the women who had been persuaded to invest voiced her doubts to friends of her late husband, high fliers in the Metropolitan police force. The night-club collapsed with arrears owing to a dozen major creditors, and Mitchell Ogilvie absconded from the gaze of his familiar public. He lay low for a while. Afterwards he had something to do with a car-dealership in Birmingham, but perhaps they had too optimistic notions on likely sales of their Bristols and Lagondas. That business also folded, with money owing, and Ogilvie spread his wings and flew a little further this time, as if thus he might soar clear of danger. The next sighting of him occurred in Guernsey, and it was the West Sussex police to whom his presence proved of such interest: two hotel bills and another for the rental of a Rover '90' saloon car were still outstanding.

Back on the mainland he progressed from financial carelessness or mismanagement to petty fraud and less petty theft. He
was living far beyond his means, and there came a point when
the non-payment of accommodation bills was a secondary matter
to the supply of 'ready' cash for unavoidable expenses: such as
securing the best tables in restaurants and earning waiters'
respect. Cheques continued to bounce on the larger sums –
he must have experienced a perversely heroic thrill every time
he signed one – but a temporary acquaintance with a jewel thief
while serving a custodial sentence in 1964 sent him off on a new
and much more satisfactorily exciting tack on his release.

His exploits were recorded on police files in Leeds, Harrogate,
Scarborough, Chester, Manchester, Bath, Torquay, Bourne-
mouth, Eastbourne and Brighton. He wasn't as subtle as he
may have imagined he was, although he did have the good
sense to change names and the initials on his luggage and to
discover the properties of half a dozen hair-dyes on the market.
His principal method of approach with each new victim was an
introductory résumé of his War, an invitation to dinner, and a
not over-long question-and-answer session (he asking most of
the questions, extracting very detailed answers and committing
them to memory) concerning his quarry's daily routine and
her physical fitness and standard of mental alertness. He was
remembered as charming, mannerly, humorous, interested,
generous of his time and money, a man who knew about his
wine and his food, and perhaps that's as fine an impression as
many of us might hope to leave behind us in this world.

By 1972 he had well and truly gone out of circulation, as
the Kensington euphemism of old had it, and in my enquiries
I felt I was dealing with a shade of the Beyond. But three
years later I *thought* I caught a glimpse of him, on a television
screen of all places for him to be seen. An ITN camera was
panning round an African airport, where white Anglo-Saxon
residents were dutifully queuing to check in for flights that
would leave before the Union Jack was drawn down by the
midnight rites and the country officially turned black. A man in
the foreground glanced over his shoulder, noticed the camera,
and averted his face again just as quickly. His hair was thinner

and darker, but the moustache remained in place, and his eyes in that leaner face were the same eyes still: intense and blue, like those of the lost boys of the Flanders time, the sort of eyes that melt hearts. I remembered Celia once telling me that his eyes did it all, never mind the chatter that would have sweet-talked the birds off the trees in Berkeley Square.

I watched a later news broadcast that evening and saw the same piece of film. Now I was certain. It *was* him, it could only have been Mitchell, and curiously the man possessed for me then a kind of innocence. For the second time at least history was grinding him through its mill.

Some of the air flights had been bound for destinations other than England: South Africa for one. Connections from Cape Town could have taken him on to Argentina or Delhi or Singapore or Sydney. He could have re-begun yet again, virtually anywhere where there was settler stock with definite – but not too distinct – memories of the motherland. He may be snuggling into a restaurant banquette this very evening, or loosening the knees of his sharply creased flannel trousers as he hoists himself on top of a bar stool: his hair is the colour of the season and not of his moustache, his cornflower-blue eyes are primed, the words are poised on the tip of his tongue to do their quietly cunning, cozening work, his mind is racing ahead to locks and bolts and chains on the doors of an apartment or hotel room, and how is he to effect an illicit, feline entrance that will not prove to be his last one.

*

April had once mentioned – had let it slip – in a conversation, that in her childhood it was an eight-mile adventure to travel up by train from the town where she lived to Ipswich. It was the first revelation of that sort which she had given me, and I wanted to follow it up. But she clearly realised that she had broken a cardinal rule of 'Circus' etiquette – and, all smiles, she firmly changed the subject before the door handle turned and someone should walk in and hear.

I had only one other intimation of a past. She had taken a head cold; I was standing beneath her on the staircase when she dropped the handkerchief she'd just removed from her bag. I picked it up. The cotton was a little time-yellowed, and not of the best quality. Sewn quite crudely in one corner was the name 'June'. She snatched the handkerchief back from me, all smiles again, but with her face reddening. 'I just use up one after another of these,' she said, through an actress's cod-sniffs.

I supposed home to have been Woodbridge, in Suffolk.

The name 'June' was to remain lodged in my mind, and I kept recalling it the day I found myself – not quite by accident – in the town, one year in the late sixties. Between its mud banks the slowly serpentining River Deben smelt of other places, carried on a fresh and salty breeze.

It was the name that led me to the Parish registers. To have a chance to consult them, I had to stay over until the next day, but I was content to do so. In the event I struck lucky. A 'June' – very fortuitously the only one I could alight on for the period – had been christened in September of 1932. There was no mention of a 'Purris' in the telephone directory, so I made enquiries at the borough offices. It required another couple of days to follow up various leads, which took me eight or nine miles out into the country, to a village with a main street and very little else. A cul-de-sac of council bungalows was tagged on at the back, beside beet fields, and there I found the Mrs Purris I was looking for.

June's father had walked out three days before her tenth birthday. Neither his wife nor his daughter were ever to set eyes on him again. His own father had married two women in two different corners of Suffolk: even if the other woman wasn't (yet) Bob's wife, and church-married, it amounted to the same thing in this land of custom and precedent.

It had been hard for the two of them left behind. His wife was reduced to charring houses by day and a chandler's shop and a notary's office in the evenings. At least the father, Purris Senior, had provided for two families while the son simply abandoned one life for another. June – named after the month of her birth, in a mistaken surge of buoyant, early summer hopefulness – left school when she was fourteen, and went to work in a bakery. But she had other aspirations. A spell in a ladies' outfitters followed, and then – closer to her own wishes for herself – she became apprenticed in a hairdresser's. She did her time there – eighteen months – before moving to an establishment with a fancier clientele, 'Woodbridge Stylings'. She was very deft with her fingers as well as imaginative, and popular with the customers, and it was she who was approached to take up a position in a new concern in Ipswich called 'Stephano's Salon'. There she found herself with her hands on the scalps of county types and also, now and then, of London socialites who escaped for long weekends that stretched to more considerable sojourns. Through one of these she received an opportunity to dress hair at a large country-house ball near Framlingham. She was invited to attend at another, and at a third. Stephano – alias Mr Tamlock – didn't dare to object, although he viewed her overtime and evident indispensability with no little suspicion.

It was at one of those occasions that she encountered whoever-it-was – as her mother had it – 'turned the girl's head'. Or maybe it was a group of them, rather, who were responsible. At any rate, for her part – a mere mother's – understanding would have been a whole lot easier if June had gone the whole hog and fallen in love, made a fool of herself, with some domestic at one of those great houses. But – I gathered, from the woman's version of her long-lost daughter's history – it wasn't quite love, it was an overwhelming fascination for a certain manner of existence, the one enjoyed above-stairs. She wasn't ever the same after that. She pored over magazines, stared at herself in mirrors, experimented with cut-out dress patterns she would re-tailor herself with those clever hands, to make them 'different' from anything any other woman in Woodbridge might be seen wearing. She spent some of her wages on elocution lessons with Madame Scutt, in Wickham Market. She put a lot of effort into adjusting her deportment, and decided her job – standing about in the salon all hours of the day – wasn't any help in that respect.

Mrs Purris was quite willing to talk up to that point. But then she became more reticent. The events of twenty years ago still struck a very raw nerve. I was left to surmise that she had been abandoned a second time. June might have had a little more guilt about it, to judge from the fact that she sent home money orders every few months in the first years, but she never again returned to Woodbridge and, in time, the despatches too became a thing of the past. 'I think,' the woman said, 'she must've died. It's all I can imagine happened. Maybe she went abroad, but she would have remembered. I moved away from the town. If she'd written, the letter would have got to me somehow.'

At the risk of aggravating the situation, I asked the woman if she had any photographs she could show me. There were only two, one of them from the girl's teens. I recognised the eyes, and the eyebrows, clipped to aloof and symmetrical arcs. The mouth was a nervous child's, the teeth were irregular, the shoulders quite thin, the chin sharp. But they were the eyes I remembered – shrewd even above an anxious and unformed, undeclared mouth, already at fifteen years old seeing ahead to possibilities and their price – and, just as much, they were the plucked arching eyebrows that might have granted solemn grace to a medieval patron's face or that of a Romanov.

*

In 1961 I saw Melinda Myer in Harrods' Food Halls. I only recognised her after I'd spotted her right hand pushing the box of truffles into the pocket of her mackintosh.

Her face was grey, putty-coloured. Her left hand fussed with strands of colourless hair that fell from beneath her black velvet beret. Her posture had gone and she stood round-shouldered and hunched forwards. The green Burberry was soiled, the velvet pile on the beret scored.

She looked as if she was only waiting to be caught in the act.

But she wasn't apprehended, not this time. No one among the shoppers or staff stopped, and nor did I.

TWENTY-NINE

The Authorised Version of English life wasn't to Chetwynd's liking. He preferred his own alternative reading. It was an equally limited perspective, and by no accident the details bore a very marked similarity. Swards of green country, poplars and cedars, mellow-stone houses, darkly intimate panelled libraries, stucco-friezed saloons, and all the rest. It seemed to be a recognisable world, but was actually its obverse image, where shadows slant in an opposite direction. Essentially it was an abstract world of symbol, a sculpted realism, stiffly draped like a Meredith Frampton painting: peopled by responsible servants, but obeying what are largely their own instructions, and no longer in the service of the old guard. Now *they* had been driven from their dwelling-places, as if all along they had been usurpers and pretenders.

*

My researches took me nearly five years all told. Chetwynd became something of an obsession for me. The search grew more and more compulsive, but my endeavours were the opposite of nostalgic. It could have been that I was wanting to uncover the worst that I could, as if that might prove I had been justified in taking Kimble's side. I didn't come to that conclusion, however, that I had been correct. The search became a clearer, dare I say *purer* exercise than that. I chiefly wanted to get hold of facts. At the outset I wanted to make a fact of myself too, within the framework of Chetwynd's story, so that rightness or wrongness was beside the point. All that events could seem to have been was inevitable.

Yet facts are variable. Truth is fickle. I think of lights

brightening and dimming at a distance. Nevertheless I've had to do what I can with them. This is Chetwynd's life as I, for one, have reconstructed it. I prefer not to use the term 'imagined'. I wish to be scientific, to keep my prejudices out of the picture. Here and there I may have failed, but not – I hope for the sakes of all of us who were his coterie – overall.

*

There are three entries bearing the name 'Chetwynd' in any comprehensive English gazetteer. One is in Shropshire, another in the West Riding of Yorkshire and the third in Dorset. I visited the first one, but drew a blank. I set off for Yorkshire without very much hope. My perseverance, however, was rewarded.

The pieces came together, more easily than I could have anticipated. I had the sensation that I was *meant* to discover, as if the clues were being laid before me at Chetwynd's own behest.

From the local talk I learned that the family which had owned Chetwynd Hall for the past two hundred and eleven years was called Defries. A southern family, Dorset grandees. The name 'Summerleaze Grange' cropped up in one conversation. That apparently was the name of the family's principal home in Dorset.

*

I had gone armed with my photographs, otherwise I might never have alighted on the true connection.

Some of the older villagers I asked could remember him, and so clearly that I presumed they judged themselves to have cause to remember. In those days he had gone by the name of 'Deeks'.

It was just after the War that he first came to reconnoitre in the locale. He was a youngish man still: thirty or thereabouts. Inquisitive but polite. He put questions to you – lots of questions about Chetwynd Hall and the Defries clan – and yet otherwise he did little to draw attention to himself. He coaxed the answers from you, even though you might have decided you weren't going to be drawn into talking. He had a way about him, it

was done so easily and painlessly without causing you to feel
you had betrayed either yourself or a confidence. A historian,
some had supposed: or even a journalist.

'A dealer?' I suggested. 'An antiques buyer?'

Possibly. But he left with no purchases, and made nobody
an offer, although he'd been told there were some well-stuffed
farmhouses in the vicinity and folk – at that time in our history
– quite hard up. He'd been a young fellow comfortably set up,
the locals decided. Not *quite* a gentleman (a gold Cartier tank
wrist-watch bright with newness, an ably-cut tweed suit worn
with *suede* shoes, an American striped tie with its colours –
whatever they represented – running the opposite way from
the British) but certainly not flashy or 'spivvy' either. Nicely,
anonymously spoken; very slightly stooped, which gave him
some gravitas; steel tips to his polished brogues which allowed
anyone to know where he was at any instant, or to think they
did. Oh, and a slight cast in one eye, which brought him the
women's pity.

Sitting by a tea-shop window I imagined the stir caused by
his sports car's arrival on the green. The appearance of the
man: a thoroughly cosmopolitan version of rural, plus (one
envious witness still recalled) buttoning driving-gloves in grey
suede trimmed with tan leather. The feeling of those days: the
country victorious but impecunious, people's appetites denied
and frustrated. Rumours of democracy, yet old sentiments
holding sway, the difficulty of finding willing labour for hire.
Unwillingness, ungraciousness, jealousy, innuendo-trading.

The stranger sitting, just like me, one prudential table away
from the window in the 'Daffodil Tea-Rooms'. He is embarking
on life anew in this (he stubbornly insists) exciting, invigorating
age of opportunity. And all the time the chief thought in the
man's head is, when – just when – to change his name?

The name of a village in three shires. The name of an Elizabethan
manor house about which he asked a good many questions on his
first and subsequent visits to Yorkshire.

Apparently he wasn't unfamiliar with the Dorset history of the family. He confessed as much, although no one was enlightened as to what the connection might be. He was the most courteous listener; he allowed you to suppose that what you had to say to him was of the utmost significance to him at that particular moment of saying it. Some of the younger women thought he became better-looking on repeated acquaintance. The men found him generous at buying drinks, and could rely on getting a good laugh out of him when they told a joke, and as blue as you wanted to make it.

But when he forgot he was being watched, his face turned quite serious, and inscrutable. By instinct his eyes would be drawn to the window of whichever room he was in, they would seek out the direction of the manor house with the dependability of a magnetic compass.

*

My next destination was the manor house in Dorset.

I parked my car opposite the front gates, with a view directly downhill. The steep avenue led straight to the ruins of the house in its hollow, between two files of venerable, gnarled chestnut trees. Only one end of the building had survived a fire in the fifties, since sealed – to make it habitable – by a great bluff-like wall with a dull cement finish. Thirty years after the blaze, the sagging mossed roof and the mottled saffron stone still carried black scorch marks from the flames.

The two pubs of the Dorset Chetwynd proved equally accommodating and helpful.

Summerleaze Grange had remained in the same family's hands until the late thirties, I learned, when Sir Anthony died prematurely of cancer and his sister chose to sell up. Consecutive buyers had acquired the property for one modern purpose after another – a stud farm, a Jewish preparatory school, a secretarial college, an eventide home, an outward bound establishment, and now the Indian swami gentleman and his followers. Nobody stayed long, and it was as if the house itself rejected – ejected – them all after some certain allotted time.

Using the local intelligence I worked back to the history of the original owners. The family, as I knew, was called Defries. They had occupied the house for over two hundred and fifty years. Their wealth had been derived from the Caribbean trades, specifically sugar and slaves, and at some point they had bought themselves into land. At the peak of their local fame, they had owned twenty-two farms. Then the family's human stock had demonstrated all too obvious evidence of decline. A succession of high-livers, gamblers, over-educated indigents and charming sensationists had sold off what they couldn't properly afford to. By the time sense and sanity prevailed again in the genes – at the turn of this century – the resources were at a low ebb. A number of investments came to nought in 1929. Sales of household effects – 'adjustments' of property – were attended to most discreetly and with a very heavy heart, in the sure and sad conviction that there could only be one eventual outcome, which all the little financial transactions, sums and subtractions, were really only putting off.

An idea, a notion, was already shaping itself in my mind before I was served certain clues that turned my thoughts in a particular, definite direction.

A woman in the snug of 'The Moonraker' chanced to mention that there had been a small scandal concerning the family at the time of the First War, although it didn't become public knowledge roundabout for another twenty years. My enquiries started in earnest from that virtually incidental revelation. I bought a computer terminal on the strength of it. There is fact to be found, although seldom in the same form with each source, and modern tastes approve of imaginative reconstruction. Maybe between the two of them, truth – the trickiest abstract of all – resides.

Home on leave, Sir Anthony – unmarried brother of the unmarried Lady Helena – had put one of the maids into the family way. She had only recently married, a local garage mechanic who had joined up and been shipped off to the Dardanelles.

The child, a boy John, was born in a distant town, and given out to an older relation of his mother, Cousin Deeks, a seamstress living in Nottinghamshire. The younger woman, Mary Froud, returned south and continued to work for a while at the Grange, but was clearly disapproved of by her employer's sister. An excuse was found to terminate her employment. When her husband came home at the War's end, he found her skivvying in the lesser of the local taps. He was at a loss to understand either what he took to be her choice of work or her see-sawing moods. After a couple of years of her eccentric – but chaste – behaviour, he grew weary of trying to reason out the causes and befriended a number of obliging women in towns he travelled to on half-days and Sundays on the pretext of plying a moonlighter's trade.

When her curiosity about her son got the better of her, the mechanic's wife invented a history for the boy and arranged that her Cousin Deeks send him for a holiday. The unenlightened husband protested too late, amazed as ever at his wife's perversity. But he found the novelty of the infant's presence not unwelcome during that first summer. It was an unsettling experience for the boy's natural mother, and she lavished on him the affection she wasn't able to give in the ordinary run of her life. The fact of her pregnancy had been kept a secret from everyone in the locale except the Defries', and the boy passed in the village as a stranger: a stranger to himself indeed. Even when the couple had their own son, and then a daughter, the older boy continued to visit them in the summer. He was responsive to the husband as his own children were too young (and, later, not disposed) to be, and his mother treated him in preference to the others, who were after all her husband's as much as hers. Every year his 'aunt' – to whom he had grown close – despatched him south to Dorset, and he readjusted the geography of his life for a couple of months. Things scarcely altered to his eye from one summer to the next, except that the couple grew older and their children more wary of him. The husband still worked in the garage and staged occasional disappearances and was spoken ill of by his mates behind his back, and his wife's existence still alternated between drudgery in the tap and drudgery in the crowded house in Goose Lane. But for the boy, approaching his teens and then advancing into them, the environs – never greatly changing in their appearance – were the one same constant source of speculation and adventure. He made wider and wider circuits of them, and sometimes had the loan of a boneshaker bicycle from which he surveyed the area like a Cortez his Darien.

A boy on a bicycle.

It's a dead spinster's bicycle. The chain has difficulty engaging, and the brakes work only fitfully, and the effort required on hills is epic. But it's a bicycle none the less, and even though it's borrowed it is the boy's access to imagined liberty and independence. Those may be a cunning illusion ordinarily, but convincing enough for him as long as these afternoons in the copses and along the bridle paths last.

Unlike the saddle, the village – to his thoughts – is tightly sprung: it's like a clasp brooch, a tarnished gilt leaf pinned to a high swathe of green.

The prettiness of these surroundings is suspect, he soon learns. The gilded or molten aspect of the stone is merely accidental, because there is little sunniness in the villagers' lives. The thatched roofs are a tangle of verminous life and owe their neglect to poverty. He wears shoes on his feet – he has always been shod: proper leather shoes would arrive as gifts at his 'aunt's' quite out of the blue – and he has always had enough in his life to eat, to allow him to grow healthier and stronger than any of the Chetwynd youth, the Goose Lane children included. He hasn't so much to complain about, in the physical sense, but he comes to understand that the village is a place only to be escaped from. It is so inward and self-involved that it has begun to consume itself in a dumb, bitter rage of acrimony and envy, rank frustration and sheer stupidity. It wants to know nothing beyond its own, frequently malicious inventions. Nor is *he* spared, and he reads the guesswork behind the tight eyes. If it wasn't that the man under whose mice-infested roof he sleeps could flatten any challenger with his bare knuckles, he would be a worse victim of the village prejudices than he is.

He establishes the distance he needs even when he isn't (strictly) mobile. He is no nature buff. Simply it's the freedom of his movements, the being where he chooses to be, which gives him his inspiration, his perspective. He can stay out-of-doors from dawn until dusk. They are the most fulfilling two months of the twelve, and surely it's inevitable that he should start considering how – notwithstanding his affection for his sorely-worked Aunt Deeks – how he might contrive to make a temporary arrangement permanent.

At the age of fourteen, with his genealogy still unexplained to him, it happened.

He was apprenticed to a cabinet-maker-and-restorer in the nearest town to Chetwynd. He was given lodgings with another apprentice in a room above a greengrocer's shop. It was a modest beginning to a new life, but one not without a modicum of dignity and self-respect.

The workrooms were attached to a showroom, where the range of House products on display attracted a regular and discerning clientele. The premises also accommodated a selection of superior antique furniture for sale, and the boy developed a precocious interest in the vast subject and – in time – a keen, instinctive eye for the 'best' against merely the 'better' sort of goods. Unlike his fellow-apprentices, he retained any information that came his way about furniture as historical artefact – the styles and technique of manufacture as well as line of ownership. He had a canny, unfailing memory for prices, both the buying-in (he succeeded in breaking the code used in the receipt books) and the much heftier sale one.

His first (witting) contact with Summerleaze Grange occurred when the firm was asked to inspect damage done to some pieces of furniture during an undisciplined party in the house. He was summoned from the workroom one morning to provide additional muscle power, and then again when a lorry was sent to collect several items for repair. But his eye had been taken by the quantity and quality of the house's effects, and his attention was noticed in turn by the repentant host of the party, Sir Anthony Defries, and by his unmarried sister who acted as housekeeper. The following year a request was made to the firm to supply the services of a french-polisher and an upholsterer and someone capable of calculating the cost of re-laying a wooden floor. Again the youth was brought along in tow, perhaps for his experience's sake but also to be on hand for the manoeuvring of furniture and rolling back of carpets. It was during a break in the proceedings that the apprentice spotted the resemblance of a writing cabinet relegated to a back corridor of the house to one illustrated in a manual of Sheraton designs kept on a cobwebbed shelf of reference literature in the company's accounts room. It had the same bowed ends, fluted pilaster columns, oval panels, ivory escutcheons, turned knob handles. Their client was absorbed by the observation and insisted that the youth speak and have his say even when his immediate superior was bidding him to remember himself and hold his tongue. The resemblance proved a genuine one when the manual was consulted on their return, and on a subsequent visit the apprentice was on hand – a specific request having been made that he should attend – when the senior Mr Hopgood corroborated the genuineness of the article. Had the cabinet not been included among contents surveyed and assessed by the very same firm five years before when a sale of minor items was in prospect, the matter might have been viewed with less seriousness on all sides. In the event the client forgot politeness as he gave vent to both his astonishment and his displeasure.

And in the event, so far as the apprentice's future was concerned, the senior Mr Hopgood over-ruled his son; as if it might negate all the embarrassment caused, he withdrew the terms of the apprenticeship and unceremoniously booted the lad out.

The news reached Summerleaze Grange. It might have been

considered of little consequence to someone in such a position but the business still rankled with Sir Anthony. His personality included a surfeit of pride, which had been quick to recognise a slight in what had originally been an accident and which now acknowledged, as well as the onerous aspect of his inheritance, the commercial worth of the house's effects, which might not after all be such a gallimaufry of objects to unload on some remote provincial saleroom. He asked the scapegoat to call on him. The sensible and generous step might have been to assist in finding him an apprenticeship elsewhere, but there was a remarkable carelessness and selfishness about the man, which saw to no more than the serving of his own interests. A handyman – joiner and polisher but also load-lifter, lawnsman, leaf-sweeper, errand-fetcher – would be a thoroughly useful presence on the premises. The youth had no other place to go and was without references, so found himself with no alternative. He was conscious of the curiosity he aroused in the titled siblings, brother and sister alike, which subsequently he was to encourage. The pay was little but (it was explained very matter-of-factly) he would eat in the kitchen as the other staff ate and sleep in an adequate attic room above the stables. For his own part he recognised it was an opportunity to keep his eyes about him, to hear what he would, and to learn: about objects, about people, about manners and the codes of conduct in a world quite alien to his own, about the value of things and the people who own them.

It was no position of favour. He didn't expect privileges, and he received none: except – which was merely accidental – his proximity to the intimates of the Defries' who had most frequent access to the house.

Those he did study, and with the cold, dispassionate eye of a true born naturalist. They were wholly creatures of habit and ingrained response, he discovered. He came to perceive – and later could codify – the series of patterns to which their behaviour corresponded. He suffered the ignominy because his wouldn't have been such an education without it. Maybe he needed to believe, or merely expected, that nothing should come to him easily. The issue itself might be appreciated better for the difficulty of its attaining – because he was helping to prove just how deserving he was. He too, but at the other social extreme from his supercilious and intrigued employer, was a man hewn from his own pride.

THIRTY

Suddenly he went missing from his job of work. For the purposes of my story he resurfaced in Bath, by way of another spa town, Harrogate.

He had gone to the latter at the express wish of an acquaintance of the Defries', to attend to some retouching – invisible handiwork, as it turned out – on furniture the couple intended to sell. A family crisis jolted their plans out of kilter, but he was paid for his labour, and he decided to take two or three days off to look about Harrogate and that reach of Yorkshire before returning home.

On his forays past the windows of the antiques shops in the town he several times re-encountered the same woman. Her face conveyed that freight of premature knowledge through suffering, phlegmatically borne, which marks out a long-term invalid – if he couldn't already have told from her pallor and darkened eyes and the slowness of her movements aided by a walking stick. She smiled to him, a little more broadly each time they met, and he saw from the lightening of her features that she meant, with comparative youth still favouring her, to be sweetly-disposed in spite of everything else.

They 'chanced' one day to meet in the Old Swan Hotel, where she was staying with her sister and whither he had followed her. In the hallway she dropped her walking stick: he picked it up for her. She didn't affect ignorance. She mentioned to him the antiques shops, and they agreed on a mutual professional interest. She removed a business card from her handbag – for an antiques and restoring firm with valuation services in Bath – and, admitting to him that standing still for any length of time was uncomfortable for her, used that as a pretext to invite the

polite and smiling, southern-sounding young fellow – a full two
decades her junior – to take a cup of tea with her.

He found an opportunity – or made one – to travel the distance
from Dorset to Bath to reintroduce himself, and as events were
to transpire he never went back south.

On news of his arrival in Monmouth Street the woman's face
had conveyed her surprise and delight. Her husband, who was
fifteen or twenty years older than she, appeared less certain, but
initially went through the motions for courtesy's sake, because
his wife waited expectantly and because he understood what
gave her pleasure.

Sprake's antiques and restoration business comprised the
showroom in Monmouth Street and a workshop and warehouse
in Walcot Street. The husband was taken by the young man's
enthusiasm and – as was quickly proved – his expertise. He
let him test his skills on a fire-damaged military secretaire, and
then a sea-battered Adam-style serpentine commode, and was
agreeably impressed; and no less so when he was persuaded to
show the visitor some of his stock and found himself answering
intelligent questions or confirming some salient and perceptive
comments. His wife convinced him that temporary accommodation could surely be found with someone among his employees,
and it was managed straightforwardly enough. The young man
was twice entertained, on succeeding Sundays, to tea at the
Sprakes' home in Prior Park. His first taste of his host's whisky
went straight to his head but he knew he had one foot in the
door, and later – when he was recovered and quite sober – was
very capable of sizing up the situation for himself.

He had assumed the name 'Lomas' and now acquired the
history of an invented persona to define him during the twenty-
three months he spent dressed in a suit learning his new
trade in the residences of Aquae-Sulis to which his employer
was summoned for purposes of evaluating effects. He proved
diligent in a somewhat detached way. He acquired few friends,
although he undoubtedly did make an impression – for good
manners and discretion, for the carefulness of his scrutiny, for
his precociously observant eye and his memory for what he'd

read and seen – on those whose homes he visited: those, that is, whose effects were of a higher worth than his employer first realised, and which had to be revalued accordingly. Sprake was in two minds: embarrassed for his own sake, but amazed at the lad's sharpness – and increasingly uncomfortable to know how to deal with him. There were blanks in the youth's knowledge, but he found he couldn't afford to leave him behind on his surveys. His discomfort was compounded by his wife's continuing encouragement, but at least he wasn't – apparently – privy to the gossip about the pair of them, master's lame wife and her robust favourite.

The tittle-tattle that did eventually reach Sprake's ears concerned another kind of approach made to his assistant. He had been ill off and on in the late autumn and had had to delegate where he couldn't postpone the visits. Another dealer, Skinley, who colluded with one of the city's firms of auctioneers, had suggested to the young man he might do better in St James's Parade than Monmouth Street.

The prospect of losing his adjutant – even on the strength of hearsay – was sufficiently serious to necessitate an increase in wages. What Lomas, stage-managing the gossip, really required however was a measure of independence. Sprake was obliged, therefore – at his wife's insistence – to allow him the leeway to undertake his own valuations where deemed appropriate, usually further off at farmhouses or in the more modest quarters of the town.

The arrangement seemed to work quite well, for a while. The protégé had gained in confidence, and his employer was pacified by the excellent reports that came his way. For his part Lomas was now easier among those with whom he was required to deal. He was duly deferential and respectful but also reassuring, uncloyingly and *helpfully* flattering, and always – his most important virtue – very well up on his subject.

Later, though, stories began to circulate in the trade that a double game was being played. Valuations were being fed back to Sprake's. But sometimes items were being, not unintentionally, omitted from the inventories. These – the more valuable

– were later sold separately through Grigsby and Nephew the Auctioneers, accompanied by a confusing welter of paper-work which invariably failed to state plainly the intricacies involving transference of ownership during the objects' recent past life.

Sprake felt obliged to act. Perhaps he judged that his wife was trying too hard to persuade him that Lomas was, firstly, an innocent man wronged – and, then, a helpless man led astray by others. He was far from stupid and had had his own unhappy suspicions for a while, on the business and domestic fronts. For him the public speculation was even worse than any actual marital deceit and doubly disloyal diversion of profits.

Consulting no one, least of all his wife, he sacked Lomas. A brusquely formal letter dispensed with his services. He offered him no thanks for his contribution to the revival in the business's fortunes. He presented no 'explanation' at all, but cryptically hinted.

Lomas's resulting fury had a profound influence on all his future life. It was because he kept that corrosive anger to himself that he only caused it to become more terrible and vengeful.

He ought to have left Bath (others opined), but perversely he decided to stay. Sprake's closest rival may not have coughed up the terms he was hoping for, but none the less was very willing to take him on. It wasn't officially acknowledged that Skinley himself was paid retainer's fees by Grigsby's in the town: but rather more interestingly he was also, as Lomas discovered, regularly in receipt of more considerable payments on the same principle from the agent of a London firm of auctioneers. It was Skinley's subtle, covert policy to work with one or the other but sometimes to take a gambler's risk in playing one off *against* the other. Lomas, still inwardly consumed after fourteen months, was fully adjusting to the complexities of the situation and its implied hazards for his new employer, Edmund Skinley.

Eighteen months later a formal police charge was brought against the aforementioned Cyril Sprake. The accusation was that he had conspired with a client to make false claims to an insurance company concerning the value of a number of items subsequently destroyed in a house fire. It was a difficult case for the prosecution, since the articles had been destroyed. Photographs were found, however – the source was never specified – which showed the objects in question: with that unexpected evidence to hand, a number of expert valuers had been approached to offer an opinion.

Sprake was found guilty in court, and given a three-year prison sentence for embezzlement. Lydia Sprake was left with the responsibility of running the business. She approached Lomas and made him an offer she was too naïve or desperate not to. He returned to work in Monmouth Street, but this time as co-owner. A year later he bought out Mrs Sprake, and when he confronted her husband with further evidence of fraudulent misdealings acquired full control of the enterprise.

This became public knowledge in time, after Lomas had left Bath and Sprake had been released from prison and gone off to set up home with the sister of a former cell-mate. His wife had left Bath for Eastbourne, where she regularly imbibed at the bars of hotels: first at the Grand, then the Queen's, then deserting the sea-front Parades for quieter private hotels in the streets and avenues behind. She talked a lot, too much, and inevitably her version of the story found its way back to Bath. She searched among the fraternity of antiques dealers, frustrated salesmen, repairers and upholsterers, in the hope of encountering any young and unattended men of personable appearance for whom she might buy drinks out of her rapidly diminishing bounty.

'Lomas' re-surfaced, not in London, but in Paris.

It's an unexpected progression. But let us suppose that he was intent on developing his interest in carpets and, to a lesser degree, tapestries, and that he understood the best means of doing so was by swallowing that inherited pride for a short while and becoming, in a manner of speaking, the sorcerer's apprentice.

The first part of the hypothesis is a more likely construction than the second. He had some money to his name from the sale of the business in Bath, even if that amounted to rather less than he had calculated on. Notwithstanding all the humiliation enforced on him earlier in his life, he possessed sufficient quantities of self-assurance and self-esteem to have made the swallowing down of pride a very tricky operation for himself. If it could be postulated that somewhere there was existing to his knowledge at that time a highly respected and eminently learned dealer, one with many contacts but who 'secretly' proved deficient in some particular aspect of his personal or business life, then one might better approach an explanation for the young man's conduct in this part of his story, bearing in mind his cold eye for any evidence of human foible.

The shop on the Rue du Faubourg-Saint-Honoré still carries the name 'Karinian', although the name's Armenian bearer died forty-five years ago and the establishment was subsequently sold to new owners. The cognomen carried great authority, and does so now. It's considered a wise move that it should have been retained when the business – which has continued to deal in carpets, to many of the original clients – was regeared for the 1950s.

The shop's position on that particularly choice thoroughfare of the Eighth Arrondissement distinguished its ambitions from even those other carpet dealers – quite august – in that *quartier*, as far as the Palais Royal. The customers in the old days included French presidents, government ministers, diplomats, financiers, the smartest globe-trotters, the *nouveaux riches* from the Avenues of the Sixteenth and the secluded villas of Neuilly, and the quietest but most dedicated collectors, the hermetic sort – a Bulgarian prince, a Greek shipowner, a Siamese clan, a Chilean whaler who used agents to acquire the finest at any price.

Karinian knew the two essential rules of his trade: to appear learned but modest, and to have such wealth of his own – fat acquired during the good years – that if the world supplies should mysteriously start to dry up or carpets begin to lose their investment value, he could either move into another commodity or – preferably – close the premises and live out his life in very comfortable retirement.

However, the sources remained true, and carpet values consistently improved. Profits rose to giddy heights, and Osip Karinian might have been as off-hand with clients as he chose to be but never was. His existence off-stage, where few saw, was like that of a Medici principe: he bought an apartment on the Avenue Montaigne, and villas at Paris-Plage and Menton. His shirts were custom-made for him at Charvet, his suits and shoes in St James's, riding apparel and tackle by Hermès' Sellerie, his luggage by Messrs Vuitton. He banked in Switzerland, and in short was the model upon whom John Lomas chose to base himself when he decided to be refashioned. Karinian also proved to be the fount of all wisdom in respect of the trade itself – he never confused the issue by calling it a 'profession' – and imparted such quantities of information as gave the future 'Chetwynd' a craving for his subject, to discover all that he might. But Karinian also knew when to withhold, if he was in any danger of jeopardising his own mystique or giving away more than he should to, not a temporary apprentice and disciple, but a potential rival in the international market in the sometime-ahead. From the man's most subtle evasions and smiling, charming withdrawals the impending 'Chetwynd' learned how to offer and yet not to offer himself, how to be an intimate and a stranger together.

It was while reading through French newspaper reports of trials in the period of vengeance immediately after Liberation that I found my first reference to the name Karinian.

His arrest in Marnay had been effected by former patriots of the Front National, and he had been transferred into the hands of the FFI in Paris. It was claimed that a former colleague in the RNP of right-wing collaborators had betrayed him, but the informant had subsequently fallen under suspicion himself; *his* whereabouts were now unknown. Karinian had signed a number of denunciations of that man and others in his turn: these were being considered, but were unlikely to prove effectual in saving the prisoner from his punishment.

Later it was reported that he had been shot; whilst –
purportedly – in the act of making his escape from the quarters
of his confinement on the Rue de la Chaussée d'Antin.

Karinian evidently had been working for both parties: pacifying
his Nazi patrons with a ready supply of the finest tapestries
and carpets, and securing a considerable fortune for himself
by dealing in the same commodities when their French owners
(political activists or collaborators, or those for whom making a
break was everything: Karinian was easy) were persuaded to
offer them as payments, inducements, to those organising their
passage out.

The Armenian, it seems, had – in the current mode of
expression – over-extended himself, not appreciating from the
comfort of his suites at the Meurice and Negresco hotels
that he inspired in others a fatal cocktail of envy and/or fear
and/or revulsion. His own major misjudgement was to involve a
business colleague so closely in his work: and to fail to act when
he discovered that his own name was being used to authorise
transactions that involved German buyers being played off one
against another.

Osip Karinian had been much too successful – and made
himself too necessary, it could be said – for his own good, for
him to remember how to save his hide.

THIRTY-ONE

I'm standing on a street corner in Hamburg, at the intersection of two thoroughfares in the quieter, leafier Harvestehude university quarter.

From my left to right runs Jägerstrasse, and from my north to my south Ulmerstrasse. I'm standing directly in front of a shiny office building with copper-tinted windows in which I can see reflected church spires and clouds. It is a construction of the most modern, international design, and five-sided thus,

with a file of substantial, semi-mature trees (they match the others on Ulmerstrasse for height and trunk-girth) in place outside the atrium fall of glass on the angled edge. Whatever was here before must have been shaped in such fashion to allow the linden trees – with their leaves shaped like playing-card hearts – to stand in the same formation.

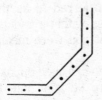

My interpreter arrives on time. Punctuality is a German virtue, and I'm coming to appreciate it.

He takes me to a café. We sit in the window where we have an uninterrupted view of the building. He tells me when I ask, yes, for a long time Hamburg has done a roaring trade in *objets d'art*. Along the northern shore of the Elbe, due west from Blankenese, connoisseurs and investors have amassed priceless collections in their white and primrose Prussian-style villas secure behind walls and gates. In particular oriental carpets have been a speciality of the city. Anything I might desire, some dealer or other would surely attempt to locate for me – at their own price, of course.

The interpreter had started asking around. He selected those who looked as if they would have longer memories. In the mid-1970s, a few years before the office building went up, the ground was cleared and hoardings erected around it, but that was judged to be preferable to having the eyesore which was previously there. The site had been occupied by a garage, which dated back to the period before the last War. Bad times hit it in the early sixties, when the proprietor seemed to lose the will and took to drink. Before that it had appeared prosperous. Well-kept and regularly spruced up with paint, it had done no disservice whatsoever to the neighbourhood. It had been the most sizeable garage roundabout – that is, in the north-western corner of the city between Alster and Eidelstedt: not a sales dealership, how big garages were nowadays, but with extensive workshops and four petrol pumps and – reportedly – the largest-volume petrol storage tanks built for wholly civil purposes in Hamburg between the Wars. The pumps were positioned on the angle between Jägerstrasse and Ulmerstrasse, and that part of the garage complex came to be known locally as 'Der Insel'. Sometimes the entire garage was referred to as the same, 'the Island' – at any rate the natives within a radius of two miles would always have known what you were meaning by speaking of it like that.

We found a woman who had lived opposite, on Ulmerstrasse, four or five years before I'd gone into temporary service at 'Underwood'. She remembered that, even when the metal shutters were brought down on the workshop area and the pumps were padlocked for the night, the lights – certain lights – stayed on in the building, that work didn't cease entirely. She told us that there would be comings and goings throughout the night. Not a great number of them, and only on three or four nights in the week at most, and always performed as quietly as they could be. She might be woken by the raising or lowering of the louvred metal gate and the turning over of a lorry's engine, but (she repeated) she realised that they were attempting to make as little noise as possible, and anyway she was a light sleeper. Sometimes, when she couldn't sleep at all, she might get up and as she was moving through the flat or sitting drinking chocolate at the dining-room table she'd catch sight of a lorry's or van's headlights or tail-lights as it crossed the forecourt, past the 'Island' proper where the four famous petrol pumps were ranged. Sometimes a car would appear – one car, but not necessarily the same model. It would be travelling slowly, with its headlamps turned off as it was driven in from the street. The car – usually no more than that one per night – would pass into the back of the garage while a couple of men operated the portcullis gate.

Deliveries of some sort? I suggested.

She'd been used to the regular delivery lorries, she said, she could recognise them. The operation at night was more organised, speedier, more – somehow – furtive. There was no revving of engines, no whistling, no feet-stamping in the cold. The lorries and vans invariably stayed awhile – behind that great shuttered gate whose works must have been frequently lubricated with oil to preserve the anonymity of the drivers of those unmarked transporters.

A mint black Mercedes-Benz limousine – the sort with the proud demeanour we used to watch Adenauer being chauffeured in – purrs up the gentle gradient of the Rothenbaumchaussee. It's late at night, nearly midnight, and the car is being driven with its headlights dipped. It proceeds past Moorweidenstrasse and Johnsallee. Six or seven hundred metres further north, past Hallerstrasse, the indicator lamp on one of the rear wings

winks leftwards, although there is no other traffic to see.
Short of Parkallee the car crosses the road on a diagonal, into
Jägerstrasse. At the intersection with Ulmerstrasse it slows.
The right-hand indicator signals, and the driver pulls across the
three empty lanes, towards a blue illuminated sign on a wall.
The letters announce 'Tankstelle-Werkstatt Immergrün' – the
'Periwinkle' petrol station and workshop. The Mercedes pulls
into the glass-roofed forecourt of the building generally referred
to as 'the Island'. As the car mounts the ramp its headlights
briefly switch to main beam. That appears to be a signal. At
the car's slow approach, at little more than walking-pace, the
slatted metal gate in the wall – like a castle bulwark – starts
to rise. The headlights are switched off; the red bulbs above
the rear wheel arches dim to nothing. Beyond the car a few
cautious wall lights hint at the dimensions of the interior space.
There are several car-hoists visible and some repair pits: the
rest is in mystifying shadow. It might be – but it's impossible
to be certain, since that is the intention – that there is another
space beyond that one, suggested by an oblong of deeper dark
on the darkness at the back of the workshop.

   The car enters and the gate begins to descend. Figures move
among the shadows. There's the sound of car doors opening
and closing. More feet are visible through the narrowing space
between the gate and the concrete floor, a man's feet shod in
highly polished Oxford willow-calfs. A voice is audible; authoritative, such as Aryans will respond to: brooking no argument.
The proper – or improper – business of the night is about to
be embarked upon. The gate meets the floor: not this time
with its customary shudder, but as noiselessly as the deed can
be done.

                               *

On the Neuer Jungfernstieg I remembered, standing waiting
to cross from one side of the street to the other. I looked
up and caught sight of some white, briskly scurrying northern clouds. Not Chinese at all, but white, and shaped very
oddly.

   They were, I supposed, providential. I heard Chetwynd's

voice – its exact cadences, the blandness of that deadly accurate staccato, truncated, simulated public school delivery.

'There's the sceptre. God's sceptre. The Chinese thought of Him as head of all the deities in Heaven. *He* is so elevated that the top of the sceptre becomes a cloud, with a little trailing tail. It means a wish. Wanting a wish to be achieved, to come true. "J". "U". "I".'

*

What happened in Hamburg?

Equipped with a list of names of War-time German patrons from Paris and Nice, he would have been able to set himself up in a wealthy trade. It might have been that certain of his customers, 'clients', wished to unload themselves of material that might incriminate, and allowed Chetwynd (or however he chose to call himself) to arrange their sale or else shipment to foreign homes. The new wealthy of Germany also required their totems of status, and Chetwynd could have discreetly dealt with the movement of *objets d'art* from one anonymous source to yet another, with authenticity proven but details of provenance and destination withheld, as always – it surely goes without saying – at a duly exceptional price.

This was where, in the space of two or three short years, Chetwynd – by that name or another – must have made his fortune and acquired his confidence. It couldn't have lasted, and he got out just in time, before he could repeat any of Karinian's mistakes. Too much success involves delegation, and a weakening of the iron links that hold the chain bound and secure.

THIRTY-TWO

The house in Portofino was rented, from an Italian princess who recognised its value to those who wanted to break into the Windsor set. None of *them* would have been willing to pay so much – be seen to be paying so much, even if they could have afforded to – for the property. But Chetwynd was.

It was a fine residence, of four public rooms and six bedrooms, in three acres of garden. Further attractions included a swimming pool, a pool-house, two terraces, and a spectacular view of the bay to Sestri-Levante.

Among the retinue of staff was a butler. It took me until 1990 to track him down, to a tiny flat in La Spezia. He was still impressive-looking: tall, silver-haired, with the stiff and uncompromising bearing of a definitive gentleman's gentleman. Clearly he'd had no doubts about Chetwynd's genuineness. How else, he implied, could he have mixed in the circle he did that season, and have had such a fine sensibility for the smallest social niceties?

On a first impression this very cliché of a former butler didn't appear likely to give anything away. But he was lonely. The world was a more vulgar place nowadays. His memories were forty years old and more, and since then he had developed a fondness for not Italian but German wines. When I told him that nobody had heard of Chetwynd or his whereabouts in a very long time, he put away any scruples he might have had and, warming to my gift of wine in ample supply, set the scene for me.

The first invitation had been sent to the Windsors, the Duke and Duchess, deferentially requesting that they honour him with their company for dinner. Renowned for their availability, they had accepted, but in their own time.

Their fellow guests were to be a surprise: assorted glamorous catches of their acquaintance – like the de Cabrols, Baron de Redé, Hubert de Givenchy – wafted down from San Remo on the Riviera of the Flowers. In the event they found themselves delayed, and the royals arrived first.

Chetwynd welcomed them but then etiquette went out the window as he begged Their Highnesses' forgiveness, he would telephone for the latest information about the others' progress. If he was – unpardonable expression – in a stew, he concealed his anxieties with some aplomb.

The Duchess, wearing a new outfit by her old faithful Mainbocher – a white crêpe dress with lime bead embroidery, tiger-head brooch fastened to starboard – and with her hair dressed by a protégé of Alexandre's with organza buds, was all smiles. The Duke nodded, rather curtly, and pulled back one side of his mouth. Before the butler, my sole but very detailed source for Chetwynd's summer adventure, the Duchess turned and glared at her husband.

The Butler's Story

I served drinks in Mr Chetwynd's absence. The Duchess said nothing as she took hers from the salver. The Duke noisily cleared his throat. I guessed that there had been 'words' on the journey over. The Duke's eyes were a little rheumy while the Duchess's shone not a little madly.

My services were dispensed with: or rather, the Duke asked me if I could be finding something else to do for the meantime.

The Duchess looked displeased, irked: by his unusually bullish departure from meek form, not on my account. I bowed and retired, opening and closing the doors behind me. Outside in the hall I debated the situation with myself for a few seconds – then I decided that, repaying discourtesy with the same, I should make myself useful in the pantry, which adjoined the salon whither access was made by way of a single and less prepossessing and less muting door.

The Duke approached the business that so concerned him with what he must have intended, and rehearsed, as a joke. He addressed the Duchess. 'I see we have that carpet-bagger on our tail again.'

The Duchess was patently not amused. The Duke's smile dried on his tanned, leathery face.

The Duchess could be most astringent when she cared to be, and not always when they were alone and in private. Since they now *were* alone and in private, more or less, I anticipated fireworks.

The Duke, meanwhile, seemed unwilling to dispose of the topic. He helped himself to a second dram, of his favourite 'J & B'. When he had done so, the Duchess, seated, thrust *her* glass into his hand. He almost made the mistake of failing to mix her dry martini in a second glass, but her intake of breath warned him. (It was bad enough that she was drinking at all.) His mind was indeed preoccupied.

As I lingered in the pantry I heard His Royal Highness address himself to the matter in stronger terms. He must have been in a determined mood to confront the Duchess when she was in a far from compatible frame of mind. Mr Chetwynd was referred to as 'that little runt'.

'Not so little, surely.'

'You know what I mean, darling.'

The Duchess smarted.

'Why did you bother to come, then?' she asked. Her delivery was glacial.

'He knows his stuff.' The Duke raised his tumbler and attempted another celebrated Windsor smile. 'No point in turning down the chance of a good malt.'

'So you'll give him *some* credit, will you?'

At that point the Duke appeared to become fully cognisant of his wife's irritation. Manifestly it caused him some distress.

'Had to be said, Wallis.'

'*Did* it?'

'I know you don't mind about him so much. But – but that's the point rather.'

She turned her head away.

'One doesn't know where that sort come from.'

'Oh, David – '

Her mouth sagged. Behind the crack of the connecting door I stood watching that ferocious, unhappy chin in profile.

'One must have one's standards, darling,' quoth the Duke. 'Even with the English.'

'Of course. But there's heaps of others to do that for us. The Dudleys, the Mosleys, the Coopers – '

'So, why should we bother with Chetwynd?'

'Because he's *not* "one of us" – '

'Darling – ' The Duke finished the whisky in his glass. 'I simply don't see the reason in that at all.'

'*Because* – ' The Duchess sighed. ' – he doesn't *matter*!'

I can appreciate now that she was not being wholly truthful. Yet the remark did seem to calm the Duke somewhat.

'Suppose not,' he said.

'This is his place. His food, his wine. His fun.'

'He *isn't* an awful lot of fun, though.'

'*Some* fun. Did you know he's trying to discover if he can get you a new set of bagpipes made?'

'Bloody damned cheek.'

'One set's enough, I told him.'

'There you are – ' The Duke stood eyeing the array of bottles on the table, the tenant's own property, a French Regency silkwood console table decorated with carved scallop shells.

'What?'

' – having your little chats. Tête-à-tête things. What's a chap supposed to make of all that?'

The Duke straightened himself. The Duchess turned her head in profile again, but with a little less force this time. She was trying to keep a watch on him out of the corner of her eye. She swallowed hard.

'I think we shall have to agree to disagree, David.'

'You'll see through him. Soon enough. He's made of paper. A paper man.'

Her lips came together with a terrible compression of will. Sometimes, I'd heard, she was quite unable to contain her anger and it would explode out of her. She had no real softness. Her robust plainness on the exterior was matched by her internal severity.

She sat back in the gondola sofa. The Duke approached the bottles, but couldn't decide, which one and if he ought to.

I coughed, from the pantry, as if *I* might assist a former monarch of Great Britain and Her Dominions to arrive at a decision.

The Duchess gave a sharp glance over her shoulder. Doubtless she knew all about cracks between doors and doorposts – just as she was reputed to know from her Shanghai days all about the relative thicknesses of mirror glass, and which conceal behind them spy-windows.

But I knew my craft too, and retreated into the shadows whence my breed emerged. The Duke put down his tumbler and walked away from the table with his hands placed behind his *derrière* in the plaid trews, tucked under the flap of his blazer. How little pity I felt for that little man then. How I sympathised with the Duchess, who in her later years would be (informally, in worldly circles) graced with the queenly designation to top them all, fag-hag par excellence.

*

Chetwynd bought his neighbours presents: soft cushions in pug shapes and alabaster pugs and a Cartier pug brooch, earrings and belt-buckle for the Duchess, and for the Duke a set of three golfing irons and, through the offices of Mr Scholte in Savile Row, an Inverness cape in Royal Stewart tartan with matching muffler, mittens and travel shawl. They received their gifts with a show of polite surprise, which must be his reward.

He entertained them several times to dinner, arranging a menu of their preferred dishes: rum avocados or lobster mousse, baked Maryland chicken or loin of lamb with mustard, an English pudding or fruit compote with pastry (to please the Duke) or even (although he couldn't rival the hot crunchy outer layer prepared by the Duchess's kitchen) camembert ice-cream. He had a number of gramophone records of Scottish reel music sent out, and played them over cards, which then set the Duke to dancing in his trews or kilt and jabot, which necessarily obliged the others to follow suit. The Duchess surveyed the arrangements with a gimlet eye, even though not queening it over her own table. She looked hard to find an error which she could make a clever pretence of disregarding, but Chetwynd and his housekeeper and cook, forces combined, were nearly a match for her and her Pierre Hotel-trained chef.

He made the journey over to Villa Dolceacqua – 'Sweetwater House' as the Duchess had christened it – as many times as he was himself host to the two former royals. They were already called the foremost Nobodies in Europe, but an invitation from the couple – who turned down none themselves – was to be treated very seriously. And anyway, the visits were not wholly social. A little time was spent 'à deux ou trois' – but usually with the Duke alone – and 'business' was discussed. Its nature remains confidential, which must be evidence of the discretion of both parties.

One can speculate that Chetwynd was a broker of some sort: either selling Windsor possessions to private buyers, or to jewellers and dealers, with himself in the guise of vendor. It's possible, though, that his function was rather more complex, to arrange the transfer – officially or unofficially – of certain items in the ownership of the British Royal Family to which His Royal Highness considered himself entitled. Rumour still surrounds the fate of Queen Alexandra's jewels, for instance: those fabulous, legendary emeralds of the Duke's own grand-mother must have excited the couple's insatiable greed more than any other stones could. It is feasible, given Chetwynd's capacity for tact and guile, that the man had some knowledge of their whereabouts and eventual destination.

The Windsors had unrefined taste in carpets – the Duchess designed her own for the mill-house near Orsay, while the Duke favoured tartan patterns for his own quarters – and the finer points of the oriental variety would have been a wasted topic in the conversation (and business?) stakes. The 'carpet-bagger' clearly had something very special to recommend him, for even such eminent Nobodies apportioned their over-abundant time and fusty, fustian dignity very, very carefully.

At a last dinner at Villa Dolceacqua Chetwynd was presented

over coffee with a token which was also to be his public pay-off: matching toiletry and writing cases, both of crocodile leather and suede-lined inside, fashioned to a design of the Duke's at Goyard. It was a brazen clue as to what he should now do, and Their Royal Highnesses (as he knew to call them both) must have enjoyed several right regal sessions of the giggles during the planning stages and in retrospect. The gift was expensive and uniquely bespoke, and they could placate themselves on that count.

In a manner of speaking, Chetwynd – I construe – was now fixer by semi-Royal Appointment. Perhaps he was also able to take a mature and enlightened view of the brushing-off dealt to him by two such borné and petty-minded benefactors.

The nature of his employment gave him confidence – I again construe – but not of an overweening sort. It proclaimed to himself – certainly not to others – what he might be capable of as a force behind the scenes, as a bunker-commander, a veritable 'deus ex machina', not unwilling to be seen with a cocktail shaker in his hands. He couldn't have failed to be flattered: that his services should have been required, for some while, by two such notable nonentities. On that score he might have re-directed himself, towards the millionaires and jet-setting socialites of the western hemisphere. But instead, with his own sixth sense for social presentation and having savoured the essence of purple crossed with hamstrung Baltimore gentility (and, however dodgy it could sometimes be, what the Windsors had was style, the élan of those for whom it is all there is to live for), he realised his forte was for the disorientated, historically dispossessed aristo class of his memory and also for the sort of eminent professionals who appreciate the old ways with a mixture of distaste and envy, who have complicated their lives with emotional repression, financial unguardedness, and that curious native stupidity in practicalities which frequently is the obverse of book knowledge or business acumen.

*

When he returned to his base of operations, England, it was to a similarly adroit method of business. He was to establish himself as the middle-man between one outmoded order and its successor, organising the transference of the objects of status from the financially embarrassed to the materially endowed. That, at any rate, is the most favourable gloss to be put on his commercial endeavours.

There wasn't enough daring in that, though, and for all the very conventionality of his appearance, Chetwynd lived in need of excitement. He must have tired of the good taste, in behavioural terms, of the enterprise. He needed complete assurance, and his wealth went a long way in a country where appearances are of the vital essence. Instead of being coyly offered objects by those wishing to sell, he chose to make his own selection of what he had a fancy to deal in. If the owners were unwilling to sell, he devised methods of persuading them. Should money not prove enough, that and the sawdering and soaping of his social betters, he devised other forms of persuasion. Companionship, through our own offices, earned him loyal gratitude in such an inhibited society as this one. Behind it all, of course, was the science of blackmail and practice thereof: or, more subtly, of the threat of threat. 'Knowledge', which he had advised me to acquire, was his modus operandi: knowledge of those with whom he dealt, in all its finite and resonating glory.

Fleur too. Fleur Simmons (as she calls herself) proves to be something of a novelty, and he can afford to indulge his curiosity.

She intrigues him during that Cornish summer of 1956 because he can fathom that she isn't who she claims to be. She does have a daughter, and she has a medical husband, but there is no married doctor of that name living in Highgate – or, more to the point, resident in Hampstead either, which is where he guesses her home actually is: a slight geographical realignment intended to put him off the scent. However, it's quite a simple matter to have someone trail one of the girls who minds the child in the house when she isn't there – the house two away from the one she has told them they've been lent for the summer – and it's almost cruelly straightforward to discover that her name is in fact 'Tobin'. A telephone call confirms that a doctor of that name has rooms in Harley Street: a gynaecologist, a protégé of the illustrious Marcus Urban, now set up with a fashionable clientele of his own. They live off Rosslyn Hill, and their daughter attends the Swinton House School; the doctor's family are anonymous, and his father-in-law (an authentic man of the law, that was, with a name – 'Mayhew' – that strikes a muffled but reverberant chord the moment Chetwynd hears it) lives in Chelsea – a laborious distance away for a man of nearly seventy with a recent history of heart trouble, and conceivably at a conveniently inconvenient remove for the good doctor, to whom the former society lawyer may have outlived his undoubted erstwhile usefulness.

From the pristinely white house by the bay in South Cornwall and, subsequently, from the solid and very substantial detached villa on its private tarmacadam road which offers the common public no thoroughfare in that select corner of Kensington, he could already see the potential of the situation, as it might bring benefit to himself.

Knowledge referred to a man's – or woman's – history, and against the full dynamic past we are all of us unable to help ourselves.

Even Chetwynd was obliged to learn that hard lesson, at the very end, that we are none of us wholly unassailable. He'd had an excellent innings, but even the golden Achilles was destined to go down in the finish.

It sounds, as I've put it, more straightforward and somehow more formulated than I imagine it really was. Hindsight smooths the business out, of its crinkles of doubt and creases of concern. He wouldn't have smiled so seriously and so often if it had been such a simple operation after all.

We constituted his web – and he couldn't afford to lose his hold on any of us. Yet at the same time, being the spider of the metaphor he was also – in another sense – a prisoner of his own artifice and compulsion.

THIRTY-THREE

From medical directories I tracked down the widowed Dr Trevor Gammon's address as being in a village on the Sussex Downs. The woman's voice which answered the telephone told me, quite briskly, that her father-in-law was now living in St Leonard's, he had done so ever since his heart by-pass operation. She seemed relieved to dispose of her explanation and gave me his number.

The man his daily-help brought to the door to quiz me had a somewhat uncharitable cast of features: or maybe his expression was that of someone who finds himself, more than others, put on the defensive – with his family, for instance. The mention of Harley Street provided more cause for apprehension – and yet I could tell that he was intrigued to discover the nature of my enquiries, enough so at any rate for me to merit an invitation inside.

The name 'Tobin' caused him to take up his guard again, but it also transported him back to that past from which his forced removal here had exiled him.

'Terrible business, the murder. No one was ever arrested for it, you know. Complete mystery. It was so savage, I thought it must have been done for a reason. Not just random, I mean. Crimes like that were still pretty much something in those days.'

He'd had great respect for Gilbert Tobin's amassed wisdom as gynaecologist and obstetrician. 'Seemed to know the lot. Maybe it wasn't just knowledge, though. He had an instinct for it. Really. Healing hands – there's something in it, you know.' He didn't suggest that his skill had gone beyond the consultative and undertaking what the law recognised as legitimate operations.

'Occasionally we had the wife or husband of the same couple. One or two of our patients did coincide.'

I asked him what sort of people were they in the main?

'Society, I suppose. London. Home Counties. But not all of them. Sometimes people would save up and come because they thought we could do for them what other doctors weren't able to, or because they distrusted the National Health. Foreigners came our way as well, of course. If you were lucky, somebody would fly you out to Geneva or Beirut or wherever. But mostly it was – well, Bond Street types. There were enough of them anyway for you not to have to go looking very much further. They'd recommend you to other people, whether you deserved it or not – '

'Didn't you? Deserve it?'

'Tobin did. He had more folk clamouring to get appointments with him than he could manage. Even though he had only one sex to get to work on and I had two! But I had as many patients as I could handle. That said, one cancer specialist can always lose his business to another. Especially if *his* prognoses are cheerier.'

I pursued the subject of Gilbert Tobin.

'You knew him socially?' I asked.

'I knew him better professionally. Get-togethers, dinners: medical ones, I mean. But sometimes our paths crossed, we were invited to someone's house. But never to one another's. I don't know why.'

'You met his wife?'

'The Mayhew girl? Oh yes, quite a few times. Very pretty girl.'

'She was.'

'Quietish.'

'But . . .'

'What's that?'

'I knew her too,' I said. 'But it struck me, she wasn't – wasn't quite ideal for it. The life.'

'Too pretty, you mean?'

'No, I – '

'I don't know if anyone was "ideal for it", exactly.'

'"Quiet" you said – '

'Didn't *you* think so?' he asked.

'Yes.'

'What – if I might enquire – what was your own association with her?'

'We knew someone in common,' I said.

'Who? Can I ask you that?'

'Yes. Yes, of course. His name – his name was Chetwynd – '

His reply was delayed for several seconds. He blinked a number of times. He rested his right elbow on the arm of the chair and placed his folded hand under his chin.

'Yes. Chetwynd – '

'You met him?'

'He came to see me for a check-up. Lex Elson sent him along.'

'A check-up?' I repeated.

'Tests,' he said. 'And you – ?'

'I – I knew him, sort of,' I said. 'Socially.'

'Entertained a lot, I believe.'

'Yes. It was through him I met Mrs Tobin, you see.'

'Where? At Chetwynd's?'

'At a restaurant,' I said. 'Where – where we all happened to be.'

He nodded, and I thought, perhaps he was genuinely unfamiliar with that part of it.

'You know,' he said, 'that he's been dead for – what? – thirty years?'

'I haven't heard him spoken of,' I countered, 'for thirty years.'

His eyes grew smaller. He didn't reply.

'He just disappeared,' I said. 'His bathing-wrap was found on a beach.'

'Presumed drowned?'

'Yes.' I heard the question mark in his voice, matching my own scepticism. 'That was the presumption.'

'I read about the bathing-wrap,' he told me.

'But you didn't hear from him again?'

'Did you think I might have done?'

'I don't know,' I answered, in all honesty.

'I didn't, in fact,' he said. 'Although he knew where to find me if he'd wanted to.'

'Why – why "wanted to" – ?'

'If he'd needed my medical advice.'

'Should he have done?'

'He was my patient.'

'But did he particularly need medical advice? At that time?'

'It was a long time ago,' he said.

'Thirty years.'

'So maybe it can be told.'

'What can?'

'He – he came to see me because he was ill.'

'Ill?'

'But it was too late. And there was really nothing I could do but tell him that.'

'Ill with what?'

'Cancer of the pancreas. In an advanced state.'

'You knew definitely?'

'Of course.' His hand gripped one arm of the chair. He spoke quietly, not irritably but with purpose. 'After God knows how long, I should have recognised something like that.'

'How long had he been – ill?'

'He'd had ulcers. Which he supposed was what the pain was, and the bleeding. Or so he told me. He'd always taken cramps, all his life, he had poor digestion. Couldn't really drink, although he did. He told me his father had taken cancer of the colon.'

'You knew about his father?'

'What about him?'

'I mean – who he was?'

'Not at all. He just mentioned his father. Having had another sort of digestive cancer.'

'You told him – what? – that it was operable? No? Terminal?'

'That it would most probably prove fatal. Before too long. In six, nine months' time, at the most.' His hands gripped both arms of the chair. 'I told him there were some placebos available. At first I beat about the bush, I thought I could get away with not telling him. Not in so many words. But he put the question to me directly. And I had to respond truthfully, correctly. Didn't I? It was only professional honesty – '

He sounded, I thought, less than sure about it.

'He accepted what you said?'

'He believed me, I think. He knew he was free to seek a second opinion.'

'He came to *you*, though. You were a cancer specialist. He must have – guessed – '

'I'd met him several times. He'd told me he had digestive problems – '

'He ate very little,' I said. 'I noticed that. He didn't always *enjoy* his food.'

'You were able to study him a fair bit?'

'He was generous with his hospitality.'

'I was just one name he had, you see – if he should have needed me.' He struck the end of one chair arm with the ball of his spread hand. 'But it's over now. Over and done with.'

'When was it?' I asked him.

'Not long before he went down to Cornwall. Four or five weeks.'

'He must have drowned,' I said. 'Out in the estuary.'

'He may have done.'

I noticed the verbal alteration.

'He wanted to know, of course. If there was anything he could do. I think we can fairly say, money would have been no object – '

'What did you tell him?'

'That he should certainly investigate every opportunity. Search any avenue at all. There *were* doctors then that I knew of, by reputation. One in Paris, one in Lausanne. They had a pretty unorthodox approach to the business – '

'He could have consulted them too?'

'Of course, of course.'

'Did he?'

'I don't know. I just don't know.'

'I could discover, though?'

'They're both dead now. Those two. There were others. In America, one in Johannesburg – '

'Could he have been cured?'

'Anything is possible. It seemed unlikely to me. But who knows, when the will is strong? A spiritual conversion – *Not* by surgery, though.'

'You discussed all this?'

'I outlined what I thought were the most suitable types of therapy. I didn't tell him "cure". He heard me out. He didn't say "yea" or "nay". He accepted what I told him, or he seemed to.'

'Did you see him again?'

'We spoke on the phone. He rang me, he let me know he was – "considering things". Those were his words.'

'And later . . . ?'

'Patients naturally get depressed – they can remain in shock – turn violent – or reckless – '

'But your contact ceased?'

'Yes. Yes, it did.'

He was watching me closely; his eyes contracted.

'I thought,' he said, 'he could take it. I have to judge these matters as best I can. I can't get it right every time.'

'Didn't you get it right with Chetwynd?'

'That is something, thank God, I now shall never know.'

*

In Lausanne he had reverted to the name 'Lomas'. Or at any rate I discovered a patient of that name in the deceased consultant's records. In the autumn of 1958 he had embarked upon a programme of experimental treatment involving drugs and diet at a sanatorium in Frutigen, in the Bernese Oberland. Innovative surgery was also mooted.

The medical files of that establishment were destroyed in a fire in 1962.

The trail at this point, as the result of the conflagration, goes quite cold.

THIRTY-FOUR

'Sit down, Mary.'

The woman hesitated. It surely wasn't her place. But the gentleman who had requested it had a quite kindly expression on his face for all his methodical manner.

So she, cautiously, lowered herself on to the edge of the chair that had been drawn before the desk in the study of the large house where she'd been employed for the last six years, where it was that her misfortune occurred.

'Now that you know who I am . . .'

The gentleman had introduced himself as the family's legal adviser: their representative and spokesman in law. Maybe he'd put it like that to intimidate her rather more, to elicit what he regarded as the proper degree of deference from her. She felt that her plight surely put her beyond such footling and mundane concerns, however.

Mr Mayhew, as he had announced himself, now proceeded to discuss with her what she'd had no idea he could know anything about. She listened, as closely as she could bring herself, to the tale of her own embarrassment. Once or twice she felt her attention straying, as if the story were in part a fiction. He never once mentioned the word 'rape'; he didn't mention anything of the violence, physical and mental, done to her.

She wondered how she could have read kindliness in his features. She saw instead the pale fubsy face of an overworked man: a man who spoke and comported himself by the book, but who addressed her in this dry, approximate, multi-purpose vocabulary with such a strangely hounded look in his eyes.

His client and her employer had absented himself for the morning, so that this discussion could take place. Really, though,

it concerned him more than it did her. It was about the
man's condition and social situation, *his* conceit and anxiety
and his alone.

The cheque was duly produced from a drawer in the desk.
She didn't even look at the figure pre-written on it in cursive
longhand script.

'I'm not interested,' she said, shaking her head to refuse it.

The man was dumbstruck.

'So that will not be necessary.' She nodded to the cheque
lying in front of her. 'I don't require money.'

'But Sir Anthony realises you will need to be – to be reim-
bursed.'

'Why so?'

'For – for medical services. As soon as possible, he told
me.'

Then she understood.

'Oh no,' she said. 'Oh no.'

'I have been instructed to assist in securing proper – reputable
– professional help. There *are* certain places to go. And – to
arrange your transport.'

'But you don't appreciate, Mr Mayhew, I think. I shall be
giving birth to this child.'

He stared at her. His mouth dropped open. *Haunted* eyes,
she decided, was what they were.

'If you wish to – to reimburse me afterwards – that is another
matter. But I should be accepting your money now – '

'Sir Anthony's money – '

' – under false pretences. I must explain that to you. I thought
that it would be quite clear.'

' "Clear"?' he repeated. 'Woman, how on earth could you – '

'But I have decided, Mr Mayhew.'

She stood up. She was uncertain where she was finding the
courage. Already she was seeing ahead, to the physical relapse
that would follow, when she was away from this room with the
door closed behind her, when she'd run the corridors to safety –
or something like it – downstairs, with more doors thrown shut
between them.

'I am quite decided, Sir.'

Yet *he* would be back, when he had calculated the lawyer would have spoken to her and neatly tidied the matter up, got it out of the way.

'I must return to my duties now,' she said.

The man's mouth curled sourly.

'Your "duties"?' he repeated.

Oh yes. She heard the warning in his tone very well. She was no fool, even if she hadn't been able to anticipate the situation – to foreread the clues to it – as she ought to have done. Defries had simply presumed her respect for his position was a flimsy cloak of concealment for her desire –

She walked towards the door. The lawyer didn't try to stop her. When she'd reached it and had the brass knob in her hand, she turned. She bobbed: a curt imitation of a curtsy.

'Good morning, Mr Mayhew.'

His eyes were directed at her feet. For these moments she pitied him: hidebound, strait-jacketed in respectability, as beholden to his masters as herself. She had less to lose than he, though, which ought to make her decisions for the future easier. She had so very little, in her own or her soldier husband's name, but still she meant to hold on to what she could. She would do it in her own way, however, taking the risks that she chose to. She was owed something at least, she deserved this sole, unique prerogative of personal choice in a whole history of helotage: for not just one person, herself, but for the other growing life she was resolute on sheltering inside her until its birth. Shame, she could still believe with the optimism of youth (even one as her own had been), might hope to make its claim on shrift.

*

At dawn a flint road unravels like frayed silver ribbon into a blurred distance. Shavings of mist curl slowly from the ploughed fields. Over running water the mist gathers in a cloud, rising like steam.

She has walked for miles, away from the wooded corner of the county she knows, from the beech and alder copses and the damp dingles of habitation. Trees here are few and far between; one will stand at a crossways, another will occur for no good reason in the middle of a field. In Artois and Picardie, she has heard, the trees have taken the bombardment of shells, they protrude limbless and at crazy angles in the very smoke and rumble of battle. The land they're fighting for is not unlike this one, she has also heard. One such landscape should be enough in the world, though. It's Dorset she would choose to see blown to smithereens, to kingdom come.

She stops and stands quite still.

Here the country is high and, in its middle portion, flat. This is the distance she used to look towards, in its mistiness, and she would wish she might stand on its height and breathe fresher air into her lungs. The layers of rolling combes like ramparts led here, but ahead of her she can now see only more combes, and she realises it's been a kind of deception, that here is no more than the point which – when she was in Chetwynd – she wasn't able to see beyond. It had *appeared* to be the final overfall of hills because of how they were circumstanced, perhaps because fate was preserving them from knowing what was only bound to disillusion them: more of the same, onwards and on and on.

She waits long enough to get her balance back and to collect her breath. She can't afford to delay a moment longer than is absolutely necessary. Time, which ordinarily hangs so heavy in this reach of England, is precious to her now – like a diamond, like a Jew's eye.

She sets off again. One foot, then the other. One foot, then the other. She keeps her head raised and her eyes focused in front of her, on the unfurling ribbon of road. It must descend eventually, but all that she can see of it in the dawn vapours is on a level.

The hedgeless fields spread from the road, beyond the ditches on either side of her. In the vale they had hedges, and all manner of life scurrying in and out, and deadness also, banked up in the soughs beneath. Here there is little evidence of the living – a hawk but no other birds, a few lolloping rabbits some way back, the bark of a fox – and yet the ditches gurgle with water. Earlier, when she had passed close to a spring and a pool, the mist had gathered, packed to a cloud, and she had imagined it hissing like steam from a kettle.

She lets a kettle take shape in her mind. Not just any kettle, but the Kettle of kettles, the archetype. Of bruised and polished copper. Squat and generous-bodied, with a proud swan-neck and viper's head. A Romany kettle. Water is busily boiling for tea over a gypsy fire . . .

One foot, then the other. One foot, then the other.

She can feel the stony hardness of the road through the thin soles of her boots. It doesn't matter to her where to, only that she gets away.

Occasionally she has sensed movements, turnings, in her belly. At the bend in the road she could have sworn she felt a tiny but decided kick: rightwards too, as if to prompt her in the correct direction, as if there's the making of a bond of sympathy between the two of them. Already she has begun to think of themselves as two in one.

She stops in the middle of the road and brings her arms up, to hold her belly with her hands. It is too soon to be certain which way round he – or she – lies, but she has the solemn weight of it inside her: a great loose bag of water slops about under her skin, but the flesh itself is as taut as a clock.

She looks to either side of her. The mist peels off the backs of the early fields. From somewhere a bird suddenly appears. A lark. In throaty flight, a lark ascending. Its tune is sweet, it sings only for her. She keeps her hands placed on her belly and follows the arc of the bird's progress until she starts to lose the shape of wings and body, the positiveness of it. It's being conjured back into its element, the dimension of blue-grey that holds the morning so still and intense. The lark's song lingers longer behind, for several moments, and she fills her muffled head with it. 'Titloo-eet! Titloo-eet!' There are no trees, no bushes, but between somewhere and somewhere else a lark emerges, winging by closely enough for her to hear. She stands immobilised, like a pillar of salt. 'Titloo-eet!' The tenderness of these moments brings tears to her eyes. She has expected nothing like it, this little intimation of mercy. The memory of the song surrounds her like balm. She forgets briefly the harshness of the road and the nip through her mittens and

headsquare. She has the important sense that she has glimpsed
something, she has seen through and beyond – but of what,
and to where . . . The lark has flown, and the mystery
perdures.

THIRTY-FIVE

I thought Liz/Lillias and I were to keep up. It seemed to me we had been together too intensely for the situation merely to be relegated to the lumber room of experiences past. We hadn't finished our story, surely.

Certainly my intimacy had not been invited by her. We had met because she had wanted to get a number of things sorted out in her own mind, to confront her own guilt. I was only to be, and now only proved to have been, a conduit of information: and a sort of sounding-board for her own ideas: and too often a slow and inappropriate prompt. I'd been given the impression so often that she didn't know where she was with me and wasn't very bothered that we should mutually understand and make amends. It was intended only that I should be of convenience to her.

But communication stopped after that. I had heard nothing from her. When I rang her flat, there was no reply. I wrote to her, with my own name and address printed clearly on the back of the envelope and a direction added on the front, 'If undelivered, please return to sender'. But not even my letter came back to me.

Nothing.

*

I contacted as many of her acquaintances, her wine bar crowd, as I could find. One said she'd gone to the States, another to an 'in' destination of that year, Australia. A third said to Milan, equally fashionable at that time. Someone else told me: Barcelona, and she loved it there.

Adventure, another person said. I'm not sure she cares what

she does, was his summing up, she just wants to get finished
with this place.

They all agreed her opinions could be caustic and harsh,
but most of all about herself. Really she thought it was a
chimpanzee's job that she had, PR work, that you could only
treat it as an extension of childhood inventions. 'This *is* my
childhood,' she'd said. 'I'm living it now.' *Her* London, she saw,
was a posh, well-appointed nursery, and in the late 1980s Nanny
was very firmly in charge.

It dispirited her too, of course, but she didn't let them see
as much of that side of her. She blamed herself quite willingly,
and it was a way of coping. Her men friends never stayed
around too long, not the ones who took the friendship one
stage further. Her elusiveness wore them out, which isn't
the way feminine mystique should work. Certain women were
disquieted and daunted by her, by her very failure to use her
natural advantages in life.

'Why Barcelona?' I asked the surest of my contacts.

'She had some tiff at work. She just took the time off.'

'Why there, though?'

'Why not? That would have been her attitude.'

'She went by herself?'

'Yes. The first time she took a hire-car when she got there
and drove. She wanted to see what would happen.'

'And what did "happen"?'

She had come back, safely to all appearances, and they didn't
discover more than that. She'd said something about wanting to
drive further south next time, over to Africa.

'Work got worse. There was something more than a tiff,
sparks flew, and then a proper disagreement, with fireworks,
and then a major row, all thunder and lightning. She just upped
and left. Said stuff your job, and vamoosed.'

'Where to?'

'Someone got a postcard, the frank mark said Gerona.
Catalonia. Evidently she wrote to a lawyer about selling her
flat here and arranging things with money at the bank, to
transfer to a Spanish bank instead. That was from Manresa.
They corresponded. The last time she was in Lérida. She

hasn't been in touch since then, it was weeks ago. It was like I've heard her say about this person or that person in the past, they'd just walked to the edge of the world and dropped right off it.'

'Into what?'

'I can't think. It fascinated her, though; I could see that. How disposable they made themselves. Like the people on drugs, only worse. Maybe she thought there was only one way to find out, so she had to do it – go that way too – to discover for herself.'

'She could be quite moral,' one of her women friends told me. 'Quite old-fashioned.'

'Like another generation?' I replied, without really thinking.

'But not her parents'. Longer ago than that. As if she was looking to find something *she* had never had, even by default.'

'And how was she "moral"?' I asked.

'Maybe I just mean, censorious. How she would look out the window sometimes. Out at all that theme-park rubbish this country has become. As if it was all that people deserved.'

'Was she moral with herself?'

'Quite primly strict. Disciplined. That came later. She'd stopped drinking. She couldn't stop smoking – cigarillo things, which had a sort of Edwardian lesbian touch that amused her. But she cut down quite a bit. She didn't "do" anything, except some exercise. No stimulants. She was really sneery about some of the people she knew who did.'

'"Sneery"?'

'You know . . . They were weak ciphers. It takes strength, will-power, courage *not* to.'

'Did she try to convert them?'

'No. She wasn't an evangelist. For a while I thought, really it was gloating. Yes, maybe like proper, awful, hell and damnation finger-pointing. But I think that actually she was intrigued. By their weakness. She could also see it as – impersonal, I guess. Sort of emblematic. A sign of the times. They were victims.'

'Could she pity them?'

'Not for being victims, no. She persuaded herself that you *become* one, by temperament, by abnegating responsibility for resisting. I don't think she could have let her heart feel anything for *them*.'

'But her mind was settled on – what? – disapprobation?'

'You just had to do better than be a victim, that was all. Pull yourself out of it. Climb up on top. However you could.'

'And how do you do that?' I queried.

'That's the trick, isn't it? If we all knew, then we'd be doing it.'

'Cut and get out?' I suggested.

'Maybe it's all there is,' she said. 'But when would you know it was time you could stop running?'

*

The year is 1988, the setting is Aragon.

I was en route for Barcelona. I hadn't come to Spain alone, but in Zaragoza Carrie and I had our bust-up. This peripeteia had actually been several months a-brewing, and it was merely unfortunate – or only too predictable – that it should happen in a strange city with an air of hostility already. We couldn't take all that additional strain in the atmospherics. The tension peaked and tempers snapped with whiplash force. Now the bridge, so precarious for umpteen weeks past, was well and truly down.

We went our separate ways. After the first forty-eight hours I hit a depression, a really bad one, and headed way off the roads routed in the maps. I wanted to get clear of people and places, to go native for a few days and forget. But it was all too easy, on those rough uphill roads where I saw so little motor-driven traffic, to ponder on the past, to bring back to mind matters guaranteed to pain me further with guilt. The heat was less than the guide-book warned, but it was remorseless none the less. The high country was bleak and rocky; the roads became riddled with potholes when it was too late to go back, and I had to drive more slowly, in the baking cabin of the car, with the windows down and dust coming in or with the windows closed and the imprisoned air in the SEAT turning fetid in minutes. My saliva dried, my tongue stuck like a lizard to the roof of my mouth. My throat was like a dead well. Grit kept blowing up into my eyes, stinging them. The wheel was almost too hot to hold, and I had to cover it with a shirt to be able to keep steering. The engine groaned and every so often spluttered little dry rasping coughs. This was as angry a land as La Mancha, and more than enough to drive a half-decent man barking mad.

Trees and vegetation fell away. I travelled into a bare ochre landscape of scattered moonrocks. It exactly matched my frame of mind. Occasionally a signpost or a crucifix loomed up from a cairn of flints. I'd watch the far distance, to spy out a lone house or the ruin of one. I was loosening the road as I went, and scree rattled behind me, beneath a billowing balloon of dust. I had lost my bearings by the map, and had no choice now but to follow the direction of the road. I passed nobody. The sky was beaten blue steel, and the sun invisible in an intense haze of fiery light directly overhead.

I crossed the second half of the afternoon. I was stunned by the tedium and by the heat. But I noticed at last that shadows were beginning to lengthen slowly in front of me. There were more houses in the distance, sometimes clusters of them, only distinguishable from the land crust by their darker roof-tiles. I was able to spot the forms of trees and bushes.

I eventually came to shade, halted there and fell asleep for a couple of hours. When I woke – thinking miraculously of nothing: or rather, without an immediate memory of Carrie – I felt refreshed and ready to begin again. I drove on for perhaps another half-hour. The country was still barren, forbidding, and only very sparsely populated. But from the sky, apparently in the middle of this nowhere, I saw a helicopter make its descent. It landed on the flattened top of a rock; which, by the time I reached it, I appreciated was crested by a fortress. Flags were fluttering on white poles. I stopped the car to look through the guide-book's hotel maps: I saw no indication of a parador in the several square centimetres of this whole district. As I watched the spot, I noticed two or three cars – bodywork flashing in the sun of early evening – climbing a road that was cut into the rock in a tilted ⋝ formation.

I found the field-glasses in the glove compartment. The cars were the last types I should have expected to clap eyes on at the end of this day spent in the Wasteland: a black BMW 735i preceding an ice-white six-door Lincoln limousine mounted with a satellite dish on the trunk, with a red Ferrari Testarossa bringing up the tail.

I was intrigued, and that's an understatement. At the slow close of this auspicious day I was in a sufficiently reckless mood to think that where four hundred thousand plus dollars' worth of automobile had gone, I might dare to follow in my hire-SEAT. I proceeded to do exactly that, reaching the zig-zagging route of ascent and a sign announcing 'Restaurant El Alcázar'. Hopeful for the first time in twenty hours, if only for the sake of my stomach, I took the first of the three gradients in second and then third gear, at 60 m.p.h.

At the top was a gravel car park, extending to battlements on either side – and beyond, majestic and stark, the camouflage donjon. The striped awnings, although wholly functional, appeared to be almost frivolous in surroundings with such a bellicose past: in that stern domain of machismo, the building was kitted out in gay, fluttery petticoats. The marquees flapped in a light breeze, the flags unfurled on their poles, the jet of a fountain splayed to an arc, sprinklers placed beside boxes of clipped hedge and carpets of pastel blooms cast spray cloudlets.

I blinked at the scene before me, as if I had accidentally crossed into a fairy tale or I was an intruder into a madman's dream. And yet – and yet none of the uniformed, braided staff in such plentiful evidence was attempting to stop me, to scare me away.

I had never seen a more spectacular collection of automotive hardware: Maseratis, Ferraris, Lamborghinis, De Tomasos, reinforced Mercedes, the gamut of American stretch-limos, a purple Bentley Turbo and, among several Rolls-Royces, one with customised solid gold Winged Victory, door handles, hub caps, even the numerals and lettering on the registration plates. Under the grimly possessive eyes of chauffeurs, posses of youths in livery were working their way among them equipped with buckets, hosepipes, sponges, chamois, waxing cloths. Further off, beyond the cars, five helicopters were parked side-by-side.

I realised I was famished. Some perversity – I was awed but also simultaneously spurred by the sight of so much pristine wealth – impelled me to park the car, between a rare Iso Grifo and a Porsche 928, and to hasten across the gravel towards the elegant sweep of steps at the entrance. My watch said quarter to eight: very early to eat by Latin standards, but then according to the map we were thirty or forty miles from the nearest fast road.

The external couldn't adequately prepare me for a full revelation of what lay within. Indeed I considered the taste of décor when I walked inside rather vulgar, although it was more sparing – in parador fashion – than it might have been: garish asceticism, let me call it. Arras tapestries, monumental portraits – cleaned and restored – of prelates in regalia and ruffed dandy *seigneurs* and *caballeros*, scroll-ended velvet sofas, shaded electric lamps converted from wrought-iron candelabra on floor stands. Cabinets were worked with fine marquetry inlay as were the side-tables, piled high with an international selection of current magazines.

That was only by way of a taster, as it were. The cocktail bar – for proper aperitifs – was indicated beyond, and beyond that was the restaurant itself. I didn't care how much the meal was going to cost me. I caught some – not offensively – superior looks before I reached the plate-glass front doors of the dining-room. The *maître d'hôtel* did not pretend that they were fully booked: about a third to a half of the tables were occupied. I had to demur when he, quite politely, explained in his Americanese that my dress was not as required: vest, pants and tie, I was informed, were 'the rules of the house', Señor. Many apologies: if I should care to make my adjustments . . . I nodded, turned, made my way back to the front doors, down the steps, and across to the car parked impudently among its expensive neighbours. I was able to change out of what I was wearing into striped seersucker jacket and white chinos without offending propriety. I pulled on a brilliantly botanical painted silk

tie, a present from my too young girlfriend to a man of her own
father's age.

My quick change proved sufficient: but only just so, I supposed, in a room where Armani, Valentino and Cerruti were the
male norms. The looks which I received were now questioning
in a more intimate way, from staff and fellow guests alike. Some
seemed bemused, the curiosity of others made them seem more
self-conscious. I can't even recall the expressions as suspicious
or sceptical. My audience were involved rather in making their
own guesses and surmises about how I happened to find myself
in this same room as themselves.

I tried to advertise my innocence, but I performed awkwardly
as I was shown to a table in a less prominent corner of the
dining-room. My surroundings, maybe for the first time in my
life, quite took my breath away. In the centre of the room,
reaching to a domed skylight, was a full-sized ornamental
aviary. On the branches of a glittery artificial tree perched
what a waiter later informed me really *were* gold birds with
sapphires and emeralds for eyes. The most artful and persuasive
trompe-l'œil of a Moorish garden decorated the walls, between
swagged silk curtains at what I thought were windows but
transpired to be extremely clever impersonations also, of the
bleached Aragonese landscape outside. When I looked closer
into the garden I saw that here and there in the mural gold
and silver leaf had been applied to make distant minarets
truly sparkle; semi-precious stones glinted in the soft pink
twilight etched close to my table, representing fabled stars.
Each table had a different setting of porcelain china – that on
mine carried the Meissen mark of two crossed swords on the
back. The cloths were of fine white brocade, the outlines of
ghostly patterns in the weave edged with the very thinnest gold
thread. The high-backed chairs were covered with tapestry
scenes of undoubtable antiquity, perhaps dissected from wall
hangings.

Within the first minute of sitting down, I was partaking
of an incomparably theatrical, and bewitching, experience.
The hot-house blooms thurified the air. I could hear the
gentle, lulling plash of water from somewhere and after a

few minutes more picked up the first chords when a pair of guitarists in evening dress started to play on the other side of the room.

I sat in state but at my vital distance, studying my fellow diners. Mostly they were men. The clothes they wore were high cosmopolitan taste: suits in navy silk with wide Milanese shoulders or in expensively crumpled unstructured linen, the crispest blazers, jackets of the softest alpaca, mohair, camelhair. I caught the flash of gold and diamonds on watches, bracelets, tie-clips and, at two tables, male ear studs.

The male clientele resembled – facially, I mean, and in details like hands and fingers – not traditional aristocrats or plutocrats, not even hawkish Sicilian dons, but men who had made their dizzying rise in a single generation, in their own lifetime. Their faces and manners showed the combined hauteur and furtiveness of the self-made who never, for all that their money will buy, can be quite certain where they stand or sit. Some had a habit of talking – in the whispers that seemed endemic to everyone – with eyes perpetually glancing half-backwards, head turning on to one shoulder or the other. The dark eyes, hooded not from applied breeding but from mutual suspiciousness, revealed native slyness and, I guessed, something of Hispanic cruelty. Their nominal ancestors had put heretics to the wheel, in the name of God, essential human purity, and the wholeness of the social organism. Here too, I could believe, were men capable of feeding their lessers to the fire, all in the name – in this age of our little despotic gods – of sacred profit and of a strictly personal glorification and salvation.

Oh, I imagined I had the measure of them all, these stooped and drop-shouldered diners in the middle of nowhere, in this mirror-less and (almost) window-less room which had them enacting their own quiet but intense rituals of alertness: recessed eyes swerving beneath knitted brows, ears cocked, words spoken under cover of food and napkin, decisions spoken into a wine glass, bonecrusher fingers unnaturally gentle with the head of a white orchid or blue gardenia.

I closed my eyes to concentrate on the musical allusions of the guitarists. I listened to their plectrum skills, the plucking out of ideas about a song, the sinuous and wiry teasing forth of components to articulate a shaded impression of a tune rather than the sober, actual, invariable dead fact of it.

I listened with my eyes closed, for I don't know how many seconds, while I felt my stomach juices run and my mouth salivate with gratitude in anticipation of the entrée, tagliatelle of oysters with cucumber.

And then when I opened my eyes, there she was. Not Carrie, who was now what she had always been, history to me. And not quite how she had looked then, in the dog-days of the summer of 1986, thirty years after that other. In certain respects she looked less like her mother than ever: broader-shouldered, flatter-chested, thicker-waisted, and with a rather too upright and unbending gait. Her hair was fairer now, sun-bleached, and I wouldn't have recognised her from that. Her face and arms and legs had taken the sun too, but it remained a foreigner's uneven tan, betrayed by little intruding angles of paler skin and a degree of orange to the parts that had been most exposed. She couldn't evade me, though. The left hand, the one I could see more clearly, was corkscrewing the top off an imaginary jar: a rotating starfish. Her other hand, the right hand, leaned across and hitched the gilt strap of the black quilted Chanel bag higher on the left shoulder. I noticed, just, before she took it away again, the crooked finger as her hand closed over the ball of her shoulder.

I half-rose from my chair and stared. My flesh chilled.

She was so supremely indifferent, to any of us. It was her manner, exaggerated by intervening time, of crossing the dining-room of the Lynton Court private hotel, pencil stilettos stabbing the wooden floor and causing the owners to look out from the kitchen greatly perturbed, mouths flexing. Here she was playing in a different league, and waiters clicked their heels, recognising to whom full respect was to be paid.

She could have been a product of my unassuaged conscience, spirited back to life in this swanking lay vision of an imaginable heaven. I stared at her, very long and hard, waiting to be disproved. Nothing else entered my range of vision or the sphere of my thoughts. I just sat quite still on my tapestry chair, staring and staring, eyes locked.

Then I realised her function. She was translating from Spanish into American and vice versa. But she did it in the shiftily authoritative manner of her companions and of the other diners, disguising the passage of words as best she could – out of the side of her mouth, under cover of food, while stretching her neck or shaking out her hair, inspecting her sleeve for loose threads. At the same time I understood that she was wholly privy to the minutiae of their business talk. Nobody came here, I could tell, to be merely social. She had the same uneasy aura of high-handedness and nervous mistrust of all the other diners. She was in it, I guessed, right up to her slender, deceptively erogenous neck.

She had come south for sun, for heat, for more adventure than she could find in that country she had such ambivalent feelings about, England. I'd had no idea how hot it could get in these parts. Tonight she had made the journey by refrigerated car like everyone else, from their coastal villas, from their Edenic citrus and cypress gardens patrolled by armed minders and stalked by unspecified danger. I noticed how the silk suits of the two men she was with had been tailored to accommodate the bulge under the oxter where the holster sat.

At last it was adding up, to make some crazy, unavoidable sense. I hadn't stepped into one of the Arabian Nights, I wasn't after all in the Caliph's kingdom under the lure of Scheherazade. The kings ruled their empires from a colonised continent now exacting its revenge, from their citadels in Bogotá, Medellín, Caracas. The room contained the 'noblesse' of the trade, but even the richest dealers in Europe were obligated to their providers. The South Americans called all the shots: the Inca and Aztec slaughter fields now waved ripely green and the spirits walked abroad, in a special sense, claiming what was theirs, billions of dollars' worth of it, from the stumbling cadavers of the other America and the Old World. Their command was cast like an invisible net from Los Angeles to Miami to Barcelona, from marbled poolsides to garbage-strewn, piss-run alleyways. They were the modern dream-merchants, and once the dreams

had worked their way into the bloodstream the end of it all –
more surely than Scheherazade's marathon – was death. The
Mercedes and Rolls-Royces were gilded catafalques, perverse
celebrations of the extinction drive that had bought them.

What was she doing here among them, if it wasn't my
imagination which was responsible for her presence? I watched
her from my coign of vantage.

She had also had her head turned (as had her mother, as had
all of us) by the enticement of, not money, but by the thrill of
subterfuge, the distraction from ennui. The table manners of
the others left something to be desired, but the translator –
her mother's daughter – had found her niche: being necessary to
people who either failed to understand or else, by an alternative
reading, understood her simple wants only too well. She wasn't
an English Rose, which was in her favour, but she represented
a not intimidating degree of classiness – her deportment, her
surgeon's precision with her cutlery, her manner of drinking
from a glass – which distinguished her from the other women
in the room. She wore a suit just like one that had occupied the
Yves Saint-Laurent window when I passed along Knightsbridge
on the bus, a full-shouldered matador-red jacket on top of a
short, tight black skirt. She had been sparing but tasteful in her
selection of jewellery: a tiny-faced watch on a gold chain strap,
a designer's heavy ivory and silver bangle à la Nancy Cunard,
and at her throat – in what might have been a setting of white
gold and diamonds – a single drop emerald.

I shook my head. Closed my eyes. Opened them again. But
she was still there, doing whatever she required to disguise
the fact that she was discussing very serious affairs: serious to
her colleagues, and in the general application. She represented
those who determine the fates of men every bit as much as
the globe-trotting diplomats and peace-brokers. If the Alcázar
Restaurant wasn't quite at Olympian level, it was on another
plane of existence from Barcelona, Marseilles, Naples, Brindisi,
Thessaloníki, Casablanca, all the vital points of contact and
exchange in their black trade.

She seemed as familiar with these environs, with their pretences, as anyone else here. Her two companions treated her

as conversably as they would have done another man. She didn't make frothy games of her femininity. Everything was on an orderly, pragmatic footing. This was their job of work, and the evasiveness of the unsaid had no part in it.

Then, after the day's mental exertions, I started to tire. Suddenly weariness was filling me like an unending source of soft, warm, weighting sand. My arms hung heavy, my legs seemed to have lost their feeling. I could scarcely lift my head on my neck. Jesus, the food, I panicked: had they doped me, Mickey-Finned me? The wine, the wine . . .

I could say that I must have dreamed the whole thing, that none of it happened. It was another dangerous illusion, in a land whose history is one of heightened, crazed perceptions.

But then she opened her quilted bag, the uniform accessory of the newly rich and the most ambitious aspirants to that condition, and removed a packet of cigarillos, not cigarettes. She extracted one and held it in her hand while one of her companions offered her the flame from his lighter. She raised the cigarillo to her lips, smiling her thanks. The man was momentarily fooled by something he detected as warmth in the smile. He might have been going to return it, but she looked away, over her other shoulder, as if . . . As if she was hearing, like me – of all impossible sounds – the scrambling and scraping of leaf husks eddying, not in Aragon, but in a Cornish garden.

THIRTY-SIX

About Monsieur Karinian, the Armenian gentleman.

Carpets and tapestries could return a good income, but I wonder if that is more than half an explanation for his ability to have lived so well, being re-measured every year for suits in Savile Row and reviewing the casts of his feet deposited at his shoemakers in St James's Street. He craved bespoke respectability and would have paid anything for the sanctity of the master craftsmen's services.

His cabin trunks and suitcases he had made to his specification in Paris, by a famous Champs-Elysées malletier. The company keeps copious records of favoured customers' transactions, and after sixty years they saw no reason not to let me consult the reconditely detailed files.

1926   One Malle-Armoire, for hats and linen. The bottom
        drawer of the five to be fitted with a false base, 2
        centimetres deep, access by a detachable lid.
1928   One Wardrobe-Large. A false back and sliding entry
        to compartment 3 centimetres deep, to be set behind
        two top drawers.
1929   One hard-sided Attaché-Case. A concealed compart-
        ment in the lid (dimensions unspecified), access to be
        offered by a spring lock hidden in left-hand side seam
        of main body.

He bought numerous other items for his extensive travels: among them a boîte pharmacie, a huntsman's sac gibier, a boîte cartouche, a couple of collapsible cruiser bags, two sacs chiens.

A clue, I was certain, must lie in the minor but significant customising of the trunks and attaché-case. He also bought money-belts from the malletier, but he may have been in the habit of transferring larger amounts of cash; or he may have required safer keeping for certain papers, or even, say, pieces of jewellery; or for any other materials or substances he chose not to declare to the authorities.

In 1937, five months after Lomas-Chetwynd appeared in Paris as Karinian's assistant, a society drugs racket became scandalous news in the press, although it was very old hat information to many in the Seventh, Eighth, and Sixteenth Arrondissements. It was a tangle of improbable associations – Beirut patricians with Marseilles hoodlums, an Alexandrian Gnostic with an errant member of the Spanish Royal Family, Parisian concierges with two directors of a London bank. For a while Karinian was absent from Paris, on the carpet trail to Baghdad and Ashkhabad, Samarkand and Kandahar, and further east to Hong Kong, Canton and Shanghai, leaving the tweedy or Bradford-flannelled assistant to keep an eye on his affairs in the Rue du Faubourg-Saint-Honoré. He returned in a different season for news, and resumed the life in which he had distinguished himself – far from his modest beginnings in the souk booths of Sukhun and Erevan.

*

Perhaps there are no proper endings, and all that's left is running down and a vague drift into an alternative condition. Clues and mementoes are scattered behind, but everything is destined to change. Experience is only the interlude between the accomplished and the inevitable.

*

Last year an item appeared in several British and French newspapers, and on an Antenne 2 TV-news broadcast I happened to catch in Paris.

A Royal Air Maroc plane flying from Rome to Rabat hit storm clouds over the Atlas Mountains. Lightning struck the tail, and the electrical system failed. The aircraft rapidly lost height, and then a fire started in one engine. There was mayhem among the passengers in the middle section. Flames leaped along the wing to the fuselage, and panic broke out all the way through the plane. It must have been the commotion of bodies which helped cause the aircraft to tilt on to its side, then to go spiralling down.

Ninety-five miles short of Rabat, it crashed on to the flank of a mountain and exploded on impact, like a fireball. Several smaller explosions followed. The livid purple sky throbbed orange.

One hundred and ninety-three passengers and the crew of ten were killed. Only two women and a baby survived.

At first it was stated there were no Britons on board. Then one of the women said in an over-dubbed Italian RAI interview that she had been sitting beside an elderly gentleman who'd spoken perfect French but informed her he was English. Probably he had saved her life, in that panicking plane, by calmly showing her how to crouch forward in her seat and how to protect her baby's body with her own. Before that he had told her he'd lived in Morocco since just after its independence, when the French laws were lost. He had joked a little about his age, saying he remembered meeting the father of Mohammed V, the king before Hassan II, the present one (but really, he'd added in parenthesis, their proper definition was 'sultans'). He had also met and got to know ex-King Farouk, the Windsors, Princess Irene of Greece in her youth, King Michael of Romania, the last Umberto of Italy, so – he'd quipped – maybe he was a bad omen for those types . . . He'd been smiling about it when the lightning struck them. Through the thunder rolls he had quietened her, instructing her how best to position herself. While everyone else around them was going berserk, he had simply refilled his tumbler of scotch whisky and pushed up his little folding table. Someone had screamed 'Fire!' Even as the plane tipped he was holding on to the plastic beaker, although most of the drink must have slopped out already. Quite composed and controlled, he had sat back in the seat in his *comme il faut* cream linen suit.

The woman remembered looking up at him for the last time, to see him inspecting his shirt cuffs, fidgeting with them, straightening the cuff-links. The elderly English gentleman who'd led such a full and urbane life smiled down at her. It was a cognisant and sad smile. As the plane banked even more steeply, canting closer to the vertical, he turned her head away with his hand, gently but insistently wrapping her over the life of the baby she held cradled in her arms.